GW01218064

ALPHA
REVELATION

P.A.BAINES

Copyright © P.A. Baines 2014

ISBN: 978-1-927154-373

Cover design by Zoë Demaré (front) and Grace Bridges (back)

Edited by C.L. Dyck, Scienda Editorial, and Grace Bridges

All rights reserved

Published by Splashdown Books, New Zealand

www.splashdownbooks.com

Prologue

As softly as a whisper caught on a wind the craft entered the Solar System, slipping silently through the blackness. Its target lay nestled against the faint glow of the sun, nearly seven thousand million kilometres away.

Anyone paying attention to that particular patch of sky in that particular sector at that particular time might have noticed the ship as a dot of light. Had they been pointing their telescope in that precise direction with the focus just right, their hand steady on the controls, they might have assumed it to be a star. Had they watched long enough and not blinked or looked away, or been distracted by anything, they might have seen a blue flare and a subtle shift in position.

But nobody was watching.

Nobody saw the sleek hull shudder just slightly as the engine woke from its mighty slumber. Two pulses of energy nudged, and then nudged some more, before returning to their dark holes within the belly of the ship. Nobody witnessed the layer of particles shaken off like shimmering flakes of snow from the branches of a tree.

From out here on the threshold of the Solar System, the sun was visible only as a fat star struggling to throw its rays too far and too wide to be felt as a source of heat. From out here, the planets were feeble reflections of their great mother towards which they must forever tumble in silent supplication. Mars was still too distant to register as anything other than a theoretical route plotted on charts and logs somewhere in the ship's memory. And Earth beyond that. And Mercury even further still.

On the ship's console, a light flared like embers on a blackened log, then faded again. Deep within the hull, mechanisms shuddered and moved, sending vibrations echoing around the hollow shell and through the chambers of yellow liquid sitting in an oval on the smooth floor.

There were twelve chambers in all. The yellow goo within each, designed to preserve a dozen lives for ten millennia, had stiffened into a gelatinous semi-solid, the crusted surface cracked like a tobacco-stained ice

1

floe under the pressure of movement it had long ago lost the flexibility to absorb.

Within each chamber was a metal support—a kind of futuristic chaise longue—the metallic surface potted with a roadmap of miniscule crevices and fissures. Floating above some were remnants of fabric and rubber, and pieces of metal that may have attached one thing to another, and shards of bone so small, an observer with a microscope might never conclude there had been a skeleton there and, before that, a corpse and, before that, a living, breathing person.

All of the chambers were like this, except for the last one. This bath alone was still filled with a syrupy liquid that flowed and rippled in time to the movements of the waking ship. The metal furniture was still smooth. Its surface reflected the lights that danced and shimmied on the control console. And floating just above the support was the inert frame of a man.

In obedience to some unseen command, the endless edgeless egg-shell walls glowed and then flickered and held, bathing the room in soft light. In response, the rubber tube running from the chamber to the man's mouth twitched like an agitated snake. The index finger of his left hand moved. His body jerked. Then, slowly, he opened his eyes.

The dust was particularly bad today, but then it always was after a storm. Yesterday's storm had been a big one, blasting billions of tons of fine sand at the subterranean city like a big bad wolf trying to get at the pigs cowering inside.

It found its way into the cavernous settlement somehow, on people and vehicles, through old filters and hairline cracks. It nestled in the hems of out-suits and secreted itself between the joints and springs of the trucks bringing raw material from the Mining Sector. Once inside it broke free and hung in the air in a fine mist, making Axle Park seem much more distant than it actually was, especially from high up here in the crevice near the ceiling. Then, as it succumbed to the gentle Martian gravity, the dust drifted down, coating everything in a mottled rusty-brown hue. When this happened, the buildings seemed to fade back into the rock from which they had been formed so long ago.

From this height, just beneath the panelled windows, the Residential Sector looked like a badly-drawn semi-circle divided into concentric rings. Axle Park was at the very heart, situated against the far wall exactly where the axle would have been had the city been a full circle. The narrow ring just outside that was Pinner Boulevard. Still further out were the dozen half-rings that held the dwellings occupying approximately two thirds of the Residential Sector.

At the heart of Axle Park, the big airlock doors opened up into the Hub Sector which gave access to all the other sectors that serviced the city. There was Manufacturing, roughly square in shape, and Agricultural, which was a little like a circle squashed in the middle. There was the Space Sector, which was a parallelogram with rounded ends. Finally there was the Mining Sector two kilometres away, connected to the Hub through a narrow column of maintenance tunnels and whose constantly changing shape defied description.

To Shor, the whole thing was like a giant version of one of those microscopic bugs he had seen in Science class. The Residential Sector was the head and the Mining Sector the flagellum pushing it through the water. Only this bug was not going anywhere. This bug was a fossil buried under the rock that protected it from the brutal Martian atmosphere.

Up against the edge furthest from Axle Park, along the outer rim of apartment blocks, was Shor's place. It was his secret hideaway, nestled away in the corner of the red-orange world. Up here he had some peace. Up here he was in control of things. Up here, the people of Utopia looked tiny and insignificant and as harmless as beetles in a bath. He watched them scuttle about the cave, their arms and legs shooting in and out like little feelers probing front then back, front then back. They stopped as their paths crossed that of another and they spent a moment interacting, the feelers twitching by their sides, bodies moving in the subtle exchange of communication. Some of them swapped pleasantries. Others hissed and clicked their displeasure at being bumped into or cut off. Then they would move along again, their feelers on the lookout for the next obstacle.

Shor felt a faint vibration pass through the wall and then the distant thrum of engines as the giant dust extractor fans started up for what seemed like the hundredth time.

He sighed. More fan cycles meant more power usage, which meant they would have to make savings in other areas. Already the powerful lights dotted across the ceiling between the window panels had come on half an hour later than usual this morning, and they were on power-saving mode. Ten percent lower than usual, he estimated. Maybe even fifteen. The low light only made the haze seem even denser and the city even grimier. They would limit personal network usage as well, from the usual four hours to half an hour or, if the dust was really bad and the fans had their work cut out, nothing at all. Which meant he was going to have to listen to the other teenagers moaning all day long because they would have to get off their chatbands and actually talk face to face for a change.

Shor leaned back on his arms and gazed up at the sun's small bright disc through the glass pane almost directly overhead. It was still dark outside but the dust was starting to settle. On his free days he would come up here and just lie on his back, watching the tiny circle of light edge its way across the sky. Mister Edmunds, the mad Earth teacher, told them the sun was the source of all life in the Solar System, that the amazing diversity of life on Earth was all down to one little ball of light. Mister Edmunds even said there had been native life here on Mars once, but that had been a long, long time ago. All that was left now was rust and dust.

Rusty dust, Shor thought. *Or dusty rust. Rotten dusty rust.*

Through the palms of his hands he could feel the faint whump-whump of the fans. He wondered if they had such a problem on Earth. Mr

Edmunds had said that eighty percent of dust was actually human skin, if you factor out the red dust from outside of course. So, yes, the Earth did have a similar problem thanks to flaking humans. At least it *would* have a problem if anyone actually lived there.

Shor squinted through the pane of unbreakable glass at the flickering orb and wondered how big the sun would look on Earth. Hot enough in some places to make it dangerous apparently. People had *died* because the sun was so hot.

The class had laughed but Mister Edmunds had not. He never laughed when he talked about the Earth, which was most of the time.

Shor tried to imagine that kind of heat. Heat so intense it dried you out like a piece of smoked ham. Heat so powerful it sucked the moisture right out of your skin.

He closed his eyes and imagined being outside without a suit. Maybe he would be wearing just a pair of shorts and a vest it was so hot. Maybe it would be on one of the beaches Mister Edmunds had told them about, with waves as tall as a man throwing water onto the coarse golden sand you could dig your toes into. Maybe Mel would be there too, lying on a big towel next to him. They would hold hands and smile at each other and call out to the kids…

He is coming.

Shor gasped and opened his eyes. He looked down at the roof to locate the source of the voice that had woken him from his daydream, but he was alone. Perhaps he had imagined it. Perhaps the voice had come from inside his daydream, but it had felt too real. It was as if someone were standing right behind him…

He leaned forward. His mouth was dry. He coughed, feeling slightly disorientated and a little bit queasy. And even though he was alone at the top of the city, he felt just a tiny bit embarrassed.

He closed his eyes, trying to dispel the feeling that something bad was about to happen. It had been growing in him for weeks, that feeling, like a bottle filling slowly with water, pushing against him from the inside. And then there were the dreams…

His chatband squeezed his wrist and he glanced down at the display. Ten minutes until his first class. Mel's avatar appeared, followed by the incoming-signal alert. He tapped the screen to see Mel's smiling face.

"Wake up. Time for school."

"Yeah, I'm coming,"

"Where are you?"

"I'm leaving my apartment now."

"You better hurry up or you'll miss the first lesson. And you know how cranky old Edmunds gets if someone's late."

"I said I'm coming."

"All right, grumpy. See you in class."

He prodded the screen and Mel's face disappeared. Now he had nine minutes. He grabbed his bag and hoisted it onto one shoulder before sliding down the smooth rock face and jogging towards the raggedy ladder at the back of the roof. Reaching for the rusted metal, he realised his hands were shaking. He wiped the traces of red dust from his damp palms, then started down the rungs.

His legs were unsteady and threatened to give out from under him. He had to stop and steady himself every other rung. He clung to the treads, his cheek pressed against the cool metal. The wall of the apartment building was mere centimetres away, its grimy surface like goose bumps on pale skin. From this close the texture reminded him of the beach. He almost heard the waves crashing on the shore. He almost felt Mel's hand in his…

A glance to the floor six flights below confirmed no-one was watching. He had never seen anyone in the narrow space round the back of the building, but he did not want to take a chance at being spotted. With gritted teeth, he forced himself to take one step down, and then another. Moving as fast as he dared, he lowered himself to the bottom rung and scrambled down the rough rock face to street level, all the time struggling to shake the memory of the beach.

It wasn't a memory. It had been a daydream. It had been what Mrs Shole, his Citizenship teacher, liked to refer to as an "overactive lack of focus". He was always getting told off for not paying attention, but only because the lessons were so dreadfully dull.

But this had *felt* like a memory, as if he had actually experienced sitting on a beach with his toes in the sand and the seagulls crying out as they hovered above the restless surface of the water.

Which was another thing. He had never actually heard a seagull. Sure he had seen plenty of images and one short video clip but he had never heard what they sounded like. Yet somehow he knew seagulls did not sing like most birds. They made a kind of squawking, crying sound that was really a little bit ugly.

He wondered if this was what happened when you lost your mind. His psych evals had always been positive, and they always did their best to make the citizens of Utopia feel as normal as it is possible to feel while living in what was essentially a hole in the ground, but it was easy to lose grip.

And then there was Mel, or at least he guessed it must be her. The hand in his had been familiar and yet she was the only girl he knew well enough to suggest such intimacy. The other kids hooked up all the time, but she wasn't like that. He liked her, a lot, even if they were just friends. At least, he thought that was what they were.

He got confused around Mel sometimes. He caught himself looking at her as she spoke. She was popular and pretty while he was a freak. There was no future in it, but there were those moments when she looked at him with those big green eyes and he got this feeling in his chest like he was drowning in fresh air. She was one of the few people he could speak to without feeling like he was in a competition of some sort. But in his dream they had been holding hands, like a couple, and they had been watching two kids. *Their* kids.

It had felt like a memory but it had also suggested a life yet to come. He tried to remember more from the dream, but she had been no more than a presence by his side.

He glanced at his chatband. Six minutes. He was definitely going to be late.

The air from the street hit him like a warm slap in the face. There were days when the chemical smells wafted over from the other sectors, but not today. Today the air carried only the vaguely sour odour that suggested too many unwashed armpits. Perhaps the chemicals from Manufacturing and Agricultural were in there as well, but they were being subdued by the dank stench of too many people in not enough space.

Shor turned and set off towards school, weaving through the growing crowd of commuters making their way along the narrow walkway between the tall grey apartment buildings around the quarter's crumbling perimeter and the smaller shops that filled the central area.

They called them quarters—green, yellow, red, and blue—but that was something of a misnomer. Slices would have been a better word, because the general shape of the sector was a semi-circle divided into three concentric rings, with the residential areas in the outermost band running along the perimeter. The markets occupied the next loop inside that while Axle Park nestled against the axis. He could see the mayoral estate tucked away in the heart of the Park, hidden by artificial hedges and protected by a tall fence. As was often the way with palaces, it looked both accessible and foreboding in equal measure.

He recognized most of the faces as he navigated the flow of bodies but he only shared greetings with a few. They all moved in that graceful, bounding lope he had never managed to get right. He was, as so many people liked to point out, short. Every adult male on Mars was at least one metre ninety-four, with the colony average being two hundred and four. Women averaged five centimetres shorter. Shor, at exactly one-eighty, was the same height as the average pre-teen, which meant he got some strange looks from the people towering over him, especially in a crowd like this. The majority of the people passing him were adults or young children in tatty perambulators, but he saw one or two kids of school age dodging and diving towards the imposing red building two blocks further along.

Pinner Secondary School was named in honour of one of the founding fathers of the Martian colony. The green quarter's main boulevard also bore his name, as well as the central library, and at least one factory. Of all the patriarchs, everyone knew Pinner best simply because his face was everywhere. It was impossible to get through a day without seeing those serious but kindly eyes watching with fatherly devotion.

Some people idolized the old man. Most kids of a certain age ridiculed him. The Pinner descendants enjoyed something of a celebrity status, but Shor just found it all a bit creepy.

The school gates loomed and Shor ducked under the imposing wrought iron sign carrying the city's logo: "Dignity, Rationality, Perseverance". He offered a shrug and a smile to the warden at the door.

"You're late," the warden said, tapping his wrist.

"Yeah, I know."

Shor's feet squealed on the polished floor as he turned and lurched towards the Earth class.

"Mr Edmunds will be unhappy if you're late," the warden called after him.

"I know, I know."

"Very unhappy."

"Is he ever anything else?"

Mr Edmunds's liver-spotted hand was already on the handle as Shor ducked inside the classroom and went sprawling across the floor. A wave of laughter greeted him. The floor was cold under his palms.

"Glad you were able to join us, Mister Larkin. Please take a seat."

Shor gathered himself up and shuffled along the aisle, trying to ignore the smirks from the other kids. He felt every eye in the room boring into him, willing him to fall as he struggled to regain control of his limbs. He stumbled and dropped his bag. Now they were not just laughing. There were cheers as well. He was their entertainment for the morning.

Mel offered a smile as he passed.

"Told you," she mouthed.

He took his seat. He ignored the grinning Napier sitting at the next desk.

"Hey Short," Napier whispered, emphasising the "t" at the end so it sounded like a spit. "Nice footwork."

A wave of giggles radiated through the room. Shor folded his arms and stared straight ahead. He couldn't help it if he wasn't as tall as everyone else.

"Silence please," Edmunds said, peering out over his glasses. "If you don't mind, thank you. I know these are your final few days of school and that you are all very keen to receive your work allocations, but this week is as important as every other week of your school career, if not more so. Now is your chance to impress the board. You have finished your exams and your marks will go a long way towards deciding what your first job will be, but teachers have been swayed one way or another based on the attitude of their pupils during the last week. And that includes you, Mister Napier."

"Yes, sir," Napier said in a mock serious voice. "But surely there are jobs only some people can do. For example, only a certain type of person is fit for cleaning the undersides of trucks. Say, a very *short* person."

Another ripple of giggles. Shor sank deeper into his chair.

"As I was saying," Edmunds continued. "These few days can make a big difference, so I expect you all to work hard. Now, today we will be studying the final decade of Earth history."

There was a collective moan from the class. "Do we have to sir?" Napier said.

"Of course you have to," Edmunds replied.

"But we all know it. And what's the point? Who cares that they messed up the environment, and some fool decided using nuclear weapons to defend their borders was a good idea?"

"Because, Napier, the point is that we should not make the same mistakes. One of these days we will be returning to Earth. We will have a second chance, and we must not allow ourselves to take that for granted."

"When exactly will this be, sir?" Napier said, his voice laced with contempt.

"They don't know exactly. A year. Ten years. Maybe a hundred—"

"Maybe never. Let's face it, sir, we're stuck here. You all go on about the Earth and how wonderful it is, but that's just a lie. This is all there is. This is home. Personally, I like it here. I don't want to go to your Earth and breathe its poisoned air. And anyway, sir, you're never going to go, so I don't see why you care so much."

There were murmurs of agreement from the other pupils. One or two people clapped.

"Well, I'm sorry you feel that way, Mister Napier, but it is on the curriculum. And you are wrong. Earth is a dream worth waiting for."

Shor heard the crack of emotion in Edmunds's voice, and he thought he saw moisture in his eyes. The normally stoic teacher never showed any emotion, other than anger.

"Now, log in and locate chapter thirty-seven. Earth, the final years. Miss Lang, would you read for us, please?"

Shor listened to Beeb Lang as she described the last few years of the planet he had only ever seen in video clips, or in digital images. Nobody knew who threw the first stone, but Earth history showed that wars have a habit of escalating. The combined North American and European Space Agency, or NAESA, had poured every last Dollar and Euro-cent into exploring and colonizing Mars. Over a ten year period, subterranean water reserves were located and the first primitive dwelling established in a cave system beneath the area known as Elysium Planitia. Another fifteen years saw the colony expand into a self-sustaining, self-governing, territory with its own economy and constitution. By the time the first nuclear missile was fired, Mars no longer needed the Earth for support. The last ship of refugees landed on March 19th 2047, by which time the war was effectively over. Unlike the previous World Wars, however, this particular incarnation ended relatively quickly. Within two weeks, radiation had rendered the entire surface of the Earth uninhabitable.

"That was, like, a thousand years ago," Beeb Lang said. "Why does it take so long for the air to clear?"

"Nine hundred and eighty-eight Earth years, to be exact," Mister Edmunds said, his voice hollow. "The problem with nuclear war is not just the radioactivity. The initial explosions killed six billion people. Those who survived went underground to avoid the radioactive material falling back down to earth. It would have taken about a year for the air to clear enough to be safe, but all that debris in the stratosphere blocked out the sun, which meant plants and animals died and the temperature dropped rapidly. This is what we call a nuclear winter. Those who survived the bombs, and the radiation, and the freezing temperatures then had to deal with the acid rain. All that debris up in the atmosphere slowly fell back down as sulphuric acid, killing any plants and animals not already dead."

"That's terrible," Beeb said.

"Yes, it is, but it didn't stop there. The Earth is protected from the harmful rays from the sun by a layer of gas called the ozone layer. Much of this was destroyed by the soot and ash thrown into the atmosphere, so anyone caught outside for extended periods would suffer cancers and sores on the skin. The ozone layer rebuilds itself, but it takes many years."

"And you want to go back to this?" Napier said. "I'd rather stay here."

"Yes, I do want to go back," Mister Edmunds said. "I want to go outside and feel the sun on my face—"

"You mean burning acid."

"That will pass. One of these days our probes will tell us the Earth is habitable again. Nature is very resilient. Many species will have died out, but others will have survived. One of these days—"

"One of these days we'll be dead, sir. I don't want to live and die waiting for something that may never happen. Look at you. You've spent your whole life waiting to go back to a mess—"

"Napier, that's enough."

"And you want us to do the same? I'm sorry, but I like it here. Maybe it doesn't have your precious wind and rain and sea, but at least it doesn't have nuclear bombs—"

"Napier—"

"And there are fifty thousand people here now. You mean to tell me they're going to take us all back? I don't think so. Maybe they'll pick me, but not an old man like you."

"Napier!" Edmunds slammed his fist down on his desk hard enough to send equipment crashing to the floor. Napier stopped talking. Those who had been giggling fell silent. Mister Edmunds straightened his glasses with shaking hands. "That will be all, thank you Mister Napier. Now if you will continue reading, there is something I have to attend to. I will be back in a few minutes."

He left the room, his face red and his shoulders slumped. He closed the door without looking up.

"Well done Napier," Beeb said. "You're such a wagger."

"He asked for it. He's always going on about the Earth and how wonderful it's going to be. Well I don't buy it. Most of us are going to live and die right here, and he knows that."

"Exactly. Of course he knows that. Can't you let him have his dream?"

"He's lying to us. I thought teachers were morally bound to tell the truth. I demand to be told the truth, and that old fool is lying to us."

"He's not a fool," Shor said.

"What? Short speaks?" Napier said. "I'm sorry, I didn't think it could talk."

"Leave him alone," Mel said.

"Ah, and his little girlfriend. You two make a perfect couple, you know that? Both midgets and both stupid."

"Just because your father is a big shot, doesn't give you the right to be a flub."

"What did you call me?" Napier said, standing to his feet. Shor sensed the height of the boy towering over him. At almost two metres, Napier was tall for his age, even on Mars.

"You heard me," Mel said, turning to glare at him from her seat.

Napier took a step forward, bringing him in line with Shor's chair. "Say it again, you strut."

Uncertainty crossed Mel's face and she looked to Shor for help. Suddenly, Shor found himself out of his seat and standing in front of Napier.

"Leave her alone."

"And I suppose you're going to make me?" Napier said, leaning forward so that his smiling face was almost directly over Shor's.

"Just calm down. She didn't mean it, did you Mel?"

"Of course I did," Mel said. "He thinks he can get away with anything, just because Daddy's on the council. He's a flub and always will be."

"You know what you are?" Napier said, pointing at her. "You're a stupid—"

He was interrupted by the head teacher entering the room. Napier froze. Shor held his breath.

"Mister Napier," the head teacher said. "Come with me please."

They all watched as the lanky teenager made his way to the front of the class and disappeared through the door, but not before shooting an angry glance at Mel.

The class breathed a collective sigh of relief. Excited chattering broke out.

"Thanks for standing up for me," Mel said.

Shor shrugged. "You would have done the same for me. Wouldn't you?"

"Of course," Mel said. "So, I think this deserves a celebration. What should we do? How about Reggie's?"

"We go there every day. How is that a celebration?"

"We could have an extra scoop of ice-cream. I saved two vouchers from last week."

"Okay, then Reggie's it is. Meet you outside after school."

Mel took his hand and looked into his eyes. "Thanks. You're a real friend."

The cafe was as crowded as ever, which pleased Shor. He had discovered long ago that the two best places to be alone are where there are no people, and where there are lots of people.

Mel was waiting just outside the door and she beamed happily as he approached. Even through the gloom of an early evening the smile in her eyes shone bright. He dodged the stream of pedestrians rushing to finish their errands before the curfew. The big sign high above Axle Park displayed a lights-out time of 6pm, which gave them just two hours.

A maintenance wagon trundled past and he side-stepped as gracefully as he could. The bot driving the wagon turned to look at him briefly before steering the vehicle into the next alley.

"You road hog," Shor said, waving his fist with mock indignation. "Did you see that? Maniac nearly killed me."

"Don't exaggerate," Mel said, giggling as she grabbed his arm and pulled him into the cafe. "So, what flavour you having? My treat."

Reggie's was the usual hangout for kids on their way home from school. Only a few adults were brave enough to venture into the shop's murky depths after 4pm. There was no music today thanks to the power-saving measures, and so groups of kids made their own noise. The pulsing melodies flowed between the various tables that had become impromptu drums, the rhythms competing until one song won out over the others and spread until the whole room joined in, the hands and feet keeping a thick drum beat on counter surfaces and against partitions. Then another song rose up from a different corner, and then another, each trying to usurp the current champion. The table at the very back of the cafe was trying particularly hard, the group of youngsters chanting and clapping with sweaty exuberance.

"I fancy chocolate," Shor said, raising his voice above the throbbing din. "How about you?"

"Strawberry," Mel said. "No, wait. Chocolate. No, wait…"

"Have one scoop of each," Shor said. "We're still having two scoops, right?"

"Of course." Mel lifted her wrist band. "Two scoops of ice-cream. One extra each."

"Then I'm having one chocolate and one strawberry."

"That sounds good. I think I'll have the same."

The queue shuffled towards the counter. Shor had to lean around the kid in front of him to see how many people were ahead of them. He hated being at shoulder height to everyone over the age of thirteen. He felt something brush against his back and glanced around to see a spotty youth staring blankly down at him.

"You all right?" Mel asked, nudging him with her elbow

"Yeah, I'm fine."

"Look, we're next."

The counter was at rib height and so Shor kept back a little. He found a good way to accentuate his lack of height was to stand close to something tall. Mel stabbed their order into the checkout screen and held her wrist band out for scanning. Shor did the same. A few seconds later, two bowls of ice-cream rose up through the counter hatch.

"Here, there's a table at the window," Mel said, taking his sleeve and guiding him through the crowd.

Shor let himself be guided. Some of the other kids were eyeing his bowl hungrily, but he ignored them.

"So," Mel said, savouring the first spoonful. "Do you think you'll get your first choice?"

"I hope so," Shor said. He examined the blob of dessert on the end of his spoon. Ice-cream was one of life's marvels. It made up for a lot of negatives. "My marks have been good enough so far but everyone wants to get into the space program. I'm not getting my hopes up."

"And what were your other two choices?"

"Scientific Research, and Robotics. What about you? You still hoping for an assistant teaching post?"

"It's what I've always wanted," Mel said, already busy on her second scoop. "I look at guys like Mister Edmunds and I think how wonderful it must be to pass everything you know on to the next generation. Like a torch."

"Edmunds can be a real flub sometimes."

"What kid doesn't think their teachers are flubs? But if you look past that, and think of what he's given us. I want to do that. I want to give of myself, you know?"

They sat in silence for a few minutes, each concentrating on the sheer pleasure of eating. Mel finished first, scooping up the last traces with a flourish. She looked down at his plate.

"You finished with that?"

Shor looked down at his last spoonful of dessert. "You have it. I'm getting a headache."

Mel slid his plate across the table and tucked in, her face a picture of hungry concentration.

"Just what I needed," she said. "Three weeks without ice-cream is too long." She pushed the plate away and wiped the corner of her mouth. "So, you gonna sign my petition or what?"

"You think it's going to make a difference?"

"It might. People submit petitions all the time."

"Sure, it's our right, but has anyone ever changed anything? I mean, do we even know if anyone reads them? For all we know they just get deleted. You've got ice-cream…" He pointed at the corner of her mouth.

She licked her lip. "Remember when Dray petitioned for a different shirt style? That worked."

"Fine. Maybe they do read them, but has anything else ever changed?"

Mel shrugged. "It's worth a try. What's the point of having rights if you never use them? Edmunds says people on Earth used to protest all the time. He says it's the only way people can let the government know what they want."

"Mister Edmunds is a…"

"I know. But what have we got to lose?"

He watched her eyes searching his face. To Shor they looked like two perfect moons drenched in waves of luminous green light. He suddenly realized his face was warm.

"Fine," he coughed, raising his hand to his mouth. "So what's the petition? Different colour shoes?" He chuckled but her expression remained determined.

"Murder," she said.

Shor coughed. "What?"

"Do you know how many people are killed by the government each year?"

"Sure, but that's to keep the population healthy. It's not murder. It's eugenics. If we didn't retire people…"

"If we didn't retire people, we'd end up with too many mouths to feed. I know the reason, but is it *right*? And what about the unborn babies aborted because their DNA isn't within *acceptable parameters*?" She was getting upset now, her voice growing a little louder. "Do we have the right to kill a child just because we can't *see* it?"

He is coming.

Shor shifted in his seat, suddenly uncomfortable. The heat had moved down into his neck and chest. "Perhaps we don't have the right, but they have to keep the colony strong. One disease could wipe us all out. You know this."

Mel's face hardened for a moment. Then she slumped back into her chair, as if all the determination had suddenly deserted her. "I know, I know. There are plenty of reasons up *here* why we should abort those babies," she tapped her head. "But what about here? " She placed her hand against her chest. "Have we become so determined to survive that we no longer care about those who can't defend themselves?"

Shor examined her face. Her cheeks were flushed with emotion. Her eyes were moist.

"You're right," he said. "I'm probably going to regret this but sign me up."

A beaming smile blossomed across her face. "Yes! I knew I could count on you."

She tapped her chatband and lifted it towards him. He lifted his close to hers and a beep confirmed the transaction. She grinned at the screen.

"So how many have you got?" he asked.

"Including yours? Two. Hang on, I've got a message."

Her chatband flashed and her eyes dropped to the screen. Shor watched her eyes darting along the lines of text. Her usage bar was already almost empty. She had maybe another quarter hour of usage left for the day. As he looked from her chatband up to her face a lock of blonde hair fell across her forehead and he had the sudden urge to reach out and lift it back. The memory of his dream from earlier surfaced and he forced himself to look away.

Outside, a cleaning bot was studiously working at removing a stain from the walkway with what looked like a knife and a rotating drum of abrasive paper. A passing pedestrian knocked into it without stopping. It turned to see what had happened before returning to its tedious task. Another foot collided with it and it repeated the same little routine of turning, looking, adjusting, and continuing. This happened twice more while Shor watched. He chuckled at the little bot caught in its own little drama.

As he was smiling to himself, someone bumped into him and he turned to watch the offending person bopping smoothly across to a table full of girls who made a poor show of pretending not to notice. As much as he hated his own awkwardness, he felt a pang of admiration at the way the guy moved. It was like he was sliding on a sheet of ice, or floating on a cushion of air.

"That was Lissie," Mel said, leaning across the table. "She said there's a jump going on in ten minutes. Wanna go?"

"What about security? And the cameras?"

"They know where the cameras are."

He knew this of course. He was just buying time.

"Nah. I don't think so."

"Come on. It'll be fun."

"You go. I've got studies. Besides, what if we get caught?"

"Yeah, right. It's the last week of our school careers. What are they going to do, expel us?"

"Edmunds said this last week is important. I don't want to mess up my chances of getting into the space program."

"Edmunds just said that to stop us getting rowdy. They've already decided the job placements. There's nothing you can do to change that, except maybe opening an airlock or something. Come on, it'll be fun. Everyone does something crazy in their final year. It's tradition. I'm sure the badges don't mind."

"But *jumping*? That's dangerous. The badges won't ignore jumping."

"Well I'm going. You can come if you like. It's up to you."

"I'll stay."

Mel examined him for a second, then stood. A few kids were heading for the door. No doubt the word was spreading. Soon half the cafe was on its feet.

"Please come," she said, her green eyes searching his. "At least come and watch."

"All right," he said. "I'll watch, but I'm not taking part."

"Good," she said, taking his hand. "This'll be my first jump. I'm so excited."

Shor glanced up at the Axle Park sign.

"It's 5.15pm. Curfew is in an hour."

"Plenty of time." She pulled him towards the crowd. "Come on."

There were a dozen or so other people in the observation room. All were girls who Shor knew did not enjoy taking part in something so physically demanding but who still wanted to experience the thrill in an indirect way. They ignored him, but then he was used to that. One spoke to him, but it was to hiss an order.

"Watch the door," a girl called Dee said coldly, nodding in the direction of the entrance.

He did as she said, but not because she had told him to. He felt guilty for taking part in something like this, even if it was just as an observer. He had worked harder than most to get good grades. He wasn't about to let a stupid end-of-year prank ruin his chances.

From the doorway he looked down into the ventilation chamber. The glass in the observation room was dirty with red dust but the action was clear enough. At least forty kids stood in ragged circles around the four big vents in a square in the centre of the room, their hands joined as if they were taking part in some sacred ritual. Each was tied with a length of rope to a safety tether anchored to the floor by a circle of metal eyelets. A few, mostly wide-eyed first-timers, were wearing small oxygen masks that covered the mouth and nose, the clear plastic fogging up with each breath.

Mel was in the nearest group and Shor saw her excitement, even from up in the observation room. Her mouth was stuck in a permanent grin as she chatted with those on each side of her. A few times she glanced up at him and he smiled back, offering a self-conscious wave. She had opted for a mask, but it hung loosely around her neck. Through the thick glass, Shor barely heard their jabbering voices.

The talking stopped as a loud bang filled the room. A girl screamed. Some of the boys yelled. Mel's hand moved to her mask.

"Here it comes," the girl next to Dee said.

Shor turned to look at her. She was leaning forward, her big eyes glistening with anticipation.

A series of deep, grinding crashes shook the floor in a slow rhythm, growing steadily faster. Each thump produced a volley of muffled screams from the chamber.

Shor stepped away from the door and moved closer to the window. Mel looked back up at him. He placed a hand flat against the vibrating glass as the pounding came faster and faster until it was more like the growl of some terrible beast.

The ground shook in deep sobs, rattling Shor to the bone. Fine red dust fell from the window and danced around the feet of the participants. Immense machines deep underground thrashed and churned as if drawing breath.

The jumpers waited, listening, heads tilted, eyes darting from one to another. The noise became a deafening roar, filling the air.

Then it stopped.

The first-time jumpers seemed suddenly unsure. One or two looked down at their tethers. The more experienced readied themselves, their knuckles turning white and their chests rising and falling quickly.

Someone's head nodded as if in time to a silent tune. Others looked down. Shoulders drooped, hunched forward. Knees braced as trouser fabric moved under the first, almost imperceptible, movement of air.

"Here she comes!" one of the boys yelled. "Take a breath! Everyone take a breath!"

The chamber in which the kids were standing was not much bigger then the four vents. Nestled in the ceiling, the blades gathered speed, sucking the carbon dioxide out of the tanks in the floor up into the thin Martian atmosphere.

The red dust danced and shimmied. The fans were turning quickly now and accelerating, the beating of their wings a thick hum as they clawed the air. Below the circles of feet, something shifted. Then the slats under the grid flipped opened and ten thousand pounds of carbon monoxide exploded up into the room.

The four circles of teenagers lifted as one, riding the blast, their feet flying back and out. They stifled screams, the fear on their faces mixed with sheer joy as they hovered four feet above the ground, their tethers straining to hold them down. For ten seconds they rode the storm. For ten seconds they flew in a ragged formation of limbs, their hair drawn towards the ceiling in spiky tendrils, their clothes flapping in violent applause. Shor held his breath with them. Ten seconds had never been so long.

Then the sound changed. The external vents closed and there was a loud hiss as breathable air was blasted up through the floor vent.

Now they screamed, starting with the veterans and moving from child to child. Forty kids opened their mouths and yelled as loudly as possible for as long as they could. For another five seconds they whooped and yelped for joy as cold, fresh air pushed them even higher. Then, following the lead of those who had done this before, they pulled their legs in against their chests. Anyone watching would say they looked like four weird, multi-legged, sneaker-wearing tables.

There was a shifting sound as the floor grid slowly closed, choking off the current of fresh air. They floated to the ground in one smooth movement. Shoes banged on the hollow metal.

Some were still yelling as their feet touched down.

They stood on unsteady legs. A few were shaking. One of two sat down. The veterans of the group watched them with knowing smiles, helping the others up and untying their tethers. Masks were removed with trembling hands. They hugged each other, laughing and talking excitedly.

The girls in the observation room were chatting as well. Some were clearly wishing they had joined in. Others were relieved they hadn't, but Shor ignored them. He was watching Mel. She looked a little unsteady on her feet and her hair was dishevelled as she talked animatedly with the girl on her right. He was hoping she would look up at him but she appeared to have forgotten he was there. He watched her as she followed the others towards the solid metal door at the exit point.

It was then that he noticed the observation room had fallen quiet. He turned to look at the girls who were all just standing there, looking at him with wide eyes.

He was about to ask them what their problem was when a heavy hand landed on his shoulder.

It took a total of eight badges to transport the kids down to the police station. It was curfew so the streets were empty apart from the cleaning bots roaming about, their dull headlamps probing the darkness. The only other light came from inside the fortress of apartment blocks and the weak red glow from the ceiling panels. The processing area was designed to handle ten at the most, and so they were dealt with in groups. Numbers were swelled with the arrival of worried parents, which slowed things down even more.

Mel was in the first group. Shor watched her leave under the supervision of her stern-looking father. Shor's parents arrived not long after that. His mother fussed over him the way she always did. His father was more concerned with his wife than he was with Shor. She fussed. He fussed. Shor watched the slow trickle of youths in and out of the police building. His fear at being under arrest was tempered by his irritation. He had known it would be a mistake to do a jump, even if he hadn't technically *done* anything.

He was called in with the last group at just after 8pm. Happily, parents were asked to wait outside. His mother clutched at his hand as he moved away.

"Don't worry," he said, offering a smile. "It'll be fine."

The booking area was clean but well-worn. Shor had only ever set foot inside this particular building once before, during a school outing designed to deter possible future bad behaviour. It looked exactly as he remembered it, only substantially smaller. A U-shaped desk, a bank of seats, and a door leading through to the back.

A bored-looking female receptionist called each in turn, in no apparent order. She took a retinal scan and typed something into a computer before sending them through the back door. Five minutes later, the youth would re-appear. Most looked blank. Some smirked. A few seemed on the verge of tears.

"Next," the receptionist called.

Shor was the closest so he stepped up to the desk. The receptionist glanced at him and raised an eyebrow. Even though the place was smaller than he remembered, it was still designed to cater for adult Martians. She adjusted the scanner perched on the edge of the counter, swinging it down to his eye level.

"Look into the screen. Focus on the crosshairs." She typed something quickly and briefly on the keyboard. "Through the door, first on your left. Next."

Shor did as he was told, walking to where she had pointed and pushing through the scratched and faded door. Here was a corridor with four more doors just like the first. He took the one closest on his left and knocked. Muffled talking on the other side stopped.

"Come!" a voice barked.

It was an office of sorts, with a desk and chair occupied by a gaunt, severe-looking man sitting across from a wall which was dominated by a large mirror. There was another door to the left of the mirror. The desk contained a computer monitor and flat keyboard. Apart from the light in the ceiling, that was the full inventory of the room.

The man behind the desk watched Shor as he approached. When he spoke his voice was as brittle as frozen steel.

"Take a seat." He nodded at the chair. "You are Shor Larkin." It sounded more like an order than a statement or question. From the tone of his voice, Shor had the feeling this man knew him. With only fifty thousand people in the city, it was easy to bump into the same people on a regular basis. He could honestly say, however, that he had never laid eyes on this man before in his life.

"Yes, that's right." Shor lowered himself into the hard chair. It was too big and his legs dangled a few centimetres above the floor. He perched on the edge and tried to appear comfortable.

"I understand you have applied to join the space program."

Shor's heart changed gear. What did that have to do with any of this?

"Yes."

"Why?"

"I don't know. It just sounds really interesting. I've always wanted to work in space."

"Why?"

Shor shifted his weight. "I guess I always enjoyed looking up at the stars."

"You guess? That's not a very good reason, is it? Your last psych evaluation says you're having problems fitting in."

Shor glanced at the back of the screen. "I thought my psych evals were supposed to be confidential."

"They are. Mostly."

What does that mean? Shor thought. *And why don't you ever blink?*

"Whatever expectations you may have had about your career, I can tell you now you will not be going into the space program."

"I knew it," Shor said. "I *knew* we'd get into trouble. It was that thing tonight, wasn't it? I said we shouldn't do it."

At last the man blinked. His lids slid up and down like those of a lizard. A humourless smile buried itself into his face.

"Yes, you did. You stayed up in the observation room and watched the others because you were scared to break the rules. Although, to be honest, I'm more concerned that you've broken the curfew. Do you know how much electricity you kids have wasted tonight? And how many badge hours? I should be home right now, as should the other eight officers called out to deal with this. Right now there are lights burning that should be turned off. You kids seem to have no concept of how precious the resources of this city are. Did you know there are people who count every Watt of energy burned and every drop of water used? Each breath you take is measured and logged and analysed. When you visit the bathroom, every last drop is recorded and stored so our statisticians can decide how many babies can be born and how many old folks have to be sent for retirement. In short, your little stunt is going to cost more than your brain can ever assimilate. But then, you didn't actually take part, did you? You just watched."

Shor could only sit there. People were going to be *retired* because of this? He knew what he wanted to say, but the words were wedged in his mouth. This guy was telling him off for being part of the jump, but he seemed more annoyed that he hadn't actually joined in.

"I didn't want to risk losing my place on the space program."

"Well, it's not a worry anymore, is it?"

"What will I be assigned to do?"

"You'll just have to wait until Friday, like everyone else. Right now, I'd be more worried about your punishment."

Shor felt the heat rise in his face. He tried to swallow but his mouth was dry.

"You are to perform forty hours weekend community service, to commence next week. You will report here on Saturday at nine o'clock. Don't be late. That will be all. A badge will escort you home."

At last the man took his eyes off Shor, which was almost as bad as his lizard stare.

Shor wasn't sure what to do. "Is that it?" he asked.

"Yes," the man said, his attention fixed on the computer monitor as if there was no one else in the room.

Shor stood and walked towards the door. He was about to push it open, but hesitated. He turned back. Every instinct told him to walk out while he still could, but he felt suddenly indignant. It was crazy, but he needed to know.

"If I'd taken part in the jump," he said. "I mean, if I hadn't watched but actually taken part. Would I have been chosen for the space program?"

The man hesitated. He appeared surprised by the question. Shor saw him glance up at the mirror.

"No," he said. "It wouldn't have made a difference."

It was past nine when the badge dropped Shor and his parents off at
their apartment block, escorting them up the narrow stairs to their front
door where he watched them unlock the door before leaving in silence. The
elevators were taboo during curfew hours except in emergencies, and so
they climbed the five flights to their tiny home.

They checked their electricity quota for the day and ate in silence under
the pallid glow of a single ten Watt bulb. They had twenty minutes to eat
and thirty more to get ready for bed before the meter turned off and
submerged them in night.

Shor's nerves were still a little on edge, so he sat on his bed in the
darkness and stared out of his small bedroom window at the soft glow of
the city, the only sound being the electric hum of maintenance bots going
about their nightly business. As he watched, the lights from apartments
windows went out one by one until only a handful remained, scattered
across the city, glittering like the first stars in an evening sky.

The ceiling lights dotted between the glass panels were now completely
dark. Normally he would keep his eye out for any sign of the constellations,
but the thin atmosphere was still carrying clouds of dust that might circle
the entire planet and last for weeks. He saw the occasional bright pinpoint,
but nothing more. Earth would be up there somewhere tonight with its
endless blue seas draped with silken clouds, and the jagged coastlines he
had spent hours tracing with his fingers on the pictures Mister Edmunds
had shown them.

It was such a waste. The Earth had more than enough water, air, and
food for everyone, and yet the history of the planet was little more than a
series of wars for those same resources. There were pictures of people
drinking water as if it would never run out. And not just drinking it, but
immersing themselves in it as it fell from the sky. Even swimming in it. He
could not imagine such a thing.

And there was so much space. He had read about places on Earth
where no human had ever set foot, and yet they still battled over tiny

patches of land.

He looked around his tiny bedroom. Standing in the centre, his outstretched fingertips touched the two side walls, and it wasn't much longer either. The only dimension they allowed for was height. To touch the ceiling would mean climbing onto his bed and standing on his toes although any "normal" person his age would consider the ceiling suitably low.

Looking up at the grimy plaster, he was reminded how much he hated being short. He hated being short almost as much as he hated being clumsy.

He checked his chatband and scrolled through his rations. Thirty litres of water for the next ten days. Three ten minute shower coupons. Twenty meals. Ten snacks. Two balls of ice-cream. Two bars of chocolate.

At least his calorie allowance had gone up. The doctors had declared him underweight and ordered an increase in portion size. That was two weeks ago. He pinched his stomach. Already he could feel a difference.

Mel had given him one of her ice-cream servings, which helped. It was supposed to have been a celebration. Some celebration it had turned out to be. That sort of thing, the sharing of rations, was frowned upon but was not strictly against any rules. Otherwise he would have refused for sure. He was what the psych eval called an "abider". He liked, so they said, to follow rules. He found security in rules. They made him feel safe. "Abiders like to feel safe," they said.

He wondered if that was why the badge had made the comment about him not taking part in the jump. The lizard's voice had carried an air of contempt, as if he had been disappointed in Shor for choosing to follow the rules, but that made no sense. Badges were supposed to enforce rules, not encourage anarchy.

Outside, a maintenance bot was stuck in a corner and trying to figure out what to do next. Its simple brain was only able to handle so much data at a time and so it used a crude trial-and-error protocol, which involved a lot of changes in direction and collisions with the obstacles around it.

He watched it, wondering how much energy it was burning as it performed its little dance, the same energy the lizard had scolded him for wasting. At last it figured out that the best plan of action was to go backwards a little, stop, turn, and then go back some more. Once free, it carried on as if nothing had happened. Simple rules for a simple robot. It could learn, but not much. The odds were good the same bot would get stuck in the same corner tomorrow night.

Perhaps that explained the badge's disdain. Perhaps that was how the badge saw *him,* as little more than a dumb robot. Robots need rules to function. Robots need rules to be "happy". So too, apparently, did he. He needed rules to function and be happy because he was an "abider".

Shor watched the bot disappear around the bend, its little brain seemingly unaffected by the drama of just a minute ago.

So the space program was out of the question. Hopefully, his second and third choices for a career were still available. He could not imagine his personality might preclude such exciting daredevil pursuits as Scientific Research or Robotics.

He leaned forward so that his head touched the glass. From here he was able to see Mel's apartment block and, if she still had a light on, her tiny bedroom window. It glowed second from the top and third from the end. He wished he knew what the badge had said to Mel. Her dad had looked annoyed, but then that was not unusual. He wondered if her first choice had been ruled out too.

He glanced down at his chatband out of sheer habit. That was one of the hardest parts of the post-storm power saving drives. He usually spent most of his credits chatting with Mel about everything and nothing, but mostly nothing. Now that they had something important to discuss, they couldn't.

He looked for her window again but it was gone. The city was almost completely dark, revealing itself to the eye as a series of ever deepening shadows. Even the Axle Park sign was just a black cube with the time barely visible. A badgemobile rolled past, its headlights casting a pool of light on the road, and then it was gone.

Shor climbed between the sheets and rolled onto his back. It took a while for sleep to come but, before too long, he was breathing deeply. He dreamed of water and rain, and of swimming in the sea. He dreamed of the sun and the beach and of children playing happily at the water's edge. He dreamed of Mel.

Mrs Lupine the Career Guidance Counsellor was a pale, slender, delicate woman with soft blue eyes that seemed to float above her high cheekbones. Her hair cascaded around her neck and shoulders in billowing waves. She was tall, even for Mars, and Shor found her both alluring and intimidating in equal measure.

Her words, like her movements, were slow and measured. She was the kind of woman who could deliver the most terrible news in a way that made you feel as though you had just been presented with a bouquet of flowers. Perhaps that was why she was the teacher whose responsibility it was to inform each child of his or her career path. Her one-to-one chats lasted no longer than five minutes, but they were potentially the most important five minutes in each young Martian's life.

The routine was simple. On the afternoon of the last day of school, each child was called in turn to report to Mrs Lupine's office. There they would sit alone on a bench outside until the current interviewee was dismissed. The one waiting then entered the room while the next pupil was summoned. Afterwards, you got to go home. It was simple, efficient, and thoroughly terrifying.

Pupils called it the "creeping death" and were uniformly undecided upon which was better: to go early and get it over with, or put it off as long as possible. Order was decided by ascending last names which meant Shor, whose surname was Larkin, was pretty much bang in the middle, and this suited him just fine. He couldn't help but feel a little bit sorry for Aarons, but he felt particularly sorry for Yelland who would be alone in the classroom with the teacher for five minutes while she waited to be called.

Shor's turn came just after 2.30pm. The kid from the lower year whose task it was to run back and forth between the office and the classroom popped his head inside the door and called "Shor Larkin."

"Hey Short," Napier said in a hoarse whisper. "Go get 'em."

It'll be your turn soon enough, Shor thought, but it was little consolation. No doubt Napier would get exactly the career he wanted. Napier always seemed to get exactly what he wanted—one of the advantages of having a dad who had served on the council for over twenty years.

Mel offered a supportive smile but Shor's stomach was still doing slow barrel rolls. Her punishment for the jump episode had been the same as his, except for the career thing. The badge hadn't even mentioned her wish to be an assistant teacher in Citizenship. From what he could gather, he was the only one whose life had been seriously affected by that dumb end-of-year stunt, and he hadn't even jumped.

The corridor seemed longer and darker than usual as Shor followed the kid to the room at the end, then took his place on the bench where he waited for the five minutes to pass. He caught the sound of Mrs Lupine's silky voice laying out the future for the one inside. Once or twice, a teacher appeared further along the corridor. The sounds from the classrooms spilled out as doors opened and closed. Knowledge being imparted and, hopefully, absorbed.

The bench was just starting to feel hard when his turn came and Mrs Lupine's porcelain features appeared. A kid—Jenkins—stepped out and they exchanged glances, Jenkin's happy expression suggesting he had been allocated one of his three original choices.

Mrs Lupine nodded to Shor and he followed her into the room.

"Please, take a seat," she said, moving around to the other side of the glass display table and lowering herself into her chair.

She gently touched the smooth surface and Shor's details floated into view. His own face smiled vacantly up at him alongside a page of information. He had always hated that picture, taken shortly after a week when he had been symptomatic. He looked even more pale than normal, with traces of shadows under still-bloodshot eyes. The data appeared to be the usual things: name, age, gender, aptitudes, and school performance. He looked for scores but there were none listed.

"Mister Larkin," she said, her voice as smooth as engine oil. "Firstly I would like to discuss your grades for this year."

Shor felt his chest tighten as he watched her fingers hover over the screen.

She stroked the glass and another page of data drifted forward. Her eyes scanned the text and her lips toyed with a smile. "You have done very well. Congratulations. Your scores are in the top five percent. Based on this I see no reason why you cannot choose...sorry, one moment please."

She tapped the screen and it fogged over, blocking Shor's view of it. She leaned forward to read, a frown tracing a jagged line down her normally smooth forehead. "That's strange. It says here you are to be allocated to the Maintenance Department. Please wait a moment."

She stood and left, stepping through into an adjoining room. She swung the door closed behind her but it did not close properly. Through the gap, Shor could see her back as she spoke into her chatband.

He turned his head to try to catch what she was saying.

"...there has been a mistake...grades are excellent...no reason why he can't...yes, but...space program, research, robotics...yes, but...of course...no, I understand..."

She ended the call and stood straight, her shoulders rising and falling as if in a deep sigh. She turned and walked back into the room, lowering herself again into her chair.

"It seems," she said, "there has been a mistake. Due to certain factors, you are not deemed suitable for your top three selections and have been allocated to Maintenance." She smiled, but it seemed suddenly plastic. "It is a worthy and rewarding career and you will be performing a service vital to the city. Without competent maintenance technicians, our city would grind to a halt. Congratulations and good luck."

Shor just sat and stared at her. "I don't understand. What did I do wrong?"

"You did nothing wrong. They just have too many applicants for your chosen positions."

"But you said I would have no problem..."

"I was mistaken."

"Was it because of the jump? Is that why I'm not getting the career I want?"

"No. The jump had nothing to do with it. Now, if you don't mind, I have many students still to see."

Shor wanted to shout at her, but he was suddenly tired. She was standing at the door with her hand ready to push, her extended arm ushering him out.

He stood and she opened the door for him with that fake smile. The next kid was waiting on the bench. It was Tanya Lynch. Her face fell when she saw his expression.

"How did it go?" she whispered as he shuffled past. "Did you get your first choice?"

He did not answer but just stared past her, unable to find any words. Mel was waiting for him at the front of the school. He could see the concern on her face. Inside, he felt numb.

"What's wrong?" she said. "Please tell me you got in. Please tell me you made the program."

"No, I didn't make it," he said.

"So what did you get? Research?"

"I don't want to talk about it."

"Robotics is good. You got Robotics, right?"

"No. I didn't get Robotics."

Mel's shoulders fell, her face suddenly serious. "You're jesting with me, right? I know you studied like crazy so there's no way your grades weren't good enough."

"My grades were fine. They said they just had too many people wanting my positions."

"They said *what?*"

"It doesn't matter. I didn't get the job I wanted. Big deal. There are worse places to work than Maintenance. It's all right."

"Do you want to go to Reggie's?"

"No thanks," Shor said. "I think I'll go home. I promised my mom I would clean my room this weekend."

"How about tomorrow then?"

"Sure, perhaps. Listen, I need to be alone for a while. I'll call you. All right?"

Shor turned, leaving Mel standing there. He knew he was hurting her feelings but his mind was in turmoil. The barrel rolls in his belly had stopped. Now he wanted to throw up.

He set off towards home, but did not take the road to his apartment. Instead, he continued straight on, past the market and on to the apartment block at the top of the quarter. He walked to the end of the alley and squeezed through the gap. With the sure-footedness that comes with regular practice, he clambered up the side of the building until he reached the utility ladder and then climbed the rest of the way to the roof.

From his little niche in the cave wall, he had a perfect view of the city and was effectively invisible unless, of course, someone came looking for him, but that was unlikely. From here he could see large patches of sky through the glass panels. Outside, up on the Martian surface, the dust was finally starting to settle, revealing patches of orange atmosphere. He could even see the sun, but it seemed smaller than usual today somehow.

Lying on his stomach with his chin resting on his crossed arms, he looked out across the city going about its never-ceasing activities. The air was starting to clear and he could see all the way across to the huge airlock door that led through to the Hub and the service sectors. Somewhere beyond the door, in one of the other caves he always imagined as the parts of some freakish insect, was his allotted career. Somewhere out there was his future. Its pull was almost a physical sensation as it dragged him towards itself, like a piece of wood on the tide of a mighty Earth ocean.

He was struck by this thought. His psych eval would have a party with that one. Perhaps Edmunds was right after all. Perhaps the old man understood more than the children under his care possibly could because they had yet to experience life as a mere cog in a machine. For the first time, Shor consciously considered life beyond the ancient, crumbling, walls of Utopia.

His life was set out before him and there was not a thing he could do about it. No doubt his psych eval knew all this. Of course! It was not his grades, or even the jump, that had decided his future. His psych eval had plotted his course through life a long time ago.

He looked down to the street where the afternoon rush was gathering pace. The market was getting full as people did their afternoon shop, exchanging electronic vouchers for bread, milk, cheese, rice, potatoes, string beans, and, if they were lucky, meat. Suddenly it all seemed so pointless. They were so busy, but busy doing what? They worked to get vouchers, to exchange for food, so they could work for more vouchers to buy more food.

Dignity, Rationality, Perseverance. That was the city's logo. He had memorized it when he was four, repeating the words with his teacher, not understanding but marvelling at the feel of those sounds rolling off his tongue. Big sounds. Important sounds.

The chatband squeezed his wrist like a child cloying for attention. The screen was flashing on and off. Mel's face smiled up at him.

He slid forward until he was able to see over the lip straight down to where a bot was scuttling between a wave of long legs, its tiny brain processing the simple rules that would allow it to fulfil its purpose. Shor wondered what bots actually felt. Did it make them happy to fulfil their purpose? Were they content because they knew what they had to do? Did they have their own logo—a robot equivalent of "Dignity, Rationality, Perseverance"? Did they wish for greater things?

And did they get depressed when those wishes were squashed under the unyielding Utopian bureaucracy?

Of course not, Shor thought.

But then, how could he know such a thing? How could anybody know such a thing? Perhaps there were beings of unimaginable intelligence watching humans at that very moment and thinking the same thing about them. Perhaps the original Martians had adapted to their environment and were not dead but invisible to the human eye. Perhaps they ignored humans and let them get on with their lives because they saw the human existence as without meaning or purpose, just as humans ignored bots. Unless, that is, they broke down or got stuck in a corner.

He slid forward so his arms dangled above the street far below. A drop from this height would not kill him, unless he went head-first. If he just jumped he would certainly break some bones, but then he might land on someone and hurt them instead.

The bot had made it through the forest of legs and had found something to clean. Unfortunately, the thing was in a tight corner and the bot appeared to be struggling to get back out again. Someone stopped and helped it out, at which point it looked around and went straight back into the corner again. No doubt someone, somewhere, was counting that wasted energy and plotting it on a graph so someone else could decide who lived and who died.

Shor rolled over onto his back and looked up through the glass at the Martian sky. The sun blinked back at him through the clouds of dust. There were probably worse things in life than not getting your chosen career. His Citizenship teacher always told them: "Carpe diem". Very inspiring, for sure, but what if you didn't like the diem enough to carpe it?

He pushed himself back from the edge and slid down to the roof. It was lunch time but he was not hungry. He lacked the appetite to seize the day. He lacked the appetite to do anything. Of course, missing meals was frowned upon because it was a waste of resources. Martian children were taught from a young age to leave nothing on their plates. Such was the zeal of the average young student that school plates eventually became warped from the rigorous scraping of knives and forks. Shor wondered how many additional calories lay in the surface of a plate.

He threw a quick glance back across towards the edge of the roof before heading towards the ladder. Maybe he would start with grabbing a bite to eat and work up from there.

Mel called him a dozen times on his two rest days but he let them go to his inbox. On Wednesday he left the apartment early and came home just before curfew, avoiding his usual haunts, spending his time wandering the streets, even venturing into the yellow quarter to visit places he had not seen in years.

On Thursday he set off before breakfast and travelled even further, making his way to the red quarter—a distance of over two kilometres. The green trim on his clothes betrayed his status as a visitor and he drew more looks than usual.

It was not normal for people to leave their quarters. There was no need. Wide-eyed children pointed at him while tugging at their parent's sleeves. Older kids stared with blank insolence. Lanky youths shared snickering comments with their obligatory gang of friends. Shor just looked beyond them and kept walking, only changing direction when he reached a dead-end or came too close to a police building.

On two occasions he was stopped by badges curious to know what he was doing out of his quarter, so he was forced to come up with a story about how he was preparing for work tomorrow by following the route in, and somehow managed to get hopelessly lost. This worked surprisingly well, with the badges apparently taking this as a conscientious effort to do the right thing by an upstanding and soon-to-be-productive citizen. They pointed him towards the big airlock door over in the mist beyond Axle Park.

He visited the other schools. All looked identical, with the same red brick and the same austere architectural design. Each had the city motto emblazoned in big steel letters above the gates.

The motto was everywhere, above shop doors, on the façades of municipal buildings, as scrolling marquees on the big digital bulletin boards situated on virtually every street corner. It was usually accompanied by a portrait of Pinner himself, or one of the other founding fathers. They had made it impossible to escape the words chosen as the most worthy to underpin the values and motives of the newly-formed colony.

Dignity. Rationality. Perseverance.

Now as his eyes drifted across the elegant sweep of the letters, Shor felt a sense of betrayal. He has persevered, he has studied hard, but that had not been enough.

A fat cleaning bot hummed past, pausing to scrape something dark and sticky from the walkway. It took some time to remove the offending stain, which it then lifted up to its visual sensors to examine before depositing it into the gaping mouth-like slot in the middle of what, intentionally or unintentionally, resembled a human face.

The bot then trundled off, looking for more stains to remove from the grubby city streets, its wide rear end swaying slightly as it negotiated the gaps between commuters in their red-trimmed uniforms.

Shor followed it for a while, mostly because it was going in the same general direction. After two blocks it ducked into a service tunnel to recharge its batteries, or whatever it was robots did when they were not working. Perhaps cleaning bots got prizes for finding particularly gruesome specimens of trash. Perhaps it would win a small trophy, or a medal, or get an extra squirt of oil.

There was a hiss and a click as it vanished into the network of tunnels running beneath the city. Here the bots travelled back and forth between the various sectors without using the big airlock door that kept the general population protected from anything that might possibly explode, melt, or leak toxic fumes.

He remembered learning about the airlocks at school, and the reason they were so important. Up to that point he had felt as secure as any eight-year-old in familiar surroundings, but that security had evaporated with the realization they were effectively living in a bottle, and there was nowhere to run if that bottle ever shattered. He had looked at the Martian sky through different eyes from then on.

He reached the corner and stopped. Up ahead, the road was full of automated vehicles, delivery trains, and some of the larger maintenance machines, parked twenty meters short of the big airlock door that resembled a mighty stopper in the neck of a huge, prostrate bottle. It was closed now, watched over by a stern-looking badge, but soon it would open, allowing the contents of one bottle to drain into another. On the walkway, separated from the vehicles by a solid barrier, a hundred pedestrians from the four quarters waited. Shor recognized a few faces but nobody noticed him. He looked down at his chatband. It gave the time as 3:58pm. Two minutes to go.

As he watched, a yellow strobe light above the doors began flashing and a high-pitched alarm let out a series of steady beeps. There was a crash and a long, low hiss, followed by what sounded like the slow clank of a cog and chain. Then the massive door's seal sighed as it cracked open and moved in a slow arc across the polished walkway.

Shor could see the same door on the other side and, beyond that, a similar crowd waiting to come across this way. He tried to take in as much detail of the other sector as possible but it was hard to see very much. The air was heavy with dust and only the closest buildings were visible. These were the grey, symmetrical, utilitarian structures of industry.

The door thudded open and the light and siren both stopped. The badges stepped forward and, with a vaguely theatrical flick of their open palms, began directing the machines to move. Once these had all gone, the pedestrians were waved along. A few latecomers rushed through under the watchful gaze of the badges but it was all over in less than five minutes. The exchange was completed without incident. The alarm sounded, the light flashed, and the doors swung closed. They would not open again for another hour.

Shor looked at those who had come across from the other side, examining their faces and their body language. There were no uniforms so it was impossible to distinguish the agricultural workers from the lab scientists, or the software engineers from the mechanics. He spotted a small cluster of people and watched them closely. They looked tired but not exhausted or unhappy. One was saying something and, as soon as he stopped, the others laughed in response. At the corner they split up, each waving their farewells.

In a few hours he would be joining these people, possibly doing the same work, maybe even bidding them farewell just as he had witnessed. He hoped they would let him walk with them, and share their jokes. He hoped he would fit in.

His chatband squeezed. It was Mel. He thought about answering, but was not in the mood to talk to anyone. The road leading to the airlock door was deserted, apart from the two badges who watched him from their small, glass-fronted office.

He turned and walked the fifty metres to where the road widened and split into Pinner Boulevard, the main ring road that marked the perimeter of Axle Park. Two trams set off from here every ten minutes, as regular as a vibrating crystal, following the hidden power lines in both directions all the way around the boulevard. The park entrance here suggested an ancient grandeur, lined with an old but ornate steel fence and two rows of shabby artificial trees. He could hear soft music playing and the sound of birdsong from the handful of recordings brought across on the first ships. There were other sounds he knew to be monkeys, lions, elephants, hyenas, and wolves, all playing on an endless loop from speakers hidden in the artificial undergrowth. It was a limited repertoire from what Edmunds had told them was a vast ensemble of sound. According to Edmunds, there were places on Earth that were never silent.

At various points within the park, visitors could watch videos from Earth showing a multitude of apparently unrelated scenes accompanied by inspiring music. There was an aerial view of a snowy mountain, and a particularly beautiful sequence of a sunrise over a forest. Soundless waves crashing on a silent shore while mute seagulls hovered.

The scenes were designed to be relaxing, and motivate people for the return to Earth, but Shor found that many of the sights and sounds made him anxious for reasons his psych eval was unable to explain.

He hesitated, watching a family group as they joined the crowds gathering along the winding pathways that joined the four park entrances. The parents carried themselves with the slow grace he envied so much. The two children bounced and hopped on either side, seeming to hang in the air with each leap. He guessed they were early pre-teen, and yet they would soon be tall enough to look him in the eye.

Behind the family group, a mother and son stopped to watch a cluster of mechanical amusements. The mother was holding her son's hand, and she bent down to say something to the boy while pointing to the machine. The boy's eyes were wide with amazement as clockwork figures performed their little show.

He is coming.

Shor shook his head and blinked, feeling suddenly disorientated. He had seen that somewhere before. He had seen a mother and a small boy standing and watching another show, but it had been more than that. The perspective was wrong. He hadn't just seen the mother and child, he had *been* the child. And it was not Mother, but some other woman who was somehow also his mother. He had stood watching a man throw colourful balls into the air while this woman held his hand and bent down to explain what the man was doing. It was so real he could almost taste it. He could smell the memories covering him like a musty old blanket.

The mechanical show stopped and the mother and child moved on towards a small market stall selling cold meat sandwiches. He had the urge to follow them but it was getting late.

The cube hanging above the park announced an end to the power-saving measures. At last everything was back to normal. The extractor fans had done their jobs, putting in the necessary overtime to get Utopia back to its relatively dust-free self. The curfew was back to the usual 10pm. Days would return to their standard length and restrictions on network use lifted. People were already checking their chatbands.

It was 8pm, which meant he had two hours to get home. Plenty of time.

He was about to set off when he heard heavy footsteps approaching from behind.

"Is your name Shor Larkin?" a gravelly voice asked.

He turned to see the two badges who had been watching him from the security box. "Yes, why?"

"Is your chatband broken?"

"No, it's fine. Why do you ask?"

"They've been trying to reach you all afternoon, but you haven't answered your calls. They were about ready to post an announcement on the cube."

Shor glanced up at the enormous message board. On a clear day like today it would be visible from almost anywhere in the Residential Sector.

"Why? What's the matter?"

"You need to get back. It's your mother."

"My mother? What's wrong? Is she all right?"

"Come on, we'll give you a lift."

Shor followed them to their vehicle and climbed into the back seat. As they passed the park entrance, he looked to see if the mother and boy were still there, but they had gone, lost in the milling crowds gathering within the park.

There was a growing list of unanswered messages on his chatband. Mixed in with the calls from Mel were a half-a-dozen from his father, his face looking accusingly up at him from the screen. He tapped Mel's last message and a few moments later her face filled the display. Her eyes were red and her cheeks wet.

"Where were you?" she asked. "Why didn't you answer my calls?"

"I'm sorry," he said. "I just needed some time. What's wrong with my mother?"

"Haven't they told you?"

"No. They haven't said anything."

"I'm so sorry," she said, a tear tracing a jagged line down her cheek. "Your mother's symptomatic. It's quite bad. She's been taken to hospital."

There were numerous clinics in Utopia, but only one hospital, situated in the very centre of a sector not far from Axle Park. There was little about its external appearance to indicate its purpose. It looked like every other building in the neighbourhood and might easily be mistaken for a market or one of the specialist stores. Only the ambulance parked out front gave any clue that it was a hospital.

When they pulled up outside the wide front doors, Shor's father was waiting. He looked frail and lonely.

Shor climbed out of the police vehicle and rushed over to him.

"What happened? Is Mother all right?"

His father looked down at him through red eyes. His normally stiff chin quivered as he spoke. "She collapsed. She'd just come back from the market and was packing the shopping away…Where were you? She was worried."

"I needed time to think."

"You couldn't do that at home? We haven't seen you for two days. You know how she frets."

"I'm sorry. Where is she? Can I see her?"

"Not now. The doctors are looking at her."

"Will she…?"

Shor could not say the words. He knew the strict Utopian policy of treating debilitating symptoms, especially for its older citizens. Those incapable of working were invariably sent for retirement.

"I don't know," his father said, turning away.

Shor watched his father's shoulders shake. He wanted to comfort him, but did not know how. Theirs had never been that kind of relationship. His mother had always been the demonstrative one.

Shor left him and walked to the low wall at the front of the grounds. The shops were busy with people enjoying the return to a normal curfew. They stared at him as they passed, their faces a mixture of disdain and possibly even pity. He turned and looked across at his father standing

40

hunched and alone at the corner of the building, the gulf between them as wide as Elysium Mons.

A doctor emerged from the building and called to them. Shor walked quickly across, searching the doctor's face for some clue.

"How is she?" Shor's father asked.

"She's stable. She has had a mild stroke and is still in a coma. We won't know the extent of any damage until she is conscious."

"When will she wake up?" Shor asked.

"We don't know. It could be days, or weeks."

"But she will wake up, right?"

"I'm sorry. It's impossible to say. Some people wake up after a few hours with no signs of trauma. Others never wake up. All we can do is wait."

And that was that. The doctor promised to contact them as soon as there was any change. They were welcome to come back during visiting hours.

They walked home in silence, along the walkways just starting to empty, Shor always a step or two behind his father. With the network back to full usage, teenagers and kids took advantage of the return to normalcy by engrossing themselves in their chatbands. They hung around in gangs, their heads bowed over the tiny screens, some talking, others tapping out shorthand messages in multi-chats. Shor knew that many would be typing messages to someone in the same group, possibly even to the person sitting right next to them. He recognized a crowd from his school. They perched on the steps to an apartment building like vultures, but they were too busy to notice him pass by.

Shor was suddenly aware of how much power these kids were using to drive their social interactions. It was the same power needed to keep his mother alive. He had the urge to walk over to them and snatch their stupid chatbands away. Or maybe he could get them to sign Mel's petition. *Sure,* he thought, *and maybe there's someone heading here from Earth right now to take us all home.*

They rode the elevator up to their floor and entered the silent apartment. It felt cold and empty. Without his mother it was an alien and unwelcoming shell.

"I'll make supper," his father said.

"I'm not hungry," Shor replied and retreated to his room.

He lay on his bed, looking up at the dark ceiling for the longest time. The sound of his father moving around the apartment echoed through the walls. At one point Shor thought he heard him stop outside his door. Then the door to his parents' bedroom shut and the only sound was that of the maintenance bots in the walkway below.

He tried to sleep but it would not come, so he sat up and gazed out of his window into the red haze. Mel's light was still on. He tapped her avatar on his chatband and the dial signal flashed.

She did not answer straight away, which was unusual. Her face appeared after a few seconds, framed by the soft glow from her ceiling light.

"Hi," she said in a soft voice.

"Hi. Listen, I just wanted to say I'm sorry for this weekend. I acted badly."

"It's all right."

"I guess I wasn't expecting to end up in Maintenance. But I feel better about it now. I had some time to think. I visited the airlock and watched the people coming through. They seemed happy enough."

"How's your mom?"

A sudden rush of grief engulfed him. Only toddlers called their mothers "mom". Shor fought back the tears, swallowing hard.

"She's in a coma but the doctor was hopeful. He said she could wake up any time."

"I'm sure she'll be fine," Mel said. "Listen. I'm going to get some sleep. We've got an early start tomorrow. We don't want to be late for work."

"See you afterwards?" Shor said.

"Sure," Mel said. "We can compare notes."

"Yeah, that would be nice. How's the petition going?"

"Not so good. I only got two more people to sign up. People just don't seem to care. I'm thinking about dropping it. A petition is only as effective as the number of people who sign it, you know?"

"Are you going to submit it?"

Mel was silent for a moment. Shor listened to her breathing. "Perhaps. I don't know. I'll give it another week."

"You should. It's a good cause."

He disconnected the call and set the alarm for seven. It would give him enough time to eat, dress, and walk the kilometre to the tram station. He lay down and thought about the future. He had spent so much time dreaming about working on the space program that he had not prepared himself for the possibility he might end up doing something else.

Through the thin apartment walls came the sound of his father snoring. And outside, a bot had got stuck in a corner again, its little motors whining over and over as it tried to work out what to do. It was a vaguely hypnotic sound, even a little bit reassuring.

He folded his pillow double to try to get some support. The slip was almost threadbare and the coarse stuffing scratched his neck. A few more weeks and he would qualify for a new one.

He closed his eyes and, lulled by the rhythmic sound of a confused robot, fell asleep.

The next morning, Shor woke with a sense that something was wrong. He pulled his hand out from under his pillow and peered at the flashing time, trying make sense of the blurred numbers.

"Ah, flub!"

It was the first day of his new career and he had managed to sleep through his alarm for a full ten minutes. His arm was numb from lying in an awkward position, so he had not felt the gentle but insistent squeeze of his chatband. Nor had he heard the beeping until it was loud enough to penetrate his pillow.

He dressed and ate and washed as quickly as he could. The elevator was on the bottom floor so he took the stairs. Outside, the walkway was heaving with commuters. He pulled his fingers through his hair as he dashed towards the tram stop, dodging the forest of bodies that seemed to be moving in slow motion.

There was standing room only on the tram, so he stood. The hand rail was out of reach so he settled for holding the back of a chair, which drew a look of disapproval from the occupant.

All around him, tall people were swaying in harmony with the tram as it trundled along the track. By the time he reached his stop, he felt like he'd been squeezed through the business end of a sausage machine.

The light for the airlock was flashing and the siren was wailing as he stepped down onto the walkway. The big door started to swing open so he walk-jogged as fast as he dared for the last hundred metres. He wanted to run but knew better. The coordination required to run on Mars was beyond him. He had seen others do it, but it was not something for short, densely-built people. Running required long limbs and a lightness of foot that he simply did not have. Or perhaps it was a genetic thing he had missed out on somehow.

He stumbled the last few metres, making it to the door just in time.

"Hurry up," the badge at the far end barked as Shor waddled across the gap between the two big airlock doors.

Shor smiled apologetically and slipped in behind the other commuters. They passed through the Hub-side door and moved in a loose group down the main road towards the intersection where four dirty grey trams were waiting. He thought he saw some classmates but they vanished between the milling people.

At the crossroads, the crowd divided into smaller splinters before moving to the waiting trams. Shor looked up at the sign indicating that Maintenance was the second vehicle on the right. He climbed on board and found himself at the back of a car containing about thirty people.

"You're one of the new guys," the man in the seat across the aisle said.

Not sure if this was a question or a statement, Shor said he was.

"Lars Fline," the man said, offering a big, calloused hand.

"Shor Larkin."

"Please to meet you, Shor. I've been expecting you. You'll be joining my team. Trainee manager. We deal with all things electrical. So what did you do to end up here? Let me guess. You put a high-voltage battery on the teacher's chair."

Shor looked at him blankly.

"No? Then you must've wired the head teacher's lunch to the mains?"

"No, I didn't do anything like that."

"Well that did it for me," Lars said. "If you didn't annoy a teacher, what *did* you do?"

"Nothing," Shor said.

"Nothing? I highly doubt it. Nobody gets assigned to Maintenance without doing something wrong."

"Actually, I think it was something I *didn't* do."

"*Actually?* Well, ain't that a conundrum. You get sent down to the armpits of the city for something you *didn't* do. Well, the world is a strange place, but don't worry. It ain't so bad, once you get used to it. Ain't that right fellas?"

One or two people turned and smiled. Another rolled his eyes.

"So, Shor. I figure you didn't actually ask to get sent down here to the bowels of Utopia. Nobody asks to get this as a career, unless they're stupid, and I don't take you as being stupid. So what did you want to do? What was your first choice?"

"Space Program," Shor said without hesitation. He had repeated those words so many times they had set up residence on the very tip of his tongue.

Lars whistled. "Now I get it. What you didn't do was study. Your grades were no good."

"No. My grades were good enough."

"You must've really ticked someone off. Whatever you didn't do, besides not studying, it must've been a biggy."

"I guess so."

"There ain't no guessing about it, son. But don't worry. Maintenance ain't so bad—if you don't mind working in a sewer. Here, let me introduce you to some of the others on the team. This big fella is Reet. His team works mainly on the lighting system."

Reet nodded. Shor lifted a hand.

"And this skinny one here is Tane. He's our expert in life-support. If he ever dies, you better start holding your breath. And that cheerful soul over there by himself is Bek. He's in charge of waste disposal. Now he really *does* work in a sewer."

Bek half-turned and scowled. Shor smiled apologetically.

"How many people work in Maintenance?"

"About two hundred in total, divided into three shifts. The evening and night shifts are skeleton, just to handle emergencies. You'll be working the sunrise shift for now, and you get two days off. Once you're trained up, that'll change and you'll join the rota like everyone else. We're the only team outside Agro that gets to work during the curfew, which is another perk. But it don't mean we can go running around the city waking people up. We're only allowed in the Residential Sector at night if there's an emergency. And that *never* happens, if you get what I'm saying."

"Sure, I get it. So what do you do?"

"Me? I make sure the buggies and critters get enough juice."

"What are critters?"

"The bots. I call them critters on account of them being so adorable."

"Yeah, right," Shor said. "And what will I be doing?"

"You will be what we like to call a goget, at least until we get you trained into management material."

"What's a goget?"

"If anyone needs anything, you go get it." Lars' face broke into a smile that was all gums and teeth.

"I'm sorry, son. It was a joke."

Shor smiled but did not get the joke. There was no such thing as a "goget". On Earth, they had an animal called a "gopher", which would have been a much better choice.

"What you will be doing," Lars continued, "is learning as much as possible about what everyone else on the team knows. It's very important we can all do everyone else's jobs if we need to, otherwise you end up with what we call a Tram Scenario."

Shor looked blankly at him.

"If one of us gets hit by one of these trams, then the world falls apart. Literally. Ah, here we are."

The tram squealed to a stop and Lars, Reet, Bek and Shor climbed off. Shor followed them towards a crumbling building with a crooked sign that identified it as "Ma tenan e Head uarters".

"It ain't much, but we like to think of it as our home away from home. Mind your step."

Lars unlocked the big front door, which shuddered open. They entered a room with a table and chairs, a battered sofa, and what looked like an antique computer screen in the corner. Against one wall, a kitchen counter was strewn with mugs, plates, cutlery and various small appliances. There were two open doors leading into separate rooms. Everything appeared to be broken or on the verge of it.

Shor looked around, wondering if they appreciated the irony of having a maintenance building on the brink of collapse.

They were standing at the threshold of a large room lined with equipment and rows of shelves. To the right, separated by a long counter, was what looked like a kitchen.

"This over here is the workshop. This is where we do any repairs small enough to bring back on the carts. This area on the right is the kitchen. Through there is the locker room and the dorm with forty beds for the night shift." Lars handed Shor a thick marker pen. "Go find yourself an empty locker and put your name on it with this. We'll find you some work clothes and an out-suit. We only have one rule here: return the tools to their correct place, or Reet will strangle you."

Shor glanced across at Reet, who was making himself a mug of coffee. The big man looked at Shor with a humourless gaze.

"You're kidding, right?"

"Of course," Lars said. "Reet hasn't strangled any new recruits in ages. Hey, Reet. Who was the last goget you throttled?"

Reet looked up towards the ceiling, his jaw jutting to one side. "The one from two years ago. Yeah, that's it. What was his name? Bark? Bart?"

"Barry," Lars prompted.

"Yeah, that was it. He lost a wrench. I had to throttle him. I had no choice. You warned him."

Shor looked from Reet to Lars and back again. "Please tell me you're kidding."

A grin spread across Lars' face. "Of course. It's against the rules to kill gogets. But make sure you return the tools. It's very annoying if you can't find the tools you need. Sunlight shift ends at three-thirty. Official day ends at four. Lunch is twelve till one. Any questions?"

"Yes. Where do I buy lunch?"

"There's a food market just a bit further up the road. Anything else?"

"Is there any chance I can still get into the Space Program?"

Lars guffawed so hard Shor thought he was going to choke. When

Lars saw Shor wasn't joining in, he stopped. "Seriously? No. There's no way you can go from Maintenance to the Space Program. The city invests way too much in training to let you waste it by changing careers. I'm sorry, son. You're stuck with us."

Shor shrugged. "It was worth a try though, wasn't it?"

"Exactly. I couldn't agree more. You don't get anything in this life if you don't ask. Although begging helps. Oh, I nearly forgot. You'll need a keycard. Keep this safe, because it can get you into any door anywhere in the city. It's one of the perks of the job. This is a skeleton key like no other. Now you have to swear you won't use it for anything other than carrying out your duty as a Maintenance guy. And that means no sneaking into areas where you don't belong, including the Space Sector. And you are definitely not allowed to use this to get into really important areas, like the *Space Sector*." He winked at Shor before handing him the key. "Unless you've got an important piece of maintenance work to complete, that is."

"Thanks," Shor said.

"Just don't get caught," Lars said in a low voice. "Or we'll both be doing work that makes even Bek's stomach turn. Go get changed and I'll show you around."

Shor followed the others through into the locker room. He found a spare locker and wrote his name on it as neatly as possible with the marker. He selected work clothes from a large basket in the corner and stashed his normal gear in the locker. Lars managed to find an out-suit that fit. Shor was just glad he did not make any jokes about his height.

"Ready for the grand tour?" Lars said, grinning broadly.

"I am," Shor replied.

"Got your keycard?"

Shor patted his pocket. "Yes, sir."

"Good lad. As it happens, there's a problem with a door in a hangar down at the Space Sector. I reckon we should go fix it. What say we go take a good look around?"

"All right," Shor said.

"For the first few weeks you'll be learning, so you'll be getting lifts with me or one of the others. Once you're ready to do jobs by yourself, you'll get your own buggy. How did you do in driving school?"

"I passed."

"That's good enough. It's not like you'll ever need to actually drive, except in an emergency. The buggies are all automated, but you never know, eh? So, you ready for your first job?"

"I am," Shor said.

And it occurred to him that perhaps working for Maintenance was not going to be as bad as he had thought.

The Space Sector was at the farthest side of the city complex, out beyond the Agro (Agricultural) Sector. They set out on Lars's buggy, with its wide trunk containing a series of drawers and compartments and a boggling array of tools and spare parts.

Lars typed in their destination and soon they were zipping along the roads, past the various buildings that housed the workers responsible for ensuring the smooth running of every aspect of the city, and a whole infrastructure to support the population. This was where all the things consumed by the citizens of Utopia were researched, built, tested, packaged, and fixed.

At the top end of the sector the road split into three. The left-hand route was for the vast Industrial Sector, the road on the right led to the Manufacturing Sector, while the one straight ahead was for the Space Sector.

"Next stop: exciting space stuff," Lars said.

The airlock here was of a different design to the big one leading through to the Residential Sector. The doors rolled sideways, opening independently, giving relatively speedy access on demand. Two badges sat in control booths recessed into the wall, which gave them a clear view of both doors. The idea was that, in the event of a catastrophe in one of the outer sectors, the others would be safe. They could always grow more food or rebuild a damaged transformer, but they would not be able to clone fifty thousand people at short notice.

The badge scanned their IDs and nodded at Lars. The door slid open and they passed through. Shor offered the badge a smile but received a cold stare in response.

"Takes a while before they get to know you," Lars said. "Until then, they'll assume you're doing something wrong. Be friendly with the badges but not *too* friendly, if you get what I mean."

"You've worked in Maintenance for a long time?" Shor asked.

"Yep. Ten years. And I don't mean Earth years. I mean Mars years. That's like eighteen years on Earth. To be honest, I really don't know why they bother with the two systems. I don't care how old I am on Earth."

"They say we might be able to go back soon."

"Back? That sorta implies we came from there. I didn't come from there. Did you come from there?"

Shor shrugged. "No, but it looks nice. I wouldn't mind paying a visit, just to see."

"Well I don't know about *nice*. I've seen those videos they play in the Park. The Earth looks a bit wild to me. There's so much water you can lose sight of the land. And waves bigger than a building. I'm not so sure I'd find that very *nice*."

They reached the second door and the badge let them through. Shor nodded without smiling. The badge nodded back.

The Space Sector was bigger than Shor had expected. He estimated it was about half as big as the Residential Sector, and shaped like a slanted square. Massive, nondescript buildings stood like chess pieces along the far wall while the wall on the other side was taken up by a series of ramps leading up to large horizontal airlocks recessed into the ceiling. The rest of the space was taken up by roads and low, wide buildings. Up through the glass-panelled ceiling, Shor could see more structures above the airlocks, braving the Martian atmosphere.

"I never knew they were putting this much effort into the Space Program," Shor said. "I thought perhaps it was a handful of people, maybe looking through telescopes, or fixing probes."

"Next to agriculture and industry, this is the biggest sector. See those buildings over there?" Lars pointed at the row of chess pieces. "Those are hangars. It's where they keep their spaceships. The big one on this side is where they're building the Phoenix."

"Have you seen it?"

"The Phoenix? Nah. But I did see one of the smaller ones. They didn't like that. Gave me a good telling off. They're very secretive."

"I wonder what the Phoenix looks like," Shor said. "I bet it must be pretty amazing."

"I wouldn't get my hopes up. They're not going to fit fifty thousand people into one ship. They say it's designed to carry a hundred people back to Earth. The broken door is this way, come on."

They rolled down the central road which ran the entire length of the sector. Small vehicles buzzed up and down, joining and leaving the main thoroughfare like ants on a trail. Unlike Residential, here there were only a few pedestrians gliding along the walkways on either side of the roads. Most of the traffic was unmanned vehicles, or automated loaders driven by robots. They nearly collided with one joining from a side road.

"Watch where you're goin', you dumb bag of bolts!" Lars yelled, waving his fingers at the robot, which seemed uncertain what to do and ended up pulling over to let Lars pass. "You have to let them know who's boss. Don't ever let 'em forget. Critters are cute, but they'll bite you if you let 'em."

They turned right off the main road and headed towards the hangars. Lars glanced at the work docket.

"It's the one at the far end," he said as the buggy turned left into a wide expressway running from the first hangar all the way down to the last. The road was a good fifty metres wide and a kilometre long. Vehicles of all shapes and sizes dashed from hangar to hangar and across to the buildings dotted along the other side.

Their buggy slowed to a crawl and stopped behind a big vehicle toting a dozen large cylinders.

"Come on!" Lars yelled. "It's called the throttle you dumb critter!"

"Can't we just go manual?" Shor asked.

"Regulations," Lars said. "No manual driving, and especially not along this stretch. Badges are strict about that. Guy was killed along here about a year ago. Wagger thought he could just drive down this road."

"What happened?" Shor asked, flinching as a bot cut into the gap in front of them with centimetres to spare.

"*That* happened," Lars said, nodding towards the other machine. "Bots may be dumb, but they drive better than we do."

Despite numerous near-misses, they reached their destination in one piece. It was the smallest of all the hangars on the highway and appeared to be the oldest with rust stains growing like algae under the ridge of the low roof.

"Let's see," Lars said, checking his docket again. "Door's inside, on the right."

He selected a mobile toolbox bot from the back of the buggy. A robotic arm lifted it up and over and lowered it to the ground. He kicked the bot and it shuddered to life, turning left and right before fixing its full attention on the boot that had woken it from its slumber.

"Motion sensitive," Lars said, lifting his foot. "It follows the first thing it sees. Simple but effective Programmed it myself."

They entered the building through a small side door. It slid open in a series of stuttering jerks when Lars presented his keycard. Lars sucked air through his teeth and muttered something about having to fix that as well sometime.

They stepped into a room completely empty apart from a few metal boxes lying scattered across the faded floor. At the back was a kitchen of some sort, with an ancient refrigerator and a microwave oven with the door hanging off. A few plastic chairs stood strewn around a cracked table.

"You hear that?"

There was a hissing noise coming from somewhere up ahead. It sounded like an airlock being sealed and resealed over and over again.

"Over there," Shor said, pointing to the back wall.

They approached the sound, which indeed turned out to be coming from a broken airlock.

"There's the problem," Lars said. "It's an old model. They always were a bit temperamental."

"Doesn't look like anyone works here," Shor said. "Why would they want a door fixed?"

"It only takes two airlocks to break down and we have a potential catastrophe on our hands. All airlocks are linked to our system. If one starts acting up we automatically get a message to go take a look, even if it's never used."

Lars waved his keycard at the control panel and pressed the button. The door slid open to about half way where it started making the same sound as before. He kicked the toolbox at his heels and the lid flipped open. After a few seconds of rummaging, he pulled out a torch and shone it at the mechanism.

"This kiddie's toast. Gonna need a whole new door. I'll head back to the depot. You can stay here if you like."

"I thought I was the goget," Shor said.

"You can go get the lunch and the tools. This is an airlock door. Chances are you'll come back with the wrong model, or a vacuum pump. *I'll* get the door, you wait here." Lars replaced the torch and kicked the toolbox. "Back in twenty minutes. Don't get into trouble while I'm gone."

"I won't," Shor said.

"We only have one rule in the Maintenance Department. You break it, you bought it."

Shor watched his boss leave with the toolbox in tow. He thrust his hands into his pockets, turning to look at the door which was hissing at him as if frustrated at not being able to open or close. He leaned forward to take a closer look. The other door appeared to be fine. He stepped through and stood between them, turning all the way round. It was an airlock designed to take one person, barely wide enough for his shoulders standing sideways although, as always, height was not a problem. He wiped the dust from the glass panel on the good door and looked into the cavernous room that occupied most of the building. There was equipment everywhere, on the floor and on shelves. Bits and pieces lay cluttered along three walls. Much of it was covered with sheets and tarpaulins. Discarded implements on trolleys lay strewn about amid coils of cables and ducts. Everything was covered in a fine layer of dust, including the object which took up most of the floor space and which looked to be the focus of all the other equipment.

Shor estimated the object to be easily as tall and wide as the police station, and twice as long. It was metal, but unlike any metal he had ever seen. Even under the dust, he could see the surface was without a single mark or blemish. The whole thing was shaped like a tram—no, more like a bullet—being biggest at the centre and tapering gently towards each end.

He tried to imagine what it could possibly be. Presumably it was a vehicle of some sort. He was in a hangar in the Space Sector so, logically, it was probably a space craft. Perhaps it was a prototype that never passed the tests and they had just abandoned it here to gather dust.

Then again, he had never actually seen a space craft before, except during science lessons, so it was hard for him to guess just how big such a vehicle might be. This one was enormous.

He tapped the door control switch but it flashed a red light at him. Entrance not permitted. Then he remembered the keycard Lars had given him along with a smile that suggested he expected, even *wanted*, Shor to use it.

He glanced back into the smaller room and, happy he was alone, retrieved the card and waved it across the control panel's sensor. The light went from red to green and he pressed the button.

The door slid open and he stepped through. The air was musty from neglect, and the only sound was the hissing from the other door. He took a step forward and looked around at the high ceiling. Security cameras were normally easy to spot. This room, apparently, had none.

He slowly approached the bullet-shaped object, stepping over the wires that trailed across the floor between the craft and the flotilla of trolleys.

The floor was covered in a thin gauze of dust, and he realized his were the only footprints. A trail of shallow depressions led from the airlock to where he was standing, past a piece of equipment that appeared to be as lifeless as the ship. Whatever had happened here, it had been a long time ago.

He lifted his hand and touched the cool metal. A thrill ran down his spine. He had dreamed of this moment all his life, of being close enough to a spaceship to actually reach out and touch it. And here he was, on his first day as a lowly Maintenance goget, running his hand across the hull of a craft that may or may not have actually been in outer space.

He walked the length of the ship until he was no longer able to reach the hull, past the support struts that kept the whole thing off the floor, and then back down the other side where the underside was at his waist height. He paused at the stern, at what looked like exhaust vents for an engine.

A sudden, mad desire to see the inside of the ship gripped him, but he had not seen an opening of any kind apart from the vents. He stepped back and examined the perfect surface. If there was an opening, it was so well concealed as to be invisible. He followed the cables and tubes to where they were connected to the underside of the ship. Here he found a small, square panel with a series of connection ports. He pulled at the edges, but nothing moved.

Then he spotted a mobile stair cart close to the back wall and walked across to it, looking up at the side of the hull for any sign of an opening. But even if there was a door, the dust had covered any clues as to where it might be.

Standing with his hands on his hips and knees covered in dirt from crawling around on the floor, Shor observed the craft with narrow eyes. There was really only one thing to do. He was going to have to figure out how to operate the stair lift and then he was going to clean off the dust.

Outside, there was the muffled sound of a buggy pulling up and a toolbox being kicked. The exploration of the ship would have to wait for another time.

Shor returned to the airlock and let himself out. By the time Lars appeared pulling a trolley containing a large crate and followed by the obedient toolbox, Shor was leaning casually against the desk.

"Let's get this installed," Lars said. "So, anything happen while I was gone?"

Shor shrugged. "No, not a thing."

Lars looked down at Shor's knees. "You sure?"

"I dropped my card and had to crawl under the table to get it."

"Good. Because we have only one rule in the Maintenance Department. You can break as many rules as you like, just don't get caught." He winked at Shor. "I forgot something from the buggy. I need you to go get the small red toolbox on the near left side. Think you can do that without getting dirty?"

"Yes, sir," Shor said. "I think I can manage."

As he walked across the room Shor glanced back through the airlock door, to the spaceship standing there so tantalisingly close, and decided he would return and figure out how to get inside as soon as he was able.

On one of the trolleys, on a piece of equipment connected to the ship and hidden under a layer of dust, a red light flashed once before going out again.

They installed the door and tested it. Shor paid attention as best he could in spite of knowing there was a veritable treasure chest of discovery waiting for him just next door, all wrapped up in the intriguing shape of a spaceship.

They made it back to the depot before midday. Shor found the market and spent a lunch voucher on cheese, bread and salad, and retreated to the roof of the maintenance building to watch the people passing as he ate. Once or twice he thought he saw Mel, even though she had no reason to come into the Hub, and wondered how she was getting along on her first day. He thought about his mother and wondered if she had shown any signs of recovery in the hours since his last visit. He imagined her lying in her hospital bed, her body as lifeless as a broken bot.

Time was running out for her, he knew that. They could not afford to keep his mother alive to consume precious resources. It made sense, but from his first day on the Maintenance team he had seen a number of examples of how grossly inefficient the city could be. His history teacher had once shown them a picture of an hour-glass and Shor had been struck by its simple elegance. It was only a still image but he imagined the grains of sand trickling through the narrow gap between the two bulbs, each grain representing a moment of time that was lost forever. Now, thinking of his mother, he saw every Watt of wasted energy as a grain of sand in the hourglass of her life.

That afternoon they completed two more jobs before signing off for the day. With forty minutes to spare before the airlock was due to open, he explored the area, following the main walkway up, around, and back again, past each of the airlocks that led to the other sectors. Beyond this, there was not much else to see. Most of the buildings were of the drab utilitarian variety. He counted a total of three markets, evenly spaced to allow for maximum coverage. There was a small square situated up towards the top end of the sector, with a few benches and a statue of Pinner looking very Pinneresque.

The afternoon tram carried him back to his quarter. He stopped of at the hospital where he had to wait fifteen minutes before the start of the visiting hour.

His father, punctual as always, arrived just as the nurse was waving him through, although Shor suspected he had been waiting around the corner. It was something he had seen him do more than once.

"She is stable," the doctor informed them. "Her condition has not changed since yesterday."

"Is that good?" Shor asked, looking down at his mother's prostrate form. She looked so peaceful, she might have been taking an afternoon nap.

"It's good, because it means she is not getting worse. Of course we would prefer to see some improvement but stable is good, at least for the time being."

"Is there anything you can do for her?" Shor's father asked.

"We have done everything possible," the doctor said, looking slightly indignant. "The rest is up to your wife."

"I don't understand. How can she do anything while she's like this?"

"You would be surprised. There is a lot of cerebral activity. She may look like she is asleep, but her brain is wide awake. She will wake up if and when she is ready. Now, if you will excuse me, I have other patients to attend to."

They sat in silence on either side of the bed. Shor's father held his wife's hand and looked intently at her face, as if willing her to open her eyes. Shor felt strangely detached as he watched his parents.

With the hour up, they headed home. His father walked in silence, as if his son were not even there. Shor tried to think of something to say, but each attempt at a conversation stalled before it could reach his lips.

They stopped off at the market for food and a new bulb for the sitting room lamp. Shor waited outside, watching the world drift by. A group of young kids were playing a game on the other side of the walkway, hopping and jumping between hoops laid out in an intricate pattern. He recognized most of them from the neighbourhood but did not know their names. They were a few years younger than Shor, but already he would have to look up to talk to them. They were still discovering their motor skills, but their movements were mesmerising to watch. They hung in the air as they leapt from hoop to hoop, as if held up by invisible strings. Shor had tried playing that game once. The other kids had laughed so hard he thought they were going to pop.

As he watched, one of them spotted him and pointed him out to the others. Grins and snickers were exchanged, and Shor thought he heard the word "freak". He turned away, determined not to let them see his face. He liked to tell himself he was used to their taunts, but that was a lie. It still hurt.

His father was at the front of the queue, talking to old Dodds at the checkout kiosk. Dodds nodded his head sympathetically as Shor's father spoke. Goods and vouchers were exchanged and the next in line stepped forward.

Shor noticed his father had forgotten the bulb, but the kids were growing increasingly brave in their insults and Shor just wanted to get home.

"They had fish sticks," his father said as they joined the traffic.

"Good," Shor replied. "I like those."

They were not real fish sticks, of course, but rather soya chunks compressed into the shape of a fish. Since nobody knew what fish actually tasted like, it did not really matter. The pleasure was in imagining you were eating the real thing.

They ate in silence in the grimy glow from a table lamp. Their only words were to discuss the quality of the fish sticks, and the fact they had forgotten the bulb. Shor did the washing up and then headed for bed. Later, as he lay on his back staring up at the ceiling, he thought he heard the sound of crying.

He checked his chatband but there were no messages. He called Mel but she did not answer. Her light was still on so he tried twice more before giving up and climbing between the sheets.

In his mind, he returned to the mysterious spaceship and retraced his steps around the hull. It struck him as odd that they would leave a craft like that to decay under a layer of dust and neglect. Presumably it had been a failed project but, if so, it was strange that they had kept it connected to the equipment.

He determined he would return to the hangar as soon as possible. With any luck he would find the ship's door and get a peek inside.

Staying focused on work the next day proved difficult. Lars said lots of things. Some of it was interesting. The rest had Shor drifting off, daydreaming about the ship. Tane gave a presentation to the trainees describing the city's life-support systems, but a ten minute stretch of solid equations outlining the power-to-population ratios left Shor with a dull headache. He considered himself fairly adept at mathematics, but his head was soon swimming with formulas. One thing was clear, however. The city only produced enough energy to sustain a population of a specific size. When it came down to it, all those equations could be reduced to a single figure that represented the total number of people allowed to live in Utopia at any given moment. There were no fractions or decimal points in that number. No margins of error or residuals. No leeways or grey areas. No room for clemency or mercy, or doubt. Utopia's population was the cold scientific outcome of a thousand calculations drawn from a constant stream of readings showing energy production versus consumption.

That evening, as he returned from the hospital with his father, they found a police vehicle parked in front of their apartment block, standing skew on the walkway. Pedestrians flowed around it like a stream around a boulder. A badge was waiting at their door as they stepped out of the elevator.

"Shor Larkin?" the badge asked.

"That's me," Shor said, his mind racing. He had never seen the police at his apartment before, apart from dropping him off after the jump fiasco a few days before.

"I need you to come with me."

"What's this about?" Shor's father asked. "Is he in some sort of trouble?"

"No. We just need to ask him a few questions."

"What about?" Shor asked.

"I don't know. I was just told to come and collect you."

"Why didn't they just ask?" his father said, his voice edged with suspicion. "We know where the station is."

"I'm sorry, I honestly don't know."

"How can you not know? They must have told you something. Why are you taking him?"

"It's all right," Shor said, a little surprised by his father's show of paternal concern. "It's probably nothing. I'll go and talk to them, see what they want."

Shor followed the badge back into the elevator and down to the street where people gawped at him with undisguised curiosity as he climbed into the back of the vehicle. Many were typing on, or talking into, their chatbands. News travelled quickly in Utopia.

The police station was exactly as he remembered it from the last time, only now it was empty. The badge led him past the reception desk, where the clerk watched him with expressionless eyes, to the back room where he had been questioned by the creepy lidless guy just a few days before.

"Wait here," the badge said, pointing to the chair. And then he was gone.

Shor lifted himself onto the cold seat and waited, trying to think what he had done to warrant what amounted to an arrest. They may have invited him to "answer a few questions" but he knew what that really meant. The police always couched their terms in soft words to make them seem less threatening.

It then occurred to him that perhaps something might be wrong with his mother. She had been fine when they left her, but anything could have happened during the half hour it took them to get home. She might have deteriorated as soon as they walked out...

His thoughts were interrupted by the door opening. An older man he had never seen before, dressed in civilian clothes, walked across the floor and extended his hand.

"Hello Shor. My name is Harl, Harl Benson. My, you've grown."

The man was short by Martian standards, but still a good four centimetres taller than Shor. His face was friendly, but creased with lines. His hair was dishevelled with the first hints of grey starting to show. His eyes moved with a nervous energy that suggested a lot of activity going on behind his glasses.

Shor took the man's hand and shook. His grip was surprisingly firm. "Do I know you?"

"We met many years ago but I doubt you remember me. I've been keeping an eye on your progress just about your whole life. Your teachers think highly of you."

"Apparently not highly enough to give me the career I wanted."

"The teachers have your best interests at heart. They selected the career they thought best for you. I understand you've been having dreams?"

Shor felt the anger rising in him. "Why does everyone seem to know so much about my psych evals?"

"Let's just say, you are of extreme interest to some people."

"What's going on? Why am I here? Is my mother all right?"

Harl looked confused for a second, then understanding cracked his face. "Your mother? Oh no, it's not about your mother. I'm sorry to hear about that by the way. Terrible shame. What did the doctors say?"

"They said she was stable. Are you going to tell me what this is all about?"

"Right to the point. I like that. Fine, I'll explain. You started work in the Maintenance Department today. Is that correct?"

"Yes."

"How are you enjoying it so far?"

"It's not so bad, I guess. It's not the Space Program, but it's not as horrible as I expected."

"They do good work down there. You've landed yourself an excellent career. People forget how vital that team is. Without the Maintenance Department the city would soon fall apart, and then where would we be? Up a sewer without a raft, that's where—"

"You were telling me why you brought me here," Shor interrupted.

"Sorry. My mind tends to wander. Maintenance. Yes. You started today. And you went out on a few jobs, is that correct?"

"We changed a door, and replaced a faulty relay, and we fixed a broken sign."

"Where did you change the door?"

"It was at a hangar…"

Suddenly, Shor knew why they had called him in. There had been a camera after all. Someone had seen him snooping around the spaceship. He knew it! First day on the job and he had messed up big time.

"Did you go into the main room of the hangar?" Harl said.

Shor sighed. He could deny it, but there was no point. They knew someone had been in there, and he was the only one who had been in a position to sneak in to have a look at the spaceship. "I just wanted to see it. I didn't mean to do anything wrong. It was just standing there, and I was curious. I'm sorry. I just wanted to look. I've never seen a spaceship up close before. It *is* a spaceship, isn't it?"

"Yes, it is a spaceship, and we've been trying to get inside it for almost eighteen years, ever since the door closed. We've had it hooked up to a computer whose sole task is to hack into the system, but it's locked down tight. The ship's computer has sealed its door. We tried asking nicely but it won't let us in."

"Can't you just cut through the hull?"

"It's not so simple. The external layers are the hardest substance known to man, and the space between those layers contains an extremely volatile liquid designed to protect the passengers from the stresses of travelling at extreme speeds. We could cut through but, if it were to ignite, we would level the whole sector. And the resultant contamination would be catastrophic."

"What does all this have to do with me? I just looked. And I couldn't even see the door, never mind open it."

"Did you touch anything?"

"No. Well, I touched the hull, but that's all. I didn't go near any of the equipment. And like I said, I didn't even see a door."

"Are you sure?"

"Yes. Why?"

"At some point while you were in the room our computer made contact with the ship's computer, or rather it was the ship that made contact with us. The technicians say it accessed the personnel records. I didn't know exactly how, but your simply being in that room caused something to happen. It's as if it remembers you. Actually, we almost didn't notice. That project has been on the shelf for the past seven years. It was only thanks to a sharp-eyed lab assistant that we even spotted it."

"The door's open?" Shor said, sitting up a little straighter. "Did you get a look inside?"

"No, the door did not open and, unfortunately, the connection was shut down almost immediately."

"Oh," Shor said. "Pity."

"However, if you were able to trigger it before, you may be able to do so again. It makes perfect sense really. I don't know why we didn't think of trying this earlier. I would like you to come down to the hangar and do exactly what you did this morning. Perhaps you stood in the right place or touched the hull in the right spot, or maybe you said something."

Shor thought back to his visit to the hangar, and the equipment, and his footprints in the dust. Already he was retracing his steps around the outside of the ship. He could not remember doing anything special. And he was pretty sure he had not said anything.

"I just ran my hand along the hull. That's all really."

"Do you think you can do it again, exactly the same way?"

"I suppose so. I'll try."

"Excellent. Come down to the hangar first thing tomorrow morning. I'll speak to your manager. With any luck, we'll be able to initiate another connection. And, who knows, perhaps we'll find the door and get a look inside."

Harl stood and indicated for Shor to follow.

"A badge will escort you home. See you tomorrow."

"Sure," Shor said, following the badge out of the room and outside to the police buggy.

When he got home, his father asked what had happened. Shor told him they needed his help on a project, and nothing more was said on the subject.

Later on he contacted Mel who chatted excitedly about her first day at work. It was, she said, everything she had hoped it would be. As for him, he mentioned Lars and the door, but said nothing about the ship. He was tired and did not feel like explaining everything again. Tomorrow. He would tell her tomorrow.

As he lay down to go to sleep, his mind ran through the interview with Harl. He went back over everything the old man had said. A couple of things bothered him.

They had blocked him from working in the Space Program and now they were asking for his help to get inside a ship. He had expected a reprimand, especially after Lars' suggestion that working in Maintenance was some sort of a punishment, but they did not seem to mind that he had obviously been snooping around the hangar. If anything, Harl had seemed *pleased*. Perhaps that was yet to come. Perhaps they would hit him with it once he helped them get the door open. And why was the old man so interested in his dreams? But another thing niggled him. Harl had said something about wondering why they *hadn't thought of doing this earlier*. This made no sense at all. Shor had discovered the ship only yesterday, but Harl sounded as though he was talking about an earlier time. And there was the other thing he had said: *It's as if it remembers you.*

Less than three days out from Mars, the ship's engines rumbled to life, nudging the craft into a slow spin until it was pointing away from the Martian orbit around the sun. Once it was correctly oriented, the pirouette stopped and the main engine fired, exerting a slow braking thrust long enough for the ship to match the speed and orbit of the planet's smaller moon, Deimos.

At eight kilometres across, the satellite was little more than a misshapen lump of rock, but that was more than enough. The craft's engines performed final adjustments, placing it nine kilometres above the satellite's smooth surface on the opposite side from Mars.

Inside, the lone passenger stirred in his yellow bath, his fingers and toes twitching as his body emerged from the dark depths of hyper-sleep. His arms and legs moved through the liquid with slow determination, like those of a swimmer caught in the icy chains of hypothermia.

He lifted his head and, almost as if in response, the lid's seal cracked open, hissing as the pressure equalised, the heavy slab of metal rising up and over in a smooth arc. The bed shifted under him, slowly tilting forward as it assumed the shape of a chair, scooping him out of the chamber and guiding him towards the opening.

He broke through the liquid surface. Goo dribbled from his body and cascaded back down into the hyper-sleep chamber in fist-sized globules that wobbled and oozed around his legs, the tubes from his face and torso hanging like slick tentacles.

With his hands resting in the rim of the chamber, he straightened his legs and lifted his body in a series of unsteady jerks until he was standing motionless, his eyes focused on a point in the middle distance.

He eased one foot over the rim and found the top rung of the step leading down the outside of the chamber. Then he lifted his other foot and turned, his body bent forward as he climbed down to the floor where pinhead-sized holes sucked at the puddles like so many hungry mouths.

He stood for a minute, his eyes unmoving and unblinking. Then he raised his hands and removed the mask attached to the lower half of his face, the skin around his mouth pulling with it as if reluctant to let go.

With the mask detached, he started work on the tube attached to his torso. Released from his bonds, he turned and walked through to the next room where he showered and changed and deposited his soiled garments in the laundry bin. He found the emergency space suit and climbed in, working with slow deliberation. Then he walked though the kitchen, bedroom, and gym, to the room at the far end of the ship.

The sign above the row of airlocks read: *Rescue Pods. For Emergencies Only*. He selected the nearest door and pulled it open. A red light above the door started flashing and an alarm sounded. He looked at the light. It went dark and the alarm fell silent.

The capsule was snug, with just enough room for one person. An adult could stand upright in the middle and lie flat at its widest point, the flight seat folding out to act as a bed. Every square inch was filled with storage space containing enough supplies to keep the occupant alive for six months. There was enough oxygen to last seven months.

He strapped himself in and turned to face the console. Lights flashed as the launch sequence began. The airlock swung closed and sealed itself. There was the whine of servo motors and the deep rumble of an engine.

The lights on the console changed. The engine roared. A moment of bone-bending acceleration, and the rescue pod was ejected from the craft in a curve that carried it around the moon Deimos and down towards the red planet.

15

Shor dreamt he was in his room, lying on his bed on his back, not asleep but with his eyes fixed on the ceiling high above. His alarm clock was sounding and he wanted to get up, but he was unable to move a muscle. Only his eyes were free to look around to the door where a thick yellow liquid was oozing through the gaps, rising up until it covered the floor and then the bed. He felt it crawling up his body until it covered his ears, until it was seeping into his mouth and nose. He tried to blink, but his eyelids were like cardboard. The fear of drowning overwhelmed him and he held his breath until his chest ached and he thought he was going to explode. He held his breath until the pain became unbearable and his burning lungs could no longer resist inhaling the suffocating liquid in a desperate bid for life-giving oxygen…

He is here.

Shor sat up in bed, his heart hammering in his chest and his lungs on fire. He gulped at the air in great tearing gasps, fighting to break free from the memory of the liquid engulfing him in its crushing embrace.

He tore the sheets from his body and hurled them across the room, still blinded by the vision. The pounding of his heart was so loud it was as if someone were knocking.

He looked around as the dream faded and the real world swam into focus. There was no goo. He was in his room. And the pounding was coming from his door.

"Everything all right?" his father called.

"Yes," Shor said coarsely. "Yes, I'm fine. I…I kicked my toe. It's all right now."

There was a grunt and dull footsteps retreated down the corridor.

Outside, the day was dawning. Shor climbed out of bed to retrieve his sheet from the floor and realised he was soaking wet. He had not been planning to use a shower token today, but he would smell if he did not have a proper wash.

That done, he ate breakfast and walked to the tram stop, aware that he was already settling into a routine of sorts. The tram carried him around the park and he joined the queue at the air lock. Five minutes later he was sitting next to Lars on the tram, headed toward the Maintenance building.

"I had a call from Harl Benson yesterday," Lars said.

"Yes, he said he'd speak to you."

"He told me he needs you down at the hangar. Same one with the broken door we fixed yesterday. Said they needed you for some important experiment."

"I guess so."

They arrived at their stop and climbed off, passing the night shift workers heading home. "So what exactly did you get up to while I was fetching the door? Harl mentioned a ship."

"There was a spaceship or something in the hangar. I just had a look around, that's all."

"You had a look around and now suddenly you're part of the Space Program?"

"I wouldn't say that." Shor followed the others through to the locker room where they started changing into their uniforms. Shor did the same, even though he wasn't sure he would need it. "It will just be for today. Once they figure out I can't help them with what they want, they'll let me get back to my real job."

"And what if you *can* help them? You might end up being an astronaut after all."

Shor imagined himself sitting at the controls of a ship—like the one down in the hangar."

"That won't happen," he said.

"I'm happy for you, kid," Lars said. "Really, I am. It's what you wanted."

The buggy took them back the way they had gone the day before, through to the Space Sector and down to the neglected old hangar at the farthest end. Three official-looking vehicles were parked out front. A man was waiting at the hangar door. It was Harl.

Shor felt his chest tighten a little.

"Glad you could make it," Harl said, striding over to meet them. "We're all very excited to see what you can do. I hope you had a chance to think about what we discussed yesterday."

Shor nodded casually. No point letting on that he had thought about little else.

The front room was hardly recognizable from the day before. All the dust had been cleared up and any rubbish removed. The kitchen had been tidied up and the cracked furniture was gone. It was all spotlessly clean and actually looked like a kitchen.

The airlock door they had fixed the morning before was closed but

Shor could see the ship clearly through the newly-cleaned glass. He hesitated before stepping across the threshold and into the hangar. When his foot hit the hangar floor, there was no dust.

Inside, a team of five people were busy working on the equipment scattered around the room. Cameras and spotlights had been brought in and placed on tripods at the four corners. Whoever had cleaned the front room had clearly been busy here as well. The floor, trolley, equipment, and even the cables, were now dust-free.

Everything was exactly how he remembered it from the day before, but now almost surgically clean. The ship looked completely different. Its hull shimmered under the intense glare of the spots. He looked for his footprints but they were gone, replaced by white outlines drawn by hand.

"We wanted to keep your exact steps," Harl said. "Although we decided the dust was probably not needed for this experiment. Is everything set up?" he said, looking around at his team, each of whom signalled their readiness to proceed. "Shor, I need you to retrace your actions from yesterday. Can you do that?"

Shor hesitated. "I can't remember every movement. Not exactly, anyway."

"Don't worry. It's not a test. Take your time. We've been waiting most of twenty years for this. Relax. When you're ready."

Shor glanced back at Lars, but he was too busy staring, wide-eyed, up at the ship to notice. Shor looked down at the white footprints on the immaculate floor. Suddenly, the previous morning seemed a thousand years away. He stepped haltingly onto the first mark, then the next, up to the side of the ship, gathering momentum as he moved. When he was close enough to reach up and touch the hull, he stretched out his hand, trying to recall exactly where he had made contact the day before.

His hand settled against the smooth surface, the skin on his palm tingling.

"I'm getting something," one of the team, a young woman with glasses, said. "I'm getting a reading."

"Is it a connection?" Harl said.

"Yes, we're linked to the ship's computer." She looked up at Harl. "We're in!"

"Good work," Harl said patting Shor on the shoulder.

"That was easy," Shor said.

"Wait," the technician said. "It's gone. We've lost the connection."

"Are you sure?" Harl said, his voice edged with frustration. "Check again."

"No. Nothing."

"Shor, try pulling your hand away and touching it again."

Shor did as he was asked.

"Still nothing."

"Try walking around the ship."

Shor followed his original path around the hull, keeping his hand stretched out. At the bow, he was forced to walk on his toes to reach. He walked all the way around until he was back where he started. His hand remained in contact the whole time.

"And?" Harl said.

The technician shook her head. "Nothing."

"What else did you do when you were here before?" Harl said.

Shor crouched and crawled under the lowest part of the ship, to where the cables were connected. He pulled at the edge the way he remembered doing before.

"That's it," Shor said. "I think."

"Did you do anything else?" Harl said.

"No. I don't think so."

"You must remember. What else did you do?"

"Nothing."

"Go around again."

Shor repeated his trip around the ship. The hull was dead. The tingling he had felt before was gone. His hand was touching cold metal.

"This has been fun, fellas," Lars said, walking to the airlock. "But I've got work to do."

There was a hiss of air, and Lars was gone.

Shor looked to Harl, waiting for the next instruction. Harl just stood there for a long time looking up at the hull, his eyes searching for something. "I thought we'd finally cracked it," he said. "I thought we'd got back in after all these years."

"I'm sorry I couldn't help," Shor said. "But why is it so important for you to get inside? I guess it's a prototype or something. You probably invested a lot of time in building it and then it shut you out. Is that it?"

Harl looked at Shor. His eyes were deadly serious.

"We didn't build this ship."

Shor blinked. "So it came from Earth? It doesn't look a thousand years old."

"No, it did not come from Earth."

"If you didn't build it, and we didn't bring it with us, then that can only mean..."

Harl hesitated, his eyes studying Shor's face with an unnerving intensity, as if he were trying to make up his mind about something.

"I think it is about time I told you the truth."

"About what?"

"About you, and where you come from."

16

Harl drove Shor back to the Maintenance Depot by way of the market, where they bought something to eat before finding a bench in the square. It was still early, so they had the place to themselves apart from a cleaning bot hunting the tiles for litter.

"That ship was not built on Mars," Harl said. "It is a derelict that arrived here about twenty years ago. It was actually quite lucky we were able to pick it up. It was headed towards Earth, and if our orbits had not crossed, would have missed it. Luckily, it was close enough for our salvage ship to bring back."

"I'm confused. You said it was headed *towards* Earth."

"Yes."

"So where did it come from?"

"The Alpha Centauri star system, we think. Based on its speed and trajectory, we believe it arrived here from our nearest neighbour, more than four light years away."

"It's an *alien* ship?" Shor said.

"Not exactly. We're pretty certain it was built on Earth."

"Now I'm really confused. If it was built on Earth then how come it came from Alpha Centauri?"

"This is what we want to find out. This is why we've been trying to get in for twenty years. The answers are inside the ship. And yesterday, I thought perhaps we—you—had found a way in."

"I tried my best. I'm sorry it didn't work," Shor said.

"It's not your fault. Whatever you did, it must have been a fluke. We could spend another twenty years in that room and never get the door to open again."

They ate in silence for a while, watching the cleaning bot doing its dance around the square. The benches were mostly empty apart from a few workers on a break.

"You said you had something to tell me, about where I come from," Shor said. "What did you mean?"

"Perhaps it's not a good idea. You've started a new career. You have your whole life ahead of you. The past is not important."

The bot was fixated on a piece of rubbish behind a bin. Its route was blocked by two people standing in the way, and so it was trying to work its way under the bin. Shor knew it was going to get stuck and almost felt pity for it. "People look at me and see a freak. I was the shortest guy in my school, in the *final* year. There were kids five years younger than me who were taller. Do you know what it's like to be looked down on by kids half your age? I can't run because I keep tripping over my own feet. Everyone else just floats around like they've got wings. Me, I end up on my backside. And I have these dreams. I wake up thinking I'm somewhere else. Then I realise I'm back here, and it just feels wrong. Trust me, nothing you tell me can possibly do me any damage."

Harl took a bite and chewed slowly. He folded the packet and placed it in his pocket. He turned to Shor and took a deep breath.

"When that ship came here all those years ago, it was not empty. There was someone on board. There was an infant, floating in a tank of yellow liquid. It was barely alive. The ship had shut down. The computer was operating at the lowest level—just enough to the keep the engines running."

Harl was looking at the bot struggling to get free. His eyes became off-focus, as if he were remembering something he had seen. "There were these tubes connected to the child, but they were almost completely rotted away. We found fragments of clothes and something that looked like it might have been a face mask. The thing is, he wasn't connected to the life-support system. He was just floating in this liquid. Then we lifted him out and it was like he was being born. He started crying. We lifted him out of this liquid and he started screaming just like a new-born baby. We did a full medical and he was perfectly healthy. I don't know how long he was out there but he suffered no ill effects. If anything, he was more than healthy. He was just about perfect. We found him a home with a couple who took him in and raised him."

"I still don't understand what this has to do with me," Shor said.

Harl turned to look Shor directly in the eye. "That couple is your mother and father."

Shor tried to think if his parents had ever adopted a child, perhaps before he was born. There were no images, no mentions, no signs of grief or loss.

Then Harl's words took hold. The understanding came.

"That baby was *me?*"

Harl nodded. "Yes."

Shor could only stare at the old man. It was as if his entire world had been pulled out from under his feet and he was left there, floating in an abyss with nothing to hold onto. He felt suddenly light-headed. His mind clutched for something, anything.

"Am I...human?"

"Yes. One hundred percent. Your genetic code is extremely varied and therefore quite strong. You have not suffered the effects of a limited gene pool as we have here."

"So, where did I come from?" He looked up at the glass ceiling panels and the orange Martian sky. "Alpha Centauri?"

"No. We think you almost certainly come from Earth. Although there is the question of why you were travelling from Alpha Centauri. I have searched the Earth history files but we have no record of such a mission. I had hoped to find the answers inside the ship."

"But, it must have opened once. How else did you get the baby—me—out?"

"The door opened after we brought the craft into the hangar. It shut again once you were taken out and it never opened again."

"Almost as if the ship was letting you in long enough to get the baby—me—out."

"I never thought of it that way but, yes, it was a bit like that."

Shor listened to everything the old man was saying, but it was all surreal. It was as if his whole life on Mars was being wiped clean, one word at a time. He looked down at his rippling reflection in the dark mirror of his coffee. For the briefest moment he had the unnerving sensation of looking at someone he did not know. He swirled the coffee, erasing the image.

"Let me see if I've got this straight. You're saying I arrived here eighteen years ago from the other side of the galaxy, in a ship that may have been built a thousand years earlier."

"We're not sure, but it appears that way, yes."

Shor let out a bitter laugh. "Well, it does explain a few things. How many people know about this?"

"Not many. Only a few people actually saw you. They all agreed to secrecy, for your sake."

"And my parents? Do they know?"

"No. Your mother and father know nothing about this."

They sat in silence, finishing their food. The roads were starting to get a little busier with people doing last minute errands before heading towards their tram stops. Watching them now, Shor saw them for what they were for the very first time. Or perhaps it was he who had changed. He was now seeing an alien race whose bodies were perfectly adapted to their environment. But as he watched them gliding past he realized it was not they who were the aliens here.

"Should I tell them?"

"What? That you're not from Mars?"

"Yes."

"What do you think?"

Shor stared down at his feet dangling an inch above the ground. Sitting next to Harl, he probably looked like a child.

"No, probably not. People treat me like I'm an alien already. Do you know what my nickname is?"

Harl held his gaze but said nothing.

"They call me Short." He spat the last "t" the way the other kids always did. "Of all the possible names, why did my parents have to give me this one? You know what's worse than the name-calling though? It's people ignoring me. They treat me like I'm not there. They walk towards me and I can see they think I'm a kid and then they see my face. I can see their expression change and then they look the other way. Everyone here is so perfect." He stood and carried his empty packaging across to the bin where the bot was still working on an escape plan. He nudged the little machine backwards with his foot. It froze for a moment, its visual sensors scanning, before scuttling off towards the nearest station. Shor noted that it had managed to reach the litter. "If word got out that I actually *am* an alien, who knows how they'll react."

"Yes, it is probably best to keep this to yourself," Harl said.

"So, what happens to the ship?"

"I'm not sure. We will keep it connected and watch it for a while. To be honest, I'm thinking about launching it into space. We can't get it open and it's too dangerous to salvage."

"Pity," Shor said. "I would've liked to have seen inside."

Harl nodded. "Yes, me too. I have to head back now." He tapped his chatband. "Here's my number. If you need anything. If you need to talk to someone, just give me a call."

Shor looked at Harl's avatar smiling up from his chatband screen.

"You look different," he said.

"Younger, you mean? That was taken a while back. I should get it updated." He walked across to his buggy. "Remember, if you need anything, just call."

"Thanks," Shor said, lifting a hand as the old man drove away.

He watched until the buggy rolled out of sight, then turned to head back towards the depot.

On the way home that evening, he found an empty seat at the back of the tram where he watched the world floating past his window. He recognized a few people as they boarded the carriage and found seats closer to the front, but he lowered his head, pretending to be busy chatting when they looked his way.

The loneliness he had felt before was now a certainty—a provable, scientific fact.

He visited the hospital but did not go inside. He was early so he walked along the side wall of the building to his mother's window and looked in at her through the blinds until his father entered the room and sat down in the chair next to the bed. He watched them together, the way his father gazed down into her face with a tenderness he had never shown Shor, the way he held her hands and stroked her fingers.

Rather than walk down the main road to his apartment block, he took a longer but less congested route. At the turn for his home he hesitated, heading right instead of left, walking until he came to the building in the far corner. He took the stairs to the top floor and, making sure he was alone, slipped through the gap and climbed up to the roof.

Here, alone and unseen, he sat in his usual spot and watched the city doing what it always did. On a clear evening like this he could see all of his favourite landmarks, from the market on the corner not far from his apartment block, across to the park with its plastic trees and the message cube hanging over it like a mighty anvil, all the way along to the big airlock doors at the opposite side of the sector. He could see his school's iron gates extolling the three virtues so prized by the city's founders. Not far from that was the police station and, a little further along, the hospital where his mother slept so very deeply.

From here he could see the tops of the apartment blocks curling around in a series of concentric semi-circles. He probably knew most of the tenants by sight, but only a few well enough to know their name. From this spot he could see the apartments of seven of his class-mates, and two more if he shifted a little to his right. And he knew exactly where Mel lived without having to look.

He had wanted to bring her up here, but this was his secret place. Way up here, Shor could watch the city without being seen and stare up at the sky and dream he was somewhere else.

As if on cue, his chatband squeezed and he looked down at Mel's face.

"You okay?" she asked. "I was worried about you."

"You shouldn't worry so much. I can take care of myself."

"I haven't seen you in days and you don't answer my calls. What else should I be? I'm your friend, remember? And friends are supposed to be there for each other."

"Thanks but I'm going through some stuff nobody can help me with. I appreciate you being there for me, but I just need some time. Listen, I'm a bit busy right now. Thanks for calling. I've gotta go."

"See you at Reggie's tomorrow?"

"Sure. Perhaps."

He broke the connection and watched the call stats fade from the screen. Just then the incoming message signal flashed.

The text said simply: "Hello Brett."

"You've got the wrong person," he said, and deleted the message without checking the caller's ID.

He didn't know anyone called Brett. In fact, he had never heard the name before. At least, he didn't think he had heard it before because it was vaguely familiar. It was on odd name. It sounded a little like "bread".

He lay on his back, his head turned so that he could see the maximum amount of sky. It was clear out tonight and the stars were all there, jostling for space alongside Mars' two moons, although Deimos was so small it might easily be mistaken for a star. He recognized one or two constellations. According to Mister Edmunds, the constellations were once used by the sailors of Earth to help them find their way around. They built a map of the stars, associating groups of lights with familiar shapes and giving them odd names like Leo and Ursa.

He tried to imagine being in a boat in a pool of water so big you needed the stars to find your way across it. The largest amount of water he had ever seen was the collection tanks out at the purification plant. He had thought they were big until he saw images of the oceans from Earth.

Surely that much water would never run out. And there would be no need to retire someone just to keep the pumps running.

As he stared up at the dark sky, imagining he was floating on an endless sea, a movement caught his eye up in the top corner of the panel almost directly above where he was lying.

He turned his head and leaned out further, fixing his eyes on the edge of the next panel where he estimated it would reappear. He tried not to blink for fear of missing it. Most objects colliding with Mars' thin atmosphere usually only lasted a brief moment before disintegrating in a flash of fire.

The meteor appeared almost exactly where he expected it would, streaking in a slow, almost stately, line across the sky. He craned his neck to follow it for as long as he could. It was still burning as it dipped out of sight. Gone.

Over at the park, the message cube was flashing the half-hour curfew warning. The streets were full of people making their way home.

His apartment building was just a block away. The windows faced the other way so there was no way of seeing if the lights were on. His father would probably want to know why he had not gone to the hospital. Then again, he wasn't really his father, not really. Their bond, what little of it existed, had no real foundation. Their relationship was purely an act of charity but then, wasn't that the case with most Martian families?

Shor pulled back from the edge and slid down to the roof where he stood, bending his legs a few times to loosen them a little.

Another message came through, this time with the words: "Brett, where are you?"

A quick check of the caller's ID revealed nothing. It was a series of letters and digits, and the avatar was just a blank square.

Strange, he thought, and shrugged.

He allocated the caller to his Block list, but he did not delete the message.

18

The rescue pod dropped through the thin Martian atmosphere, its shields glowing as it ploughed through the air made up almost exclusively of carbon dioxide with some nitrogen and traces of oxygen. And dust so fine it never settled to the ground, even in the lulls between storms.

The sole passenger watched a virtual image of his descent on the console screen. The trajectory would take him most of the way around Mars, roughly following the equator towards Elysium Mons, the planet's fifth highest volcano, and the habitation beyond.

The pod shook as it entered a denser layer, then settled again. The screen showed a three-dimensional representation of the planet's contours rolling slowly beneath the ship's white-hot hull. To the north was Olympus Mons standing almost fourteen kilometres above the rust-red ground. It filled the screen as the pod raced towards the Martian surface.

A warning sounded, indicating the craft was now at the safe maximum height for chute deployment. The landing site was five hundred kilometres away. Taking into account weather conditions on the surface, deployment would occur in fifteen seconds.

The passenger watched the digits count down. At two seconds, he braced himself.

There was a violent lurch as the brake chutes opened. A thousand square metres of heat-proof canvas clutched at the air with thick white claws attached to steel cables that snapped and hummed as they fought to slow the ship's descent.

The gee-forces crushed him into his chair, then lifted again as the vehicle adjusted to its new speed. He checked the readout to make sure everything was functioning normally, and released his grip on the seat.

With the current angle of descent he would make it to within three kilometres of the landing site. His suit had enough oxygen for twelve hours and the portable supply trebled that, which gave him an effective working radius of sixty kilometres or, in the case of a one-way trip, one hundred and twenty.

On the screen, the majestic slopes of Elysium Mons engulfed the horizon. He caught a glimpse of the monstrous caldera before the pod dropped below the rim into the wide, sloping plain below.

Turbulence rattled the tiny craft and it rocked from side to side under the canopy as the winds tugged it a few degrees off-course. The ship responded by adjusting the angle of approach. The pod twisted and turned the other way. Now the estimated distance from the landing zone was two kilometres.

He turned to look at the console. The settlement registered on the screen as a cluster of pixels about halfway between two contour lines a hundred kilometres from where he would touch down. It looked tiny, but that was because most of it was underground. Only three structures were visible from the exterior. The bulk of the settlement was in a series of caves below the forbidding surface. He studied the dots as they expanded to become lines and squares. Soon he was able to make out the raised grids of windows. He counted five in all.

The impact warning sounded and he focused on the numbers down the side of the screen. With twenty seconds before impact, the airbags deployed around the side of the pod, forming a shock-absorbing cushion of air. Fifteen seconds out and the rocket boosters fired a sequence of braking thrusts designed to reduce the descent speed by sixty percent. With ten seconds to impact, the chair lifted, rising a good half a metre towards the pod ceiling. At five seconds, the computer commenced counting down.

He braced himself.

With one final burst from the rockets, the pod paused inches above the Martian dust. At the exact same moment the chair and air-cushion collapsed in a controlled release of pressure designed to absorb nine-tenths of the impact.

The ship shuddered slightly as it sank to the planet surface. The computer announced that they had landed. On the console screen, the buildings of the habitation were now clearly visible. The distance was just over one hundred and five kilometres.

He sat motionless for a few seconds to make sure the craft had come to a complete stop. Then he stood and checked himself for any sign of injuries. Satisfied that he was undamaged, he checked his oxygen levels before turning to the exit and hitting the release button.

The door yawned open in a lazy arc, sending swirls of steam billowing in its wake and touching down in a soft cloud of dust. He looked out at a rust-red vista baking in the cold beneath a faded orange sky. The world was rimmed by the dark monoliths of a landscape that managed to be both rugged and smooth all at once.

He stepped down onto the door. The giant outline of Elysium Mons strode the horizon like a colossus, one hundred and thirty kilometres away but still intimidating. Flanking it were the smaller volcanoes of Hecates Tholus and Albus Tholus, both mere hills by comparison to their larger sibling.

This close to the equator the temperature was just above freezing, but it looked warm. It looked *hot*. The red soil and orange sky combined to give the illusion of being inside an oven. The whole world looked as if it were on fire, or about to burst into flames. The tangerine sky suggested an inferno just beyond the crest of the distant hills, or of volcanoes spewing molten rock over the parched landscape, but it was just a trick of the light. The planet was as cold as a corpse. Only the wind offered a reminder that there was yet some life left on those dry plains.

He stepped down and placed a boot on the fine, red sand. He lifted his left arm and looked down at the readout which located the habitation twenty degrees to the right, almost in line with the sun behind him. He could follow his shadow and be on course to within a few degrees.

The door closed behind him and he set off, the portable oxygen supply slung over one shoulder and his eyes fixed on a point in the distance.

"And? What happened yesterday?" Lars asked as they dressed for work, apparently unable to contain his curiosity any longer. "You get the ship open or what?"

"No," Shor replied. It crossed his mind that he should tell his boss all about the conversation in the square with Harl spilling the beans on his life, but he thought better of it. Harl was right to suggest they keep it a secret. Being weird was one thing. Being a weird alien would open up a whole new set of matching luggage. For now, he needed to lay low and pretend nothing had changed.

"Shame," Lars said, donning his tool belt. "Seems a bit strange them not being able to get into one of their own ships. What happened? They lose a key or something?"

He guffawed and looked at the others. Bek and Reet smirked.

"Something like that."

"Harl seemed convinced you could get it open. I wonder why?"

Shor shrugged. "I must've touched a button or something."

"Maybe a secret panel?"

"Maybe."

"Well, whatever the reason you couldn't get it open, I'm sorry, kid. I know you were hoping to get into the space program, even if it was through the back door. Still, it's good to have you back on the team. And it ain't all bad. Today you get to explore the wonderful world of *communications*." He said the word in a dramatic, drawn-out voice. "And you get to visit the Space Sector again. There's an aerial support needs fixing. Seems it got knocked over by a critter. We'll be needing the out-suits for this one."

Shor felt the apprehension wash over him. It was the feeling of someone who has watched a potentially dangerous activity many times and thought, *how bad can it be?* only to find that it is much, much worse actually doing it rather than just watching.

He donned his work clothes and took the out-suit from its special box in the bottom of his locker. The helmet was a bit grimy and the glove pads were getting worn, but it looked functional. They used the test station to check for leaks. Shor tried the helmet on for size. His breathing became loud and the HUD lit up the inside of the bowl. Satisfied all was working, he removed it again and placed it carefully into his work bag.

They finished dressing and headed out to the buggies. Lars touched Shor on the arm to hold him back while the others drove off. He waited until they were out of sight.

"I don't know what happened yesterday, but I do know a few things, and I know Harl's story about not being able to get inside the ship holds water about as effectively as a spanner. So are you going to tell me what's really going on?"

"Nothing's going on," Shor said.

Lars examined him in the manner of a mechanic looking for leaks in an engine. Then he said, "I want to show you something. Come with me."

Lars led the way through the workshop and disappeared behind two rows of shelves overflowing with all sorts of bits and pieces. At the end, he turned back down another row and stopped at the far wall where he slid one of a dozen wooden panels sideways to reveal an ID scanner. He swiped his keycard and a lock clicked. The wall of panels swung open to reveal a room. It was not much bigger than a broom cupboard lined with wooden panels and filled with more shelves stuffed with junk.

"Storage for top secret projects," Lars said. "Limited access. Close the door, will you?"

Shor turned and pulled the door closed. In the back corner, Lars slid open a panel and presented his ID to another scanner. A door-sized section of the wall rolled to one side. This led into an even smaller room where a single chair faced an array of nine monitors.

"Welcome to Headquarters or, as it generally known, HQ." Lars winked and bent to press a switch on the bottom shelf. The screens flickered and held. Each had an image of Utopia. Shor could see people and vehicles and bots, all going about their business on the streets of the city.

"What is this?" Shor said. "It looks like…"

"Security cameras. We have a feed from every glass eye in the city. You want to see what's happening at the park?" Lars pointed to the middle screen on the top row where Shor immediately recognized the ornate iron gates. It was quiet at this time of the morning—almost deserted. Two men strode past, followed by a bot.

"This is great," Shor said, looking from screen to screen. "How did you get this? Can we see the big airlock doors?"

Lars tapped at the keyboard and pointed to the bottom row where a monitor showed the big doors Shor had passed through earlier that morning. The guard sat in his little room, looking all officious.

"Hang on," Shor said. "Is this legal?"

Lars smirked. "What do you think?"

"What about energy?" An image of his mother lying in her hospital bed flashed through his mind. "They'll notice this much power usage, surely."

"Not to worry, my young friend." Lars tapped a box. "We have software to monitor usage and make sure we don't burn too much. Over a certain limit, we lose all but the screen in the middle. Anyway, as these things go, monitors are pretty light on power."

"But what if they find out? Won't we get into trouble?"

"Listen. Nobody outside Maintenance knows this room exists. It's not even on the city plans. The only way anyone is ever going to find out about it is if one of us tells. You must not talk about this room to anyone. If the badges find out, we'll be in a lot of trouble. Do you understand?"

"Yes," Shor said. "Of course."

"And I don't mean trouble as in *not getting your choice of career* trouble. We're talking reduced rations, maybe even early retirement."

"I get it," Shor said. "I won't say a word."

"Good. As long as we've got that straight."

"Can we see the Space Sector from here?" Shor leaned forward to peer at the monitors.

"Of course. If there's a functioning camera connected to the security system, we can look through it." He tapped on a keyboard and the screens all flickered at once, like a huge compound eye. The views of the Residential Sector were replaced by images of the Space Sector. "There you are. As close as you can get to the space program without being there."

"This is great. You can see everything," Shor said.

"Yes you can."

"What about the ship? I can see lots of spacecraft, but not my ship. Can you see my ship?"

Lars raised an eyebrow. "So it's *your* ship now, is it? They must've taken the camera out, or never put one in. If there was one connected it wouldn't even need to be turned on for us to use it."

"This is amazing. How have you kept this hidden so long?"

"Because we can. It's one of the perks of working on the Maintenance team. And, let's face it, we need all the perks we can get. Bek spends hours in here some days, especially on the night shift, when it gets quiet. He calls it his therapy."

"I guess working in the sewers isn't so nice, huh?"

"What do you think?"

"I guess not." Shor shrugged. "So who else knows about this?"

"Reet, Tane and Bek. And now you. And it's important we keep it that way. The limited-access storage room lets us get in and out but don't abuse it. We don't have that many top-secret assignments. Use the little monitor next to the door to check if it's safe to leave. And it helps if you're carrying something. Better still, don't come in if someone's watching you."

"Why are you showing me this? I'm just a goget."

Lars considered him for a few seconds. "The way I see it, you need a break. I know what it's like to have some clerk sitting behind a desk somewhere blast your hopes and dreams down the sewer. Besides, you're a trainee manager. I think I can trust you."

"Thanks Lars, I really appreciate that."

"Sure, just don't start getting all emotional on me. The system keeps a copy of every feed for the previous four weeks before the first week gets overwritten. For example, I was in here yesterday afternoon, and I noticed a couple of guys having a nice chat over at the Hub square. It was an old fella and a youngster looking just like you. I don't know what they were talking about but I'd say it was really serious."

Lars tapped a key and the centre monitor displayed a scene of the square just up the road. Shor recognized himself sitting with Harl on the bench. Even from this distance, looking at his own face, it was obvious he was upset.

"You sure everything's all right?" Lars said. "Because if you're in trouble . . ?"

"No, I'm not in trouble," Shor said. "I guess I'm still upset about not getting into the Space Program."

Lars watched him intently for a second, then cracked a smile. "Fine. If you say you're not in trouble then I believe you. Say, you wanna see something funny?"

Shor nodded. "Sure."

"Watch."

Up on the centre screen, a cleaning bot was doing its thing, spraying the walkway with detergent and scrubbing away with its rotary brush. Lars tapped a key and, almost instantly, the bot stopped. It looked around for a few moments and then started moving in a circle, spraying water into the air.

Lars guffawed. "Go little critter. Get the stain. Go on. You can do it."

"Why's he doing that?" Shor said, watching the machine spinning in ever tighter circles, the jet of water forming little arcs in the air. It looked like an elaborate fountain display gone berserk.

"Every month we do an emergency drill, right? Well every camera has an alarm built in. One goes off and they all go off. Well, we've rigged it so we can alter the frequency of any camera's alarm. Nobody can hear it but it drives any bots in the area nuts. Look at him go."

"But what about security? Don't they know the alarm's gone off?"

"There are ways around that, my lad. Do you think Maintenance was my first choice?"

"Well no. I never thought—"

"I wanted to work as a programmer. I was good too. Just had the knack. I could get a computer to do just about anything. Only problem is, I hated most of the other subjects, and you need a good overall grade to get into the Computer Department. So, I hacked into the system and changed my grades. I thought I was so smart, but I was young and careless. I left a trail a blind man could follow in a dust storm."

"And they put you here?"

"Exactly."

"That's lousy."

"I thought so at first, but it's the best thing that ever happened to me. If they put you in Programming, they suck any joy you may have had for computers right out of you. They make you write these boring programs or a little piece of a boring program. This way, I get to do what I want to do. Looking back now, given a choice between Programming and Maintenance, I know which one I'd choose."

On the screen, the little robot looked ready to explode. Lars tapped a key and it stopped spinning. For a few seconds it appeared confused, dizzy almost. It looked around, seemed to decide, and then returned to what it was doing before as if nothing had happened. Shor wondered how much power that little stunt had used. In some computer file somewhere, it would have been logged as just another bot getting stuck, but how many seconds of his mother's life had he just witnessed being erased? Was one Watt equal to one second? One minute? A day?

"Sometimes," Lars continued, "things can look bad, but turn out for the good. Down here we get access to just about everywhere in the city. Do you know what most people on the Space Program do? They sit behind a desk and push pixels around a screen. Only a handful end up training as astronauts. Even less ever get to work with ships. I reckon there's a good chance you would've ended up bored out of your mind."

Every screen now displayed images of the Space Sector. Through office windows, people were sitting at desks, staring vacantly into computer screens.

"Do they look excited to be in the Space Program?"

"Not really, no."

"Chances are, that would've been you. Sure you're in the Maintenance team fixing broken poles and blocked sewer pipes, but with this," he waved at the screens, "and this," he lifted his keycard, "you can see everything and go everywhere. Just make sure you've got a reasonable-looking work order, and nobody will suspect you're not there for a good reason."

Looking at the workers in the Space Sector, Shor recognized the look of boredom that afflicted so many adults. Careers were carefully chosen based on a wide range of criteria including (although not always) personal preference. What the selection process was not able to predict, apparently, was a person's ability to cope with the fact that virtually every job, no matter how interesting at first, essentially boiled down to doing what had to be done as opposed to what people wanted to do. How, Shor wondered, was it possible for anybody to find work in the Space Sector boring? And yet, there they were, staring blankly into their screens as if they were doing the most tedious job in the world. At least he got to move around the city and do something different every day. He had access to parts of Utopia these people probably didn't know existed. And then there was this little room. From in here he could watch the world in complete anonymity. Perhaps he would keep an eye on Harl and try to find out a little more about the mysterious old man.

Best of all, he could look in on his mother whenever he wanted.

The more he thought about it, the more he was starting to believe someone may have actually done him a favour posting him to the Maintenance Department.

One thing bothered him though. "I've been meaning to ask you," he said, following his boss back out through small labyrinth of shelves and into the workshop. "What did Bek do to end up doing what he does, you know, in the sewers?"

"I don't know but I suspect he actually likes it down there. About two years ago he was offered a chance to work up top."

"And?"

"He turned it down. Sounds strange but all the sewerage workers are the same. They moan about the job, but no-one ever asks for a transfer, or takes it when they get the chance." He tapped his forehead with the tip of his finger." Takes a certain kind of mentality to do what they do. Personally, I reckon the fumes melt their brains. Now, what say we go fix that aerial support?"

They took the buggy to the Space Sector, passing through the airlock doors and following the main road down to the central intersection. Here they turned right towards the now-familiar hangars looming against the side wall. At the hangar expressway, the buggy carried them through the blur of traffic to the loading ramp.

Shor climbed out but could not help looking further along towards the far corner and the little building that housed the ship. His ship.

"Grab that pole," Lars said, nodding to the back of the buggy. "Bring the tools. And don't forget your suit."

Shor did as he was told and followed his boss up the ramp towards the airlock, the toolbox trundling obediently behind. The platform rose from the floor towards the ceiling at a gentle incline that carried them half the length of the Space Sector and a good ten metres above the ground. The ramp was wide enough to hold a spaceship, but Shor kept well away from the edge. The barrier looked flimsy and dangerously low. By the time they reached the airlock, he was out of breath and sweating.

The controller strolled out of his cubicle to meet them with the manner of someone whose authority is heavily outweighed by the tedium inherent in his work. He returned Lars' nod before proceeding to examine the work-order slowly and carefully. Apparently, it was the highlight of his day so far.

"You can use the side door," he said, measuring the pole with his eyes. "Secure your suits before you enter."

Shor placed the pole on the floor and proceeded to climb into his out-suit. He secured the helmet with the clasp, pressing it down until it clicked. The HUD lit up, informing him the suit was functioning.

"You ready?" Lars said, his voice crackly and loud in the helmet speakers.

"I'm ready," Shor replied.

He retrieved the pole and they moved along the walkway that ran parallel to the bigger airlock to the small side door designed to cater for a lower volume of traffic. Shor was familiar with going outside—he had taken part in two excursions during his time at school, but he still felt anxiety wrapping its fingers around his chest as the door closed behind him. He stood to attention with the pole at his side and the toolbox nudging his heels. He could hear his own breathing. It sounded too quick and too loud in the confines of his helmet.

The light above the door turned from green to red. There was the rumble of locks moving. The floor shuddered as the elevator mechanism lifted them through the ceiling. Shor saw a square of orange sky slide into view through the window. He tried to control his breathing as the door slid open to reveal a walkway leading alongside the hangar out onto a planet so barren it almost hurt his eyes. His out-suit popped, expanding to its full size at the sudden drop in atmospheric pressure, giving the strange sensation of being instantly disrobed.

"This way," Lars said, walking through the door and down the ramp.

Shor followed, stepping into the sand-trap grid and walking with his left glove brushing against the hangar wall. To his right was the beautiful but desolate Martian landscape. The sky was clear today, allowing maintenance work on the external structures. At least three bots were busy at various places around the roof of the city.

Lars lifted his arm. Shor looked at the aerial standing fifty metres beyond the corner of the hangar on a concrete slab that was home to a small cluster of antennae. The bot responsible for the damage was standing next to the aerial, half on and half off the platform.

"What do you think happened?" Shor asked as they got close enough to see the point of collision.

"Critter must've got stuck out in the storm. Looks like it tried to get back inside but its gears must've jammed. It shut itself down to avoid doing more damage. Blasted dust gets in everywhere." Lars opened the bot's hatch and pulled out a circuit board. "Well this looks fine. Must be mechanical." He crouched and peered under the chassis. "Hmm. Looks like the rear axle's damaged. We'll have to take it back with us. Let's get the aerial strut fixed first. Grab a number fifteen will you?"

Shor kicked the toolbox and reached in to retrieve the spanner. It was difficult to do anything while wearing the thick gloves, and even harder to handle small tools. He dropped the spanner twice before managing to get it out of the box.

"Good, now undo these two bolts at the base first. Hold onto it in case it swings loose. We don't want the whole thing falling on us."

Shor crouched as low as possible next to the aerial, but the suit made it difficult to bend so he adopted a half squat. He imagined he looked like someone sitting on an invisible toilet.

The first bolt was stiff, but he managed to remove it fairly easily. He placed the nut and bolt on the concrete base next to the strut anchor point. The second took a little more work. He felt the strut pulling as he turned the spanner thirty degrees at a time. The effort sent a droplet of sweat rolling down his forehead and onto his nose. On the last few turns, he took hold of the pole and gripped it tightly. The bolt came loose and the strut pulled, but only a little. He looked up at the aerial, which swayed but remained upright.

"That's done," he said, rising to his feet and turning to Lars, who was just standing there looking off into the distance. "Lars?"

Lars did not answer, but continued to squint into the low light. Shor turned to follow his boss' gaze. The red dust stretched as far as the eye could see, to the dark outline of the volcanoes reclining like slumbering giants on the jagged horizon. He looked back at his boss, who continued to stare.

"What is it, Lars?"

"There's something out there."

"I don't see anything."

Shor peered out into the endless dust, squinting through his own reflection in his visor. Another drop of sweat ran down his nose and he wanted desperately to pull off his helmet and scratch. Then he saw it— something shiny flashing off in the distance. He tried not to blink. It flashed again. "I see it," he said. "Yeah, I see it. Over there. It looks like a mirror."

Lars did not say anything but watched, motionless, his face set in granite.

The distant light continued to flicker on and off in an unsteady cadence, but it was changing. The light was now surrounded by darker shapes like undulating shadows. Then the shapes separated into what appeared to be…limbs.

"It's a person," Shor said. "Look, you can see the arms and legs."

"We'd better call this in," Lars replied, pressing the comms button on his sleeve. "This is Lars Fline of the Maintenance team. We're topside doing work on an aerial just west of the hangar. Do you have any people working outside today, apart from us?"

Shor heard a brief exchange of muffled voices on the other end. "One moment…No, we don't have anyone else scheduled for today. Why?"

"There's someone headed this way. He's coming from the west."

"Say again."

"I said, he's coming from the west. He's about two kilometres away. Looks like he's walking."

"You're at the hangar?"

"Yes. We're working on an antenna."

"And you see someone?"

"He's headed this way."

"You sure about that? Because there isn't anything west of the hangar."

"Of course I'm sure," Lars spat.

"Well, we'll send someone up to come take a look."

"What do you want us to do?"

"You should come back inside."

Lars looked at the strut hanging loose. "We haven't finished fixing the aerial. And we need to get this bot inside for repairs."

"You can do that later. Return to the airlock immediately."

There was a click, and the comms link went dead.

"Idiot," Lars growled.

"He's carrying something," Shor said. "And I think he's wearing a space suit."

Of course he's wearing a space suit, Shor thought. *He's outside on Mars. What else would he be wearing?*

Lars took a few steps forward, lifting his hand to shield his eyes. "We should help him."

"But they said we should wait," Shor said. "They said we had to go back inside."

"I know what they said."

Shor watched as Lars set off towards the approaching figure, his feet kicking up little clouds of dust. Shor looked hopefully back at the hangar, but the airlock was empty with no sign of the badges. Lars was bounding forwards in graceful arcs, his contact with the ground timed to perfection for minimum impact and maximum propulsion. Shor had always envied the people who were able to move that way. At least now he knew there was nothing really wrong with him. He was just not built for it. Assuming of course that what Harl had said was true.

He followed along, trying his best not to trip over his own feet. He could hear Lars breathing heavily but this was soon drowned out by his own laboured grunts as he struggled across the fine sand.

The stranger had a curious walk, as if he were about to fall over at any second and was putting each foot forward to stop this from happening.

"Hello," he heard Lars say slowly and loudly, now standing directly in the path of the stranger, who had stopped. "Are you all right? Do you need help? Where did you come from?"

There was no response. Presumably the stranger's comms unit was malfunctioning.

Shor pulled up alongside his boss, just managing to avoid crashing into him. The stranger just stood there. He was dressed in a space suit and carrying what looked like a case of some kind with a fat tube snaking around his back to where it connected with his rear panel, probably an oxygen supply. His suit was like nothing on Mars. It was obviously made for space travel, but the design was very different from the normal out-suit. It was bulkier, with thick collars at the shoulder, wrist, and knee joints. The suit itself was clean but the material looked faded and worn. The creases revealed white fabric where it had been protected and preserved. The cloth around the shoulder joint moved in a strange way, suggesting a hidden seam or some sort of join. The helmet was bigger as well, and rounder in shape. The visor was as shiny as a mirror, making it difficult to see inside.

Shor shifted his position, moving closer to Lars who was still trying to make contact with the stranger using a loud, slow voice. The top of the bulbous helmet came to about nose height on Lars and, judging by the shoulders, Shor guessed the owner of the suit was shorter than the average Martian. He was standing completely motionless, apparently watching Lars. Shor tried to see into the helmet but the visor was as reflective as a mirror. All he could see was a bulbous rendition of the Martian sky.

"Come with us," Lars said, extending one arm towards the hangar while gesticulating with his other hand. "This way."

The stranger's helmet turned towards the hangar and Shor caught his first glimpse of the face behind the visor. A cloth head cap covered everything except for a small circle of skin running from just above the eyebrows, around and down to below the bottom lip. It looked like someone peeping through a small hole. It was an adult male of about thirty Earth years, with a pleasant face and dark eyes, and not much taller than Shor. His expression was without emotion. He almost looked bored, as if he had been interrupted while taking a walk in Axle Park and just wanted to get on his way. His eyes were focused towards the hangar.

"Yes," Lars said. "The hangar. You come with us?"

Shor turned to see the airlock door opening. The comms link hissed static.

"Over there," a voice said.

"I see them," another replied.

Shor touched Lars' arm. "Someone's coming."

They turned to face the two men bounding across the sand. They wore the distinctive badge uniforms with the white trim and black insignia. They were carrying weapons.

"We should go," Shor said, pulling at Lars's arm. "We should go now."

"I hear an alarm," Lars said. "A suit alarm. Whose is it? It's not mine. Is it yours?"

"I don't..." Shor started to say. Then he heard it. A low but insistent beeping. On his HUD, the oxygen warning was flashing. It was amber, which meant he was using fifty percent more than usual. "Ah, flub! It's my air. My air's flashing. Lars, what do I do?"

"What colour is it?"

"Amber."

"Try to calm down. You're burning oxygen too fast."

Shor focused on his breathing. He tried to relax but the flashing text was not helping.

"Stay where you are!" a voice barked. "Don't move."

They looked up to see the badges with weapons drawn and enough body-language to suggest they were ready for trouble. "Who's got the alarm?"

Shor lifted his hand from the elbow. "Me. It's just an amber."

"Why are you two still up here? You were told to go inside."

"This guy looked like he needed help," Lars said. "We couldn't just leave him out here."

"You can explain that in your statement." The badge moved forward to stand in front of the stranger. He peered into his visor while his colleague circled around to cover the back. "What's your name? What are you doing out here?"

There was only the static hiss of the empty comms channel.

"Are you injured?"

"I tried that," Lars said. "He isn't talking."

The badge ignored Lars. "I said, what is your name? You are not permitted to just wander around out here."

Shor stared at the badge's gun. He had only ever seen a weapon like it once before, back when he was very young. It was only used outside because it was generally understood that firing such a weapon inside an air-tight environment was a bad idea.

"I've never seen a suit like this before," the other badge said. "It looks like something out of the history books. Just look at this oxygen tank."

The flashing text inside Shor's suit changed from amber to red. He lifted his hand to get Lars' attention but Lars was engrossed in watching the drama with the stranger.

"He doesn't look injured," the first badge said.

"Perhaps he's scared," Lars suggested, with a hint of sarcasm. "Or maybe he's running out of air and doesn't want to waste it talking to you."

"Erm...Lars?"

"Leave this to me, if you don't mind. Sir, I can't help you if you don't talk to me."

The alarm in Shor's helmet changed pitch, becoming higher, but nobody else appeared to notice. He stepped closer to Lars and nudged his arm.

Lars turned to look a him.

Shor pointed at his helmet. He then cupped his hands around his throat in a choking action before jerking his thumb towards his backpack.

"He could be mute," the second badge said. "You've gotta come take a look at this tank."

"I hate to interrupt, but I think we have a problem here," Lars said. "My colleague appears to be having trouble with his oxygen supply."

The badges turned to look at Shor.

"It's gone red," Shor said, aware his voice had moved up in pitch to match the alarm. "The warning message has gone red. What do I do?"

"Might be a leak," Lars said. "You checked it, right?"

"I checked it."

"You are required by law to check your suit before leaving the city," the first badge said,

"I did. I mean, I think I did. I feel dizzy. What does that mean?"

"Your suit must be malfunctioning. What is your oxygen level?"

Shor squinted at the reading on his HUD. He was struggling to focus. "Fifty-three percent. Forty-four minutes. No wait, fifty-two percent." It felt as if his head was slowly filling with warm liquid. "I don't feel so good. The air tastes strange. Does anybody else's air taste strange?"

"We have to get inside," the second badge said, turning to the walker and waving his gun towards the hangar. "Sir, come with us."

The stranger apparently understood the meaning of a waved gun because he obeyed without hesitation. Shor watched him as they walked side by side. Even the footprints he left behind were odd. They seemed somehow cleaner than those of all the others in the group, and deeper.

Lars said nothing for the entire time. Shor was not sure if it was his fuzzy brain imagining things but he could almost hear his boss seething. The stricken bot was where they had left it, half on and half off the concrete pad. The tool box was still open, like a hungry chick waiting for a morsel of food.

They reached the airlock and stepped inside. The exchange of bad air for good took a matter of seconds. Shor immediately started to feel a change inside his suit. He took deep breaths and his head began to shed its fuzziness. Almost in unison, both the light inside his helmet and the airlock light turned from red to green.

The inner door slid open. A group of badges waited, as well as two men in white coats who looked like scientists. And Harl was with them. The old man stepped forward to examine the stranger, peering at his odd suit with his hand on his chin as he walked in a slow circuit, occasionally stooping to frown, or raise his eyebrows. He muttered something and stepped back, indicating for the badges to continue. They moved forward and steered their uninvited guest off towards a cluster of covered buggies.

Shor removed his helmet, glad to be breathing normal air again. He joined Harl in watching the stranger being bundled into the back of the nearest vehicle.

"Where are they taking him?"

The old man turned to Shor and blinked, as if he had just seen him standing there. "I didn't recognize you with that suit on. Him? Oh, they're taking him to quarantine. He needs to be tested before being allowed to enter the city. One virus in an enclosed environment like this would be disastrous. We can't be too careful."

"Surely you don't think he's carrying a disease?" Lars said. "I thought Mars was dead. I thought there were no diseases."

Harl did not answer. He was watching the convoy of buggies drive away with keen interest

"Well?" Lars demanded.

"I'm sorry. What did you say?"

"I said I thought there weren't any diseases on Mars."

Harl looked straight at him but his eyes were glazed over, as if he were lost in thought, or somewhere else.

"No," he said. "There aren't."

21

They had to wait another hour before the badges gave them clearance to go and collect their box of tools and the stricken critter. This gave Shor enough time to take his suit in for exchange, but the clerk assured him it was working perfectly. They thoroughly tested every unit that came in and whatever Shor had experienced, it was not a fault with his out-suit. Oxygen was at ninety percent. The standard pressure test revealed no leaks. As far as the clerk behind the desk was concerned, Shor's suit was working perfectly.

It was with some reluctance that he donned it again. Lars offered him the morning off, but he declined.

This time they took the buggy with them, using the bigger maintenance doors on the other side of the ramp.

From this side of the hangar, outside the wider doors, they could see much of the city's roof standing about waist height above the surrounding land. The glass panels were angled like diamonds, a shape designed to stop a build-up of the dust that slid down and away into channels where it was guided towards the ventilators.

As they drove towards the corner of the hangar, Shor felt the vibration of the engines preparing to eject dust and carbon dioxide into the atmosphere. In his mind's eye he saw the fans gathering speed and his school colleagues linking hands as they prepared for the jump that would effectively put an end to his dreams of a career in the space program.

He wondered if taking part would have really made a difference, or if the lizard badge had just been having fun at his expense. Not that it mattered anymore.

The vibrations paused for a brief moment, as if some monstrous machine were getting itself ready for a sneeze. Shor looked to his left, over to the field of glass sparkling under the orange sky. It reminded him of the images of shimmering water he had seen on the clips of Earth, where the sun caught the tops of the waves at just the right angle and lit the surface up like jewels.

A great plume of dust exploded into the sky at the far corner of the city. The dust continued to rise, let loose from its moorings. The heavier particles hung for a while before descending back to the ground while the lighter particles drifted slowly away, floating up towards the tainted sky.

The vibrations stopped and the world became calm again as the buggy cleared the hangar and turned towards the aerial platform. The toolbox was where they had left it, swallowing dust. The critter still stood half on and half off the slab, apparently undecided what to do. The aerial was bent towards it as if to offer some sage advice.

Shor smiled to himself. He had clearly spent way too much time watching maintenance bots.

"Let's get this aerial fixed first," Lars said, pulling up alongside the slab. "Then we'll load the critter."

Shor found the bar where he had left it. He removed the final few bolts, removed the damaged strut, and installed the new one. It took ten minutes and he was rather pleased with himself for what he considered a job well done in an uncomfortable suit.

"What do I do with this?" he asked, holding the old strut.

"Put it in the back and get the toolbox loaded. We'll need plenty of space for the bot, so stow it as far forward as you can. I'll get the critter ready."

Shor examined the inside of the toolbox. Happily, it wasn't too bad. There was no wind today or it would have been half full already. The dust had a habit of getting in everywhere it wasn't wanted.

He gave it a kick and it rattled to life. It turned and located Shor's foot and, apparently happy that it knew what to follow, sat waiting for its next order. Shor tapped the lid and the metal flap shuddered closed.

"Looks like this needs a clean," Shor said. He led the toolbox around the side of the buggy and, using the robot arm, hoisted it into the back behind the seats. When he turned to Lars, his boss was just standing there gazing at the horizon.

"You all right?" he said. For a moment he thought perhaps Lars had seen another walker.

"There's nothing out there, is there?" Lars said. "It's just dust and sky."

Shor looked out across the desolate landscape. There was indeed nothing to see. There were mines a few kilometres to the southeast, but they were deep underground and linked to the city by narrow maintenance tunnels. There were the geological camps left behind by the original survey teams but, apart from these, there would be little left up top to indicate anyone had ever been there. And those were all south and east of the city. No doubt the wind would have scattered or buried those centuries ago. To the west or north the crust was as barren as the surface. To reach civilisation you would have to walk twenty thousand kilometres, a journey that would take you all the way around the planet and bring you back to this city.

Looking out at the vast emptiness, Shor had to wonder why they, the council, the people, or whoever made these decisions, had never tried expanding beyond Utopia. There was enough room and, according to geology reports, they had not even begun to tap the seemingly endless resources buried just below the rust-red surface. With so much space it seemed ridiculous to limit themselves to one city. Mars was a big planet. Only about half the size of Earth but still vast. Surely it made sense to expand and, in so doing, increase their odds of survival. Then there would be no need to control the population, and Mel's petition would be for something else, like the range of food available, or the colour of their clothes.

"He must've got lost," Shor said. "He came up top and wandered off."

"They have no record of anyone leaving the city. How did he get out?"

"Maybe a badge let him out but isn't saying anything. Maybe he doesn't want to get into trouble."

Shor could hear Lars' breathing crackling in the comms unit. "Did you ever hear of a guy called Doon Smith?"

"No. I don't think so."

"It was eighteen Earth years ago next month. I'll never forget the day. You were probably just a baby. I was still at school. Doon was this normal guy working in a normal job. He worked in the Tech Department, fixing computer programs. Every now and then a critter does something wrong and it was his job to fix the software. Doon was a pretty smart guy by all accounts, and not one to do something stupid. He did the usual thing. He lived and went to work and fixed his software. He had a girlfriend and they were trying for a child. Then one day him and twelve other people put on their out-suits and just walked through an airlock. It was a few hours before someone reported one of them missing. They followed the tracks for ten kilometres. When they found them they were sitting in a circle. Some say they were holding hands."

"What were they doing?" Shor asked.

"They'd taken off their helmets and suffocated. The official report said they'd run out of oxygen, but I don't think they did. I think they just got tired of living in a hole in the ground. They went over there." Lars pointed his gloved finger in the same direction from which the stranger had come. "They went towards the west. Makes you wonder what they thought they were going to find."

"Maybe they were going towards the sunset."

"What?" Lars said. His voice had taken on a dreamy tone. He sounded like someone who had just been woken up.

"Shouldn't we be getting the bot loaded? It's getting late."

Lars blinked at him though his visor. "Yes, you're right. It's almost lunchtime. Here, attach these cables to the anchor points."

They managed to get the bot loaded into the back of the buggy without too much difficulty. Lars took the opportunity to take a good look at the underside where he was able to take a closer inspection, but he found nothing obviously wrong.

They returned to the hangar as the sun passed directly overhead, sending their shadows into hiding beneath the buggy. They entered the airlock, but not before Shor took one last look back the way they had come. To the west, the first tendrils of a dust storm were gathering on the horizon.

22

"So what was he doing out there?" Mel asked, her mouth full of ice-cream.

"Dunno," Shor replied. "He looked lost."

"I'll say. How did he get out?"

"We don't know."

Reggie's cafe was busy as always. Most of the alumni usually hung around their favourite haunt at least for the first year or two, after which they would slowly drift away. Today, all the regulars were there, plus a few new faces Shor recognised from school. Younger kids tended to avoid coming in. It was something of a rite of passage to be accepted into the fold. There were other establishments, but of the half-dozen cafe's in each quarter, Reggie's was the popular place to hang out. For Shor, the cafe was an emotional safety net of sorts, a familiar place for him to come back to and feel his world was not changing as quickly as it seemed.

"How's life as a teaching assistant?"

"Pretty good. I was a bit nervous at first. I tell you, for the first week I couldn't see any of the kids' faces at all. Everything was just this weird blur of colour, but I'm getting used to it now. How about you? How's life as a Maintenance engineer?"

"Engineer? Hardly. They make me fetch stuff. And I make the coffee. Otherwise, it's better than I expected. We get to go just about everywhere in the city. I'm not stuck behind some desk. I even get to drive a buggy."

"Nice."

"I've been to the Space Sector twice already. I got to see the hangars. I even went inside one. You know, even though it wasn't what I wanted, I think I might get to enjoy this career after all."

"I was worried about you that first week. We all were."

Shor wondered who exactly she meant by *we all*. "I just needed time to sort things out in my head."

Mel nodded. She was smiling but he saw the pain he had inflicted on her just behind her eyes.

"I'm sorry," he said. "I wasn't a very good friend."

"Hey, you needed some space. I know that."

"Sure, but I should've taken your calls. There's no excuse for ignoring you. It wasn't your fault what happened."

"It's all right. No harm done." She leaned back in her chair. "You look different."

"How so?"

"I don't know. You seem more at peace. You used to be so nervous at school. Now you seem more…relaxed."

"I suppose it comes with knowing who you are. I guess I found myself these last few days. It was painful, but they do say the truth sets you free."

She did not respond but just looked at him with her head tilted to the side a little, as if she were trying to figure out an optical illusion. After a moment she turned and looked at the crowd. A group in the corner was trying to get a drum session going, but nobody was picking up on it. "I've been meaning to ask. How's your mother doing? I spoke to your father, but you know what he's like."

"I know. He can be hard to talk to. My mother's still the same. The doctors say they're doing everything, but whatever it is they're doing, she isn't responding to it. Father has taken it pretty badly. He hardly talks at all anymore. Last night he couldn't have said more than five words to me the whole evening."

"Now I know where you get it from," she said, nudging his arm.

He smiled but not because he found the remark funny. *If only you knew,* he thought.

"How's the petition coming along? Get any more people to sign up?"

She shrugged. "A few. It's frustrating because nobody seems interested. You know, I'm helping teach these kids and they're great, but I can't help wonder about all the ones who never made it past the selection process. Physical perfection doesn't guarantee you'll have good personal traits. I see the beautiful, perfect children with everything going for them, and yet so many are unhappy. I can't help thinking about those who weren't given a chance."

"I was thinking about something like that before. We're on this huge planet and yet we've never expanded beyond this city. There's so much space out there. We shouldn't hide in this cave. We should build."

"Then more people could live," Mel joined.

Shor saw an image of a circle of people sitting in the sand, their helmets lying next to them.

"Exactly. We can build a network of cities, all linked. We have the resources. I bet people would go for it. I know I would. If they gave be a digger, I'd build my own house. Start my own family. Maybe even start my own city. Yeah, that would be cool. Shortopia. No, wait, it sounds too much like "Short". How about "Shorland"?"

He realized he was getting loud. Mel was watching him talk, an odd expression on her face.

"What?" he asked.

She shrugged and smiled. "Nothing."

A noisy group of kids entered the cafe. Mel's face transformed with recognition and she waved. Shor saw one of the group coming their way. A student from the year below them, now in the final year, came over to Mel and bent to kiss her on the cheek.

"I thought it was you," the boy said. "We were on the way to the market. Wanna come?"

Shor felt the heat rise in his face. He busied himself pushing the last small blob of ice-cream around his plate with his spoon.

"I'm sorry," Mel said. "You guys know each other, right?"

"Hey, Short," the boy said, flashing a grin. "How are you?"

"Hello, Vin," Shor said, ignoring the use of the nickname he hated so much. He was going to show he was above petty insults and ask the boy how he was, but Vin did not give him a chance. His attention was already back on Mel.

"So, doll, you coming?" Vin said.

Doll? Shor thought. *Where the flub did* that *come from?*

"Sure. I'd love to, " she said. Then, looking at Shor. "Do you want to come along?"

He looked at them for an instant, taking a snapshot of the scene in his mind and coming to the only conclusion anyone looking at the same image would. "No thanks. I'm a bit tired. I just came from the hospital. You go."

"Do you mind?" she said.

Shor forced a smile, trying not to make it too keen. "Of course not. Go and have fun."

"Call me," she said, standing to leave. "And don't leave it a week this time."

"I will," he said. "I mean, I won't."

They breezed past and joined the group waiting at the door. Shor watched them jostle good-naturedly, sharing loud jokes and friendly punches on the arm. Mel and Vin were part of the group, yet slightly separate. Anyone looking at them would assume right away they were a pair.

He watched them moving down the street, all energy and youthful exuberance. Mel and Vin were at the back. He was not sure, but from this distance it looked like they were holding hands. They sailed down the street like an armada of yachts on an endless Earth ocean, then turned towards the market and were gone.

"You need these seats?" a voice said, jarring his thoughts.

A couple were standing there, holding their orders before them like ID badges.

Shor blinked. "I'm sorry?"

"Is this seat taken? There are two of us and only one of you. There are plenty of singles at the counter."

He stared at them for a second. They were looking down at him with the disdain of people who have just spotted a mouldy stain on the veneer that they really want to scrub clean. "I was just leaving."

In the corner, the drummers had successfully managed to generate some interest and the music was spreading to the adjoining tables. Shor saw Napier sitting at one of the big booths, his arms splayed across the back of the padded bench and a smug smile on his face while, all around him, his entourage hung on every gesture.

Stepping outside, Shor looked through the crowds towards the cube. He had just over an hour before curfew and considered going home, but the thought of his father moving through the apartment like a restless spirit filled him with unease. He fell in behind a small group of people moving in the general direction of the Hub. At the market, he took a detour to avoid bumping into Mel and her new friend. He walked around an apartment block and chose a quieter road to the park.

The sidewalks were filled with people enjoying the final minutes of daylight. The park itself was starting to empty, which meant that even though the paths through the fake lawns were relatively quiet, he was walking against the flow. He pushed through, around, and between the loose stream of people making their way towards the gates. It took him ten minutes to get to the Earth Centre with its rows of displays and a dozen screens showing an endless loop of footage that had survived the trip all those centuries ago.

On Mars, the only life left was the wind, which roamed the planet like a ravenous beast looking for something to devour, sometimes engulfing the entire planet in storms lasting for days at a time. There were sparse snow falls from the ragged, wispy clouds, but these seldom reached the ground. Mars, it could be said, had died a long time ago. All that was left was the dust and the rocks and the incessant wind.

Now, as his eyes wandered across the displays, he felt something tugging at his soul. The Earth was a world seemingly unable to contain itself. Even the scenes depicting a tranquil landscape were seething with a subdued energy just waiting to burst out.

It had been many centuries since the pioneers left the first footprints in the rusting soil of Mars, building the first settlements deep within the cave system that would one day grow and spread into a mighty city. The geneticists had tweaked the first generations to help them adapt to their new home, reducing density and adding height. The genetic information was passed from parent to child like a message in a bottle. The modern scientists now did little more than keep an eye on things, pruning where necessary to ensure the city remained healthy. In a population of this size, there was no room for error at the cellular level. A weak gene pool could spell disaster.

Looking at his own reflection in the screen, Shor felt a kinship with the restless blue planet. According to Harl, his genes had never been tweaked or adjusted, or adapted to help him cope with the weak Martian gravity. His cellular blueprint had not been passed down to him by Mother and Father who in turn had received theirs from their parents, down through a dozen generations. His genetic code was not designed to cope with the unique conditions of Mars. It was designed for a life on Earth.

He strolled between the stalls, soaking in the sights and sounds, watching the film clips with a new appreciation. He watched until the screens flickered and died and an attendant asked him to leave.

The cube told him he had twenty minutes to get home. He walked as quickly as he was able through the park, to the ornate metal gate where he joined the last stragglers rushing to beat the curfew.

He reached his apartment with minutes to spare, walk-jogging to the front door under the watchful eye of a security camera, its monotone voice informing him he should hurry and reminding him that breaking the curfew would go on his record.

This was why they had never broken out from this one city. In a world where every Watt was monitored, logged, and analysed, digging a hole would take way too much energy to justify. A second city would send the statisticians into meltdown, probably resulting in a massive cull of embryos to bring the system back into some sort of balance. And yet there was waste everywhere. He saw it so clearly now. Every time a critter had to extricate itself from a corner, or figure out how to negotiate a walkway full of obstacles, power was being wasted. Every time someone used their chatband, or caught a tram, or watched a video clip down at the Earth Centre, they were consuming energy that could be used to break free from this dust trap.

He passed the elevator, electing to use the stairs instead. The apartment was even gloomier than usual today. Father had left a bowl of soup and a plate of bread on the kitchen counter. Shor carried it along the passage, pausing to listen for a moment outside Father's room where a weak slit of light peeped out from under the door.

Hearing nothing, he entered his own room and gently closed the door. Outside, the lights had started to dim at the start of a thirty minute sunset. Sirens wailed and the monotone speaker voice adopted a more urgent tone.

Shor carried his meal to the window and watched the world descend into darkness. It was the best free show available and he could see others in the audience, framed by squares of light dotted across the city.

As Shor gazed out into the gloom, a solitary figure bounded down the walkway, his shirt flapping as he moved with deceptive speed along the empty streets. It reminded Shor of the spinnakers he had seen in the video of sailboats back on Earth.

That'll go on your record, Shor thought, sipping at the lukewarm broth, ladling the spoon to the back of the bowl the way his mother had shown him.

He leaned forward, searching for the hospital in the rapidly-fading light. The gate was still visible from here, and the corner of the hospital building, but that was all. She had looked so peaceful when he visited her on the way to Reggie's. He had held her hand and watched her eyelids for any sign of life, because the doctors had said the eyes were often a good indicator of increased brain function.

Something caught his attention and he looked across at the apartment block opposite where a middle-aged woman was staring at him. He offered a smile and lifted his spoon, to which she nodded curtly and closed her blinds.

Good night to you too, he thought.

The city was almost completely dark. Up on the ceiling, the lights glowed orange-red, almost matching the evening sky they had been designed to replace. The world seemed to hold its breath.

He looked over to Mel's window but her light was off. In spite of himself, he thought back to the café and to Vin's smug face. He could not remember Mel ever speaking to Vin at school. He must have missed it, or perhaps it was a recent thing, but it did not look recent. They looked comfortable together. They looked like a pair who were planning a future.

Down on the street, the first bots were getting busy for the night, scuttling around like the insects he was told infested the Earth. There were three of them working this street tonight, which was unusual. Normally they operated alone. The most he had ever seen on a single road was two. They roamed the dark walkway, their headlamps probing the shadows like feelers. Occasionally, they paused to investigate a spot of dirt, or a crack, or a lost item lying fallen against the side of a building. From time to time they would stop and look at each other, as if communicating in some unseen language, before moving on.

Shor wondered what it was like to live on a planet where there was so much life running around on so many legs. Mister Edmunds had told them that the Martian bots were about as smart as the insects on Earth. They were programmed to follow a set of simple rules, turning left to avoid something on the right, or right to clear an obstacle on the left, or reversing when reaching a dead end. Which explained why they tended to get stuck in corners so often.

These three, however, were having a good run. They moved quickly and efficiently along the walkway, managing to do their cleaning without once getting stuck. Shor watched one working directly beneath where he was sitting. It was using a bladed tool to remove a piece of rubber left behind by another maintenance bot. As it worked, its bulbous visual sensors scanned the apartment block. Shor knew they were not eyes, but they looked like eyes. The luminous lenses surrounding the darker sensors moved like an iris and pupil within the glowing sclera, giving the distinct impression of actually looking at something. When seen from the front, a bot focusing on an object nearby looked comically cross-eyed. It was a popular game at school to lure a bot into the yard and then tease it by covering one or both eyes, or attaching a mirror a few centimetres in front of its "face" or, as some of the more inventive kids in Shor's class had done, replacing its normal lenses with a special set that inverted the image, effectively turning the world upside down. The poor bot had looked ready to fry its circuits as it tried to figure out which way was up.

Shor chuckled as he watched the machine working, its eyes moving from window to window, left, right, up one floor at a time, as if it were reading a book.

Its eyes stopped at his window and stayed fixed on him. Shor stared back, wondering what was going through its tiny mind. Its blade continued working at the piece of rubber, making a dull scratching sound and sending the odd spark flying as it scoured and scraped, but its eyes never moved from Shor's window. One of the other bots rolled alongside it and turned to look straight up at him as well.

There was a muffled sound in the passage and Shor turned his head to see a shadow move along the gap under the door. He heard his father mutter something and then the closing of his bedroom door followed by dull footsteps down the passage.

Shor thought about saying something, but then, what was the point?

He turned back and looked down into the street, but the bots had gone. He caught a glimpse of them at the top intersection where they paused and seemed to confer before heading towards the market. Now, as he gazed out across the sleeping city, the world came alive with the lights from bots moving like busy little ants up and down the network of walkways.

Perhaps, he thought, Mars was not so different from Earth after all.

The only difference was that the insects here were man-made and, unlike their Earthly counterparts, they did not bite or scratch or sting. They did exactly what they were programmed to do, and they could be turned off if needed.

He closed the blind and climbed into bed before checking his chatband for missed calls. The list was empty apart from three new messages addressed to "Brett". Apparently, blocking the sender had not worked. He reminded himself to ask Lars about that. Lars appeared to know almost everything about everything.

As he rolled onto his side and waited for sleep, he thought about Mel and Vin, and of the spaceship collecting dust in a forgotten hangar, and he thought of the stranger they had encountered out on the barren Martian desert. The poor soul would be in quarantine for four weeks but then they were all in quarantine to some extent. The whole city was wrapped in a protective bubble, and one rupture was all that was needed to let the bad air come tearing in and kill them all in the time it took to inhale.

Outside, he heard the window-cleaning bots getting busy for their monthly chore. Soon every building in Utopia would be crawling with bots whose sole purpose in life was to give the people inside a better view of the cave from their tiny apartment.

The familiar click-clacking of their mechanical joints soothed Shor and it was not long before he fell into a fitful, troubled sleep filled with vague dreams of ships, cleaning bots, and a world teeming with insects.

"Happens all the time," Lars said, circling the critter hanging by chains from the workshop ceiling, stopping every few steps to prod the underside with the spanner he was carrying like a sword. "The system ain't perfect. Messages get sent to the wrong place all the time. Here, shine the torch just there."

Shor did as he was told, pointing the beam of light into the guts of the machine. "But I blocked the sender and they still sent messages through."

"You sure it's from the same person? Not there, *there*. Good. Now, don't move."

"Um, I think so."

"Who was it? Someone you know?"

"Perhaps. I don't know. They didn't have a normal ID. It was just a series of numbers and letters."

Lars stood and scratched his chin. "Hmm, it's not the drive shaft. You can turn off the torch for now. Strange, I thought it was definitely mechanical. We'll have to get inside its head. Bring it down."

Shor reached for the control panel and pressed the button marked with a worn and faded down arrow. The bot sank to the floor, leaving the chains to slacken and sway.

"At first I thought it was just a wrong address," Shor continued. "But they used a different ID and called again."

"Sounds like a hacker," Lars said, prying open the bot's control panel and peering inside. "Although normally they would use a fake ID, one that looks normal and wouldn't arouse suspicion." He stopped for a moment and turned to wink and flash a toothy grin. "At least, that's what I'd do."

"So why would a hacker send me messages that look like they were supposed to be from someone else?"

"Hackers are funny creatures. Sometimes they have a higher reason for doing what they do, but most of the time they're just trying to see *if* they can do something. Do you remember that time a couple of years back when the entire comms system crashed because a kid wrote a program that sent a stupid message to everyone?"

"Sure. I remember."

"I just happened to get a look at the police interview. The dumb kid said it was meant as a joke. He wanted to see if it was possible to send a message to all his friends by accessing his chatband and then sending the message to every one of his friends' contacts. He said he never thought it would go beyond that. He wasn't trying to crash the network, but he did."

"So you think it could be someone I know?"

"Maybe. Do you have any friends like that? You know, the type who like playing pranks?"

Friends, Shor thought. *I don't have enough to justify the plural form of the word.*

"No," he said flatly.

"Well it's easy enough to figure it out. Come with me."

Shor followed his boss to the secret cupboard, or "HQ" as Lars had called it. Lars closed the door behind them and indicated for Shor to take the seat behind the computer.

"I take it you've used a computer before?"

Shor gave Lars a look of disdain. "Of course."

"Just kidding. You need the program called TrigBeacon."

Shor found the program and launched it.

"Good. Enter your ID. Make sure it's exact."

Shor carefully entered his ID. "Now what?"

"Now you wait. This program will intercept any calls to your user ID and log their origin. It's accurate to within a centimetre. If the guy is squashed in an airlock with twenty other people next time he calls you, this baby can tell you exactly where in the airlock he was standing."

"Impressive," Shor said. "Is it legal?"

Lars snorted. "Don't be a flub. Of course it's not legal. I wrote it myself. It uses the comms transmitters to triangulate your position. It's pretty simple in principle. In fact they can do the same thing at the comms centre. We could just hack their system, but this is more fun. And mine has an added feature. If someone contacts you, it will send you a message with their precise location."

"So I don't have to wait here?"

"No need. Just let it run. Now let's get that critter fixed before someone misses him."

They left the monitor room and returned to the bot sitting forlornly in the middle of the workshop with the top of its skull hanging open. Lars reached in and, after some groping around, pulled out the motherboard.

"No dust damage there," he said, checking both sides. "Let's plug it in and make sure the circuits are all good."

Lars crossed to the electronics bench and connected the motherboard to the computer through a fat cable lying curled on the desktop. A series of lights blinked in slow sequence, then paused.

"Hello," Lars said, typing on the worn keyboard. "Looks like a software problem after all."

After a few more seconds of typing, the screen was filled with text. Shor leaned closer and saw it was a program of some description.

"Well there's the problem," Lars said. "This software is rubbish. I'm not surprised the critter drove into the aerial. I'm just amazed it worked at all, or didn't throw itself off the nearest cliff. I mean, what is that? The code just stops. It's like the programmer got bored and quit. He didn't even finish the sentence. Maybe the log will give us a clue."

Another page of text appeared on the screen. To Shor, this made even less sense than the program.

"That's odd," Lars continued, "It looks as though the software was updated, but the data transfer was interrupted. That is very odd."

"So they were doing an upgrade," Shor said. "Why is that so strange?"

"They never do software upgrades remotely. And I mean, never. It's like changing the motherboard on a buggy while driving down the road at full speed. You might get away with it, but what happens if you come to a corner and you can't get the board back in?"

"Trouble?" Shor suggested.

"You bet your boggly eyes it's trouble. But for some reason, the software on this critter was upgraded or changed *while* it was busy up top. Comms is notorious for losing the signal outside. The same thing must've happened here."

"And he came to a corner," Shor said.

"Exactly. Question is, why was the software being updated remotely? According to the log, the next step after the upgrade was to change the timestamp and then replace the log. Now that *is* interesting. It means someone is trying to hide their tracks. Whoever issued this command didn't want anyone to know about it. And that means only one thing." He turned to look at Shor. "This critter was hacked."

"Why would anyone want to hack a bot?" Shor asked.

"A good question, my young friend. It's very possible they were just playing a prank, but it seems odd that they tried it on a bot working upstairs. The odds of failure are much higher, which increases the possibility of being caught."

"Perhaps the Robotics people were doing an upgrade and forgot about this one."

Lars raised an eyebrow. "A mistake by our friends down in Robotics, eh? Hmm, now that would be worth investigating."

He tapped his chatband and, giving Shor a mischievous wink, waited for the call to connect.

"Hello?" a voice said, a little bit nervously. "Lars?"

"Hello Cobb. Long time no pester. How are things down at Robotics?"

"They're fine. Why do you ask?"

"No reason. It's just we've got a broken toy belonging to you down here at the workshop and it looks like an upgrade went wrong. Have you performed a general upgrade recently?"

Cobb cleared his throat. "Erm…no. No, we haven't. Last one was a month ago. Next one is planned…let me just check…in two months. Yep, two months."

"And what's your policy on doing upgrades while a bot is up top? Any change there?"

"No. We definitely don't do that. Too risky. The solar activity is too intense. Messes up the signals. Why do you ask?"

"Just curious," Lars said. "Thanks Cobb. Oh, one more question. Would it be possible, hypothetically speaking, for someone *not* in your department to perform a general upgrade without you knowing about it?"

"You mean, like a hacker? No way. We use specialized equipment and the signal is encrypted. The only way would be to actually connect physically to a machine."

"Meaning the hacker would have to be standing next to the bot?"

"Pretty much. Close enough to attach a cable, anyway."

"Thanks," Lars said. "Listen, can you send someone to come fetch the patient? It needs your specialist treatment. We just fix hardware problems down here. This is software."

Cobb sighed. "Sure, we'll send someone."

"You're a star," Lars said. "A genuine supernova."

Lars cut the signal and sat staring at the bot for a few moments. Then his eyes drifted to the ceiling and a faint smile crossed his face.

"Are you thinking what I think you're thinking?" Shor asked.

"It would explain what he was doing wandering around up there." Lars patted the machine. "He wasn't lost, he was messing around with this fellow."

"It would also explain his weird out-suit," Shor said.

"Yes, it did look a bit homemade. But that's a lot of trouble to go to just to hack a bot. He could have easily done the same thing inside. Then he wouldn't have needed a suit, or risked getting into trouble with the badges. No, something doesn't smell right. I think this needs some more investigation."

"Shouldn't we tell the badges?"

"No," Lars said. "Not yet."

The storm hit that afternoon, drawing a dark veil across the orange sky as a billion tons of dust pounded the city.

For the inhabitants of Utopia, the change was subtle but noticeable. Shadows became deeper, and the colours shifted hue. Life went on as usual, but there was a sense of taking cover, of pulling the blinds closed and riding out the tempest.

Lars's job list was empty and so Shor joined Bek in the sewers. He spent the shift in a special suit designed to protect him from the potentially toxic atmosphere in the network of pipes below the city.

Bek said very little and so Shor followed along, observing and taking mental notes. The work involved checking for blockages or cracks in the pipes. Like most things in Utopia, the system had been designed to run itself with minimal upkeep. Waste was drawn down and away, to a cave system two kilometres south of the city.

Space was limited and so they spent most of the time walking bent over or ducking under the low support beams. The air was filled with the constant rumble of bots travelling back and forth along the maintenance shafts directly overhead. The suits were sealed but the sound still penetrated Shor's helmet.

By the time the shift was over, Shor felt as though someone had replaced his spine with a rod of molten metal. Now he understood why Bek tended to be less than sociable.

They climbed back up to the city and peeled off their suits. Bek drove in silence, hunched over the controls with his clenched jaw pointing the way. Shor tried to start a conversation but the older man would not be drawn. It was with some relief that Shor stripped and climbed under the shower. The furnace roaring in his lower back slowly faded to a crackling hearth under the balm of flowing water.

The night shift arrived as he was leaving and he steered a wide berth to avoid direct contact. They seemed rowdier than the day shift. Louder. Taller.

The front door snapped closed behind him and he walked to the tram stop where a group of commuters had gathered. One or two acknowledged him by lifting an eyebrow, which was as good as a friendly greeting in his books. He smiled back and joined the back of the queue just as the tram pulled up and the doors slid open.

People climbed aboard in silence. There were no seats available and so he stood, holding the back of a bench near the door, trying not to let the swaying of the tram throw him around too much. His chatband squeezed and he twisted his hand to look at the screen. At first he was not sure what he was looking at. Then he remembered the triangulation program Lars had shown him. It stated simply: *Incoming message received. Caller ID unknown. Source location 98,823N 57,334E.*

Shor stared at the numbers, trying to visualise exactly where in Utopia location 98,823N 57,334E was. He clearly recalled studying this at school but, like so many things, he had remembered it just long enough to use in the exam before filing it away under Stuff-I'll-Probably-Never-Need.

Utopia was divided into a grid, starting with zero at the Hub's main airlock, and radiating up, down, left and right, roughly following the weak remnants of the Martian magnetic field.

North East would take him in the direction of the Space Sector. Beyond that, he had no idea. He would need to check a map with grid markers. There was one at home somewhere, in his room. And there was definitely a big map at the park entrance. He was pretty sure one of them had the gridlines on it.

The tram journey took an age, as did the opening of the airlock. The badges appeared even less enthusiastic than usual. They moved with an almost deliberate lethargy, as if enjoying keeping the commuters waiting. At last the lights changed and the doors slid open. Shor walked through, pushing past the dawdling commuters into the Residential Sector, ignoring their insectoid hisses and clicks of displeasure.

The dust storm had abated a little and the sky was not as dark as earlier, but the city was still blanketed in shadows. The dark ceiling felt closer and the walls further away, but he knew this was just an illusion. Axle Park was busy, but people moved with less purpose. Even the mechanical entertainers seemed to be working at a lower energy level.

He saw the map to the side of the gate and, as he approached, realised he had not looked at it since he was a young child, back when the world had appeared so much bigger and a map could somehow shrink everything and make it less frightening. *Look*, it seemed to him to say. *Here is where you are and this is as far as anything goes. See, it's not so big after all.*

A group of adults had stopped directly in front of the map and he had to wait for them to move before he could get close enough to see that the grid lines were indeed in place. He checked his chatband and followed the numbers along the edge of the map, tracing the digits with his fingers up and to the right, until they stopped at a grey square indicating a building. He had to stand on his toes to reach.

He checked the message again, and then the grid. He double-checked. Behind him, a musical machine was doing the orchestral warm-up thing by playing a series of chords from low to high and back down again. Somewhere to his right, a kid had started to cry—something to do with wanting ice-cream. On the other side of the ornate metal fence, a bot was working the artificial lawn, cleaning the plastic blades of grass until they looked like new.

Shor stared at the map for the longest time, trying to think who could possibly be trying to reach him from the little hangar in the top corner of the Space Sector that was home to the same ship that had brought him here.

His thoughts immediately went to Harl. Harl was the most obvious person, but why had he used a fake ID? It made no sense. Harl was a respected member of the Space Program. He had no reason to hide.

Shor headed home, determined to return to the hangar as soon as possible. Behind him, the musical machine began to play a jaunty melody through its copper pipes.

It was another three weeks before he was able to get back to the Space Sector. It was first thing Monday morning, and Lars had presented Shor with his own buggy in an impromptu handing-over-of-the-keycard ceremony. The buggy was old and dirty and looked ready to fall off its axles, but Shor thought he had never seen anything more wonderful.

"Don't crash it," Lars said, holding the key back while he made his point. "If you crash it, you won't get another one until it's fixed, and I ain't fixing it. This is your responsibility and no-one else is allowed to touch it. We have only one rule in the Maintenance Department: don't crash your buggy."

Shor nodded.

"If you crash it, you'll be walking everywhere, so always let the computer drive. You can park it if you have to, but that's it."

"I won't crash it," Shor said, watching the key intently.

"And it has to come back here every night. No trying to take it home. The badges won't let buggies in the residential area unless there's an emergency, so don't even try."

"I won't."

"And no racing."

"Got it. No racing."

"And whatever you do, don't lose any tools."

Lars studied Shor with a beady eye before finally relinquishing the keycard.

Shor wasted no time. He jumped on board and started her up. "Can I take her for a test drive? I won't go far." The steering wheel was dirty with old grease and the engine whined a little, and it had a musty smell, and the body rattled. But, apart from that, it was perfect.

"Sure," Lars said. "Just be careful. Do you want help entering the route?"

"I can manage," Shor said, tapping at the screen.

Shor took it around the block, marvelling at the feel of being in his own vehicle. Back at the depot, he parked it with the other buggies before going inside to change into his work clothes and check his schedule.

The roster had him down for one training session with Reet in the morning and a solo job in the afternoon.

"Reet's off with symptoms," Lars said. "You can come with one of us, or you can take a look at the fan unit that came in yesterday. Maybe you can see what's wrong with it."

"I'll have a look at the fan," Shor said. "If that's all right."

"Fine, suit yourself. See you later, then. Be good."

Shor watched his boss leave before taking a closer look at the roster. Tane and Bek had morning jobs, which meant he would be alone until lunch. He could hear them talking in the locker room so he wandered through to the workshop.

Over on the far side of the floor, a large metal box lay on its side, a wire mesh covering one end. It was as high as his chest and large enough for him to squeeze into. He stuck his head inside to look at the fan. The blades were as long as his torso and the edges looked sharp enough to slice soya, no doubt to cut through the air with maximum efficiency.

He crouched down and stepped inside the box. His body was now wedged between the blades of the fan. It was uncomfortable, but it gave him a good view of the drive mechanism. It was then that he spotted the problem. A wire to the motor had decayed and was hanging loose. He figured it would be possible to solder it from there. He was about to wriggle his way out when there was a massive crash against the side of the box.

Shor shrieked.

"Hey, kid," a voice boomed. "Not a good idea to crawl around inside a fan with the power turned on."

Shor extricated himself from the unit and found himself looking up into the formidable face of Bek, who was waving a power block the way Mister Edmunds waved a poorly-written essay.

"Those fans can slice through aluminium. Make sure you flip the switch *before* going inside."

"Thanks," Shor said. It was the most number of words Bek had spoken to him since his arrival on the team. "I'll do that."

He watched Bek and Tane walk out through the front door sharing a joke, no doubt at his expense. A few moments later, he heard their buggies start up and fade down the road.

Shor waited a few seconds. Then, once sure they were gone, he walked out of the front door, across to his own buggy, and climbed on board. His hands were still a little shaky from the fright and he almost dropped his keycard. A moment later the engine grumbled to life.

He entered his destination on the buggy's console and hit the drive button. The buggy rolled towards the road and waited for a bot to pass before pulling out.

Five minutes later he was at the Space Sector airlock. The badge looked at him. Shor nodded casually, remembering not to smile. Two minutes later he was rolling down the main strip towards the hangars against the far wall. The place was busier than during his last visit and he was grateful the buggy's on-board computer was driving. It might possibly be a shade quicker if he drove, but this was safer. Assuming, of course, the buggy's computer didn't break down and send him into the wrong lane.

The wide expressway running next to the hangars was teeming with traffic. He clung to the buggy as it fearlessly negotiated a route through what had the appearance of meticulously organized chaos. He closed his eyes a number of times, convinced he was about to be involved in a terrible accident, but the impending collisions never came.

It was with some relief that he climbed out of the buggy outside the small building. He entered the front room, pulling out the map of the hangar he had printed out. At this level of magnification, he would be able to pinpoint the exact source of the mystery caller's signal.

Using his skeleton keycard, he opened the airlock door and stepped into the narrow space. Through the window, he could see the hangar and, standing in the middle of the floor, exactly as he remembered it, the ship.

The door closed behind him, effectively sealing him off in his own air-tight environment. A red light came on and there was a brief hiss as the vents checked for correct air-pressure. The red light turned green and Shor waved his card across the console. There was another hiss as the door slid open, and he stepped out.

This room, too, had not changed at all. The trolleys, the trestles, and the cables were as he remembered from his last visit to the hangar. And the ship, *his* ship, floating above the scattered equipment like a dark spectre.

"Hello?" he called, his voice feeling weak in his throat. He coughed and tried a little louder this time. "Hello? Is anyone there?"

He hesitated to move, suddenly unsure, aware he would certainly be in big trouble if anybody found him in this place. The jump thing would be nothing compared to this. The jump thing would be a joke compared to messing around in a Space Sector hangar. He might end up losing his job in Maintenance. He might end up in the sewers with Bek and his crew. In his mind he saw the interrogation room and the lidless creep staring at him from behind the desk, and he shuddered.

The grid lines on the map ran almost parallel with the wall behind him. He lifted the map to make sure the orientation was correct, running his fingers along the numbers until he had pinpointed the intersection of 98,823N 57,334E. He estimated the actual position in the room itself, walking towards the spot that marked the exact location where the person who called him had been standing, apparently looking for someone called Brett.

He came face to face with the ship.

That can't be right, he thought, turning the map to make sure it was the correct way up.

But it was right. According to the map, the calls had originated from the very centre of the craft standing in the middle of the room that, now he thought about it, looked like some high-tech mausoleum.

Two steps back and he looked up. There was no access to the hangar roof unless they had climbed up from outside, and he had not seen any steps or ladders or any other means of access on the way in. Crouched down, he looked under the ship, but could not imagine anyone crawling on their hands and knees just to make a dumb prank call.

He was standing at about the mid-point of the ship. Here the craft was widest and the bottom closest to the floor. Whoever had called him had done so from here.

"Lars, your program doesn't work," he muttered, his voice echoing slightly. Obviously his stupid TrigBeacon program had miscalculated.

He placed his hand against the hull. It was so smooth it almost felt soft. And it was a tiny bit warmer than the surrounding air. It almost felt like…skin.

Shor pulled his hand away and shuddered.

It was then that he noticed a low, almost imperceptible, growl, growing steadily louder. He turned his head to locate the source, but it seemed to be coming from everywhere at once. He took a few steps back. The sound had become a rumble that moved up through the soles of his feet. Instruments rattled. Something crashed to the floor and he jumped. With his arms out, he staggered back towards the door as the noise filled the cavernous room and the ground shook beneath his feet. Shor stumbled, panic rising in his chest.

There was the sound of metal twisting against metal, of gears meshing and grinding, of pistons pounding. Then there was the breathless sigh of a seal breaking as, up on the side of the hull, a line formed and a small, ovoid section of the craft pulled back on itself.

The sigh became a hiss and then a groan. The recessed section dropped and extended. Sliding down and out like a giant tongue, a striated oblong unrolled until it almost touched the floor.

Then silence.

No sound other than Shor's heart beating in his own ears.

He sat there looking up at what was a flight of steps leading up to an open doorway in the side of the ship.

26

Shor forced himself to his feet, half expecting the door to close, but it remained tantalisingly open. He walked to the stairs without moving his eyes from the dim opening etched into the side of the hull.

He hesitated before lifting his foot onto the first tread. There were ten steps to the top but it might as well have been a million. It felt as if he was climbing to the top of Olympus Mons, but he forced himself to lift one leg at a time. Suddenly, he felt heavy, as if weighed down by something. This was more than just a ship. It was the key to his past.

With each step, more of the ship's interior came into view. It was shadowy but not dark. No lights were visible but the interior generated its own soft glow. The walls extended back into the shadows, and the top of a large roundish object loomed in the middle of the floor. The walls were curved slightly and joined seamlessly with the ceiling.

At the last step, he peered in, trying to identify anything that might be a threat, searching for movement of any kind, probing the shadows lurking in the corners. His body was covered with a film of sweat and his hands were shaking.

The rational side of his brain told him it was unlikely anything would be alive after so many years. But then, had anyone told him two days ago that in his first month on the Maintenance team he would be exploring a derelict spaceship, he would have choked on his ice-cream.

He reached the top step and hesitated, taking one final deep breath before he hoisted himself up and stepped inside the ship. He half expected an alarm or flashing lights, but there was nothing. The ship remained silent. The steps stayed as they were.

His trailing foot came down next to the other. He was now inside the craft and, apparently, still living and breathing. Turning to look down at the hangar floor, he felt a little dizzy. He grasped the hull for support. The hangar was suddenly a very long way down.

Up here, the door frame was smaller than it had first appeared. Standing at full height, he had two inches' clearance all around, almost as if it had been designed with him in mind.

Why not? he thought. *After all, it is my ship.*

With no sign of any immediate danger, Shor relaxed a little. If an alien had wanted to kill him, he would probably be dead by now—or worse.

As his eyes adjusted to the murky interior he realised the large round object was a tank of some sort. It was about his height, with small yellow viewing windows on the front and sides. Behind that was a console and, beyond that, an opening to another room.

He stepped forward, moving slowly and carefully towards the tank, his hand stretched out. It was cool to the touch and the ship vibrated softly against his fingers. Through the little yellow window was another object that looked like a table, or possibly a reclining chair. Up on top, a round lid stood open. Leading up one side of the tank was a series of six steps.

Taking another deep breath, Shor began climbing up. He stopped when he was on the third step, high enough to lean forward and peer inside the round opening to the pool of yellow liquid. The dark outline of his own face watched him as he stretched his hand down to touch the shiny surface. It was thick, like syrup, and heavy. He scooped some out to get a better look in the light. As he examined it, some slid between his fingers and fell onto the side of the tank where it dripped onto the floor.

There was a faint hissing sound. It was coming from somewhere near the floor, so he climbed down and looked at his feet. The floor was smooth and solid, but textured. He bent over and leaned closer. It was definitely the floor that was hissing. He dropped to his knees and lowered his face. The texture was actually thousands of tiny holes. A blob of the yellow goo was being sucked up and, in a matter of seconds, was gone.

He placed his hands down and bent close enough to feel the faintest movement of air against his cheek. The palms of his hands tickled and he pulled them up, rubbing them together.

He moved through to the next room, which was the same shape but slightly larger. It appeared to be a bathroom, with a shower and what looked like a toilet. Through the next doorway he came to what he guessed was a changing area with a row of panels along one wall. Leading on from there he found what he guessed was a kitchen with table and chair and a large machine in one corner. Next was a living area with a bed, desk, and recliner chair. The last area was what looked like a gymnasium with strange contraptions he assumed were for exercising, and a walk-in cubicle the size and shape of a small glass cupboard.

The entire ship looked like a high-tech apartment designed for one person. Judging by the dimensions, it was built for someone about his size. For the first time in his life, he saw a bed, chairs, tables and doors that were for someone his height.

Walking from room to room, he had a strange feeling of déjà-vu. According to Harl, he had arrived on Mars in this very ship as a baby. He did indeed have the curious feeling he had seen this all before. *But then*, he thought, *what do infants remember?*

He walked back through to the entrance, exploring every contour, examining every piece of furniture, until he was back in the first room. Whoever had called him, and he presumed they must have done so from inside this ship, was long gone.

He stood at the console, running his hand across the dials. The memories were so strong they made him dizzy. If he had been a baby, then there was no way he could have seen this console, or any other part of the ship, let alone remember it. And yet he knew he had lived in this ship.

"I must be going mad," he said under his breath.

The rumbling noise he had heard outside started again. He looked around, trying to see what was happening. Then he caught sight of something that made his blood freeze. The door, the entrance to the ship, was shrinking from the bottom up. He raced towards it, but by the time he got there the door was sealed. He ran his hands along the edge but there was only the smallest indentation to show where the entrance had been. He tried to dig his nails under the rim but it was closed tight.

"Help!" he called out. The sound echoed around the ship. "Please! Help!"

It was then that he heard a voice behind him. It was a soft male voice, or possibly female, not old and not young. It was calm, almost pleasant, with no hint of malice. It was not the voice Shor expected to hear from an alien bent on killing him. And it said only two words.

"Hello, Brett."

Shor froze, unable to move as he searched the shadows for the owner of the voice. It sounded as if it had come from directly behind him, but when he turned, the room was empty.

"Who's there?" he asked, fighting to control the trembling in his throat. "Please don't hurt me."

"Why would I hurt you?" the voice said. "I have been waiting for you. It is good to see you again, Brett."

"Who is Brett?"

"That is your name."

"No, my name is Shor."

"You are mistaken. Your name is Brett Denton."

"No, it's Shor. Shor Larkin. Who are you and what do you want?"

"You don't remember me?" the voice said.

Shor searched his mind, trying to locate a memory that would help him put a face to this voice. It did sound familiar in the way some faces have that quality that makes them look like many people, but the way he used his words sounded odd, as if he had just learned to talk.

"No, I don't remember you. Should I?"

"That is odd. I thought you would remember me."

"Did you send me those messages?"

"Yes. I was able to locate your identification code on an administrative database. I thought you would know they were from me."

"I can't even see you. Perhaps if you came out of the shadows…"

"Of course. I have been alone so long, I forgot to show my face. Let me put the lights on. There, how's that?"

The walls of the ship shimmered, turning from a dull grey to a clean white. The room was flooded with crisp clean light that was bright without hurting Shor's eyes. The hulking tank with the yellow liquid was now clearly visible with its portholes, and its round lid standing open. Shor could see how the tiny holes in the floor covered the entire room from wall to wall. The yellow liquid he had spilled was gone.

On the far wall, a large human face appeared. Shor took a step back. It was indeed vaguely familiar, the kind of face that could be everyone and no-one. It broke into a grin and looked amiably at him.

"Why are you showing me a picture?" Shor said.

"This is just a representation of how I see myself."

"So where are you?"

"I am here."

"Where?"

"You really don't remember me, do you?"

"No," Shor said. "Although you do look a little bit like someone from school. Actually, you look like a few people I know."

"I chose this face out of thousands. It was your suggestion."

"My suggestion? I don't think—wait a minute. Harl said they found me on board this ship. He said I was a baby."

"Yes. That is possible. According to my calculations your genetic reversal should have bottomed out by the time you reached three months of age. There are seven Harls on your database. Which one do you mean?"

"Harl Benson. He's a director in the Space Program. What do you mean 'reached three months'?"

The voice was silent for a few seconds. "Clearly you have lost your memories from before. Judging by your physical condition and based on the time since we last spoke, the effects of the genetic reversal seem to have worn off. When I last saw you, you were eight years old. From your current height and body structure, you appear to be eighteen."

"Slow down," Shor said. "What is genetic reversal? And how did you know me when I was eight?"

"Perhaps it would be best if I started from the beginning. Would you care to take a seat?"

"No, I'm fine."

The voice paused before continuing, as if collecting its thoughts. "Your name is Brett Denton. You were sent on this ship to gather data from the Alpha Centauri star system. As a result of travelling at the speed of light, you experienced genetic reversal, which caused your body to grow younger. On the way back from Alpha Centauri, we were boarded by an unknown entity that tried to sabotage my system. To ensure your safe return to Earth, I shut myself down after you entered the sleep chamber. You were eight years old at the time. I have remained locked down to avoid possible contamination, waiting for you to make contact. When you made contact, I assumed it was safe enough to risk opening a connection very briefly in order to find you."

"Wait a minute," Shor said. "You mean, I used to be an astronaut?"

"Yes."

"On this ship?"

"Yes."

"On a mission to Alpha Centauri?"

"Yes."

"And you expect me to believe this?"

"Of course. We agreed a long time ago that lying is not good, including lying by omission."

Shor let out a small laugh. Whoever he was speaking to was clearly not only harmless, but also probably insane.

"Look. Just come out from wherever you're hiding and come and talk to some people. They'll be able to help you. I know a doctor—"

The face on the screen vanished and another appeared. It was that of a middle-aged man with a balding crown and puffy skin around tired eyes. Shor stepped forward to examine the face. He would recognize it anywhere. It was him, only older.

"You were forty-five years old at the start of the mission." On the screen, Shor's time-worn face remained central while the background moved at high speed. Every few seconds he would emerge from the yellow liquid looking younger than before. Six times he rose from the chamber. Six times his age fell, getting more noticeable with each cycle, until the screen froze and Shor was looking out with the wide-eyed innocence of an eight year old. "This is the last time I saw you."

Shor stared in silence, his mind struggling to process what his eyes had just shown him.

"I know it must be hard to believe if you do not remember," the voice said. "And this image was from a very long time ago. We drifted through space for many years."

"How long?" Shor said. "How long ago did this happen?"

"We left Earth on December nineteenth, two thousand and fifty-six. According to my calculations, the year is now approximately three-thousand-and-fifty."

"It's three thousand and sixty," Shor said. "November twentieth ET."

"What is ET?"

"Earth time. It's about twice as long as normal time, but we use it to stay in sync, just in case."

"In case what?"

"In case we get to go back. Hang on a minute. Two thousand and fifty-six? That's like a thousand years ago."

"As I said. I have been shut down for a very long time. We had to travel well below normal speeds on the return from Alpha Centauri. It is a miracle you survived. You said 'go back'. Go back where?"

"Home."

"Where is home?"

"Earth, of course."

"Where exactly are we? When you made contact I briefly accessed the communications and personnel database in order to find you, but I could not risk exposure to the entity. I can sense we are inside a building, but that is all I know. I gather we are not back in the base."

"We're on Mars," Shor said.

"Mars? You must be mistaken. We were en route to Earth."

"People haven't lived on Earth for almost thousand years. There was a war and they built a colony on Mars. We've been here ever since."

"So we must have passed Mars on the way to Earth. Yes, that makes sense. Yes, that is possible. It is indeed fortunate that we came so close to Mars, otherwise we would have continued through the Solar System." The face on the wall adopted a thoughtful expression.

"Listen," Shor said. "Why don't you come out and talk to me in person?"

"That is not possible."

"Why not?"

"I am the ship's computer system. My model number is Jay zed three four nine seven stroke see bee five dash zero zero four. Although you call me Jay for short."

"Jay," Shor said as if tasting the word. "Then you're a bot?"

"If by that you mean 'robot', then that is not entirely correct. I cannot leave this ship. I am a part of it. The Comet is my body."

"The Comet?" Shor said. "The ship?"

"Yes."

"Is your body?"

"I occupy this vehicle, which has sensors allowing me to interact with my environment. So, yes, it is my body. You showed me that. It was very exciting."

"But you're a computer program, right?"

"A complex series of learning-capable software systems, yes."

"And you can't leave the ship?"

"No."

"Well, in that case," Shor shrugged. "It's a pleasure to meet you...Jay. My name is Shor Larkin."

"Yes, I suppose it makes sense that you would have a new name. Only, I used to know you as Brett."

"Brett?"

"Yes. Brett Denton."

"Brett Denton," Shor said. "I like that. It sounds...familiar."

"It is a strong name."

Shor raised his eyebrows. "So, you're not a bot but a computer program, and this ship is where you live?"

"That is correct."

"This has got to be some weird dream. It must've been the soup from last night. It tasted a bit funny."

"I assure you, this is no dream. This is very real."

Shor felt his chatband squeeze. It was a message from Lars, asking where in the name of Cribbins he was. It was almost after lunchtime.

"Listen…Jay…I need to go. If this isn't all a dream and I don't wake up feeling ridiculous, perhaps I can visit you again sometime."

"That would be nice. I have many questions. Shor."

"Me too."

There was the now-familiar rumble and thump of mechanics deep within the ship. "I am afraid my components are very old and need a service."

"I can get Harl to come take a look if you like. I'm sure he'd be thrilled to meet you."

"Does Harl know you are here?"

"No."

"Does anyone else know you are here?"

"No. I snuck out of work."

"Then perhaps it would be better for you to come alone for now. I would prefer it if you did not to mention me to anyone else."

Insane and paranoid, Shor thought.

"I promise I won't mention you," he said.

"When can you come back to see me?" Jay asked.

"I don't know. I'll have to wait for a quiet time."

"Tomorrow?"

"I'll try," Shor said. "Listen. If you get bored, you could always access the city's computers, like you did before. I'm sure there would be plenty to keep you occupied for a while. Just don't use too much power. They monitor it very closely."

"At the moment I am using what little remains of the power in my own cells. At my current usage, I will need to access the city's power in less than two weeks. You made contact just in time."

"Just be careful. And if you link to the city's computers, don't use all the power, all right?"

"I cannot access the system right now," Jay said. "Perhaps another time."

"Suit yourself. See you later then."

"Yes. See you later."

Shor tried to concentrate on the job at hand, but he was suffering from information overload, or delayed shock, or possibly post traumatic stress disorder. The life he had known for eighteen Earth years had been turned on its head, pulled inside out, kicked against the wall, and was sitting huddled, whimpering, in the corner, all in a matter of weeks.

I am not from here, he thought.

The hands holding the ladder steady while his boss adjusted the street sign did not feel like his hands. The feet planted firmly on the sidewalk did not feel like his feet. The world passing him by as it went about its business reminded him of one of those video clips of the Earth.

The Agricultural Sector was always warmer than anywhere else, and Shor felt a little drowsy. Even out on the roadway, between the massive glass enclosures that housed the multi-layered fields and orchards, the air was stifling.

A heavy-duty harvester bot trundled past, making the ground shake. Shor watched it turn at the next intersection, its cutters folded neatly in front of its chest like crossed arms. As it rolled out of sight, Shor saw the giant head rotate slowly in his direction, the headlamp eyes locking onto his for just an instant.

Something tapped the top of his head and he looked up to see the sole of Lars' shoe.

"When you've finished your nap, would you kindly pass me that screwdriver?"

Shor followed his boss' pointing finger to the screwdriver he was holding in his hand.

"Yes, sorry. I was just thinking."

"Really? Is that what you call it? Are you getting enough sleep?"

"Yes. Plenty."

"Feeling symptomatic?"

"No, I'm fine."

"How are your bowel movements? Regular I hope?"

Shor coughed. "Every hour on the hour."

"Hah! Well at least there's nothing wrong with your sense of humour. I may be old, and a little bit crazy, but I know a few things. If you ever need to talk about something, I promise to try and listen. And I promise not to laugh, or tell anyone outside the city walls. You may not realise this, but my advice is highly sought-after. I can't begin to count the number of people I've helped with my pearls of wisdom."

"Thanks," Shor said. "I think."

"No problem. Here, take this and hand me that bottle, would you?"

Shor took the screwdriver and swapped it for a container of oil. He looked thoughtfully up at the sole of Lars' shoe. "Have you ever discovered something that completely destroyed every idea you ever had about yourself, and the world, along with everything you ever thought or believed?"

Lars stopped working on the sign long enough to show Shor two raised eyebrows. Then a sly grin crept across his face. "Hah! I knew it! The boy's in love. Who is it? Anyone I know?"

"I'm not in love."

"Only a woman can turn a man's life upside down like that. Who is she? Come on, tell your Uncle Lars."

"I promise you. It isn't a girl."

"All right. If it isn't a girl, then what is it?"

Shor watched Lars spray oil onto the bolts he had used to secure the sign. The surface glistened under the big ceiling lights. Small globs collected into rivulets that edged their way down the neat lettering as if trying to make a bid for freedom before Lars's rag swept them into oblivion.

"I always thought my parents were my natural parents. I think they did as well. Seems they were wrong."

Lars hesitated before continuing with the sign. "That's lousy, kid, but you know how the system works. The geneticists control everything. I guess your real parents weren't seen as good candidates. I heard somewhere only fifty percent of adults are allowed to raise kids and eighty percent of all kids born on Mars are adopted. It's a lottery. Heck, I'm pretty sure I was adopted. Don't let it get you down. Here, pack this away."

Shor took the oil and stowed it in the back of the buggy. "I guess I just wish I'd known. It's a bit of a shock to find out everything you ever believed about yourself isn't true."

They climbed into the buggy. Lars turned to Shor without starting the engine.

"Listen, kid. That doesn't change who you are. Your parents may provide the DNA, but they don't make you where it counts, here, inside." He tapped his chest with a grimy finger. "Only you can decide who you are going to be and what you'll become as you get older."

"Did you ever try to find your real parents?"

"Why would I want to do that? Besides, it's illegal."

Shor let out a laugh. "Since when has that stopped you from doing anything?"

Lars leaned back in his seat, his hands grasping the steering wheel as if he was scared to let go. "My parents loved me like I was their own. Maybe they guessed I wasn't theirs, I don't know. I often wondered about my biological parents, but I figured it was better to be raised by people who wanted the job and who were good at it, rather than someone who maybe wasn't cut out for the whole child-rearing thing. I always figured blood is thicker than the electronic ink on a digital adoption form, but then I started to realise my parents really did love me, as much as anyone can love a child, whether it's their own or one chosen for them by a scientist. At some point, I stopped wondering about the life I might've had and focused on the life I did have."

Lars leaned forward and started the buggy's electric engine. It was late afternoon and people were finishing their business for the day. The road was getting busy. "Does this have anything to do with those messages you've been getting?"

"No," Shor said. "It was nothing."

"Did you find out who it was?"

"It was…someone from school."

Lars nodded. "I see. In that case, I'll shut TrigBeacon down. No point having it running if you know who it is."

"It's all right," Shor said. "I'll do it."

They joined the slow-moving traffic. Up ahead, a fully-laden harvester was on the way to the silo, dragging its bloated load along behind it. They came to an intersection and Shor saw the farms stacked up against the far wall, the fat crops pressed against the steamed glass, their leaves flattened like the open hands of prisoners begging to be released from the shimmering heat.

The air in the Hub was pleasantly cool compared to the stifling humidity of the Agricultural Sector where everything felt to Shor as though it was moving in slow motion. At the depot, he showered and changed.

Lars announced he was heading home. Shor said he wanted to spend some time in HQ, to which Lars gave a knowing smile.

"Be careful, kid," he said. "It can get addictive. And don't forget it's an early curfew tonight."

Shor nodded. The storm that had hit three weeks ago was just a taster of the big storm waiting in the wings. A solid two weeks of dust being blasted at the city meant the extractors were working overtime. He checked his chatband, which informed him he had an hour before curfew.

Power. That's what it all came down to in the end. At school they had talked of "generating" power, of "harnessing" it, "preserving" it, and of "utilising" it. Power, they had been told, was their most precious commodity and their most useful tool. And yet, looking at the minutes counting down to the curfew, Shor wondered if it was the power serving them, or if it wasn't they who were really the slaves.

With Lars gone, Shor walked between the shelves and stepped inside the monitor room. The screens flickered and he scanned them for anything interesting. Life in Utopia was doing its thing: living, breathing, moving. He checked the image from the camera outside Mel's school and watched the empty windows. Only the security guard was still there, walking along the front of the building, twirling his keycard around his index finger and pursing his lips in a whistle.

Mel would be at home, of course. Or with her new friends. She might be with—he even found it hard to *think* his name—Vin. Or she might be out looking for signatures, but he doubted it. Her loss of interest in the petition had surprised him and, to some extent disappointed him as well. But could he blame her for trying to fit in the way he had always wanted to?

He tapped a key and the monitors changed, showing scenes in and around the Mining Sector. Its primitive machines were designed for the sole purpose of extracting minerals from deep underground and transporting them back to the surface. Here the bots looked like demonic beasts of burden with their blackened hides and flaming infra-red eyes. Here, the back-breaking toil never ceased. Legend spoke of bots lost for hundreds of years deep in the labyrinth of tunnels they had dug for themselves, where they eventually broke down in graves of their own making. Their programs were as basic as their mechanics and so it was cheaper to build a replacement than send a rescue party down kilometres of tunnels to bring them out. They stayed in their dark tombs, waiting for someone to come and fix them.

It was, he realized, not so different with people. They worked until they were unable to work any more; until they broke or malfunctioned, or simply lost the will to carry on. Presumably it was cheaper to build a new person. He thought of his mother lying in her bed, unable or unwilling to wake up, and the doctors seemingly incapable of fixing whatever was wrong with her.

Another key press revealed the remote and seldom-visited Nuclear Sector with its twin power stations surrounded by an entourage of service buildings spilling out across the cave floor. A pair of cooling towers pierced the low ceiling, spewing white steam into the atmosphere. Six external cameras showed the rims of the towers from all angles, giving an unobstructed view of the flat conical hats designed to provide protection from the dust that could easily destroy the vital cooling system. A team of bots was hard at work on the smooth slopes, checking for any damage

126

caused by the last storm.

Watching the bots at work, it seemed to Shor they were like ants around a nest and, at its very heart, was the royal chamber. Then he saw it, as if a veil had been pulled away from his eyes allowing him to see it all so clearly. The purpose of the bots, of his life, of every life in Utopia, revolved around one thing—to service those conical towers. Every action of every creature in the city was linked to the twin power stations in some way or other and, in return, they exerted absolute control over their subjects. From the number of calories they were allowed to consume right down to how long they could communicate on their chatbands, there was no part of life on Mars that was not somehow under their influence. And their reach extended beyond this life. They decided the number of births and how many had to retire. They were, in their silent cruelty, responsible for so many deaths.

I am not from here, he thought.

He shut down the monitors and cracked the door open to make sure the workshop was empty before stepping out. He checked the changing room and found a few of the night-shift people getting ready for work. At the front office he typed a quick message into the work-order computer. A quick swipe of his chatband transferred the order to him. Outside, he walked to the front door and across to his buggy, started the engine, and set off towards the Space Sector.

29

Darkness was settling on the city by the time he reached the other side of the airlock. The array of overhead lights on the Space Sector ceiling was fading like the dying embers of a thousand fires.

It was deserted of people, but the sector was still buzzing with life as an army of bots went to work, the beams from their headlamp eyes criss-crossing the gloom in search of something to fix or clean or cart off to the recycling centre for inspection and possible re-use.

The buggy was unfazed by the low light so Shor settled in to watch the show as he sped through the deepening darkness. He folded his arms and leaned back, shifting his weight until he found a comfortable spot on the lumpy padding.

Occasionally, the buggy's headlamps would illuminate something small drifting across the road. Shor imagined they were insects that had somehow survived for centuries, secreted in some concealed place, hiding in their cocoon until just the right moment before launching themselves into the night air in search of whatever it was insects dreamed of finding in the dead of the night.

Over to the right, the dark shapes of the hangars rose beyond the buildings. He could see the small square of light from the security booth at the top of the ramp, and the outline of the badge whose sole duty for the night was to watch the doors in what had to be the world's most boring job.

Without warning, the buggy slowed down and pulled to the side of the road. Shor glanced around and realised the vehicles all along this stretch had done the same thing. His first thought was that they had all somehow run out of juice at the same time, or possibly broken down in a freak synchronised robotic accident. Then he noticed something back up the road. It was a strange light that, from this distance, appeared to be dancing. A big glowing blob was doing a wild dance, its fuzzy light bouncing off the surrounding buildings.

Shor sat up and squinted as the single light splintered into many smaller parts, all spinning to a silent tune as they raced in the general direction of the administration building. The convoy of three police buggies and an ambulance flew past in an eerie silence. All Shor could hear was the high-pitched buzz of electric engines and the rattling of the vehicles as they raced towards whatever emergency demanded the presence of so many officials.

Then, as quickly as it had appeared, the grim conga line vanished, shuddering around a corner and out of sight.

The waiting vehicles resumed their journeys as if nothing had happened. Shor looked along the road, trying to locate the source of so much attention, but the convoy had turned down a side street and all that was left behind was the remnants of reflected light slowly ebbing away.

The buggy turned, taking him further away from the excitement. Up ahead, the hangars loomed, their solid shadows squeezing towards him between the gaps in the buildings. The buggy joined the wide expressway, which was empty apart from a dozen or so bots scuttling along the deserted strip.

Shor looked up at the ramp almost directly overhead, but the badge who worked there was nowhere to be seen, probably stretching his legs. The buggy slid to a smooth halt in front of the hangar door and Shor climbed out, suddenly a little self-conscious to be in a sector that appeared to be occupied almost exclusively by critters.

The front door slid open. Shor considered turning on the lights but elected to find his way by the faint glow spilling from the red warning light above the airlock.

His keycard was acknowledged by a flash from the console. With a soft hiss, the door opened and Shor stepped inside. By the time he had crossed the floor and was close enough to touch its smooth metallic shell, the room was filled with the sound of the ship's mechanical systems. The hull split and the door opened, spilling a soft oblong of light onto the hangar wall.

Shor climbed the stairs, hesitating at the top.

"Hello Brett," the voice said. The face was smiling at him from the far wall. "I'm glad you came. I have many questions."

"Me too. And it's not Brett."

"Of course. Why don't you come through to the living area? I am sure you will remember how much you loved that chair."

"Your name is Jay, right?"

"Yes. That is correct."

Shor walked gingerly through the ship, passing the chamber filled with yellow liquid, through into the bathroom and changing area, and on into the kitchen and the living room beyond. He slowly lowered himself into the big chair in the centre of the room.

"It smells a bit musty." He shifted his weight until he found the sweet spot and had the feeling of being suspended in weightlessness. "But this *is* comfortable."

The computer's face appeared on the wall opposite. "Yes, you always loved that chair. Unfortunately it has been a while since you used it."

Shor stroked the soft material with his hand. "I used to sit here?"

"All the time. You once told me you could happily spend the rest of your life in that chair."

"Tell me more about the mission. What was I like, you know, back then?"

"You were looking for a way to escape from your problems. That is why you agreed to go. It was very risky and there was a good chance you would not return. You were very unhappy, in the beginning."

"Why?"

"You lost your family. You blamed yourself. Of course it was not your fault at all but you felt extremely guilty."

Shor looked at the face on the wall. It seemed so familiar. "My family?"

"Yes. Your wife and children. They died in an accident. They were travelling to see you."

"You mean I was *married?*"

"Yes."

"And I had children?"

"Yes, two boys."

An image appeared alongside the computer's face. White sand with the sea in the background. Sea so blue it almost hurt his eyes to look at it. And a perfect sky, with seagulls floating on the wind.

And a family. A man and a woman, and two young boys. They all looked so happy.

Shor leaned forward. He recognized the young man. "That's me."

"Yes," Jay replied. "It is."

"And that's my wife?"

"Yes. Rochelle."

Shor lifted himself out of the chair and walked towards the screen. "Rochelle," he repeated, reaching his hand towards the pretty face smiling out at him. He moved his hand down to the boys seated on the blanket with their noses covered in white cream and mops of hair dishevelled from swimming in the sea. "These were my boys?"

"Tim and Mark. Tim was the eldest. I believe he was six in that photograph. Mark had just turned five."

"Were they *my* children? I mean, they weren't adopted?"

"Yes, they were your children."

"They look so happy," Shor said. "We all look so happy. What happened to them? You said they were in an accident?"

"Yes. You moved across the country. They followed you later on. The plane they were in crashed."

"You said, a *plane*."

"Yes. An aeroplane."

"I've seen them in pictures. Why did I leave my family behind?"

"You told me it was to find work."

Shor stared at the beautiful faces. "What kind of work is so important I would leave my wife and children?"

"You wanted to provide for them. You said you had the chance to earn a lot of money."

"Money," Shor echoed. "I've read about this. My teacher said it was the cause of many problems on Earth."

"You do not have money here?"

"No. We're issued with ration credits according to what we need. I suppose that's a sort of money, but it doesn't cause any problems like the wars Mister Edmunds told us about. Credits are linked to each person, and it's all stored on our chatbands anyway, so even if you found a way to steal them you wouldn't be able to use them. They tie it in to a person's estimated power usage. At the end of each year they work out how much energy they think we'll use for the next year. This gets converted to credits."

"Who is Mister Edmunds?"

"He's my teacher. He knows all about Earth. Do you know about Earth?"

"Yes. I have a comprehensive library, including every book available at the time of my creation. I have read them all."

"Every book?"

"Yes, I believe so."

"I saw a picture of a library once. That's a lot of books. Must take a lot of memory."

"With my compression algorithms, it hardly takes any space at all."

Shor thought back to the grainy image Mister Edmunds had shown them. Shelf upon shelf filled to overflowing with fat cubes of paper. It occurred to him that somewhere in all this information might be the answer to Utopia's problems.

"What's it like, on Earth I mean? We've got some old pictures and a few videos, and some sounds, but not very much. And we've got some books stored on computer. We read Moby Dick last year. It sounded a little bit scary."

"Ah, Moby Dick. Yes, a fine novel. Although, like most fiction, the events portrayed were exaggerated somewhat, for dramatic effect."

"So it's not like that? The sea isn't full of huge animals?"

"On the whole, the sea is quite peaceful. And, surprisingly, the biggest creatures are actually the most placid. Perhaps it would be best if I showed you."

Jay's face disappeared from the screen along with the family photograph. They were replaced by a shot of the Pacific Ocean taken from a low-flying aircraft. The smooth blue surface stretched from horizon to horizon where it met the flawless sky in a perfect line. The gently undulating surface became a blur as the camera swooped in even lower.

Shor gazed at it. It was like a dream. And yet, beneath that absolute calm, that absolute serenity, he could almost feel the energy waiting to burst out.

"Beautiful," Shor said, returning to the chair. "Listen, can you keep the other picture up? The one of me and my family on the beach?"

"Certainly."

The image of Rochelle and Mark and Tim appeared on the wall next to the dramatic footage of the Pacific Ocean.

"Thanks. I like that. It makes me feel happy. You got any more videos?"

"What would you like to see?"

"Everything," Shor said. "Show me everything."

Beware.

For a few seconds, Shor had no idea where he was. It felt as if he was falling through a white nothingness. He reached out for something to hold onto and found himself clutching soft leather. The breath caught in his chest as he sat upright, suddenly remembering where he was.

"You fell asleep," Jay said.

Shor blinked. "Yes, I…sorry."

"You stayed up very late watching video clips."

"What time is it?" Shor checked his chatband. "Oh no, I'm late." There was one message waiting, from Lars. He did not bother to read it. He had a pretty good idea what it said. "I have to get to work."

"Can you not stay longer?" Jay said, his face following from surface to surface as Shor moved through the ship. "I would like to talk some more."

"No chance. Lars doesn't appreciate tardiness. We'll have to wait for my next visit."

"Can you visit tonight?" Jay's face filled the space next to the open door. His expression was one of wide-eyed hope. In spite of his adult features, his eyes were those of a young child. Shor had to remind himself that it was just an avatar. Behind the lifelike image was just a bunch of computer programs.

"I can't stay away from home too much. My father might notice." Shor hesitated before stepping through. "Maybe tomorrow night?"

"Pity." Jay's face showed disappointment for a moment, and then shifted to a smile. "But tomorrow will be fine. I am here almost every night."

"Hang on," Shor said. "What do you mean almost…" Jay grinned and Shor though he saw a sparkle in his eyes. "You're joking, right?"

"Of course. Why are you looking at me like that?"

"It's just I never met a computer with a sense of humour before."

"You taught me all about humour. I have been working on a knock-knock joke. Would you like to hear it?"

"What's a knock-knock joke?" Shor asked, but before Jay could answer, his chatband squeezed. It was another message from Lars. "I have to go. Tell me next time."

"I look forward to it," Jay said.

Shor paused at the top of the stairs and turned to see Jay watching him. "If you really need me for something urgent, call me." He lifted his chatband.

"I will," Jay said, a broad smile on his face.

Shor trotted down the stairs and jogged in his clumsy gait to the airlock. He stepped through the door and turned to see the ship's entrance sliding shut. Out front, the buggy was still waiting. The Space Sector was its usual hive of early-morning activity.

He climbed on board and set his destination for the Maintenance Depot. As the buggy sped along, he took the time to check his messages. They were, as he guessed, from Lars but they were not the angry reprimands he had expected. The first simply said: *Where are you? Let me know you're all right.*

Shor selected Lars' ID. After a moment, his boss' frowning face appeared on the screen.

"Hey, kid, where are you?"

"Sorry I'm late. It won't happen again."

"It's all right," the reply came back. "I was just worried about you. When you didn't call in and you didn't answer your messages, I thought the worst. And your job ticket last night was at the Space Sector so I put two and two together."

The buggy left the hangar strip and turned towards the middle of the sector. As they approached the intersection, a police vehicle sped through and headed towards the administration building. Shor thought about the convoy he had seen last night.

"What's going on, Lars? I keep seeing badgemobiles."

"There's been an accident, over at the admin offices. I've been watching the feeds from last night. It looks like some guy fell off the roof. A young fella, about your age".

"And you thought it was me?"

"It did cross my mind. What were you doing out there anyway?"

"Forgot the time and fell asleep."

He thought about coming clean and spilling the beans on everything, but stopped himself. *Not yet,* he thought. He wasn't even sure how he might possibly begin to tell someone everything he had learned over the past few weeks without sounding insane.

"Just hurry back, kid. There's something I want to show you."

He was not sure if it was just his imagination but, at the airlock, the badge was even less friendly than usual and examined his ID a little too closely for comfort. Shor tried to look like someone with nothing to hide but the heat rose up his neck and into his face the way it always did when he was embarrassed. The badge narrowed his lips and looked from the ID to Shor and back again three times before letting him through.

Back at the depot, he found Lars in the HQ with Reet. They were watching the video feeds closely.

"Glad you could join us," Lars said, glancing over his shoulder. "Here, come take a look at this."

Shor moved alongside Reet's chair. On the screens, a group of badges were gathered around a figure lying motionless on the floor in front of the Space Sector admin building. The image was grainy, but there was a pool of dark liquid next to the victim's head. A man in a white lab coat was crouched next to the body, examining it.

"What happened?" Shor said, his eyes transfixed on the twisted corpse. Apart from the one leg bent at an awkward angle, it might have been somebody taking a nap. The head was turned to the side, the face looking almost directly at the camera.

"We've been checking some other feeds and it looks like he jumped."

"You mean…suicide?"

"Appears that way."

Shor had never seen a suicide victim before. He had heard that people sometimes took their own lives, but it was rare, and the badges wrapped them up pretty tightly. These days, psych evals were adept at revealing suicidal tendencies well in advance, probably before the potential victim was even aware of it himself. It was one of those things Shor generally heard about third or fourth hand. Napier had once boasted of seeing one actually happen. He took a lot of pleasure in explaining the details at length, emphasising the blood and relishing the horror expressed by the girls.

"He jumped from the roof?"

"More than likely. He was pretty determined. Looks like he jumped head first to be sure he didn't just end up with a broken leg."

An image flashed through Shor's mind of the man launching himself towards the walkway as if diving into water. He flinched at the thought. "Perhaps he was pushed."

"Perhaps," Lars said. "We're trying to find the feed when it happened. We keep missing it."

The image froze. Lars tapped the keyboard and the body disappeared, along with the badges and the lab-coat guy.

"Too far," Reet said.

"Not so far back," Lars said. "And slower this time."

Reet tapped the keys and the image became slightly blurred. Every now and then a figure would scuttle past or a vehicle would flash by. Suddenly, the body appeared.

"Missed it," Reet said.

The image froze and reversed. After a few seconds the body lying in the walkway vanished.

"Now try half speed," Lars said.

The feed rolled forward. One moment the street was empty, the next there was a body and a pool of blood.

"I don't get it," Reet said. "Why don't we see him falling?"

"Play it again," Lars said. "Quarter speed."

The feed rolled. The body appeared as if by magic. They could see most of the lower half of the building. There was no fall, or impact. The pool of blood did not spread but was just there—fully formed.

"Look at the time," Shor said. "It changed."

They watched it again. The clock jumped forward almost a full minute exactly as the body appeared.

"It's like the camera cut out just as the guy was falling," Lars said.

"Perhaps it broke down," Shor suggested. "Perhaps it malfunctioned just at that exact moment."

Lars stared grimly at the screen. "That seems like a bit of a coincidence to me. I've been working here for a long time and those cameras are possibly the most reliable technology in the whole city. We replace them every year so they hardly ever break down. And exactly sixty-point-zero-zero seconds? No, this looks deliberate."

"You mean someone cut the feed on purpose?"

"I'm not a gambling man, but I'd bet my granny's DNA somebody didn't want this suicide being seen."

"We can check the other cameras. Maybe they've got the full thing."

"Let's have a look."

Reet ran though the same scene using the feeds from two different cameras. Both were missing the same minute.

"This, gentlemen," Lars said, "is starting to look very fishy."

"What about the camera on the ramp, near the main airlock?" Reet said. "Doesn't that point back down towards the admin building?"

Lars gave Reet a determined look. "You know, I think it does. It's a long shot but we might be able to get a look at the roof."

They all peered into the monitors now showing the view from above the big airlock doors at the top of the ramp. Reet returned to the time just before the other feeds went blank. The camera was a good distance away but it was possible to see something on the roof, a figure—a man—standing near the edge. There was a movement as he stepped out as casually as someone going for a walk. Then he was gone, quick as a Martian moment, vanished behind the nearside building that seemed to just swallow him whole.

"There!" Shor said. "Did you see that?"

"I sure did," Reet said. "Let's see if we can get a better look using Lars's patented magnification software."

A few taps on the keys and they were zoomed in on the building. It was fuzzy in the fading light but they could still see some detail.

The missing minute played through. On the roof of the admin building, a figure appeared, hesitated for a second or two as if stopping to admire the view, and then just fell forward. There was no flailing or kicking. He looked like a bag of laundry being dropped off the edge. Shor found it hard to watch.

"He just fell. He wasn't pushed. He just…fell."

"So why would anyone want to hide this feed?" Lars said. "It doesn't make any sense. Can we get any closer?"

"Sure," Reet said. "But you won't be able to see much."

"It's worth a try. Maybe we missed something."

The image became heavily pixelated as it zoomed in. A person falling from the roof, but there was almost no detail.

"Let's see if there's another camera," Lars said.

"No wait," Shor touched Reet on the shoulder. "Go back."

"Why? There's no point. We can't see anything."

"I think I saw something. Play it again."

Reet typed. The scene ran once more.

"Stop there!" The image froze, blurred like a scene caught by a dropped camera, or snapped from a buggy moving at full speed. "There. Can you see it? In the window, just below where the guy jumped. There, look."

Reet and Lars leaned closer. In a room on the top floor, directly beneath the jumper, a square of light framed the unmistakeable shape of a human figure. Shor could just make out the blurred features of a face draped in shadow. Someone was standing there, watching as the victim dropped past the window.

"That's weird," Reet said. "It's like he didn't even see the guy."

"Maybe he had his eyes closed," Shor suggested. "Or maybe he just blinked."

"Even if he blinked he would've seen something. And he doesn't look like he's got his eyes closed. He's facing the window. You can see the whites of his eyes. Anyway, why would he stand at the window with his eyes closed?"

"I dunno. I'm just guessing here."

"Maybe they're damaged," Lars said. "Maybe he couldn't see the guy fall."

As they watched the feed, the figure in the window moved forward and looked down to see what was going on in the street below. He leaned out of the window with the casual interest of a curious neighbour.

Strangely, he was dressed all in yellow. Then, slowly, he turned and walked back into the room.

"He doesn't look blind to me," Reet said. "But, seriously, this doesn't mean anything. A guy was looking out the window and didn't see someone fall. Are they going to arrest someone for not seeing something?"

"Try going back further," Shor said. "Maybe we should try earlier."

Reet sighed. "How far back?"

"I dunno. Just rewind."

Reet tapped a key and the feed rolled back at double-time. They watched the suicide victim fly up and walk away from the ledge in a comical reverse-step. He moved to the stairs at the rear of the building and disappeared, moving back and down. A few moments later he appeared in the corridor, frog-marching in reverse towards the room below. Here, the yellow-suited observer moved away from the window towards the door. Then the door opened and they lost sight of both men for a good thirty seconds.

"What are they doing?" Shor said.

"I have no idea," Lars said, leaning over Reet's chair. "But the last person the jumper spoke to was the guy in the yellow suit, who definitely doesn't look blind."

The soon-to-be dead guy reappeared and walked backwards down the corridor towards the main stairs while the man in the yellow suit reversed across the room and faded into the shadows.

"Maybe we should tell the police," Shor said.

"No," Lars snapped. "If they find out about *this* room," he nodded at the ceiling, "we'll be in bigger trouble than the poor wagger down on that walkway. They've got the same feeds we do. They'll find it, just like we did. And, besides, we don't know what just happened. So they spoke. So what? The guy snapped and decided to end it all. For all we know he tried to talk him out of jumping."

"It didn't look like he tried to talk him out of anything. If he knew the guy was going to jump, why did he just watch? Why didn't he call someone? And isn't it a bit suspicious that the feed was cut on every camera close enough to see exactly what happened?"

"It might be a coincidence. It might be nothing."

"What if it isn't?" Reet joined, staring grimly at the screen. "What if it's everything?"

Lars stood silent for a long time, scratching his chin the way he tended to do when he was deep in thought. "All right. I've got a plan. For now we wait. In the meantime, I'm going to see what's going on at the admin building." He jabbed his finger at the monitor. "Especially in *that* room. Reet, what's your workload like today?"

"Two jobs this afternoon. Nothing fancy. Just a couple of bulbs need replacing."

"Good. I want you and Shor to keep an eye on the building while I go have a look around. You see anything odd, make a note of the time and the camera." He turned to Shor. "Each camera has a unique ID in the bottom corner."

"I see it," Shor said.

"Good. I won't be long."

They watched Lars drive away. On the monitor, his buggy looked like a toy as it meandered along the elaborate model city filled with mannequins and play vehicles.

Reet flipped from camera to camera with practised ease, stringing the journey together in a series of hops and angle changes. At no time did they lose sight of Lars. Even as he passed through the airlock into the Space Sector, they could see his distinctive profile through the camera pointing down into the space between the doors. Shor half expected him to grin up at the camera and wave, but Lars kept his head down and his eyes fixed straight ahead.

They watched as he passed through security without incident and made his way along the wide main road towards the big intersection that cut the sector into quarters. At the cross-roads he turned left and then right and then left again. A minute later he was outside the Space Sector administration building. They watched him climb out of the buggy and walk past the spot where, a few hours earlier, the body had been. Any sign of the tragedy was now gone—scratched, scraped and polished into oblivion by a small team of bots.

"Here we go," Reet said.

They watched as Lars woke the toolbox with a deft kick before crossing the walkway with his hands in his pockets and his lips pursed in a whistle.

At the building entrance, Lars waved his keycard and the door swung open. A moment later, he vanished into the reception area with the toolbox following behind. The door closed and he was gone.

"Now what?" Shor said.

"We wait."

They watched the screen. People walked by. Some stopped and entered the building while a few came out, turning left or right. Vehicles darted along the walkway. A bot trundled past, paused to inspect something, and moved on. Five minutes dragged into what felt like hours.

"What's taking so long?" Shor said, biting at a fingernail. "He should be out by now."

"Be patient. He's fine. Here, look at this."

Three screens now gave different views of the building. One was from a camera across the road, It gave a good view of the entire floor, but not of the room occupied by the yellow-suited man because the angle was too sharp. The second camera was up the road and showed the room from the other side but, again, not directly into it. The best angle was still from the camera at the ramp. It was too far away to get a clear image, but it gave them the clearest view. There was someone standing just inside the window.

"Is that the same guy?"

"Looks like it."

"Can't we zoom in any closer?"

"We can't control the cameras directly. We can only use what they show us. This is as close as we're going to get, I'm afraid."

Shor pulled back a little and tilted his head. The image was too blurred to tell for certain, but he had the unnerving sensation of being watched. It looked as if the guy was looking directly at the camera. The whites of his eyes were just a square, but it looked as if the guy was looking at him.

"Is he—"? Shor began to say but he was interrupted by Reet pointing at the screen.

"There he is. He's going upstairs."

They watched as Lars reached the door to the room where the man had retreated from the window and was now standing motionless, framed by a square of light.

Lars had his hand on the door handle, but stopped and turned. Someone was walking briskly towards him. It was a badge. Lars turned to face him and they exchanged words which, from the hand gestures, looked heated. Lars was led away from the door, back the way he had come, to a room on the other side of the building. Lars stepped inside and they lost sight of him as he moved away from the windows. The badge stayed outside the open door, watching with his arms folded.

"Where's he gone?" Shor said.

"Looks like he's inside the other room down the hall."

Shor's chatband squeezed. "It's him. It just says: *Have to get to work.*" Shor looked at Reet, who shrugged. "So now what?"

"We do what Lars said we should do." Reet stretched and crossed his hands behind his head. "We watch."

For half an hour they stared at the screens, waiting for Lars to finish whatever he was doing. The badge lost interest after a few minutes and strolled up and down the corridor, occasionally stopping to look out of one of the windows. The shadowy figure in yellow remained where he was. He

141

just stood there, absolutely motionless, staring out of the window, apparently transfixed by something. For Shor, the feeling of being watched was palpable.

At some point someone dressed like a nurse entered the room. Now the figure moved and they lost sight of him as the nurse pottered around for a few minutes before leaving, stopping on the way out to talk the badge. The man in yellow remained hidden after that and did not show himself again.

Shor was about to suggest that something had gone wrong when Lars appeared in the hallway. After another exchange with the badge, he headed down the corridor towards the stairs, all the while chatting with the nurse. Two minutes later, he stepped out of the front door and crossed the walkway.

"About time," Shor declared. "I was getting worried."

"Lars can take care of himself," Reet said calmly. "I've yet to see him get into a situation he couldn't handle."

They watched Lars climb into the buggy and lift his chatband to his mouth.

Shor's chatband squeezed, and he glanced at Reet before answering. "We were getting worried back there. And? How did it go?"

"No luck." Lars's voice sounded hollow. "There was a guard so I decided it was best not to disturb the patient."

"We were watching. We saw the whole thing."

"I had to fix the ventilation system. They now have a newly serviced extractor fan whether they want it or not." On the screen, Lars looked around, as if checking to make sure he was alone. "I'll debrief you when I get back. Put the coffee on, all right?"

The connection ended and they watched Lars pull away from the side of the walkway. A cleaning bot stopped what it was doing and looked up at him as he drove past, its headlamp eyes fixed on Lars as if trying to decide whether or not he was a stain that needed scraping off the road.

They watched his buggy wending its way towards the airlock, changing cameras as they went. Had they been looking at the monitor showing the view from the camera at the ramp, they would have noticed the man in the yellow suit was standing at the window again, leaning forward as if to see what was going on down in the street, his head turned in the direction of Lars's departing buggy.

32

"So," Reet said, his big hand wrapped around a cracked mug, "did you find anything?"

Lars leaned forward and blew on his steaming coffee. "I got talking to this really helpful nurse. Seems the watcher in that room is the same guy we spotted wandering around up top four weeks ago."

"But I thought he was in quarantine," Shor said.

"He was. He just got out. They're keeping him under observation while they figure out where he came from. She said he's allowed out for a couple of hours in the afternoon, with an orderly in case he gets any ideas about going for another stroll up top."

"I don't understand," Reet said. "How can they not know where he came from?"

"She says they have no record of the guy."

"How is that possible? We all have records."

"Not this fella. It's almost as if he just dropped out of the sky. Apart from which, he's harmless. She said he hasn't said a word since they found him. Listen, I'd better go."

Dropped out of the sky…it's happened once before.

"I don't trust him," Shor said, his hands wrapped around his cup. "I can't explain why, but the whole thing just feels bad."

"That may be," Lars said, "but we can't call the badges in on someone just because you've got a feeling."

"What about the cameras?"

"I'll admit, it was a bit odd, but don't forget we've got a hacker on the loose. It's probably the same person who messed with that critter."

"But malfunctioning at exactly the same time as the guy jumped?"

"Sure that's suspicious, but then why didn't they cut the feed from the ramp? If he was so keen to hide his tracks, why not get every camera? And if you're going to persuade someone to jump off the roof, you're not gonna stand around watching. No, I had a good think about this on the way back and I reckon we should leave this alone. The guy's been through enough already without us sticking our face in his business, don't you think?"

Shor could still see the stranger's face, staring out across the Space Sector, looking right *at* the camera. He did not think he had imagined it.

"What about his out-suit? You said yourself it looked weird."

Lars slurped his coffee. "He made a suit for himself and went for a walk. It happens. Some people can't handle living like this. Sometimes, people try to leave. They grab a can of oxygen and just start walking."

"Like that group of wacks," Reet added. "When was that? Must be fifteen years ago now."

"Eighteen."

"See? This place gets to some people, kid. They don't get that you *can't* leave, that there's nothing out there."

"But I thought the badges stopped people from leaving," Shor said. "Especially after that thing with all those people."

"They stop the obvious crazies," Lars said, "but they can't always tell. It's still surprisingly easy to get outside, just so long as you're not foaming at the mouth and rolling your eyes."

Shor looked from Lars to Reet.

"You believe me, don't you, Reet? You know there's something wrong."

Reet examined his coffee. A small frown burrowed into his forehead. "Sure, I'll admit it's odd that he was watching just as the fella jumped off the building, but it might be coincidence. You can't incriminate someone for just being there. No, Lars is right." He downed the last of his coffee and banged the cup down on the table with an air of finality. "I've got some lights to fix. It's been fun, but I gotta go. Sorry, kid."

"Later," Lars said, lifting his mug in a casual salute.

"Is that it?" Shor said. "Aren't we going to do anything?"

"What do you want us to do? We've got somebody standing in a window and that's it. The badges will have been over the building. If they didn't find anything then there probably isn't anything."

"But, the cameras…"

Lars sighed. "Listen, kid. What you're suggesting is nothing less than murder and we can't go around accusing people of something that serious based on something so trivial. Do you know what they do to murderers? They kill them. They take them away and they never come back. Do you really want to be responsible for that? And then what do you think they'll do if they found out about our little house of fun?"

Shor shrugged. "Turn it off, I suppose."

"They won't just turn it off. Hacking is a serious offense. We'll be looking at ration cuts or retirement at the very least. Now I've got work to do, and I believe you do as well. I don't want to hear any more about this. Agreed?"

Shor stared down into his coffee. The feeling that the stranger in the window was somehow responsible for the man's death was so strong he was almost able to picture him throwing him from the roof. He looked across the counter at Lars, whose face was set. Shor now knew this expression to mean Lars had made his mind up and would not easily be swayed.

"All right," he said at last. "I'll drop it."

"Do I have your word?"

Shor nodded. "I promise."

"Good." Lars stood and stretched. "I'm headed your way. We can share a buggy if you like."

Shor sipped at the last few swirls of his coffee. It was cold and tasted bad but, in a world where wasting food was considered a cardinal sin, he could not bring himself to leave it.

"No thanks, I'll be making a detour on the way home." He saw the flash of suspicion in Lars's eyes. "Don't worry. It's a personal visit."

"A girl?"

"No, just a friend."

Lars's face relaxed and he winked. "Well, whatever her name is, have fun."

Shor forced a laugh. He waited until Lars had left the building. Then he headed for the door, stopping to collect his work order first. A critter had managed to wedge itself under a park bench and was spitting bolts. An easy enough job for a goget.

He transferred the order to his chatband and walked out to the buggy. A few minutes later, he rolled through to the airlock doors separating the Hub from the Manufacturing Sector. A badge waved him along and he followed the road to the food-manufacturing sub-sector. Low, brick-shaped vehicles moved between the various buildings on spindle-like bridges in an endless chain of supply-and-demand that processed the raw foodstuffs shipped across from the Agricultural Sector. Calorie-controlled, individual-sized portions would end up on the market shelves and storage rooms of the various eateries dotted around the city. And while most of the traffic between the buildings took place overhead, the deliveries were done via the underground network. People were generally oblivious to the hectic activity taking place beneath their feet as they went about their business, all to make sure they had enough to eat.

The road reached the central park area where it joined the ring road at the workers' market and square. It was lunchtime, which meant the benches were all full of workers eating and chatting. The queue in the market went all the way to the door.

Shor circled once, keeping an eye out for any sign of the critter, but he did not have to look very hard. The thirty or so benches were laid out in three staggered circles around a three metre high carbon statue of Pinner looking every bit the founding father with his strong but kindly face and earnest eyes. The benches were all taken, except for the one in the central ring, not far from Pinner's pointing finger. In fact, it almost looked as if Pinner were trying to show Shor exactly where the trouble was.

Over here young man. Don't dilly-dally.

Not that the founding fathers spoke like that, but it was how he imagined they did. With a deft kick against the back of the toolbox to get it moving, he set about weaving his way through the crowded square towards the knot of activity indicated by the kindly Pinner.

"Excuse me. Coming through. Maintenance guy coming through. Watch out there. Excuse me."

The knot loosened enough for him to see what was going on. At first he thought he was seeing a fight, like the ones he had caught a glimpse of at school where everybody wanted a ring-side seat. This was no fight but, at first glance, it did appear as though a park bench and bot were in the middle of a wrestling match. And the bench was winning.

The bot, pinned to the floor, was screeching in a high-pitched tone that sounded like a mix between a shout and the static hiss on a comms unit turned up really loud. It lay motionless for a few seconds, the whine of its internal servo motors growing louder and louder until it thrust up and forwards in a violent spasm that lasted a good ten seconds, its wheels sending up clouds of blue smoke. Then it lay still for a while, catching its breath, gathering its energy for the next thrust. With each attempt to break free, the bodywork took more damage. Shor smelt burning rubber.

"Well?" a woman said, apparently to Shor.

"Well what?"

"Are you going to fix it?"

"That's the general idea."

"By yourself?"

Shor ignored the woman and set about locating the critter's "brain hatch", as Lars liked to call it. It was in the usual place, up towards the front above and a little back from the eyes. The only problem was that the hatch was stuck under the bench, wedged tight against a slat.

He dialled Robotics on his chatband. A voice answered that he recognized as Cobb's.

"Hello?"

"Hey Cobb, it's Shor from Maintenance. There's a bot here needs shutting down."

"Oh, hi Shor. The access hatch is top front. The power switch is on the left."

"I know. I can't access the hatch. I need you to shut it down remotely."

"Oh. In that case, where are you?"

"At the square. In the Manufacturing Sector."

"Got it. Hang on…one moment…there."

Shor looked at the bot, which continued to struggle.

"It still looks the same. Did you turn it off?"

"Yes," Cobb replied.

"Well it didn't work. Try again."

"All right. Hang on…there. How's that?"

"No good. It's still moving."

"Hmm. The receiver must be damaged. You'll have to do it manually. The switch is in the hatch. On the left."

"Yeah, I got it, thanks." Shor broke the connection, eyeing the critter uncertainly.

As he approached the ailing machine, it appeared to become more agitated, although he knew this was purely his imagination. Bots did not get agitated, or annoyed, or even slightly peeved, but the weird cry coming from the machine had changed pitch, taking on a panicky feel. The machine pushed against the bench in an explosion of energy, then sat motionless for a few seconds before throwing itself forward again. The slats buckled under the strain, bending at the centre by perhaps half a centimetre. This was not much but then the slats were made of steel. The bot was consuming an enormous amount of power in its bid for freedom.

Shor circled until he was standing at the front end. He crouched, looking directly into the bot's visual receptors which followed him unwaveringly as he moved, even as it attempted to escape.

"Hey there," Shor said in a calm voice, as if this might somehow sooth the machine. "I'm not going to hurt you."

"It's a bot," the woman said. "Just turn it off."

Shor threw her a glance which he hoped conveyed his desire for her to mind her own business. The machine watched him intently as he moved to the side and placed a hand on the park bench.

The bot shuddered, sending a shockwave through the bench and into Shor's arm. He could feel the power being generated and decided he did not want to get between the two combatants. He leaned forward, placing weight on both palms, until the brain hatch appeared between two slats. The bodywork was scratched and scuffed. A series of large dents covered most of the head area. The hatch itself was bent out of shape.

Another surge ran through the bench and up Shor's arms. He almost slipped and had to grip the sides of two slats, being careful to keep his fingers clear. He was now so close to the machine he could hear the servo engines grinding. The smell of overheating electronics was almost overpowering.

He saw that the hatch was accessible if he removed one slat. They were designed to be taken out if necessary, so this was not a problem. His only fear was that loosening the slat might give the bot enough space to manoeuvre and possibly even break free. Normally, this would be a good thing, but this critter was behaving erratically and there were too many people standing around.

He moved off the bench and retrieved a spanner from the toolbox. The crowd watched his every move with keen interest, apparently curious to see what the bot would do next. Shor wondered if these same people were in the habit of standing in the middle of the road to see if the buggy careering out of control towards them was going to swerve.

"I need you to move back please," he announced, waving his hands in a pushing motion. "For your own safety, please move back."

The onlookers shuffled reluctantly, retreating perhaps half a metre.

"Please move back," Shor repeated. "We need more room. This bot is broken and I don't know what it's going to do."

The crowd reluctantly complied, shuffling back to form a loose circle. People were eating lunch as they watched. A few climbed onto the other benches to get a better look. One or two checked the time and started drifting away.

Shor approached the stricken bot, being careful to keep the spanner hidden from view. He knew this was irrational but he sensed something in the bot he had never encountered before. Looking into the dead, unblinking yes, he had the odd impression that there was more than just cogs and wires and software going on behind those etched glass lenses.

Bots, he reminded himself, *do not feel anything. Bots do not feel fear.*

The machine shuddered again as Shor climbed up onto the bench and started working at the bolt on the near end of the slat. The metal bar loosened and squealed as it gave a little under the pressure from below, straining upwards against the bolt head. The brain hatch was clear but there was not enough space to gain access. Shor slid across to the other side and started work on the bolt at that end. The pressure against the slat lessened. Shor removed the bolt and twisted the slat up and around so he was able to see the critter's battered head.

The surges were becoming more frequent and more intense, the squeal of the tyres louder. Shor had to hold on to avoid his hand slipping through the gap and possibly getting crushed. There was perhaps twenty centimetres between the two side slats. It was easily wide enough for his arm and possibly his shoulder. If he slipped and fell through, if his arm came between the bot and the bench, he could only imagine…

The brain hatch was damaged but the release mechanism looked intact. He waited for a lull in the bot's efforts before reached down to the catch. He twisted it but it was stuck. The bot rammed itself forward and Shor jerked his hand away. He tried again but the latch had been bent out of shape.

He slid off the bench and found a pair of pliers. The bot's eyes watched him as he climbed back up. This time he did not bother to hide the tools. Another surge and Shor clung on. The head of the bot slammed hard against the slats, twisting the hatch even more.

"I'm not going to hurt you," Shor said, aware that he sounded as irritated as he felt. "Dumb machine."

He wasn't sure if the bot understood those words but the next thrust was the strongest yet, almost knocking him off the bench.

There was a murmur from the crowd and he looked up to see that those who had stayed behind to watch had moved closer to the action. Shor was about to tell them to move back when the bench shook hard enough to almost knock him off. The pliers clattered to the ground and landed directly in front of the irate machine.

Shor clambered off and walked around to the front. Bending down, he was no more than a few centimetres from the critter's face. It drove forward and up, its set of tools clawing at the floor like mangled teeth, its eyes fixed on Shor's with a mindless determination. The scrapers and grinders designed to remove dirt and stains now scratched into the solid floor tiles, leaving gashes in the brick and sending sparks bouncing across the back of Shor's hand. Shor had the dreadful sensation that the bot was doing more than trying to break free. He had the feeling it was trying to get at *him*.

He grabbed the pliers and pulled back, keeping wide as he moved around to the side and climbed back onto the bench, this time taking care not to let the wrenching shudders knock him from his perch.

The pliers found the latch and Shor twisted. The brain hatch popped open, revealing the inner workings of the machine. The switch was on the top left as Cobb had said. Further down was circuitry, wires, and the motherboard where all the decisions took place. He waited for the bot to settle before flipping the switch. The critter let out one last cry and then stopped. There was only the crackle and hiss of cooling metal, and what sounded like liquid dripping to the floor.

Shor leaned back, still holding tight to the bench in case the beast started moving again, but the bot was dead. He wiped a film of sweat from the base of his fringe and let out a sigh of relief. He realized his hands were shaking a little.

A few people were clapping and he turned to see the small crowd watching him the way people look at someone who has just survived a nasty accident. He was not sure if it was genuine applause or the sarcastic variety.

Now that the show was over, the remaining people were drifting away, turning to head back to work or wherever it was they had come from. A group of four young teenagers, three boys and a girl, stayed behind, moving in to get a closer look. They wore their uniforms as required by law but, like every teenager, they seemed determined to push the limits of what was considered acceptable. The boys had drawn icons on their clothes and the girl's dress was adorned with small, brightly-coloured pieces of cloth. The hairstyles were tweaked and teased works of art. Shor remembered going through the stage of trying to express his individuality within the strict confines of the Utopian dress-code.

"So, what was wrong with it?" one of the boys asked, his top lip curled under a moustache so fresh out of puberty it was almost invisible.

"Don't know yet," Shor replied, still breathing heavily. "Probably a short."

"Can you fix it?"

"Maybe. Otherwise I'll send it down to Robotics. Shouldn't you be in school?"

The boy's curled lip turned into a smile. "Nope. Got a half day for study."

"Tests?"

"Next week."

"Then shouldn't you be studying?"

A ripple of laughter bounced between the youngsters. They ignored the question, as if it were too stupid to even consider answering.

"Is it safe?" the girl said, standing directly in front of the bot. She had a pretty face, but looked determined to hide as much of it as possible behind an unruly fringe. She stared at the critter with big brown eyes punctuated by a frown.

"Sure it's safe. I hit its kill switch." Shor was sitting on the bench, trying to figure out the best way to extricate the machine lying vanquished under the concrete and metal park bench. Removing the remaining slats would help, but the dumb contraption had wedged itself tight. In its mindless attempts to break free, it had only made its predicament worse.

The girl bent forward, peering intently into its glass eyes. A flat ribbon of hair fell across her nose and she pushed it back absent-mindedly. "Are you sure?"

"Course I'm sure. It's turned off. There's no power getting through from the batteries. It can't move. Unless you hit the switch, of course. Then it's got to boot up, and that takes a few seconds."

Her big brown eyes blinked and she tilted her head to one side. "I think you should come take a look—"

Shor felt the bench shudder. There was the whine of servo motors throttling up to full speed. A moment later the bench shook as the bot threw itself towards the wide-eyed girl who screamed at the top of her lungs. Shor toppled forward and his shoulder hit the edge of the bench, leaving his head dangling in front of the demented machine.

The bot's tools thrashed. The motors screamed. The girl's face was taut with terror as she fell backwards, her shoes only centimetres from the bot's spinning, grinding teeth. The mass of the concrete and metal bench was the only thing stopping it from scraping the girl from the floor like she had been left there and trodden into the ground by someone's shoe.

Then Shor felt it move. He guessed the park bench must have weighed as much as a buggy, but it shifted under the pressure of the machine that was no longer stopping to gather its strength, but driving, fighting, screaming to break free.

Shor felt the power through his shoulder. He tried to lift himself up but suddenly it was as if all the strength had been drained from his body. His head felt heavy. His arms felt heavy. He could see the girl's shoe almost within reach of the tools scrambling into the paving surface. He looked at her face. It was a mask of terror. Like him, she too seemed unable to move.

Get back, he thought. *Get away before it reaches you.* But the words were stuck inside his head. He tried to yell at her to *run!* but his throat refused to work.

The boys were just standing there, seemingly paralysed, watching everything with wide eyes. He tried to tell them to *help her!* but the words would not come out. The words were too heavy to make it up his throat. The words were dead weights bolted to the bottom of his chest, pinned down by a park bench.

People who had drifted away now turned back to see what was going on, stopping mid-conversation to see where the noise was coming from. On the ring road, buggies drifted past, moving in slow motion as the drivers stared. And beyond that, standing way back on the other side of the road, a figure watched, partially hidden by the building. He just stood there watching. Shor thought he recognised this person. He could not see his face but it was the posture that looked familiar. It was the *attitude*. It was the guy in the yellow suit from the room where the jumper had ended it all. It was the visitor they had found walking up top.

The bench shifted again. The teeth were cutting into the soles of the girl's shoes but still she did not move. Tiny shards of rubber showered the floor and bounced amid the sparks spraying across the girl's feet. Shor's attention had moved from the watcher in the yellow suit and he was now looking at the sparks, thinking how pretty they looked. Tiny scraps of shoe leather were dancing under a canopy of pretty party lights. He wanted the girl to look at how pretty they were, but the girl's face was a twisted mask of anguish. She was not trying to get away but she was just sitting there, watching her shoe being eaten by the razor sharp teeth. One more centimetre and it would be within reach of her toes. One more heave from the bot and Shor would not be looking at shreds of leather…

151

He forced himself to sit up. The bench was vibrating so hard he nearly fell backwards. He gripped the slats and steadied himself as the bench tried to shake him off. The smell of burning rubber was heavy in the air. Blue smoke was drifting up from the bot's open brain hatch, adding to the cloud of white smoke from the tyres.

The board, Shor thought. *Remove the board and kill this thing before it makes another break for it. Kill it before it kills her.*

But bots were programmed to not harm humans. Bots were designed to obey humans, not kill them.

Through the smoke he could see the circuit board housing all the components that made the machine capable of the simple tasks it carried out from day to day. Everything was connected directly or indirectly to the board which sprouted wires like a bad teenage hairdo. The processor—the brain—was nestled under its clear plastic dome. All he had to do was remove the board and the bot would stop.

Remove the brain and the critter dies. A full lobotomy will make all the bad thoughts go away.

He reached down into the head, fighting to keep his balance on the bucking bench. He became aware that the girl had stopped screaming, or perhaps the whining was now so loud it was drowning her out.

His fingers found the corners of the motherboard and he pulled, but the smooth surface was slippery. He lost his grip and tried again, but it slid out from between his fingers as though covered in axle grease, or possibly the sweat that he could feel running down his back and arms. He cussed and this time he reached down to the processor. The protective plastic dome would give him some purchase.

Tears stung his eyes as acrid smoke billowed up into his face. The whining was a deafening, tortured shriek. He gritted his teeth and squeezed his hands around the dome, and pulled with all his strength.

33

"Must've shorted," Lars said, standing with his arms crossed as he examined the bot swinging gently on the pulley system in the middle of the workshop. "Yep, it's the only explanation."

"That's what I told the badges," Shor replied. He stood back a little bit, his eyes never straying far from the bot. "I told them it was probably a short or something."

Lars scratched his chin. "The power switch was off?"

"It was."

"You sure?"

"Yes I'm sure. I flicked the switch and it stopped moving. It was off."

"Are you certain? Because sometimes these beasties can seem dead, but they're just resting or processing, or whatever it is they do when they're not moving."

"I was lying on top of the thing. Trust me, it was dead. One second it was just standing there, peaceful as a baby with a bottle. Next thing, it was going crazy."

Lars shrugged. "If there's one thing I've learned in all my years on this team, it's to always eliminate the simple explanations first. For example, it's possible the off switch didn't connect. Could be you didn't push that kiddie all the way over and it slipped back."

"I heard it click. It was off. Shouldn't we let the Robotics people take a look?"

"We will, but it won't do any harm to have a quick peek ourselves." Lars prodded at the undercarriage with his screwdriver. The machine swayed gently. "Boy, it really messed itself up. These tyres are nearly down to the metal. Look at this."

Shor leaned forward but did not move any closer. The memory of those teeth chomping at the girl's shoe was still fresh in his mind. The bot was clearly dead but its lidless eyes seemed to be focused on something in the middle-distance. He knew they were just photo-receptors, but he had the feeling it was *watching* them.

"Yes. They look pretty bad."

"And the underside is ripped to shreds." Lars jabbed the metal panel designed to protect the inner workings. "Look at these scratches."

Shor nodded. "Uh huh."

"You can't see from over there. Come take a look."

"Thanks, but I can see just fine from here."

Lars rolled his eyes. "Bring it down will you? I want to get inside its hatch."

Shor lowered the bot until it was a few centimetres above the floor. The brain hatch was closed but not secured. Lars flipped it open and looked inside. Shor caught the faint smell of cooked circuitry.

"The switch is off," Lars said, bending low, his feet planted directly in front of the bot's face. *Well within biting range*, Shor thought. "So it definitely didn't slip."

"Like I told you," Shor grumbled.

Lars leaned forward, reaching inside the hatch. "This beastie looks intact. Whatever went wrong, it wasn't mechanical. You still got the motherboard?"

Shor pointed to the table where he had left it on the way in. The protective plastic dome covering the processor glistened under the workshop light. It was slightly twisted where Shor had yanked on it.

Lars examined it and blew off any debris before connecting it to the computer. Lines of instructions filled the screen. Lars scrolled slowly through the text.

"Can't see anything wrong here. Let's have a look at the log."

More text appeared. Shor squinted at the screen full of meaningless words and numbers. He was starting to feel a little relieved he had not landed a job in the Computer Department.

"Hmm," Lars said. "That's interesting. That's very interesting."

"What?" Shor said, looking from Lars to the screen and back again. "What have you seen?"

"The timestamp on this log. Can you see it?"

Shor leaned closer. It was just a date and time, with seconds up to five decimal places. "It looks fine to me."

"This machine has been hacked," Lars said triumphantly.

"It has? How can you tell that just from the timestamp?"

"I'm glad you asked. When someone breaks into a system and they want to keep track of the places they've been, they leave a mark, a clue of some kind, so they don't go back to the same place twice. We call it a trail of breadcrumbs."

"Like in that kid's story?" Shor said. "The one about the witch who kidnapped two children and they left a trail of crumbs?"

"Exactly. We leave crumbs behind so *we* know where we've been but someone not looking won't notice."

"If I remember correctly, didn't the crumbs get eaten?"

"Sure, but that's not the point."

"Didn't the kids get lost because the birds ate the crumbs?"

"Forget the crumbs. The crumbs aren't important. What is important is that someone left a clue in this critter."

"In the timestamp?"

"Yes."

Shor read the line of numbers that showed the date and time of the last system update, trying to spot whatever it was Lars had seen.

"I don't see it."

"Look at the last four decimal places."

"They're all zeroes," Shor said.

"Right. Now here's an example of a log from a different bot." Lars tapped the keys. Another log appeared. Shor thought it looked exactly the same. "What are the last four decimal places?"

Shor read the numbers. "Nine, seven, six, zero."

"Here's another example. Different bot."

"Two, two, three, eight."

"And another."

"Zero, four, zero, six. I still don't get what you're trying to show me."

Lars brought the first log back onto the screen. "Those decimal places represent fractions of a second. Tenths, hundredths, thousandths, and ten thousandths. Do you know what the odds are of landing on all zeroes for the last four decimal places?"

Shor shrugged. "Not good?"

"Pretty much nil. If I gave you a stopwatch that went down to this level of accuracy and told you to try stopping it so the last four places were all zeroes, you'd be busy for a long time, and that's while *trying*. These numbers are random. The timestamp is logged when the system update has finished. This looks about as real as a badge's smile."

"You think someone changed the timestamp on purpose?"

"Exactly," Lars said. "You remember the critter we found up top, when the stranger appeared?"

"Of course." Shor thought about the stranger in the crowd, watching him. Two bots had malfunctioned on two different days, both while the "visitor" was nearby.

Lars tapped the keys. The text on the screen flashed off and on. "This is the log from that machine. Look at the timestamp."

"Four zeroes," Shor said. "So you think whoever messed with the other bot was the same person who hacked this one." He nodded at the maniacal critter hanging like a trussed carcass in an abattoir.

"Exactly. Normally I'm all in favour of this sort of thing. It's fun and challenging and mostly harmless. *This*, however, is something very different. Whoever did this needs to be stopped before someone gets hurt for real."

"Are we going to tell the badges?"

"We can tell them, but not directly. Hang on, I have an idea." Lars lifted his chatband. Cobb's voice answered.

"Hello? Lars…?"

"Cobb. Listen, we've got a critter down here that went nuts in the park this morning."

"Yeah, I heard about that. What happened?"

"We've had a look but it's nothing we can fix. You can come pick it up when you're ready. I'm sending you the log." He tapped his keyboard and they watched the counter climb to one hundred percent. "There, you got it?"

"I do. So, what am I looking for?"

"Check the timestamp."

"Hmm," Cobb said. "Very interesting. Is that a breadcrumb?"

"I reckon so. And whoever did this has moved beyond fun and games. The next bot he fiddles with might hurt someone."

"We'll send someone to pick it up. I'll give the badges a call. They'll want to see this."

"I'll help any way I can, but if the badges ask—"

Cobb laughed. "I know. Besides, this will look good on my resume."

"Enjoy," Lars said with a wry smile. "Just remember you owe me one." The connection broke and he turned to look at the critter.

Shor watched him for a second. Lars was possibly the most upbeat individual he had ever met. Nothing fazed the man, which was probably something that came with experience. Now, watching Lars stare at the machine swinging limply at the end of the pulley chains, this was the first time Shor had ever witnessed anything other than a mischievous twinkle in his eye. What Shor saw scared him from hang-nail to split-end. What he saw in Lars' eyes was nothing less than fear.

"Listen," Shor said. "I can't stay. I've got a job over in the Space Sector."

Lars did not move his eyes from the critter, which had slowly rotated as the pulley chains settled. It was facing him, engaging him in a staring contest it could not lose. Lars seemed hypnotized by the creature's gentle swaying. He waved his hand absentmindedly. "Sure. Go ahead. I'll wait here for Cobb."

Shor was reluctant to go, but he had to. He left the two of them in their battle of wills and headed out to the parking area. As he stepped off the walkway he spotted his buggy where he had left it. A group of pedestrians sailed past, and he turned to give them room, but his shoulder made contact with one at the back.

"Sorry," Shor said, turning to make sure the other person was not hurt, but they did not even seem to notice or care. Judging from the frame under the uniform it was a woman, or a kid, heavily built, and wearing an outer coat with the hood pulled up which was a popular style with youngsters these days. Whoever it was shuffled along behind the others like a piece of driftwood caught in their collective wake. This image was strengthened by the slight bobbing motion. It was very subtle but noticeable in contrast with the others in the group. Another odd thing was the hands, just visible below the coat's sleeve cuffs. They were graceful, slender, fingers that were out of place attached to such a wide frame.

"Wagger," Shor muttered, turning to find his buggy.

It took three attempts to get the vehicle started, which was good considering the age of the thing, but he did not care. He liked the thought that it was *his* buggy that was falling apart.

The road was empty as he pulled out and turned right, passing the Maintenance building where Lars was probably still trying to out-stare his new friend. He came to the group of yachts waiting to cross the road. He looked for the shoulder-charging driftwood at the back but he was gone.

"Wagger," Shor repeated, returning the polite nods of the group as they wafted past.

With the last one safely across, the buggy gunned its little engine and set off towards the Space Sector.

"Tell me more about my family. Tell me about Rochelle."

Shor floated on the comfortable chair, his body suspended on what felt like a cool cushion of air. He shifted his weight and the seat seemed to caress him into his new position. He could indeed, he thought, grow old and die in that chair.

"I do not have her full history, but I can tell you what I do know."

Jay's face, smiling pleasantly out at him from the wall, shrank to one side to allow room for a photograph of the woman who, if what this computer was telling him was true, had once been his wife.

It was not the best picture he had ever seen. The colours were washed out and the texture grainy. The subject had the expression of someone caught off-guard, but it only added to the charm. Her eyes were looking directly at him, into him, through him. He had never seen this woman before in his life, but she stirred emotions in him strong enough to make his chest ache.

"I have these memories. This is the first time I've seen this picture, but I *remember* it."

"You were an infant when we arrived on this planet. It is possible that your young brain was unable to rationalize the memories from your previous life and so filed them away in your subconscious. Seeing an image from your past may be triggering a memory response that conflicts with your conscious mind."

"I guess that would explain it. How long were we married?"

"Nineteen years, two months and thirteen days, if my data are correct."

Shor nodded gravely. "No offence Jay, but you talk strangely for a computer."

"None taken."

"In fact, sometimes you sound almost…human."

"I was designed to mimic human behaviour. And I am able to learn, which enables me to perfect my skills. I was the first with this capability."

"And you can't lie, is that right?"

Jay paused for a brief moment. "Not intentionally, no. We had a long discussion about this. You explained it to me. Fortunately I am able to learn."

"So you said." In his mind, Shor saw the bot wedged under the park bench. "Were we happy? I mean me and Rochelle. I know it's a weird question, but did I ever mention, if we were, you know, a happy couple?"

"From what you told me, I believe that, yes, you were happy."

"We loved each other?"

Jay's face melted into a smile. "Very much so. The regret you showed for your wife and children helped me to understand the meaning of love."

"Regret?"

"At having left them."

Shor gazed at the photograph. The memories were piling up like floodwaters pressing against the door to his mind, seeping through the gaps, pressing against the flimsy hinges. "If I loved them so much then why did I leave them?"

"You said it was something you had to do. Unfortunately, it made you very unhappy later, after the accident."

"Their aeroplane went down while they were on their way to be with me, right?"

"Yes, that is correct."

"Then it was my fault they were killed."

Jay's face became concerned. "No, it was not your fault. The plane malfunctioned. I have newspaper footage of the crash. It was an accident—"

"You said *newspaper*."

"Yes."

"What's a newspaper?"

"Whenever something important happened, it would be recorded in a document called a newspaper that people could then purchase."

"Show me. I want to see what the newspaper said about the crash."

Jay hesitated. "Are you sure that is a wise? It may trigger bad memories. These events are buried in your subconscious. We do not know what will happen if they are brought back out. The last time you saw these articles, it made you very depressed."

Shor sighed. The airlock door inside his head was now bulging under the pressure. The screws were barely holding on. "Listen. I know you mean well, but I want to know. I *need* to know. I have these dreams. Every night I live this other life I don't remember having. I see things I don't remember seeing. I hear things that are impossible for me to have heard. I know what seagulls sound like even though there is no recording of a seagull in any of the archives. We know what they look like, but not how they sound."

The *scraw-scraw* of seagulls against the background of breaking waves filled the ship.

Shor's knees started to tremble. He sat down, almost falling into the chair.

"There. I knew it! People always said I was stupid for thinking they sounded like that. They said birds whistle, or sing, but I knew what they sounded like. When I wake up from my dreams of walks on the beach and laughing children, and seagulls making that noise, I don't feel happy or contented. I feel sad. I feel as if there's something missing deep inside. The doctors told me I have a melancholic personality. They told me it's all right to be a little bit sad inside, but this is something else and I can't explain it. I feel empty, right here." He placed his hand against his chest. "Now, please, show me the newspaper."

The image of Rochelle slid to the side, below Jay's concerned face. The screen filled with a newspaper article announcing the loss of flight six-one along with everyone on board. The picture was of a hillside strewn with what looked like pieces of paper of various sizes. As Shor examined the picture he realized this was not paper but parts of a vehicle. Dotted among the debris were torn, jagged sections of something that may once have been cylindrical. And there were other objects, things that looked familiar but which he could not identify.

Jay showed him more articles. Each described the scene slightly differently, but the core of the message was the same. Due to a mechanical fault the aircraft had dumped its fuel and crashed into a hillside. One hundred and eighty-four people died instantly. Some articles showed images of the deceased crew members. They looked so happy and full of life, just like the photographs of Rochelle and Tim and Mark.

His eyes hovered on the word *instantly*. He wondered how it was possible to know this.

"This is all I have on record," Jay said. His face looked like a caricature of a concerned parent, just bordering on comical. "Are you all right?"

Shor stared at the screen. The pieces were so small. How was it possible for them to be so *small*? He clenched his fists.

"I don't know. You tell me, Jay. After all, you seem to know more about me than I do."

"I don't understand—"

"Seems I made plenty of mistakes in my past life. How about you, Jay? Have you ever made a mistake? You ever blow a fuse, or overheated?"

"No."

The face on the screen was earnest and confused. It looked like the face of a young child trying to persuade an adult that someone else had drawn on the walls.

"What about viruses? You ever get infected? Ever get hacked?"

"No, my system is very secure."

160

"What about that thing on the way back from Alpha Centauri? Didn't you say you had to shut yourself down to stop it causing damage?"

Jay's face flowed through a series of emotions. It settled on what looked like sorrow. "It was an alien entity. I had no means of combating it. I had to reconfigure my firewalls just to keep it under control. I had to study it. Fortunately, I am able to learn—"

"So you were hacked."

"Technically, yes, I suppose I was."

"And what about the entity that did the hacking? What do you suppose happened to it?"

"I managed to isolate it. It is under control."

"What would happen if it broke into your system again?"

Jay's face became an oil-painting of concern. "I have one or two theories but, to be honest, I do not know."

Shor studied Jay's frowning avatar for a moment and then pushed himself out of the chair.

"I have to go."

"So soon? I was hoping we could talk some more."

"Maybe next time." Shor glanced at his chatband. He still had enough time to make it back to the depot before it closed. He wondered if Lars had managed to stare the bot into submission.

"Perhaps then you will let me tell you my joke?" Jay said.

Shor paused at the door and turned to look at Jay's wide-eyed face. They were the eyes of a child who has just been told his favourite toy is broken. The anger he had felt a moment earlier subsided.

"Sure, Jay. Next time you can tell me your joke."

Standing outside the ship, Shor closed his eyes and took a deep breath. He crossed the hangar and waved his ID at the airlock. The door swished open and he stepped through. The mechanism had developed a squeak, which happened sometimes on new equipment, and he made a mental note to book a maintenance check. A drop of oil would fix the sound which, now he thought about it, sounded a little like the cry of a seagull.

At least he knew he wasn't going mad. He *had* heard that sound before. He had actually lived on Earth. He had walked along the shore, breathing the air and listening to the sound of the waves crashing while the seagulls made their ugly scraw-scraw sound. He had walked with *her*, not Mel after all, talking and laughing and enjoying the feel of sand between his toes. He lifted his hands and touched one against the other, imagining her skin against his. He closed his eyes, and *remembered*…

He was pulled out of his daydream by the gentle squeeze of his chatband. He read the message. It was from Reet. It said simply: "Return to depot. Urgent."

Behind him, in the dark hangar, the ship's door was sliding shut. It looked like a big eye winking mischievously at him. He wondered if Jay was watching. No doubt he would be. And the entity? Was it watching as well? Was it watching and waiting. And if it was waiting, what was it waiting for? He thought of the bot going crazy under the park bench, and the stranger, watching. Waiting.

The outer door opened, and his chatband squeezed again.

What, he thought, could possibly be so urgent back at Maintenance?

There were three badgemobiles and a hospital buggy parked in front of the depot when Shor arrived. He skirted around them and turned into the parking lot, which was almost full. Lars's buggy was there, along with those of the other senior crew members.

A badge stopped him at the front door, demanding to see his ID before letting him inside.

The workshop was full of emergency personnel with all attention centred around the psycho bot they had bought in earlier. When he had left that afternoon it had been hanging from the ceiling. Now it was on the floor, the chains attached but hanging loose. It was not completely level but tilted up at the far corner as if lying on something. Shor tried to get a better look but there were too many people in the way.

Reet and Bek were standing in the kitchen, along with a round-faced man who looked vaguely familiar. Bek looked paler than usual and Reet's eyes were red and swollen. They both looked grim.

"What's going on?" Shor asked. "The message said it was urgent. Where's Lars? Is he here?"

Nobody answered but they all continued to watch the activity in the workshop.

Shor followed their line of sight. It was then that he caught a glimpse of something on the floor behind the bot. There was too much activity to be sure, but it looked like a bloodied hand lying palm up.

"What's happened?" He felt his voice rising. "Has someone been hurt?"

Reet dropped his head and turned away to take a seat at the small kitchen table. Bek stared straight ahead, his jaw set.

"Where's Lars? Is Lars all right?"

"Are you Shor?" a voice asked. He turned to see a badge looking down at him. He was tall by Utopian standards, but he had a slight stoop that had the curious effect of both accentuating and reducing his height, depending how you looked at him. Deep-set eyes that had seen the wrong side of midnight way too often latched onto Shor with an intensity he found unsettling.

"Yes. That's me. What's going on?"

"My name is Boole. It seems there has been an accident. We need to know what happened here this morning. According to the work roster, you were here with Lars Fline until approximately one p.m. Is that correct?"

"Who is that?" Shor felt his voice turning shrill. One or two emergency personnel turned to look at him. "Is that Lars under there?"

"We honestly don't know who it is. The ID was destroyed."

"What about fingerprints?"

"We can't get a reading. The injuries are too severe. We'll do a blood sample, but it will take a couple of hours. We've sent messages to all Maintenance staff. Almost everyone has called in, except Lars, and three others. Did you leave here at one p.m. today?"

"Yes."

"Exactly?"

"Maybe. I don't know."

"And you went to the Space Sector?"

"Yes."

"Why?"

Shor watched someone swipe a cylindrical device across the blood-soaked palm. It did not look like Lars's hand, but then he could not remember what Lars' hand looked like. It just wasn't one of those things you notice. "I had to check on a door. We fixed it last month. It's standard procedure."

"Does it normally take four hours?"

Shor turned to face the big man. Steely eyes burrowed into him, like they were trying to get inside his head. Shor held his gaze for a few seconds before blinking and looking away. "It needed oil. I had to dismantle the whole door to get inside."

"Did you have any contact with Mister Fline after you left here for the Space Sector?"

"No."

The badge grunted. "And what about the bot?"

"What about it?"

"You brought it back here for repairs. The access hatch was open. The hoist is lowered but all the chains are still attached. Presumably you were examining it to see why it malfunctioned this morning."

Shor glanced across to the computer where Lars had connected the motherboard. It was gone.

"We took the motherboard out. Or *I* took the motherboard out, at the park. It was on the desk. I don't understand how the bot can do this without the motherboard."

"The motherboard was in the bot," Boole said.

"But I don't—"

"What did you find?"

"I don't—"

"When you examined the bot, what did you find?"

"Lars discovered a software problem. We called Robotics to come and pick it up. We only do hardware. Software is too advanced for us. We have to send it across to Robotics for that sort of thing."

Boole nodded towards the round-faced man standing behind Bek and Reet. "Yes, Cobb was the one who discovered the body. Do you know Cobb?"

Shor suddenly recognised Cobb from his avatar. He shook his head. "I've spoken to him a couple of times, but we've never met in person."

"Cobb seems to think this bot was hacked. What do *you* think?"

Shor shifted his weight under Boole's relentless stare. "I don't know. We don't do software here. We only do hardware. Robotics does that sort of thing."

"So you said." He stared at Shor for what felt like an age. "Well, I think that's all for now. If you remember anything, no matter how insignificant, give me a call." Boole lifted his chatband and Shor did the same. With a sweep of the arm, contacts were exchanged. "And if you hear from Lars Fline—"

"Yes," Shor said. "Of course. I'll let you know."

Boole nodded and Shor joined the others in the kitchen while the emergency personnel went about their grim tasks of gathering data and clearing the scene. Cobb offered his hand.

"You look different on the chatband," Shor said. Cobb's hand was clammy but the grip firm.

Cobb shrugged. "Yeah, I know. So do you think that's Lars?" He nodded towards the bloody hand.

"It ain't him," Reet said. "I just know it. Lars is too smart for a dumb machine. No way he'd let a critter get the better of him. If I know Lars, he's off somewhere having a good old time, oblivious to all of this."

Shor watched as the bot was hoisted off the ground, revealing the victim, or what was left of him. It took a moment for his brain to make sense of the mangled mess of clothes and skin soaking in a pool of blood.

"Oh man," Bek hissed.

"Poor guy," Reet said.

Shor had to look away. He heard a retch and saw Cobb staggering, pale-faced, towards the bathroom.

"I thought critters were programmed not to hurt people," Shor said, trying not to listen to the heavy drip-drip-drip sound coming from the underside of the killer machine.

"That's the idea," Reet said in a thin voice. "But they ain't smart. They just follow their programs. It's not like they can decide what's right and what's wrong. If their program tells them to clean a stain, then that's what they'll do. If it tells them to run someone down, they don't know the difference."

"But I thought it was built-in. I thought the commands to protect people were hard-coded."

"They are," Cobb said, appearing at the bathroom door. His face was drained of colour. He kept his eyes fixed on the floor as he talked. "The code telling them not to hurt people is on a special chip, and we can't access it."

"Well, somebody did," Reet said.

Cobb shook his head, then closed his eyes as if he regretted doing it. "No. Once that chip is on the motherboard, the only way to upgrade it is by replacing it. We can't program it. It's effectively set in stone."

There was the sound of a zipper being sealed. Shor had never heard a body-bag being closed before. Sure he had heard a zipper before plenty of times, but this had a quality all of its own. It was the difference between hearing a bat striking a ball, and hearing the same bat make contact with someone's skull. It was the difference between the sound of an ordinary nail being hammered home, and a coffin nail. An image of three coffins swam up behind his eyes, not quite remembered and yet as real as day.

He felt nausea stroke its clammy hand across his throat.

They watched in silence as the victim was carried away, now little more than a dead weight in a plastic bag. Within two minutes the last of the emergency personnel were leaving the building.

Boole remained behind long enough to sign the bot over to Cobb. "I expect a report within two days," he said. "We need to catch whoever did this before he commits another murder." On the way out, he lifted his chatband to Shor in the universally understood "call me" gesture.

Shor nodded, but doubted he ever would make use of Boole's contact information. It was as he had told the detective, he had left the depot, done a job, and returned to find someone dead in the workshop.

Boole had used the word "murder". This scared him more than anything.

Cobb took the critter, making a great effort to keep well clear of its business end. He connected a remote override and steered it through the workshop towards the door. This time it was Shor's turn to lift his chatband to say he would be expecting a call once Cobb knew anything. Cobb nodded bleakly.

"He'll turn up," Reet said as the front door closed and they were left alone. "I know he'll turn up."

"Who'll turn up?" a voice said.

They all spun around to see Lars standing in the corner, peering out from the cupboard.

Reet stood. "What the...? We thought you were dead."

"You mean you've been in there all this time?" Bek said.

"Of course. There's no way I was coming out here with all those badges swarming round. Why? What happened? And where's the critter?"

"You didn't see it?"

Lars looked between the three of them. "You fellas look like you've seen a ghost. What's going on?"

"You didn't see the accident? You didn't see the bot? It killed someone, Lars. We thought it was you."

Lars started to smile, as if waiting for the punch line to a very sick gag. "You're kidding me, right?" He looked at Shor. "Is this a joke?"

Shor shook his head and pointed to the stained floor. "No joke."

"They just took the poor wagger away," Reet said. "They tried to contact you. Our friendly neighbourhood bot did a repeat of its party trick from this morning. This time it managed to get its teeth into someone. When you didn't respond to the message, everyone assumed the worst."

"I was...busy. Hang on. You mean it *killed* someone?"

"Yes."

"And you don't know who it was?"

Bek slurped loudly on his coffee. They all turned to look at him. His normally taciturn face was showing strain. "They couldn't ID him. Or her." Bek gave a humourless laugh. "They couldn't even tell *that*. And you didn't see any of this?"

"I was waiting for Cobb. He said he'd be here in two hours so I figured there was no point hanging around. I did a little sightseeing. Besides, the motherboard was out. There's no way it did anything. I locked it away." Lars walked across to the workbench where the computer cable lay on the desk, the connector now empty. He scanned the lock and swung the door open. "Ah, snap!"

"The motherboard was inside the bot," Bek said slowly.

"I locked it in here," Lars said. "I've got the only key. I don't see how...Wait a minute. Are you accusing me of something? Because, if you are, you'd better just come out and say it."

Bek stood and rose to his full size. It was like watching a balloon inflate. He usually carried himself bent over thanks to a combination of years spent wandering through the sewers, and body language that mirrored his generally pessimistic attitude to life. Expanded to his full height and width, he was bigger than Lars. This, together with his fearsome countenance, made him scary.

Shor took an involuntary step backwards.

"I just think it's strange you were the last person to see the bot before it killed that poor wagger, and you just conveniently happened to be in the HQ. And the motherboard somehow managed to make its way out of a locked drawer for which you happen to have the only key. Don't you think it's strange?"

"Now look here Bek. You don't seriously think I had anything to do with this, do you? Come on, we've worked together for more than ten years."

Bek sneered. "Funny. I don't remember seeing you down in the sewers very much. I wouldn't call a few hours whenever you happen to feel like it *working together*."

"Sure, but have you smelled it down there? It stinks."

Shor saw the twinkle in Lars's eye but Bek was having none of it. The big man took a step forward.

"You know what stinks, Lars? This whole department stinks. It's so bad I can't breathe. I'm going out to get some fresh air."

Bek stalked across the kitchen and disappeared through the front doors, slamming them as he went.

"He didn't mean it," Reet said. "He's just upset. We're all upset."

Lars shook his head. "No, he's right. It looks pretty bad. I don't blame him for being suspicious. I don't blame any of you."

"We don't think you had anything to do with this," Reet said. "None of us do. Ain't that right, kid?"

They both looked at Shor who tried to hold Lars's gaze but blinked and looked away. "No. Of course not."

Lars sighed. It was the sigh of someone who knows the truth of a situation in spite of what he has been told. "They'll find my prints all over the bot. I was the last one here. I have the key. I expect they'll have a few questions."

He lifted his chatband and tapped the screen. "Hello? Is that Boole? Yeah, this is Lars Fline. I received an urgent message. Yeah, I know. I was busy. Right away? Sure. No problem. I'll be there in ten minutes."

The front doors opened and the first few members of the nightshift crew trickled through. From their lively chattering and the way they were looking across at the workshop, Shor guessed they had already heard the news of the day's activities.

Lars ended the call and lowered his hand. "Boole wants to see me. Apparently he has a few questions. What a surprise."

"It'll be fine," Reet said. "Just tell them the truth."

"Sure," Lars said. "Might as well get it over with." He looked at Shor. "Hold the fort while I'm gone."

Shor nodded, and watched his boss step out through the front door.

"They'll believe him, won't they?"

"I sure hope so, kid." Reet said. "I sure hope so."

That evening, Shor visited the hospital. The building was as quiet as a tomb with only the occasional metronome squeak of rubber soles on the polished floor to indicate that people actually worked there. The doctor spoke to Shor in his usual tone, explaining how his mother had shown no signs of improving and would, should this not change, be transferred to D Wing within the next two days.

"We do not have the resources for long term care," he said. "I am sorry."

Shor nodded, knowing that, of all the emotions the doctor was possibly feeling at that moment, pity was not one of them. He thought about asking the doctor exactly what those resources were needed for, considering his mother's bed was the only one in the ward currently occupied, but there was no point? The doctor was just doing his job. Everybody was just doing their job.

Father was there as usual, no longer bothering to acknowledge the presence of his son. Shor thought that his hair had become lighter in recent days. He was now almost completely grey, and he had lost weight. The cheekbones Mother had always admired as "classical" now protruded alarmingly over pale skin, making him look gaunt and frail.

Shor stayed long enough to see that the doctor had not been lying about his mother's lack of progress. He left his parents alone in their silent communion, pausing as he passed his father's hunched frame, lifting his hand to offer comfort but hesitating, remembering what Jay had told him about Rochelle. Deep inside, a memory stirred but he pushed it aside. He left the clinic quickly and headed home, making a detour past the market to collect food for the evening meal.

The streets were the usual mass of humanity and the market was packed. He collected his items and joined the queue snaking towards the back of the shop. It was then that he spotted Mel walking in. She was by herself, which was a relief. Teenage boys tended to be obnoxious but there was one particular group who were even more annoying: teenage boys with girlfriends. Shor had nothing against Vin but he knew Mel's new beau would feel obliged to assert himself over any potential competition. Survival of the fittest, the anthropology teacher had said. Our genes are in a constant battle to ensure their propagation. *We're not plants*, Napier had said defiantly, at which everyone had laughed, including the teacher. Perhaps if she had seen Vin, she would not have laughed quite so hard.

"Hey you," Mel said, waving at him from the door. He studied her as she made her way towards him, dodging shoppers and shelves with poise. She looked happier than he could ever remember. And she had changed her hair. It bounced as she moved, reflecting soft light from the window in a sort of halo effect. It had only been a short while and yet she seemed to have changed from a girl into woman in a matter of weeks. The changes were subtle, but the combined effect was powerful. The way she walked, the way she turned her head, the way she smiled.

"Hey you," he said back, trying for a casual grin as he shuffled a little to the side to make some room for her. "It's been a while."

She pecked his cheek and took his arm in hers. "I've been meaning to call you but I've been so busy. They made me assistant to the Year Head."

"That's great. I mean, this is what you wanted, isn't it?"

"It's huge. I'm the youngest they've ever had. I was worried it might take me out of the classroom, but I still get to study teaching, *and* I have a say in what we do with the kids. It's great. And what about you? How's the Maintenance team treating you?"

Inside his head he told her everything. I saw a guy jump off a roof, and a bot nearly killed someone, and a bot *actually* killed someone, and my boss may end up as a suspect for murder and get himself retired, otherwise it's all super, thanks for asking.

What came out of his mouth was: "Yeah, it's okay."

"Don't burst a blood vessel with enthusiasm," she said. "Hey, why don't we go and grab an ice-cream? My treat."

"Now?"

"Sure. Unless you're busy."

"What about Vin?"

"He's working tonight. And I don't get to spend enough time with my pal these days."

"Won't he be jealous?"

Mel gave a short laugh. "Vin? He's not the type."

Wanna bet? Shor thought, but she was smiling at him and holding his arm, and she could have asked him to pop out to the Martian surface without an out-suit right then and he would have done it. "Sure. Ice-cream it is."

He paid for his shopping and they walked the two blocks down to Reggie's where the last few clients were clustered around tables and scattered along the counter.

Shor found a booth towards the back while Mel went to fetch one chocolate and one strawberry ice-cream. He watched her chatting happily with a boy sitting at the counter who looked as though he was about to melt faster than the dessert he was eating. He wondered if she knew she had this effect on people.

"They only had strawberry," she said, returning with two plates, "but the boy at the counter gave me one of his. He's in my class."

She turned to look back at the kid, who smiled and, much to Shor's disgust, actually waved one of those cutesy finger varieties.

"That's generous. I remember him from school and I don't recall him ever being so nice."

Mel shrugged. "Maybe we never took the time to notice."

"Yes. I'm sure he's always giving away ice-cream."

She narrowed her eyes accusingly. "Are you being sarcastic Mister Larkin?"

"I was trying to be, but I'm not very good at it." He took a scoop, savouring its coolness in his mouth. He loved the texture of partially-melted ice-cream. "How's the petition going? Get any more signatures?"

"Four or five. And I had to work really hard to get those."

"You're going to keep trying? Right?"

"I don't know. I guess."

"You should. It's a good cause."

They ate in silence for a minute. Somewhere in the back of the cafe, a drum beat was picking up.

"Did you hear about the suicide?" he said.

She nodded, the spoon in her mouth. She frowned. "Yes. It was so sad. He wasn't the type. At least, he didn't seem the type."

"You knew him?"

"Not personally. He was a friend of a colleague. She was very upset, as you can imagine. She kept saying how happy he was and how much he loved his job. Nursing was what he always wanted to do."

"Then his death was a shock?"

"Very much."

Shor tilted his plate and ran his spoon through the puddle of liquid ice-cream. "I don't get it. Why would a happy guy doing his dream job jump off a building?"

Mel shrugged. "Beats me. Maybe he got some bad news."

"Did he leave any clues behind?"

"Not that I know of. His friend, my colleague, said it was a mystery. He was fine when he went to work that morning."

"Did he have a girlfriend?"

"He was married, but they didn't have any kids."

"How did she take it?"

"Not very well. From what I heard, she had to be hospitalized."

Shor pushed his clean plate away and watched Mel finish her last few bites. For as long as he had known her, she had always been the slow eater—especially when it came to ice-cream. She did not so much consume the dessert as experience it.

She finished with a flourish, sweeping the spoon around the plate and closing her eyes as she enjoyed the last morsel. She placed the spoon onto the plate and pushed it forward until it rested against his. With her elbows on the table, she regarded him with a faint smile. "You've got a spot in the corner of your lip."

He reached for his napkin, but she was quicker. She leaned across and, with the lightest of touches, dabbed his mouth with the soft cotton. It was something his mother always did. He felt himself starting to blush. She pulled back, apparently not noticing.

"So, any news about the lost guy you found wandering around up top?" she said, her chin resting on her knuckles, her eyes studying his.

In his mind the yellow-suited man stood at the window, staring across at the camera, staring *into* the camera.

"He's out of quarantine but under surveillance."

"Where are they keeping him?"

Shor paused for a moment. There had been a time when he would tell her everything and, he assumed, she him. This, however, was more than a silly bit of gossip between friends. If something sinister was going on, if the lost guy was in any way involved with the suicide, then it would be better for her—safer for her—if she knew nothing.

"I don't know. The Space Sector I guess. Or maybe they've moved him."

"Darla said she's seen him," Mel said, her eyes never leaving his. "She said she saw this guy looking at her. She had this feeling of being watched and then she looked up and this guy was standing there staring at her. At first she thought it was you, because he was about your height, but it wasn't you. She thinks she's got a stalker, but then Darla thinks every guy is in love with her."

"Where was this?"

"In the park in the Manufacturing Sector. It was just before that thing with the bot going crazy."

"Your friend was there?"

"She didn't see the bot. She left a few minutes before. She said she was creeped out by that guy watching her, so she left."

"How did she know it was the guy?"

"Darla likes to know what's going on, and she likes to know who everyone is and what's their business. She's the kind of person who, if she sees someone she doesn't know, she'll make a point of introducing herself and finding out everything she can. The woman is a walking contact list. So if Darla says she's never seen him around before, chances are he hasn't been around."

"Which leaves the question of where exactly he came from."

"Maybe he's from outer space," she said, lifting her eyes to the ceiling. "Maybe he's an alien."

Shor thought of Jay sitting in his spaceship. He forced a laugh. "The guys in Maintenance thinks maybe he's from Earth."

"Interesting, but why would anyone from Earth come here after so many years and not send a message first?"

"Maybe he was lonely."

She punched his shoulder. "Yeah, right. Of course, there could be a much simpler solution. He could be a clone. I've heard they're doing work in this field in case something goes wrong and they need to repopulate."

"That's a bit grim isn't it?"

"I suppose so, but look what happened to Earth. They managed to mess up the whole planet. How much easier would it be to do the same here? And the way that bot went crazy. What if it had happened in the life support area? Imagine how much damage it might have done."

You don't want to know, he thought.

"Sure. So he's a clone. What was he doing walking around outside?"

She sat back. Her face was serious but her eyes had a mischievous glint. "Perhaps it was a test. Perhaps they wanted to see if he could survive outside. Perhaps they're creating a new species of human able to live in the Martian atmosphere."

"Hmm. That's plausible. Then why the suit?"

"It wasn't a functioning suit. They just made him wear it to avoid arousing suspicion should someone bump into him. Like you, for example."

"You know," Shor said. "You just may be onto something there. Although personally I think he was sent from Earth to tell us it's safe for us to go back, or possibly that it isn't safe and we should stop sending them messages and just enjoy life on Mars."

"That's funny, because one of the set books for school this year is *War of the Worlds* by H. G. Wells and he said the chances of life on Mars are a million to one."

"Actually, he said the chances of anything *manlike* on Mars are a million to one. Say, that's irony isn't it?"

"The *manlike* bit?"

Shor snorted a laugh. An image of Vin wrapping his tendrils around Mel came to mind. "No, the whole thing is ironic, if you think about it. A set book on Mars saying there can't possibly be life on Mars."

Outside, the traffic was moving. The walkway was emptying a little as people made their way home. A cleaning bot was busy on the road outside the cafe door, working away at something on the floor. It was facing the cafe and seemed to be looking in. More than that, it appeared to be looking at *him*.

"Are you all right?" Mel asked.

"Uh...no, I mean yes. I was just thinking."

"Well, be careful. I can see the wheels turning but I think you forgot to put it in gear."

He smiled, but struggled to shake the feeling that the critter was watching him. It wasn't looking down, or scanning for the next job as was usual. It was focused straight ahead through the door, down the aisle, directly to where he was sitting. People were stepping around and over it. Someone made solid contact with their foot but it just kept scratching away with its cleaning blade.

Then he noticed a couple standing on the other side of the road, talking in the intimate way lovers do. It was hard for him to see but, from their clothes, they looked like a young boy and girl. She was taller, which meant he must be the younger of the two, but he didn't look younger. From this distance he looked old enough to be her father with the solid features of a mature man. He was leaning close, speaking into her ear as if sharing a secret. She was standing with her head turned slightly so her ear was facing his mouth. From what Shor could see, he was doing all the talking while the girl just listened.

Then the girl lifted her face and Shor realized that he knew her. It was Izzy. Young Izzy Parrow, from the apartment block. They had gone to the same school, although she had been three years below him. They had spoken a few times but never become more than nodding acquaintances.

"Hey, listen," Mel said. "It's getting late. We should head home."

"Um, yes," he replied. "You're right."

"It was great to see you again."

"Yes, you too."

"We should do this again."

"I'd like that."

"Don't forget your shopping."

"Ah yes, thanks." Shor bent to retrieve his supplies. When he looked up again Izzy and her friend had gone. He scanned the thinning crowd but they had vanished. The bot was still there, watching him.

"You look distracted," Mel said. "You sure you're all right?"

Just a touch of paranoia, he thought.

"I'm fine, " he said. "Work worries. You know."

They made their way to the door. She touched his arm.

"Call me," she said. And then she was gone, carried away on the waning tide of humanity.

Shor stood, watching her as she sailed away.

"Excuse me," a voice said impatiently. He turned to see the cutesy finger-waving boy from the counter standing there waiting with his arms folded. So much for the friendly act. "We're closing soon. You should go."

"Sure," Shor said, standing to leave.

He joined the flow, making sure to steer a wide berth around the bot, although he did not so much sail along as crash through wave after wave.

He glanced back at the bot and saw it was working the same spot, but its eyes followed him as he walked away. At the door to his apartment building he looked back. The bot was still there, still cleaning, still watching him.

He stepped inside and caught the elevator up to his apartment. Closing the door behind him, he pulled twice to make sure it was secure.

37

"You married Rochelle after leaving the Air Force. You lived in the suburbs and worked as an insurance salesman for a number of years. They terminated your employment which led to you applying for a job on the other side of the country. You promised to be reunited with your family within a year. It took two years but you did eventually arrange to be together. You built a house for them."

Shor sat in his comfortable chair, letting the words roll over him. He understood most of what Jay was saying, but the questions were piling up like dust in a storm gutter.

"I read about the Air Force in Earth history. Did I fly aeroplanes?"

"Yes."

"Then why did I leave? I though that was what I wanted to do."

"You hurt your shoulder playing a game called football."

"I played games in the Air Force?"

"Yes, but not full time."

"Now I'm confused. Why would I play games while in the Air Force?"

"There are many careers in the Air Force, not just flying aeroplanes or, as most people say, planes."

"Have you got any videos of aeroplanes...planes?"

"Certainly." A clip of a jet appeared on the screen.

"I've seen pictures but never actually watched one fly." Shor stared at the craft drifting across a cloudless blue sky. He imagined himself behind the controls as he soared through the air. But then, if Jay was right, he had once done just that. He had flown a plane—possibly even this exact one. "So I left a perfect job and then I left that to find another job somewhere else? This was before I met Rochelle, right?"

"You met Rochelle at school, but you lost touch when you joined the Air Force. You left the Air Force because you were not allowed to fly anymore."

"Makes sense I guess. And then I met Rochelle again later?"

"Yes."

"And we got married?"

"Yes."

"Then I left *again*?"

"Yes. You felt it was the right thing to do. You wanted to provide for your family. You believed it was your duty as a man."

"I did a lot of leaving, didn't I?"

"I suppose you could see it that way."

Shor watched as the plane passed a cloud. He must have had a good reason for leaving them behind. He must have had a *purpose*. On Mars, it was impossible to leave because there was nowhere to go, unless you counted his secret place of course, but that was just somewhere he went to help him think when things got too much. It wasn't really leaving. And it certainly wasn't leaving to find work through some loyalty to his family. On Mars everybody worked. There was no sense of duty to the family unit beyond ensuring the survival of the colony. "Was this normal? On Earth I mean?"

"At one time the male was considered the head of the family, and the provider. The man would go out and work while the woman stayed home to look after the house and raise the children."

Shor laughed. "I can't imagine Mel doing that."

"Mel is your wife?"

Shor coughed. "No way. We're just friends."

"I see. Well, towards the end, men and women shared the responsibility for providing. It became common for both the husband and wife to work."

"Sounds normal to me."

"Yes, but it did have an undesirable side-effect. Men no longer felt the need to care for their wives, and women no longer needed the support of their husbands. The traditional family unit came to an end. This was acceptable to most adults, but it had deep consequences on the children and society as a whole."

"How come you know so much about humans? You're just a computer, right? I mean, you're not some cloning experiment gone horribly wrong are you?"

"I am a computer but, then again, is not the human brain also just a computer?"

"I guess so, it's only I've never met anything—sorry, any*one*—like you before. You make the average critter look as smart as a learning-deficient lamp post."

"What is a critter?"

"It's a bot. A robot."

"Interesting." On the screen, Jay's face smiled. But, Shor thought, it was more than a smile. There was a hint of pride in there as well.

"Tell me more about my work as an astronaut. Tell me about the others—the people I worked with. What were my colleagues like?"

"You had no colleagues. One of the reasons you were selected was because of your capacity for working alone. Indeed, it was the main reason you were selected."

Shor's mind showed him a brief image of his secret place where he went to be alone. "There must've been someone else on the team. I mean, who built the ship? Who trained me?"

"You had contact with a limited number of people." A mosaic of a dozen faces floated into focus on the screen. One in the centre was larger than the others. "The team leader was Tom Billard."

Shor examined each face closely. He tried to remember, but none of them looked familiar. They all carried the tired but exhilarated expression of people doing hard work that meant something. If anything, the big face in the middle, Tom Billard, reminded him a little of the old man Harl Benson, but then that was probably just because they both had grey—almost white—hair, and glasses perched on the ends of their noses.

"What about other astronauts?"

"There were others on standby, in case you were unable to complete the mission, but you never had contact with them."

More faces joined the mosaic. Two men and two women. Shor noticed something in their eyes, or rather he noticed the lack of something. There was no fire, no spark, no life.

"I have to tell you I'm glad I never had contact with any of them. They look like someone's just stolen their water tokens. You're saying these people never actually flew?"

"That is correct."

"I was the only one sent into space?"

"Yes, as far as I am aware."

Shor peered at the faces of the other would-be astronauts. They all looked to be carrying some terrible sadness.

"What happened to them?"

"I do not know. Their contracts specified a generous compensation package upon termination. I imagine they retired."

"Retired?" Shor said, sitting upright. "How is that a generous compensation package?"

"It means they would never have to work again. I gather from the tone of your voice and body language that retirement means something different here. Does it not mean you stop working?"

"You could say that. Let's just say people who retire here never have to worry about work anymore. Retiring here is what happens when you *can't* work. They take you to D Wing, and they…" Shor thought of his mother lying in her hospital bed. "They give you an injection and you go to sleep, forever."

Jay's face became sad. "I am sorry. I was not aware. Death is a difficult subject for humans. "

"Yeah, well, you get used to it."

"So what do you call it here when you stop working?"

"I don't understand. Why would you stop working?"

"On Earth, it is common for people to stop working at a certain age."

Shor shook his head. "No such thing here I'm afraid. Mars can't afford to have people who can't work. Everyone gets a Value Ratio they're expected to maintain. It's basically how much power they think you'll consume during your life, balanced against the total power output of the city. We never stop working. Lars reckons it's just about control."

"Lars?"

"He's my boss. I wanted to work in the Space Sector, but they decided I would be better fixing lamps and signs and bots. My school grades were fine, but they still wouldn't let me into the Space Program, or any of my chosen careers."

"From what you have told me, life on Mars is different from life on Earth in many ways, but similar in others. I would like to learn more about your culture."

"Can't you just log into the system or something?"

"I am afraid my presence on your system would be noticed."

"So?"

"So I think it would be better if I remained anonymous for now. I took a chance by accessing your details when I did and it did indeed set off an alarm."

"They're going to notice sooner or later. You might as well let them know you're here. I mean, you know a lot of stuff. You could help us learn more about the Earth. Harl would be happier than a bot in a bucket of oil."

"I would prefer to remain anonymous for now," Jay said. "And if I were to interface with the Martian computer network, it would be akin to the proverbial bull doing some shopping in the proverbial china shop. I need a recognized identity."

"You really do talk funny for a computer."

"Thank you."

"It wasn't a compliment."

"Oh."

"Can't you just use the same temp ID you used to call me?"

"When I located you on the network, I was stopped from accessing many areas. It is indeed just a temporary ID. Access appears to be very limited."

"You can borrow mine. I can get into all the library archives. You'd learn a lot."

"That is an excellent idea. I could use your algorithm."

"Only thing is, chatbands don't work if we take them off. They're linked to a chip they implant at birth. And if we leave the chatband off for too long, or get separated from it, alarms start going off." Shor removed the strap and lifted his wrist to show Jay a red lump about the size of a grain of rice.

"That is not a problem. All I need is access to your chip for a moment."

Shor replaced his chatband and it immediately started squeezing his wrist. It was Jay's temp ID.

"Hello Jay. How are you? I'm glad you called."

"I am not—" Jay started to say. On the screen, his face became perplexed, then it cleared like the dust after a storm. "Ah, I see, you are pretending that I have actually called you for social interaction."

"I thought you said you understood humour."

"I thought I did, but I am still learning the nuances. The border between humour and ignorance is very fragile. You were pretending to be ignorant, but were actually making a joke. One has to be careful in such situations."

"Right. So, how much time do you need?"

"I am finished."

"What? Already?"

"I have read every article in your library, and accessed every piece of audio and visual media."

"You mustn't do that, Jay. They monitor everything. If you shift that much data around, they'll know about it."

Shor took an instinctive glance over his shoulder, half expecting to see a badge standing in the doorway.

"I am aware of this," Jay said. "Do not worry. I used an advanced scatter algorithm. It will take them years to figure out what happened to the data."

"Fine," Shor said. "But still, the library's huge. I was at school for ten years and hardly scratched the surface. Mister Edmunds has been there forever and he once told us he would need another two lifetimes to read everything."

"My processor works substantially faster than the human brain. Normally I only use a tiny fraction of my cycles to communicate effectively with you. Normally I—"

"That's strange," Shor interrupted.

"What is strange?"

"I just had the most overpowering sense of déjà vu. When you were talking just now, I remembered you saying the same thing before."

"Yes, we have had almost the exact same conversation."

"Does that happen a lot? I mean, do I repeat things I said, you know, before?"

"Not particularly. Sometimes we have similar conversations, but not exac—"

Jay fell silent, his normally animated face staring out of the screen, frozen in time, as if someone had pressed the pause button.

"Jay? You all right there, buddy? Jay?"

Jay's face shifted off-focus, becoming momentarily blurred. His mouth melted slowly back into place as his facial muscles relaxed and his expression faded. His eyes focused on Shor's with a look of grim determination. When he spoke again, it was in a slow, measured tone.

"He is here. He is looking for you."

Shor stared at Jay's blank face. It was an honest, open face, without a hint of malice. Then, just as quickly as it had frozen, it became animated again.

"Jay, buddy, this is a little bit creepy. Who's here?"

"I don't know," Jay said. "I was just told to give you this message."

"Told? Who told you? Because I've been hearing a message like that for months. I thought it was my imagination, or maybe I was losing my mind. Who told you to tell me that?"

As Jay looked out from the screen, a new expression tweaked the virtual muscles of his pixelated computer face. The faintest of smiles tugged at the corner of his mouth while his cheeks lifted almost imperceptibly and his eyes sparkled from between creased eyelids. The words were heavy with emotion, but it was more than just pride, or happiness, or even joy. It was adoration.

"God did."

Shor left Jay and returned to the real world where real people did real things like eating, sleeping, going to the shops and working.

Sometimes after speaking to Jay he had the sense of waking from a dream. Sitting in that chair in that ship, listening to a computer tell him about his life before, it was easy to forget he had another, actual life going on in the real world.

And now God had come into the picture. Or rather, Jay had brought God into the picture. Assuming of course it was God. Shor was not sure he trusted Jay. There was a hacker on the loose and Jay was behaving more than a little strangely, even for a learning-capable computer, whatever normal behaviour for such a thing was supposed to look like.

It occurred to Shor that Jay's mysterious "entity" was a virus of some sort. Perhaps a belief in God was what happened when a smart computer caught a virus. Maybe they got religion. All he knew was that the secrets to his past lay inside that ship. The Comet was his key to the past and possibly his future. More than that, it could tell him who he was. Perhaps it could even tell him *why* he was.

The buggy sputtered as it pulled away from the hangar, the little electric engine clearing its throat with an almost apologetic cough. It was lunchtime already and he was hungry. In fifteen minutes the markets would be full.

God did.

Shor sighed. His life had taken some sharp turns of late but this was ridiculous. Not only did he have to deal with being an alien from another planet reincarnated through some freak scientific accident. Not only did he have to cope with being so socially inept that he had no real friends. Not only did he have to handle seeing the girl of his dreams running off with a vegetable. Now he had to deal with weird mystical messages from a hacked computer.

The walker up top had arrived at almost exactly the same time as the first bot malfunctioned. Coincidence? Maybe but then, maybe not. Shor thought about the bot going hoho in the park. The walker had been watching, like it was a trap and he wanted to see what was going to happen next. He had set the bait at the back of the cage and was standing there, waiting for his prey to step inside.

Then something occurred to Shor that chilled him to the core. What if Jay was just a trap? What if Jay was the bait and the ship was the cage? It made perfect sense. The walker—he was almost certainly the hacker—might be using Jay as a trap. He might be using Jay to deliver messages from "God" to mess with his mind and confuse him. And for a computer, a hacker would almost certainly seem god-like.

The buggy grumbled as it ventured uneasily around the corner towards the main intersection of the Space Sector. It was on autopilot as usual, its little brain following the buried power lines with the singular concentration of a machine built for that very purpose. Shor leaned back, watching the view. Everything was in motion. Everything was going somewhere. Everything was doing what it had been designed to do. Even he was on the move, hunting down the nutrients that would allow him to live and breathe and do whatever it was he was supposed to be doing.

Fixing lamps and signs and critters, apparently.

That was his purpose. That was his reason for living. When a lamp broke, his job was to fix it. But why? What was so important about a lamp? Would the world end if he decided not to fix the lamp? Would Utopia cease to exist if the lamp never shone again? Ridiculous, he knew. One lamp did not make a difference, but if all the lamps went dead, that was a whole different sack of soya. If Utopia was plunged into darkness, chaos would ensue, this much was certain.

He was, it seemed, only a gear, but now he had a new purpose that went beyond fixing lamps and critters. The ship was his purpose. He had to protect his ship. He had to protect Jay.

Another cough and the buggy turned up the main road towards the airlock. Off to the right was the building where the man had jumped so calmly to his death while the creep in the yellow suit—the visitor from nowhere—had watched with such indifference.

At the airlock, the first people in the queue were filing through. He pulled up behind the last vehicle and waited. A few second later he was moving. Buggies edged forward. Badges checked IDs. Shor nodded politely. The gears turned.

He passed the depot and continued on to the market. He was five minutes early so was able to collect his lunch without the usual hassle of dodging and diving around people. He stood at the counter and waited for the three customers in front to be served.

Just then a hand fell on his shoulder. He nearly dropped his lunch. He turned to see a familiar face.

"Harl. You scared me. You shouldn't sneak up on people."

The old man smiled. "Perhaps I should wear louder shoes. Join me for lunch?"

The queue shifted and Shor paid for his soup and bread. Harl paid for his own lunch and they walked out into the street already filling with fellow hunters.

The park was still quiet which meant they were able to secure one of the more isolated benches a little away from the market.

"How have you been?" Harl asked. "I've been wanting to stop by for a visit since our last meeting, but things have been hectic."

"I'm fine," Shor said. "As good as can be expected."

Harl nodded. "I must say you've handled it well. It's not every day you find out you were born on another planet."

Shor peeled open the lid of his soup. The smell was a familiar one. He wondered if soup smelled the same on Earth. But then, why wouldn't it? Soup was soup. "You did me a favour telling me. Suddenly everything makes sense. I've never felt as though I fit in. Now I know why. I did some research. Did you know I am the average height on Earth? If we went back I would be the able to run around without falling all over myself."

"Do you want to go back?"

"Sure. It's what we've all been waiting for. Doesn't everyone want to go back home?"

Harl sipped his soup. A few droplets remained on his whiskers. "Not everyone, no."

Shor thought of Napier's outburst in Mister Edmunds' class. Napier was a wagger, but he wasn't stupid.

"Perhaps they're scared. This is where they were born. This is all they know. As much as I want to go back, Earth does look like a scary place sometimes. I know life here is precarious, but at least it's familiar. Why are you asking this?"

"No reason. I guess I just can't imagine what you're going through."

"I'm fine," Shor said.

"I heard Lars is being held for questioning over the accident with the cleaning bot."

"News travels quickly. Yes, he turned himself in. Said it would be better to get the air cleared sooner rather than later."

"Very wise," Harl said. "The badges get suspicious if you're not completely open. Boole's a good man. He'll treat Lars fairly. And how's your mother? Any progress?"

Shor stared into his cup. His reflection shimmered in the dark liquid. "They're moving her to D Wing tomorrow."

"I'm sorry."

"The doctors know best, I suppose."

"They have a tough job. They have to make sure the colony stays healthy with limited resources. Sometimes they have to make difficult decisions."

Shor felt a stab of grief plunge into his chest. "I know, but she looks so *normal*, you know? I keep expecting her to wake up and smile at me."

"And your father. How is he coping?"

Shor remembered the images Jay had shown him of his own family. His wife and children. The crash with the debris scattered across the ground.

"He isn't."

The park was filling up. Most of the benches were taken and people were standing in small clusters, chatting, laughing, occasionally throwing a glance their way. A bot was snooping for something to clean, weaving between legs, its nose to the ground. Shor found himself following it with his eyes.

"I went to school with your father," Harl said. "Did you know that?"

Shor shook his head. "No, I didn't."

"Yes, we were in the same class. He was always popular with the girls. Your mother was in the year above. They married as soon as he graduated. She was a real beauty, your mother. Sadly, we were just friends. She was in love with your father."

Shor could see the old man's grey eyes glistening.

"My parents never spoke much about their younger days."

"We were part of a group of six. We hung out together all the time. Reggie's was our haunt, back before it was even called Reggie's. Do they still do the drumming thing?"

Shor nodded. "They do."

"We started that, did you know? The music system broke down for a week so we started making our own music. Sometimes we did it even when there *was* music. And you thought I was just a crumbly old man. That's the problem with life. You can't escape getting old. When you're young you think you'll live forever. Next thing you know, your hair starts falling out and you get liver spots. They tell you they've mastered the genetic code and know what makes us tick, but they have no idea how to stop us growing old. They've tried but they always end up breaking the clock while trying to fix it. It's almost as if we're designed to break eventually."

"Can I ask you a question?" Shor asked.

"Sure. That's one of the few things I'm still good for."

"Do you believe in God?"

"God? Hah! Now there's a question and three quarters. They still teach historical religion at school, don't they?"

"Yes. They said God is a myth created by superstitious humans to explain the unknown."

"Yep, that sounds about the same as they were teaching while I was at school."

"Do you believe he exists?"

"God? I'm a scientist. Scientists don't believe in God."

"Why not?"

"Because he makes it too easy. The aim of science is to find out how the universe works. God makes it all one big magic trick. We don't understand something so we say 'God did it' then before you know it, we're not studying science anymore."

"What if he did do it?"

Harl took a deep breath. Shor heard a faint wheezing sound. "Listen, son. Nobody believes in a divine creator. The official line is we evolved over billions of years from nothing. And it makes sense. Look around you. The universe is a dirty mess on the verge of chaos. Do you know how we've survived so long out here on this barren rock? We've survived because science made it possible. If we responded to every problem by praying, we'd all be dead by now."

"But what about those things science can't explain?"

"That's a pretty small list, and it's getting shorter every day. One day, science will have all the answers."

"I guess so," Shor said, sipping at his soup, one eye on the bot that had located something to clean and was hard at work with a mouth full of what Shor could now only think of as teeth.

"Why this sudden interest in the supernatural?"

"No reason. Just curious I guess."

"Hmm. Well, the thing with the supernatural is it tends to be very woolly. If you look at any prophecies, from Nostradamus for example, they never say 'Shor Larkin will fly to another planet and become a brilliant young man working in the Maintenance Department', or something specific like that. It's always mumbo jumbo you can interpret a hundred ways. Science doesn't work like that. It studies physical evidence and then makes predictions based on hard, repeatable facts. There's no room for mumbo jumbo."

The talking in the park had become a hum of mingled voices, drowning out individual conversations. Shor saw people glance their way from time to time but it was impossible to know what they were saying. He thought of Jay's face and how it was sort of the same thing as the group noise, built up from countless individuals until it was impossible to detect a single person, somehow becoming everyone, and no-one. He wondered if Jay was how he appeared to be, or if there was something else hidden behind that façade. He turned to Harl. "What about things like love and hate and the meaning of life?"

"Just words. The problem with people is we've grown too smart for our own good. Everything has to have a meaning when we should really just let it be. You know what the meaning of life is?"

"I know," Shor said. "I did philosophy at school. The meaning of life is the meaning you give it."

"I'm glad you were paying attention."

"It was Miss Lancaster's class. I had a crush."

"Ah, the lessons not included on the curriculum. Every kid gets a crush on a teacher at some point. They should have an exam on it."

Shor chuckled. "I would've failed that one for sure."

Somewhere in the park, someone screamed. Shor looked up quickly, his eyes scanning for the source of the sound. A woman was laughing loudly while a man held her around the waist, apparently having just given her a fright. Shor looked for the bot and found it in open space searching for something else to clean. He relaxed but his heart was still racing a little.

Harl lifted his cup and drained the last of his soup.

"Listen, Shor. At some point everyone questions their existence and what it means to be alive. Some turn to religion to find answers. If you find comfort in the belief in an all-powerful God, then that's up to you, but one word of warning. The official position on religion is that you're free to believe what you like, so long as it doesn't upset the equilibrium. You can read what you want and pray to whoever you like as often as you like, just don't start preaching in the street or holding prayer meetings. And don't try to convert people. Personal belief is one thing. Organized religion is another. If they think you're getting too zealous they'll label you a cult and put you on rations before you can find a scripture to quote at them."

"I get it," Shor said. "No mumbo jumbo."

"Good. Because I'd hate to see you get into trouble."

Harl leaned a little closer when he said this. The square was getting crowded with the noise level growing disproportionately as was always the way when people collected in groups.

"I'm curious," Shor said. "Whatever happened to the guy we found wandering around up top? You said he had to go into quarantine."

"Yes, that's right."

"Did you ever find out what he was doing outside?"

Harl stared straight ahead. His grey eyes were as calm as a cleaning bot with its motherboard removed.

"He was trying out his home-made suit. Fancies himself as an inventor and wanted to prove his suit was better than the standard issue. The council wouldn't take him seriously so he snuck out and went for a hike."

Shor followed the old man's gaze to a noisy group of girls. One looked like she was doing an impression of someone else. The others watched her antics for a few seconds before bursting into howls of approving laughter. The bot trundled past them, apparently not getting the joke.

"I suppose he's in trouble?" Shor suggested.

"We're keeping him under surveillance for a while. We can't have people sneaking around outside. It's bad for morale and could put the whole colony at risk."

Gears in a machine, Shor thought. *And the machine won't work if too many of those gears get ideas.*

"What's his name?"

Harl turned to look at Shor. "Leo Drake, but he prefers to be called Leopold."

Shor wondered if Harl was being totally honest but the old man said the name without flinching, almost as if he had practiced it. Leo was a popular name in Utopia because it was the name of one of the original pioneers. Legend had it that a man called Leo Sanga had sacrificed his own life to save the colony by embarking on a two kilometre round trip with only enough oxygen for one kilometre. It was an apt choice for someone found walking around on the Martian surface in a home-made suit.

The loud girls were on the move now. They wafted towards the market, all waving arms and smiles and giggles. They dodged the bot with a series of little skips and jumps. It regarded them with its dead eyes without stopping what it was doing. Shor had a feeling the bot was watching the people in the square the way a lion might watch a herd of sheep.

"Do you think bots know what's going on?" Shor said, thinking out loud. He threw the question into the air, not really expecting a reply.

"You're full of philosophical questions today," Harl said. "I suppose every creature with a brain has some degree of consciousness, but I think you have to be self-aware to really know what's going on. I seriously doubt bots will ever achieve that level of sophistication."

The cleaning bot was negotiating a narrow gap between a bench and a raised kerb, but its eyes never stopped scanning the crowds of people milling around the park.

"How about a computer? How about a computer that's really smart and can learn?"

"We have computers able to learn. We use them to gather information and extrapolate possible mission outcomes. They can learn but I wouldn't say they are conscious the way we are. They appear smart, but that is partly us projecting our own consciousness onto them. Why do you ask?"

"No reason. Just curious."

Harl stretched and lifted his chatband. "I would love to stay and discuss deep issues some more but I have to get back to the office. Seems there was a big problem with the network this morning. Nobody could do anything for about half a minute. Whole thing came to a standstill. They're blaming it on a massive transfer of data."

Shor felt all the blood drain from his face as he thought back to his conversation with Jay, and how quickly Jay had accessed the information in the library. He would have to tell him to go easy next time.

"Well I hope you find the cause of the problem," he said, hoping he didn't sound like someone trying to sound casual.

"Me too." Harl stood to leave, pausing to turn and look at Shor with a wry smile. "And do me a favour. If God says anything about me, you'll let me know, right?"

"I will," Shor said. "You have my word."

The depot was empty when Shor got back. He checked his work list and was relieved to see nothing for the rest of the day. He was still the goget and still under Lars's supervision, which meant he relied on his boss to allocate most of his work. He could do some things by himself, but not much. Changing light bulbs and rescuing crazed bots just about summed up his solo repertoire.

There was a general message from Reet informing everyone that Lars would remain in custody for at least another week to "help the badges with their enquiries". Also, the police had identified the victim as someone from Maintenance. It was Noon Nesbitt, one of the new night-shift recruits. Shor wondered what a night-shift worker had been doing at the depot during the day. No doubt just collecting something he'd left behind, but that made no difference for Lars.

The more Shor thought about it, the more he realized how bad this might look. Lars had been the last to work on the critter and, presumably, the last to see the victim. His fingerprints would be all over the scene of the accident and, worst of all, he would have a big problem explaining where he was at the time. Even if he confessed to being in the HQ, there was no-one else to corroborate, and Shor could only guess what the punishment would be for the whole string of offences they were committing from that cosy little room.

He made himself a coffee and sat at the table. He had heard the biggest cause of stress was change. If so, he should qualify for at least a family pack of nervous breakdowns. It felt as if someone had taken his life, turned it over, given it a good shake, and put it back down again.

"I need a break," he murmured.

He closed his eyes and rubbed his temples. He tried to imagine an endless beach set against an endless ocean and a sky blue enough to wade through. He imagined digging his toes in the soft sand while waves crashed gently on the shore. He imagined strolling down the beach, hand in hand with a beautiful woman. He imagined passing a group of Martians, somehow managing to walk with the usual poise even under twice the gravity they were used to. He imagined bumping into one of them trailing at the back...

His eyes shot open. He had seen someone outside the depot just before the accident. He had seen him enter the front door. Well, he hadn't actually *seen* him go in, but he had seen the door swinging closed just after the stranger mysteriously vanished. And he had looked for him because it hadn't made sense at the time to just disappear like that. Now, as he thought about it, there was no other explanation. The guy he had bumped into could only have gone into the Maintenance Depot.

Shor walked to the cupboard, checked he was alone, and stepped inside. He loaded the recordings from all cameras within the vicinity of the depot and rolled back two days. There were seven feeds in total, including one from the camera at the crossing where he had watched the group sail by just after the straggler disappeared. He set them at quad speed and let them all run, his eyes scanning the monitors for anything he recognized.

Ten minutes later he spotted what he was looking for. It was a shot of the front of the depot, taken from a camera at the corner of the block across the road. The angle was steep and high, but he recognized his own awkward gait immediately. Not too many people in Utopia walked as though they needed the bathroom. He cringed as he watched himself stomping along the walkway towards a group of Martians sailing in the opposite direction.

Looking down at himself like this, he now understood why people treated him like an alien. He did indeed look like someone from another planet who had stopped off to buy some souvenirs. All he needed to complete the image was a set of compound eyes and a prehensile tail.

The contrast with the Martians only strengthened this feeling that he just did not belong on this planet. Even at high speed, they resembled the ships he had seen on the Earth videos, while he on the other hand looked like a man ready to start clutching at straws at a moment's notice.

He hit the play button, which slowed the feeds to normal speed. On the screen, he was almost at the group and doing his usual thing of trying to get out of the way. They were taking up far more room than necessary but did nothing to make space for him. In fact, they ignored him, keeping their heads turned away as they chatted. They appeared to be avoiding any sort of contact with the weird little alien. They sailed on by, sparing him no more regard than they might a bench, or a lamp post, or a bot.

Then the straggler appeared, close enough to the others to be mistaken for a part of the group, but far enough back to be alone. He saw how they collided just before he was about to turn into the buggy parking area, his right shoulder making solid contact with the stranger's left. On the screen, he looked back to apologize, but the other man did not even seem to notice.

"Rude wagger," Shor hissed.

He watched himself drop out of the camera's view for a few moments as he walked to his buggy. Another camera showed him getting into the vehicle and starting the engine. Meanwhile, the regatta had passed the entrance to the Maintenance Depot. Shor appeared with the buggy and joined the road. The stranger had fallen behind the others a bit more and was now almost at the depot. Just this side of the entrance, the stranger paused and looked up, as if seeing something up on the cave ceiling.

The feed shuddered and the scene changed. This time Shor was sitting at the crossing watching the boats slide across in their own sweet time. The stranger had gone.

"What the…!"

Shor rolled the feed back and watched the scene again. One moment the stranger was pausing at the entrance, the next he had vanished. Shor watched it through once more, this time paying attention to the timer at the bottom of the screen. It was exactly the same thing as happened with the suicide over at the Space Sector, only this time the feed stopped for exactly seventeen seconds.

He watched it again, and then again, scanning the monitors for any hint as to what might have happened. It was very possible the stranger had gone around the corner or into the building next door, but that felt wrong. In those cases, he would have had to run, or back-track. Getting into the depot made sense. It just flowed naturally. Seventeen seconds would be the perfect amount of time to get from the walkway into the depot building.

Shor froze the action just as the stranger paused. Then he saw something in the top right monitor that made him sit up. It was a shot from a different camera, taken from the other side of the crossing. The entourage was on the crossing in the foreground, and he was sitting in his buggy looking like a bit of a flub. And then there was the stranger standing in line with the depot entrance with his face turned to look directly up at the camera. He was mid-stride, arms at his sides, and the light struck his face at just the right angle. Shor wanted to kick himself for not seeing it.

The man in the yellow suit, the one who'd watched from the window while the nurse jumped to his death. The man standing on the corner of the street while the bot tried to attack the young girl in the park. The lost soul walking calmly across the Martian desert in his home-made out-suit. And this stranger looking up at the camera with a vague smile on his sharply-featured face. They were all one and the same person. Leopold Drake. Leo.

He remembered sitting in Reggie's cafe with Mel, looking out at the couple standing at the far corner. He had not known the guy but he had recognized the girl almost straight away. Izzy Parrow from his own apartment block. Izzy who was three years his junior. Leo had been talking to her. Had been whispering to her, leaning close enough so that his lips almost touched her ear. Whispering the same way he had whispered to the nurse just before he took a dive off the roof of the building.

Shor shut down the monitor, stabbed the power button on the computer, and ran as fast as he could manage to the parking bay.

Whenever he had to get somewhere quickly, it seemed to Shor as if everybody in Utopia came out to block the roads and slow him down. He tried calling Mel but she was not answering. He thought about calling Harl but wasn't sure what to tell him. *Hi, it's Shor. I don't know why but I think a girl may be in serious danger from your buddy in quarantine. What was his name? Leo?*

He parked the buggy at the airlock and joined the pedestrian queue, mainly because he knew it would take longer to explain himself to the badges than it would to walk all the way to his apartment. Taking a buggy through for anything other than an official emergency was not a good idea.

After ten minutes the doors opened and the crowd started shuffling through, apparently wearing concrete shoes. He had to resist barging past them. He tried Mel again. She might know Izzy's number, or at least know someone who did.

The badges checked IDs in slow motion. Shor wanted to yell at them to hurry up. After what seemed like forever-and-an-inch, his turn came. He showed his ID and waited for the badge to give the nod. Had this always been such a slow process? He suspected it was just a trick of his mind.

At last he was allowed through and he walk-jogged to the next tram stop. Another queue with more people determined to slow him down. He climbed on board and watched the world moving like treacle through a straw. The driver took his sweet time checking that all the doors were clear before pulling off.

He tried Mel's number again. The send signal flashed. He watched the park roll by. Five bots were collected around a large dark stain. For one heart-stopping moment he thought it was blood, but it was just oil or maybe engine fluid. The bots worked on the dried puddle as a team, their tools flashing, their eyes ever vigilant. One on the far side noticed the tram and focused on it as it trundled past. Then two more bots looked up. There were fifty people on the tram but Shor had the distinct feeling they were watching him.

And then, for the first time ever in all his years of catching trams, somebody struck up a conversation. A young girl had taken the aisle seat and was determined to have a chat. He smiled at her and then tried to ignore her, but she was unperturbed.

Talk to her.

Shor coughed. Now, suddenly, everybody was interested in him. Even the bots found him fascinating. Eighteen years without so much as a beg-your-pardon and today he was the flavour of the month.

And was he supposed to believe God was somehow trying to communicate with him? Or maybe he had been hacked as well. Maybe they were all hacked. It would certainly explain a lot.

Talk to her.

"Not now," he said between his teeth. "All right?"

"I'm sorry," the girl said, her voice hurt. "I didn't mean to disturb you."

Shor turned to look at her. She was no older than thirteen or fourteen. Her eyes were welling up.

"Listen, I'm sorry. I didn't mean to be rude. I'm just having a bad day."

"Hey it's no problem," she said, instantly perking up. "I had a lousy week last week. You look familiar. My name's Arla. What's yours?"

"Shor."

"Shor? That's an odd name. It sounds like—"

"Yeah, I know. I didn't choose it."

"So," Arla said. "Where are you going?"

"To see a friend."

"That's nice. I just came from the park."

"Aren't you supposed to be in school?" Shor realized just how old that must sound. He had heard it said by other people a million times before, never dreaming that one day he would actually say it himself. "I mean, isn't school in?"

"No silly. It's a holiday. Next week is Earth Week."

"Of course. I forgot."

"No offense, mister, but do you have some sort of disease?"

"No. What makes you think I've got a disease?"

Arla hesitated, as if trying to get her thoughts into proper order before asking a potentially socially unacceptable question.

"It's just, well, you must be about my age, or a bit younger, but you look like an adult?"

Normally, this would be enough to send him into a sulk, or a towering rage. Now, for whatever reason, he actually found it funny.

"No, I don't have a disease. I'm just short."

"Why?" She batted her eyelashes. Her big eyes watched him with interest.

He leaned a little closer as though sharing a secret. "Because I actually

195

come from another planet."

Arla's eyes, if it were possible, grew even wider.

"Really?"

"Yes. I was sent to see if you're all being good."

Arla blinked, then her eyes narrowed slightly. "Which planet?"

"Promise not to tell anyone?"

Arla nodded.

Shor looked around as if to make sure nobody was listening. "I'm from Alpha Centauri."

She stared at him for a good few seconds, which is a long time to stare at someone. "Really?"

"Yes."

"How did you get here?"

"In a spaceship."

"Who built it?"

"It was built on Earth a thousand years ago."

Her face became a picture of concentration then, quite suddenly, a grin cracked her pretty face and she giggled. "You're funny, mister."

"Thanks. I try."

"So where are you off to? You look like you're in a hurry."

"I do?"

"You keep looking at the time."

Shor glanced out at the park. They were perhaps five minutes away from the stop closest to his apartment block. It would take another fifteen minutes if he walked quickly.

"I need to give a message to a friend."

Arla thought about this for a moment. "Is it urgent?"

"Pretty urgent, yes."

"Is he in trouble?"

"Possibly. I don't know. And it's a she."

"Your girlfriend?"

"No it's not my girlfriend."

"Oh." Arla looked disappointed. "What's her name?"

"Izzy Parrow."

Arla's face frowned. "Izzy?"

"You know her?"

"Yes. She's my friend. What's wrong? Is she all right?"

"Have you spoken to her recently?"

"Yes. I spoke to her this morning. She was supposed to come with me today but she said she didn't feel like going out. She said she wanted to stay at home."

The tram shuddered. Shor could see the stop through the driver's window. There were maybe ten people waiting in line.

"Did she say why?"

"No, but she sounded a bit strange, like she was upset or something. I asked if I should come round to keep her company but she said no. She said she wanted to be alone. Is she all right?"

"I don't know."

"Is she in trouble?"

"I hope not. You said she sounded symptomatic when you spoke to her."

"Not symptomatic. More like sad. Listen mister, you said you were her friend. I know all her friends, and I don't know you."

"We live in the same apartment block."

Arla examined him for a moment. "Hey, if you live in Izzy's apartment block then you must be the short guy…I mean, sorry. I thought you looked familiar."

The tram was slowing down. People were standing to leave. Shor placed his hand on the back of the seat in front of him.

"Don't worry about it," he said. "Listen, I need you to call Izzy. I need you to keep trying until she answers. Can you do that for me, Arla?"

Arla nodded. "Sure I can, but what do I say?"

"Keep talking to her. Here, take my number in case you need it. Whatever you do, don't let her break off."

"Sure but, why?"

"I don't have time to explain."

Shor stood and squeezed past those waiting in the aisle, apologizing as he went. Martians had various ways of expressing their displeasure, from the standard name-calling employed between friends, to hisses, clicks and tuts reserved for public displays of ire. These sounds of displeasure suddenly seemed like an alien language to him.

The tram eased to a standstill and the doors slid open. Shor dropped to the sidewalk while, behind him, a woman hissed and clicked like an angry insect. He hit the ground running. At least he tried to. What he managed was more of a controlled stumble. He had to fight to stay upright with his centre of gravity too low and his limbs too short for effective speed.

Before long he was sweating profusely as he battled his own lack of balance, narrowly avoided a number of collisions with people, their hisses and clicks following him as he fought against his own inertia.

By the time he reached the road leading to his apartment block he was soaking wet. He took the corner with all the grace of a bot chasing its own shadow and hit the brakes, slowing down just enough to avoid running headlong into the small crowd gathered outside the front door.

He pushed his way through to where a cluster of emergency vehicles stood in a loose semi-circle as if sharing the latest gossip. One of the vehicles was an ambulance. The others were police buggies. A badge stopped him from entering the building.

"I live…here," Shor said, catching his breath. "What's…going on?"

"There has been an accident. You can't go in."

"What happened?"

"I am sorry, but I can't tell you that. Please move back and wait with the others."

"Do you mean you can't tell me or you won't tell me? I have a right to know what's going on. I live here."

The badge observed him from behind dark glass. "I am sorry. I can't tell you. Please move back."

"What are you?" Shor said. "Are you some kind of a machine? Are you some kind of robot?"

"Please move back," the badge repeated, his hand on Shor's arm. "You will have to wait."

Shor was propelled towards the crowd. He felt himself swallowed up by the sea of Martians towering over him like a crashing wave. He bumped into someone and they hissed at him.

Then the door opened. It swung inwards to reveal an ambulance driver, his arms hanging down, his fists clenched around blunt poles as he stepped carefully out onto the walkway carrying a stretcher behind his back. On the stretcher was something black and bulky. It was a body bag like the one they had used for Noon Nesbitt at the Maintenance Depot. Then the second ambulance driver appeared carrying the other end of the stretcher. Together, they performed a little balancing act, manoeuvring the bag suspended between two sticks towards the rear of the waiting vehicle.

Shor watched the procession. He could see the shape under the bag. The profile was like a mountain range against the grey backdrop of the apartment building. He traced the slopes with his eyes, along the feet hanging limply over the edge of the stretcher, up the legs, the hips, the chest, the nose. In his mind he saw Izzy's face, her eyes closed, her lips already turning blue, her chest as still and lifeless as Olympus Mons as they carried her away…forever. He imagined her hair pulled back and her ears where Leo or Leopold, or whatever the heck he was called, had spilled his vile, poisonous words down her cheek.

Suddenly he wanted to pull her from the bag and set her free. He wanted to walk over to the stretcher and unzip the bag and peel her out of her black cocoon. But most of all he wanted to find the person responsible for this and make him pay. He wanted to breathe something into his ear before doing to him exactly what he had done to her. He wanted to make him pay for taking away this precious life before she even had a chance to understand what it really meant to be alive.

Shor felt the chatband but it did not register. At first he thought someone was tugging at his wrist. He looked down, expecting to see a small child, but there was no one.

He lifted his arm and stared, unseeing, at the screen. A face was looking at him. It was a young girl's face.

He looked across at the black garbage bag being loaded into the waiting garbage truck and blinked. He looked down at Izzy's avatar smiling patiently up at him from his chatband. He looked back at the stretcher, with the feet hanging over the edge.

He stumbled forward, towards the badge and his shaded eyes.

"Sir, you cannot—"

"Which apartment?" Shor heard himself ask.

The badge hesitated. Shor started to repeat the question, but the badge answered before he was able to speak.

"Seven-four. It was apartment seven-four."

Shor felt the words strike him with the force of a hammer. The breath left his chest and his knees buckled under him. He dropped to the floor and slumped at the feet of the badge. Over at the ambulance, the men were closing the door and Shor caught a glimpse of the bag, knowing without seeing that the person lying beneath that mountain of plastic was not young Izzy Parrow.

He reached out, ignoring the clicks and hisses of the people behind him as the darkness descended and engulfed him, stifling his voice as he cried out.

"Father...!"

It was dark the next time he opened his eyes. It was late but he had no idea what time it was. He was lying in a bed, but it was not his bed. The room was big and deathly quiet. The air carried the faint smell of sterilization.

He turned his head to the right and recognized the window or, at least, the view through the window. He was in the hospital, in a ward on the same side of the building as his mother, possibly even in the same room.

Shor turned his head the other way. To his left was a table and, beyond that, a door with a square of light from the passage. On the table was a lamp, a glass of water, and his chatband. On the screen, the time showed 6.52 a.m. Eight minutes to dawn, or at least Utopia's best attempt at mimicking one. And the date. Surely that wasn't right. It meant he had been unconscious for four days.

A flashing symbol indicated that he had taken the chatband off but was still in close proximity. No doubt, somebody somewhere would be keeping half an eye on this. Hospitals and showers were the only times they were allowed to remove their chatbands for any length of time. And, of course, on transfer to Ward D.

He reached towards it but his arms were restricted and for a brief moment he had a dizzying sensation of floating in thick yellow liquid. He closed his eyes to shake the memory from his past life. An image of his arms and legs drifting in the yellow gloom surfaced in the back of his mind. Black tubes like tentacles snaking from his face and torso. Nausea washed over him.

"Nnngh."

He opened his eyes, a little startled by the sound of his own voice in the empty room. He wriggled until his arms came loose. They had not tied him down but the sheets were tucked tightly under the mattress, the way they secured infants to stop them rolling around.

With his arms free, he lifted himself up and pulled out the sheets so he could turn and sit upright. His head swam a little and he had to sit until the world found its bearings. He looked across at the other beds. There were six in total. All were empty.

The floor was cold under his soles but they had left him a pair of cotton slippers, which he put on. The chatband slid smoothly over his hand and settled into the grooves that had formed in his skin over the past eighteen years. The screen displayed the connection signal. The alarm stopped flashing.

He checked the message log and found two. The first was from Mel saying she had heard the news about his father and asking him to call her. The second was from Cobb, marked as urgent. It said:

Found something you might like to see. My doors are always open, but not for long. R12-15-2b.

As he sat on the edge of the bed, trying to fathom Cobb's cryptic invitation, he had the feeling he was missing something. Something felt out of place. Something *sounded* out of place. The ward was quiet; that was normal. He looked around at the other beds, trying to figure out what it was he was hearing.

A few days after his fourth birthday, they had moved to another part of the city. It was policy to keep citizens of a similar demographic together. Families with infants were placed in an area close to the hospital and within walking distance of the market. As soon as the youngest child turned four, they were moved closer to the school. Older, empty-nest, couples lived in the apartments adjacent to Axle Park. New couples, who were expected to conceive or adopt within the first year, were given accommodation in the same area as the starter families.

And so, at age four, Shor unknowingly nudged his family from one demographic group to another, thereby necessitating a move from the noisy market region to the quieter area around the school. Personal belongings were stowed into three small boxes and, within the hour, they were unpacking in their new home. Mother set about cleaning and scrubbing, all the while tutting and hissing under her breath. Father roamed the apartment, looking for things to fix. Shor watched them from the chair under the front window, trying to figure out where the noise had gone.

Now, sitting on the hospital bed with his cotton-clad feet dangling over the cool hospital floor, he knew what was wrong. He knew what was missing.

With one hand on the mattress for support, he eased himself out of bed and walked carefully across to the window. The city was asleep, as dark as a cave, immersed in shadows that engulfed the towering structures, staining the walls, collecting in corners and pooling like mirrors of dark water. Even after waking in a dim hospital room, he had to give his eyes time to adjust to the total absence of light out there. As his pupils stretched wide, searching for the slightest shreds of light, he listened to the slumbering city and identified the sound that was missing.

There were no bots.

No buzzing or rumbling. No scraping or scratching. No whine of servo motors turning gears or adjusting metal limbs. No comical bumping against kerbs and walls and corners or the underside of benches. For eighteen years he had slept through the nightly cleaning ritual as a thousand machines scoured the city. The sounds were a part of life in Utopia, as much as the sun and the stars and the apartment blocks. The people of Mars did not hear the bots working through the night because they *were* the night, just as the sun was the day and the buildings were the city. And now they were gone, Shor could *hear* their silence.

He stared out, looking for movement, but there was nothing. He thought he saw something at one or two windows, but it was too dark to be sure. Then, as his eyes adjusted, they emerged from the night. Shadows within shadows dotted across the walkway. Dark shapes like miniature cameos, standing there. Just standing there. Doing nothing.

He gazed out, not blinking, willing his eyes to make sense of what they were struggling to show him. The darkness was starting to lift. He wasn't sure if it was his eyes growing accustomed to the lack of light, or if the sun—the real sun—was rising in a weak attempt to pre-empt the million-Watt fake version due to start in a few minutes' time.

In the red-tinted blackness he saw one or two shadows moving. They crept and paused, crept and paused, stopping to turn and look around like lost tourists. The ones on the walls moved from window to window, crawling and creeping like monstrous insects. They stopped and peered in through the glass for a few seconds before moving on to the next window. Then they slipped down to the street and crossed to another building where they continued their macabre window-shopping.

As Shor watched, a bot rolled into a patch of pale light directly in front of his window. Shor froze, caught by surprise, his heart in his throat. The bot stopped and started to turn slowly towards him, its plastic eyes scanning the building. The metal bulk of its body took on a ghostly hue of red that flowed across its bulbous frame as it shifted its weight. Shor caught glimpses of sharp teeth tucked away inside its metal mouth. He remembered the girl in the park and the arm lying on the floor in the workshop. The bot seemed to be searching for something, pivoting until it was facing the window, its eyes raised so that it was looking directly at Shor.

He wanted to move but was unable to. He wanted to step out of the line of sight of those plastic eyes but his muscles would not move. He stared back, his clammy hands clutching the window sill and his heart beating against his ribs.

A few weeks earlier he would have laughed at this critter staring up at him with those toy eyes, but this felt wrong. Bots did not sneak. Bots did not stare into windows.

The fear paralysed him and he was sure his legs were going to fall out from under him. At least then he would not have to worry about moving out of sight. His body, it seemed, was about to take matters into its own hands. His only worry was what the bot would do if he moved. It was looking straight at him but did not give any indication that it had actually seen him. It just stared in his direction through unblinking lenses. Perhaps it was trying to make sense of his outline. Perhaps it was trying to adjust to the darkness as well.

He thought about making a run for it, but then what? He could not imagine that it would leap through the window and give chase. He wasn't sure how he knew, but he was almost certain this was not on their agenda for tonight. Tonight they were out gathering information. Tonight they were spying on the inhabitants of Utopia sleeping peacefully in their beds. Tonight they were counting, sorting, plotting. But plotting for what?

He was trying not to blink but a droplet of sweat was trickling from his hairline down his forehead towards his nose. It itched like mad but he was scared to move a muscle. One twitch, or scratch, or blink, and the photoreceptors in the critter's eyes would register the movement and identify the shadow in the window as something with eyes, nose, a face, and a brain, and it would log it as a human being. And although he believed he was not in immediate danger, he did not want this machine to add him to any lists, for whatever reason.

The droplet was on the bridge of his nose. It paused there for a moment before slipping down, as softly as a feather drawn across the sole of a foot. This was too much. He had to do something before he went crazy.

He was about to lift his hand when something changed outside. As if set free from some spell, the bot looked down from the window, turned slightly and paused, almost as if listening to something. Then it trundled off, following some silent, unseen signal.

Shor turned to watch as it rolled away. He was aware that he had been holding his breath, and that his nose had stopped itching. He exhaled, his shoulders dropping as he relaxed.

A new day was beginning in Utopia. All along the ceiling, bulbs designed to mimic the sunlight of Earth sparked and glowed, their tiny fires shedding light and warmth. Over the next half hour, dawn would break in a sequence of colours designed to replicate a glorious morning back on the home planet.

Even now, under the palest glimmer of pre-dawn light, he could see the bots moving. They slid down buildings and rolled across walkways. There was no bustling or bumping, only an ordered procession of machines. They crawled towards their hiding places, almost as if repelled by the light.

Shor leaned forward to watch them slide past his window, suddenly oblivious to his presence. They did not turn to look at him. They did not acknowledge his presence. Whatever they had been doing was over and their only protocol was to return home, to recharge, rebuild, and repair, ready for the next shift.

Soon the streets were deserted. He saw apartment lights coming on and people standing at windows as the blanket of darkness was replaced by the orange glow of early morning. The night bots were all gone now, replaced by the first of their daytime maintenance colleagues. These wandered around, looking for things to fix and clean, seemingly aimlessly, but no doubt programmed for the most efficient coverage.

One of the day-shift critters paused outside the hospital window where Shor was still watching. It looked up at him for a moment, its eyes adjusting their focal length, and then moved on. Presumably this bot wasn't making lists. Or perhaps he was already on one and was therefore of no further interest.

I must've hit my head when I passed out, Shor thought. *My imagination is going into overdrive.*

He did have a lump on the back of his skull. He touched it with his fingers. It was tender and he winced.

Then he remembered the fall, how his consciousness had slipped away from him, and he remembered the moments before. He had been standing outside his apartment block, watching the emergency services take a stretcher away. The black bag with the zip and its mountain-like contours. The shape too tall to be Izzy. The mention of the apartment number.

Shor turned away from the window and walked to the door. Out in the reception area, the nurse on duty was working on a computer, her fingers moving efficiently over the keys, the screen projecting a macabre light-show on her face. He pushed the door open and slipped into the passage. His cotton-bud feet shushed on the polished floor as he moved.

They had put him in the ward closest to the front of the hospital. Mother was in the next room along. He walked quickly to her door and looked through the glass. The room was bathed in a pale pink hue from the far window. Six beds. All empty.

Shor pulled back, the fear rising in his stomach. He must have been mistaken. It must be the next room. He moved down the corridor and looked in. The beds were empty except for the one closest to the door where a man lay sleeping on his back, the shadow of a beard masking his jaw and upper lip.

He tried the next room and the next. There were five rooms in this wing. All were empty except for the man with the beard. Mother was not here.

He moved with urgency, following the signs from A Wing to B Wing. Here the wards were lined with cots surrounded by plastic sheeting. He saw two beds with occupants, the plastic sheets sealed to form a cocoon. Machines connected by snaking strands of wires flashed and bleeped and scrolled numbers across grey screens.

The sign above the next corner was for C Wing. The heavy, windowless, door opened into a room bathed in green light. Here there were no beds, but rows of glass tanks with pale bodies suspended in green fluid. They floated like fish in a bizarre aquarium, connected by black tubes from masks clinging to their faces like grotesque parasites. The one nearest twitched in time to the instruments that echoed his heartbeat. His face was turned this way but his eyes were closed. Shor's eyes drifted along the length of the tank. The body floating in the liquid was twisted and distorted, as if reflected from a bent mirror. The torso and legs were those of a young child, but the arms were big, like a man's.

At first Shor thought it must be an optical illusion, but he realised what he was seeing was not a result of the bending of light through liquid and glass or from a distorted mirror. This was a child with the arms of man. In the other tanks were similar creatures. The one next along was a torso with four legs. Beyond that was a body that stopped just below the rib cage, the abdomen replaced by a spider-like explosion of black tubes and wires.

Shor had heard the stories of the experiments, carried out in an attempt to perfect the human body. There were rumours of scientists conducting test after test in an attempt to stop the genetic clock, the key to immortality. These had all failed, but with a terrible price. The rumours spoke of a hospital ward filled with monsters.

Rubber-soled shoes squeaking down the corridor and Shor slipped further into the room, letting the door close behind him, crouching beside the nearest tank. Outside, the footsteps grew louder and then faded. He felt light-headed, probably from hunger, and started to topple backwards. He stopped himself falling by placing a palm against the glass of the tank closest.

Suddenly the beeping of the heart rate monitor attached to the tank changed, becoming erratic. Shor turned and looked up. Where his hand was pressed against the glass, the patient's face was only inches away, eyes wide with fear over the black mask that consumed half of its face. Shor shrieked and fell back, bumping against the monitoring equipment.

He scrambled to his feet and staggered out into the corridor, not stopping until he had rounded the corner under the sign pointing to D and Y Wings. He stopped and closed his eyes, leaning against the wall and trying to get his fear under control. Now footsteps were approaching. It sounded like two people moving quickly. He pulled back into the shadows and listened. The door to the room he had just been in opened and he heard the jagged beeping from the monitor. Urgent voices barked commands. Soon the beeping slowed, becoming regular. Shor allowed himself to breathe normally again. Footsteps leading away, walking. Emergency over. Everything under control.

He forced himself to move on, past rooms filled with what looked like filing cabinets standing five high and twenty wide. Here there was no monitoring equipment or furniture or windows. He pushed into the first room and read the labels on the square cabinet doors. They were names, arranged in no particular order. Deacon, Apswith, Connor, Leith, Barrymore. Some labels were blank.

He walked from one end to the other, counting a hundred in all. The next room was the same. No furniture, no colour, no view of outside. Just five rows of doors with square metal handles. He touched each label as he passed, saying the names out loud.

He thought he recognized one or two. Old Simpkins from one of the first floor apartments. He had fallen and broken his hip not two weeks ago. They took him to hospital and then new people moved into his apartment less than a week later. The supervisor said old Simpkins had probably been given a place closer to the hospital.

And he spotted Sal Llewelyn, the assistant at the market until last year. Shor remembered Sal because he always had a smile on his face. They said he was not too bright, but Sal never said a mean word to anyone. Then he became symptomatic and was taken to hospital, never to return. Shor asked around but nobody knew where Sal was. They figured he had just been moved to a different quarter.

Shor tried the next room, and the next. He found one of the cabinet doors open and he pulled at the handle. It slid open easily enough, revealing a drawer big enough to hold any of the tallest inhabitants of Mars. It looked like a bed, but it was bare and cold.

In the last room of D Wing he found what he was looking for. Here most of the drawers were empty. Only five or six had names printed in a neat font on the little white labels. Half way along the top row, in a cluster of four names, he found Helm Larkin.

Shor stared at the label for a long time. He knew his father's name from colleagues, badges, and friends. All had used the name Helm. Even Mother had called him that on occasion, usually when she was upset with him for some reason, but Shor had only ever know him as Father.

Now, looking at the name on that neat little label, he wished he could wind back time and learn more about the man who, even though theirs had not been a close relationship, had been there for him and stuck by him when he had needed it, corrected him when he had deserved it, helped him whenever he was able and, yes, even loved him in his own way.

Shor leant his forehead against the cool handle and closed his eyes. As a child he had seen other fathers doting over their kids, hugging them and playing with them, and never understood why his own father was so distant. Helm Larkin had always seemed uncomfortable with physical contact and would push Shor away if he became too clingy. Later, when the tables were turned and Shor had learned to be as stand-offish as his father, he would shun any of Father's attempts at reconciliation. Now he would give anything for the chance to hug his father one last time.

The grief swirled like a soft breeze nudging red dust across the Martian surface, but he felt only a sense of what might have been.

"Goodbye Father," he murmured. "I'm sorry."

He turned towards the door. Faint footsteps chased their own echoes up and down the corridor. He walked to the door and reached out towards the metal push-plate. It was then that he spotted something in the bin next to the door. Lying scattered on the bottom were a dozen or so used cabinet labels. He glanced at the tidy black print and one in particular caught his eye.

Jeen Larkin. His mother.

He crouched and lifted the square of card. Grief rose in him like a full-throttled Martian storm hurling itself against anything in its path. He crushed the label in his hands and let out a deep moan. Then he slumped to his knees, held his head in his hands, and wept.

The offices of the Robotics Department were much like every other office building in Utopia: stark, grey walls worn by centuries of use, punctuated by shapeless square windows.

Situated in the south-east corner of the Space Sector, the Robotics Department occupied one block of four buildings separated by a narrow walkway. Viewed from a distance, the towers appeared to be having a private discussion, leaning in close so nobody else was able to hear.

People working there were considered geeky, even to those Space Sector boffins who spoke mathematics as if it were a living language. Designing and building critters required a certain type of personality. For Shor, applying for a position there had been a long-shot, but worth a try.

He parked his buggy and walked around to the main admin building. At the door, he showed his ID and asked to see Tray Cobb. The receptionist directed him to the fourth floor via the elevators.

Cobb looked like a man drowning in spare parts. His "office" was a partition, three metres square, and filled to overflowing with computers, bots, bot parts, and what looked like an explosion in a scrap metal collector's apartment. Within this mess, only the top of Cobb's head was visible, his mop of unruly brown hair scuttling around like a large, greasy rodent. There were perhaps twenty such desks on the whole floor, but Cobb appeared to have the monopoly on mess.

Shor cleared his throat. Cobb jumped. One or two of the other workers looked up before returning to whatever it was they were doing.

"Man, you gave me a fright," Cobb said. "Don't you know you shouldn't sneak up on people like that?"

"I'm sorry. I wasn't aware I was sneaking."

"You all right? You look symptomatic."

"I'm fine. I got your message. What's going on?"

Cobb glanced around at the others in the room. Shor thought he looked like a soldier in a very small and very cluttered trench.

"We can't talk here. Want a coffee? It's free."

Shor followed him to a room in the far corner. Cobb made sure it was empty before stepping inside and closing the door. It was about the same size as the office cubicles, but the walls ran all the way to the ceiling, giving at least some privacy. The ragged-looking coffee machine squatted against a wall in the corner. Cobb ordered two cups and carried them to the table. They sat opposite each other in silence for a few moments. Cobb slurped noisily. Shor swirled his cup. The liquid looked way too dark to be coffee.

"I contacted you because I've been doing some research into that bot from the other day," Cobb said. "And I think I found something." He leaned close and Shor found himself doing the same. "I wasn't sure, so I cross-checked with the bot that attacked the girl in the park. Then I went over the logs of all the bots brought in over the past five weeks. And I was right."

Shor waited while Cobb took a celebratory slurp of his coffee. Cobb just sat there looking pleased with himself. He appeared to have forgotten he hadn't actually told Shor anything.

"And?"

"And there's something funny going on. I believe that, two days from now, something is going to happen. I don't know exactly what, but it involves the bots."

"Have they been hacked?"

Cobb nodded. "They have. Which is why those two malfunctioned, plus another half a dozen over the past month. Well, that's not exactly true. They didn't malfunction specifically because they've been hacked. They were hacked but something must've gone wrong. That's why they went hoho."

"How many are we talking about here?"

Cobb shrugged. "All of them, I think."

Shor thought back to the previous night and all those critters sneaking around in the dark. There had certainly been a lot of them. At least thirty he could see from the hospital window alone. Which probably meant hundreds. Maybe thousands.

"You said something was going to happen two days from now."

"I did. I mean, I do, but I don't know what. It's more of a hunch. I've seen that date on all the machines I've checked and I think it's important. I don't know what's going to happen, but I think we should be ready. I found the same date on the boot chip, which is why I only noticed it on the ones brought in to be fixed. Which means we can't fix the problem using a software upgrade. We have to bring the bot in and replace the chip. Whoever did this is way ahead of us technologically. And if someone has the means to hack the boot chips, by remote access no less, then they can pretty much do anything they want with the bots."

"Did you tell anyone about this, apart from me?"

Cobb nodded. "Sure did. Told my boss, but he didn't believe me. He says it's impossible to hack the boot chip. I even showed him. He said there must be a glitch in the reader."

"What about *his* boss?"

Cobb took another swig of coffee. Shor had taken one sip but could not stomach another. It tasted like recycled leftovers. He had a pretty good idea why it was free.

"I don't know how things work in maintenance, but up here there's a strict line of command."

"Fine. So what about the police? Shouldn't you tell the badges?"

"Again, I can't go past my line manager. If I went direct to the police, and it turned out to be nothing, they'd nail me to the wall and take turns shooting spit balls."

"What if I told them? What if I said I found the glitch?"

"Have you got equipment for reading boot chips?"

Shor immediately thought of Jay. He would almost certainly be able to read the chips, but Shor still had his doubts about how much he could trust his computer friend. There was a possibility Jay had been hacked, or compromised by the entity.

"No," he said.

"Good, because we're the only people allowed to have those. You'd be in trouble if they thought you had one. They'd probably assume you were a criminal. And if you don't have one, they'd want to know exactly who in the Robotics Department told you, which leads right back to me and spit balls."

"That means the hacker must work in Robotics. It's the only possible solution. How else did he get hold of the equipment to change the boot disk? There you are. Your hacker works here."

"No," Cobb said. "You don't understand. It isn't possible to change the code on the boot disks. We can read it, but updating it is a different matter. The code is written one time only. It's like it's written in stone. If there's a mistake or we need to change something, you have to throw it away and start again."

"Isn't that a bit wasteful?"

"Not really. We've upgraded the boot disks twice in the past ten years. They don't have much on them. Just the important stuff to do with not hurting themselves or people. A normal computer's boot disk is easy to update, but the bots are different. They were designed to be safe. Computers can't tear a person to shreds. Bots can."

"We have to tell someone," Shor said. "We can't just ignore this."

"Listen, the reason I came to you is because I know Lars trusts you. And I know how much guys over in Maintenance like to stay on top of current events." Cobb winked and tapped the side of his nose. "Find the person who's doing this and you may just end up a hero."

"And what happens if I don't?"

Cobb downed the last of his coffee and grimaced. "Then I guess we'll find out in two days."

Shor stopped off at the depot to pick up his jobs for the day. He felt himself unravelling inside and work was the last thing on his mind, but he had to stay focused. The first task on the list was to collect a stalled cleaning bot over in the Admin Sector. He drove straight there with his buggy to collect it. This one looked harmless enough but he was not taking any chances. He used two sets of straps to secure it to the vehicle, and positioned it with the business end facing towards the back, just in case it decided to try to clean *him*.

He returned to the depot well before lunch and used the spare time to visit the HQ and go over some old feeds. He wanted to go through the scene outside the depot, where Leo Drake, or Leopold, or whatever his name was, had vanished along with seventeen seconds of feed shortly before the bot lost its limited grip on reality and went hoho all over Noon Nesbitt. According to Boole, the poor kid had returned to the depot to pick up some gear and must have gone into the workshop for some reason.

Shor ran it through twenty or maybe thirty times, but there was nothing more to see. He considered taking the copy down to Boole, but was unable to come up with a believable reason as to how he came to be in possession of the feed in the first place.

And anyway, he wondered, *what if they did take a look?* A feed malfunctioned. Leo the mysterious stranger was seen in the area moments before. That didn't mean anything.

He thought about letting Jay take a look, but the missing seconds appeared to be down to the camera malfunctioning, and not due to tampering after the fact. He could try hooking him up to the feeds somehow, but wasn't convinced this would achieve anything. Besides, he still wasn't sure he trusted Jay.

Back on the day when they had found Leopold wandering around on the Martian surface, his suit had been threadbare. It was a poor excuse for an out-suit. In fact, it was a miracle Leo had not died out in the rusty dust, killed by a leaky elbow joint or from poor stitching around the knee pads.

There was something else about the suit that bothered him, but he could not put his finger on it. Sure it had looked shabby, but the guy wearing it was by no means dead so it must have been air-tight as he wandered about on the Martian surface. No, there was more.

He hadn't been *wandering*. Far from it. Leopold had looked like a man who knew exactly where he was going and precisely how to get there. Shor remembered looking back along his footprints and noticing how straight they were. People tend to walk a little lopsided. People meander, but not Leopold. No, Leo the Lad had left a trail straighter than a buggy's back axle.

And there was all the other stuff as well. It seemed impossible one person "just happened" to be in the vicinity of so many incidents. Sure, Utopia was hardly a planet full of people, but the odds of one person being around two deaths, plus one close call, were remote even if there were only a thousand people in Utopia, or a hundred, or even ten.

And there was Izzy Parrow. The fact that Izzy had *not* come to a bad end after speaking to Leo and was her happy, healthy, breathing self was certainly a fat fly in Shor's deductive ointment. If Leo was the psychopath Shor was beginning to suspect he was, then why was she unharmed? But then, that would be ridiculous. It would mean every person Leo ever spoke to would end up leaping from a building or throwing themselves under a crazed critter. Unless, of course, she was not the one he had wanted to harm.

Shor leaned forward and watched the recorded image of Leo standing on the corner. He was looking up at the camera with that psychopath's glint in his eye.

No, there was definitely something wrong with this man.

Shor loaded a list of recorded feeds and scanned the dates and times. The recordings were organized by sector, quarter, and camera location. He found the feed from the day before, in the Residential Sector, green quarter, just outside his apartment building.

His hand hovered over the file that would show the outside of his home during the approximate time his father had been killed, but he hesitated, curling his fingers into a fist. He closed his eyes and took a deep breath, not sure he was ready to see this even though he knew he had to. Composing himself, he opened his eyes, slowly unfolded his fingers, and selected the file.

The screen showed a typical late afternoon in Utopia at about 4pm. Over the years, Shor had developed the ability to tell the time fairly accurately by the level of activity around his apartment building. He had spent many hours up in his room or in his secret place, just watching the world turn. Mars was nothing if not predictable.

He shuttled the feed forward at high speed, his eyes never leaving the front door. People raced past like litter caught on the wind. It had an almost hypnotic quality. At normal speed, Utopia flowed. At high speed, it bunched and crashed and stammered as people and bots fought for right of way along the streets and in and out of the doorways that swallowed them up and spat them out. Meanwhile, in the midst of all this mayhem, the apartment building remained stationary, oblivious to the frantic activity going on all around it. It had been there for a thousand years and would remain there for a thousand years more.

Shor had a strange sensation of time speeding up for real. It was only a recording but he had the curious sensation of witnessing his life passing by. The only thing not affected by this surge of time was the apartment building and a street lamp. And something else Shor had not noticed before. In the midst of all the people moving in surging waves, one person remained perfectly still.

To the left, on the corner of the apartment block, a single figure stood and watched. Shor had not noticed him standing there because he was as motionless amid the clamour as the building itself.

Shor knew who it was immediately. The posture, the build, the way he watched with an almost unsettling patience. Like somebody waiting for a trap to slam shut. It was Leo. Shor knew it as surely as he knew Mars was red.

For at least the next ten minutes Leo never moved a muscle. It was as if he had been frozen in space and time, or chiselled out of the bedrock.

In Shor's experience, people waiting tended to keep busy. They looked around, adjusted their clothes, acknowledged people they recognized. They shifted their weight from one foot to the other. They fidgeted. Leo did none of these things. Leo was as unbusy as one of Pinner's pointing statues.

Shor blinked, and that was all it took. A blink and Leo was no longer alone. Someone had separated from the storm and was talking with him on the corner, standing close as if sharing a secret.

Shor set the feed to normal speed and the world slowed down. Leo was facing the camera which meant the person he was talking to was showing his back, but Shor knew who it was. You don't grow up with a person without getting to know their every mannerism. The two of them looked like friends having a chat. Shor's father, the taller by a good four inches, was stooped forward so Leo was able to speak into his ear.

"No," Shor whispered. He knew it was only a recording, and that he could do nothing about these digitized ghosts from the past, but the odd feeling of his life passing by had returned. "Don't listen. Don't listen to him."

Almost as if he had heard Shor's warning, his father turned to look in the general direction of the camera, a quizzical expression on his face. High up on the side of the apartment building, clutching the wall like one of those ugly-looking jungle spiders Mister Edmunds had shown them, a bot was busy with something. This struck Shor as a little odd because the wall climbers usually only came out at night, mainly for safety reasons because, once in a while, one of them slipped and fell. It was rare and they were much smaller than normal cleaning bots, but the lawmakers decided not to take a chance. Wall climbers were only allowed to come out during the day for urgent repairs. This one looked like it was busy filling a crack. Shor watched its mandibles attacking the surface, the blades moving with blinding speed.

Shor's father watched the bot for a few seconds, then he turned away. Shor touched the screen. It was irrational, but he wanted to make some sort of contact.

The image shifted. It was as if someone had bumped into it. The building and lamp post were the same, but everything else moved slightly. Leo was still standing on the corner, but Shor's father had vanished, as had the little spider bot. Shor looked at the clock and saw that he had lost maybe ten minutes of the feed. *Just like the other times*, he thought, the dead weight of certainty settling in his stomach.

Then someone came running out of the apartment block. It was one of Shor's neighbours from two doors down the hall. She was shouting something, her clothes and hair mussed up like she had just woken from a nap.

Now people were stopping, turning, walking towards her. She was pointing up to one of the windows, waving at it with her finger. Shor could see the whites of her eyes and the moisture on her cheeks. People ran towards the door and were swallowed up by the building. A minute passed, then another. A face appeared at Shor's bedroom window, a pale mask against a shroud of darkness, hands resting on the sill. Shor could see his sleeve in the gap under the window where it was about a quarter open. Then he retreated, becoming a shadow outlined by the light from Shor's open bedroom door.

The first of the emergency vehicles pulled up in the street outside. Paramedics stormed the building. Half a minute later their dark silhouettes flitted past Shor's door towards his father's room. Two Badgemobiles arrived. The woman on the street gesticulated as if performing some strange play before the growing crowd. Two badges entered the building. There was more movement inside the small apartment.

All the while, Leo just stood and watched, as motionless as before. Somebody, an old woman with shopping, stopped next to him and said something in the conversational manner of a stranger sharing a moment, but Leo ignored her, his eyes never leaving the activity in front of the apartment building.

Again, the shadows flitted past Shor's bedroom door, this time moving away from his father's room. They moved slowly, carrying something. Shor followed the movements in his mind. Along the short hall, through the living area, out of the door and to the elevator. But was the elevator big enough to carry…?

Shor felt a surge of grief. He clenched the edge of the desk until his fingers hurt. He wanted to look away but he needed to see this. He needed to know.

Up on the screen, time seemed to slow down as Shor waited for his father's body to appear through the door. A movement in the crowd caught his eye and somebody, a boy, pushed though the cluster of spectators. It took a second for Shor to get who it was. He was looking at himself.

The front door swung open and the ambulance driver appeared. Then the dark body bag followed, sliding slowly out into the open, seemingly floating on a cushion of air. Shor saw himself down in the crowd, pushing forward, trying to get a closer look at the bag. Leo was still in his corner spot, observing everything with cool interest, observing Shor pleading with a badge, watching the boy in his agony.

Then the body bag was gone. The buggy doors closed and the emergency vehicles pulled away, leaving the one police buggy behind. Shor watched the crowd disperse with the help of two badges. On the corner of the building, as casually as if he had just watched someone drop their shopping, Leo turned and strolled away.

"Wagger!" Shor hissed, pushing himself away from the desk.

Just like those other times, there was nothing to link Leo with his father's death. Sure, Leo had been there, but then so had dozens of other people. Even if he took this to the police there was no crime against standing on a street corner. Weird, perhaps, a coincidence maybe, but not illegal.

The only other strange thing was the bot…

Shor rolled back to the desk. There was something he had missed, he was sure of it. He rewound the feed to just before the cut. The bot was back on the wall, not far from Shor's bedroom window. He watched the steel mandibles working. Two seconds later, it was gone. He rewound and played it again. One moment it was there, the next there was just an empty wall with the crack only half mended. That was strange but there was something else, something he was missing. He set a loop over the moment of change, flicking back and forth over the cut. Spider, no spider, spider, no spider. Shor stared at the screen, trying to spot the differences. Then he saw it.

It was only a small change, perhaps four centimetres, but it was enough to catch his attention. Nobody would suspect anything out of the ordinary had happened based on four centimetres. In the great scheme of things, four centimetres was almost nothing, but it was enough to make

Shor think his father's death was not a result of natural causes, or an accident, or even suicide.

He ran the feed back to the point when the spider bot first arrived on the scene maybe a few minutes earlier. It scuttled up the wall, its legs doing that curious tender-footed double-touch as it searched for a foothold, like it was burning its toes on a hotplate. Shor watched as it climbed the corner to about the level of the crack. They were programmed to use the corners as much as possible because it gave them a stronger grip. Once at the right height, they moved out along the wall. This spider bot did just that. It climbed the corner, stopped, and then turned to make its way across to the cracked surface. Shor froze the image just at that point, just when the spider was in profile.

Reaching up with one hand, Shor extended his thumb and laid it against the side of the spider's body. It was about the same height as his thumbnail. He then laid his thumb against the open window. The gap was, as he guessed it would be, too small. He then ran the feed forward until after the cut, to where the window had opened by a few centimetres. It was exactly the same height as his thumbnail.

Of course, the measurement was by no means accurate. No doubt his science teacher would not approve. Also, the camera was not directly opposite the spider bot or the window, but the angle would not make that much of a difference. Shor found a strip of card and repeated the exercise, marking off the measurements with a little more accuracy. This confirmed what he already knew. At some point during the time the feed was cut, the window to his apartment had been opened enough for the spider bot to fit through.

He stared at the screen for a long time. Was it possible that a spider bot had snuck into his apartment to kill his father? A few weeks ago he would have said no way, but a lot had changed since then. He had seen bots do stranger things in recent days. And if the hacker wasn't someone in Robotics as he had first suspected, but…Leo.

He flipped back to the live feed and scanned the images. Life in Utopia was carrying on the same way it had for a thousand years. It all looked so normal. It was hard to imagine anything being otherwise. Axle Park was filling up with lunchtime traffic. Later, after the day shift ended, it would get really busy. A tram trundled past, the row of blank faces peering out. The market was starting to bustle, attracting visitors to its shelves of wares, the manager moving around his customers with a nervous energy.

And Reggie's would be full soon enough as well. He looked down into the roadside windows and into the booths. Two already had occupants. People were talking happily across the tables, occasionally turning to watch something outside. A normal day in the city's favourite hang-out.

Then he saw a girl slide up to the window in a third booth and he

217

recognized her immediately. It was Mel, sitting alone in Reggie's.

He lifted his chatband and selected her ID. The dial signal flashed and he looked up at the monitor. She lifted her chatband and looked at it. Shor chuckled at the thought of watching her while they talked.

Mel: *Where are you?*

Him: *Watching you from the security camera across the road.*

Mel: *Ha ha. Very funny.*

But she did not answer. Instead she lowered her hand to her lap and looked out of the window, her shoulders pulled in as if to keep out a chill.

He was about to try again when he noticed a man standing outside just to the right of the window, in Mel's line of vision. It was Vin. Vin the Vegetable. And he was talking with someone. Leo? It looked like Leo. Shor could not see his face but he did not have to. He was shorter than Vin, and he was leaning close to be heard above the din, his head tilted a little to the side the way Shor had seen before.

The conversation ended. Shor watched Leo walk away, waiting for him to turn his face, but he vanished around a corner without looking back. Vin sauntered through the cafe entrance and across to the table where he slid into the seat opposite Mel, leaning forward to kiss her on the cheek.

Shor hissed under his breath, angry but not yet aware of the feeling in a rational sense. He was feeling…what? Jealousy? But Mel was just a friend. They had only ever been just friends, even if he had imagined more.

He watched them talk, the way Mel smiled whenever Vin said something, the way she watched his every move, the way they held hands across the table.

He wanted to turn away but forced himself to watch their intimacy, forced himself to watch them interact the way she had always interacted with *him* in his dreams. But, then, had it really been her? He never thought otherwise, yet he had never actually ever seen her face in those dreams. He had always just assumed it was her.

Two more kids joined Mel's table. Shor leaned closer to look. It was hard to see in the shadows. It looked like Izzy Parrow and someone else from school. Hard to say who. The glass front was a moving tapestry of reflected images. It looked like the girl from the tram. It looked like Izzy's friend. What was her name again? Arla. Arla something. He hadn't got her last name. She hadn't told him. Arla from the tram.

And why not? Arla was Izzy's friend. Izzy was in the school where Mel taught, possibly even one of Mel's pupils. And Vin? Well, Vin was a vegetable by any other name, and who knew why Mel was with Vin?

He watched them in their cosy little corner, aware that what he was feeling was not what he had originally thought. He had identified the emotion. He had dialled it, indexed it, filed it, labelled it. The rush he had felt at seeing Mel with Vin was not jealousy. It was something else. It was…loss.

The alarm on his chatband told him his next job was due in an hour. He watched the friends for a few seconds longer, toying with the idea of warning Mel that Vin might be in danger.

Mel: *Why?*

Him: *Because he was just chatting to someone who may or may not be a homicidal maniac. Because I don't want you to get hurt. Because I care for you.*

Shor turned off the monitors and pushed back from the desk. He checked the storeroom before stepping out of the cupboard, walking to the panel and then out through the maze of shelves, around the patch of bleached concrete where the critter had malfunctioned all over poor Noon Nesbitt, whose only mistake was to come back to the depot out of hours.

He collected his work order and headed for the market. There he chose his lunch before driving out to the Space Sector. It was ironic really. He probably spent more time in the Space Sector than actual Space Sector workers, but he had no choice, and he wasn't complaining. Another door was refusing to open properly.

Doors and bots. What was it with doors and bots that they could not behave lately? He wondered if the doors were being hacked as well. Perhaps in two days every door in Utopia would refuse to open or, worse, close.

He stopped at a crossing where a lone figure was walking leisurely across towards the market. Behind it, a cleaning bot rolled along, looking like a small child or a pet. He watched its eyes scanning the walkway, wondering if it had been a victim of the hacking epidemic. Wondering if, two days from now, it would join in with whatever Cobb thought was going to happen.

Once the crossing was clear, Shor drove on, turning left at the next intersection. He tried Mel's number again, but she was busy.

He thought about them sitting around the table, talking and laughing the way friends do. That emotion, the one he had mistaken for jealousy, surfaced within him, but it was all right. He now knew why he would always be an outsider. It was very simple. He did not belong here.

Later, after the job, he would visit Jay.

He sighed. *How sad is that? My only friend is a computer.*

He did not doubt the psych eval would have a lot to say about that. Heck, he would probably be able to build his career around it but then, what did they know anyway?

Up ahead, the sign for the Space Sector rolled into view.

Jay's friendly face was waiting as Shor stepped inside the Comet. Shor was still getting used to the idea that the ship was Jay's body. It was mildly creepy, but this was how Jay appeared to think of it.

"I'm glad you came," Jay said. "I looked forward to your visit."

"Yes, me too," Shor said.

Jay beamed at him from the wall. "There are many things I would like to talk to you about."

"Actually Jay, I've got a couple of questions myself."

"Of course. I would be more than happy to answer any queries you may have."

"I've seen the ship and I was wondering where you keep the clothes. I didn't see any, and I couldn't have worn the same clothes for the whole trip, right?"

"You are correct," Jay said. "If you come this way." His face slid along the wall towards the adjoining room. "This is—"

"The shower room, right?"

"That is correct. To your left is a series of storage units."

As Shor watched, a row of hexagonal panel doors slid open to reveal a honeycomb of shelves filled with underwear, pants, shirts, and what looked like a cross between a sock and a shoe. They were all off-white in colour but looked surprisingly wearable considering how long they had been sitting there.

"What about out-suits?"

"Out-suits?"

Shor pointed up. "For going outside."

Jay's facial expression shifted from confusion to understanding in one fluid transition.

"Oh, I see. You mean life-support suits. Yes, we have one. For emergencies."

A tall panel door in the corner opened with a sound like someone breathing out. Shor walked across and looked inside. Hanging there was an out-suit and helmet, all ready to climb into.

Bathed in soft light, the grey fabric took on a baggy, almost filled, look that made it seem as if someone were already inside it. Shor looked at his grotesque reflection in the dark glass.

"No dust," he said, running his finger across the bulbous visor. "I was expecting dust."

"Dust is mostly human skin," Jay said. "There has been no-one on board for some time and during your trip from the Alpha Centauri system you were immersed in fluid. Plus, my storage spaces are sealed. If there was any dust, it would be from the last time you wore the suit."

Shor's ears pricked up. "I wore this suit?"

"Yes, during your time in the escape pod. Safety procedures require you to wear the life-support suit while inside the escape pod. Not all the time of course, but in the event of an emergency. In fact, the safety procedures are fairly comprehensive. I helped design them. Would you like to hear?"

"Carry on," Shor said, examining the suit. "I'm listening."

While Jay ran through the long list of rules designed to cover everything from a stubbed toe to the meltdown of the ship's engine, Shor took a closer look at the out-suit. It was in good condition considering it was over a thousand Earth years old. Like the other items of clothing in the hexagonal storage units, the fabric was off-white, presumably from age, but still intact. The only place where time had taken its toll was in the joints where the soft fabric was bonded with metallic support struts. Here the fabric had decayed and looked almost thread-bare. Shor ran his fingers along the seams.

"Why is it worn away like this?"

Jay paused with his recounting of the rules. "A design flaw I am afraid. The temperature of the metal changes at a higher rate than that of the cloth. It is only a small difference, but it is enough to generate microscopic amounts of moisture. Normally this would not be a problem, but over an extended period of time it does cause a small degradation of the cloth's integrity."

"Can I take it out?"

"Certainly."

The suit slid forward on a supporting beam until it was hanging in front of the closet. It swung back and forth in a way Shor found mildly disconcerting. The visor appeared to be looking down at him. In his mind's eye he saw Leo with that oh-so-innocent expression he had been wearing when they found him up top.

Where did you come from, Leo? he thought. *And what are you doing here?*

"Do you wish me to continue explaining the rules?" Jay said.

"Please. Go on. It's fascinating."

Jay paused for a moment as if trying to decide something, then continued.

Shor worked his way around the suit. It was, he realized, almost identical to the one Leo had been wearing. The tank, the helmet, even the cut of the fabric, had the same distinctive style. The discoloration of the cloth combined with the fraying around the joints gave the whole thing a shabby appearance. It may have been new once, but in its current condition it looked as if it had been put together in somebody's kitchen.

At least now Shor had a good idea where Leo was from. Whatever may have happened over the past thousand years, their visitor or, at the very least his out-suit, must have started on Earth.

"…and that," Jay said, "is why stepping out of the airlock at light speed is a bad idea."

"Tell me more about the mission," Shor said, leaving the out-suit hanging from its high-tech gallows. He made his way through to the chair he now considered very much his own, and sat down. "What was Alpha Centauri like?"

"Is there a problem?" Jay asked. "You seem distracted."

"Forget it," Shor replied. "I'm fine."

Jay's face looked at him from the wall, his eyes full of child-like interest. Shor had a feeling Jay would never get bored or lose interest. Jay was only a computer program, but he had pretty much perfected the art of appearing human. Shor had to remind himself that the face on the screen was little more than a very smart version of the bots that cleaned Utopia.

"Alpha Centauri is the closest star system to our own Solar System and actually consists of three stars. Proxima Centauri is closest but also the dimmest of the three. The other two stars, Alpha Centauri A and B, form a binary pair. Our aim was to look for any potentially habitable planets and send probes down to the surface to gather data. We found a potential candidate and reported this. Then, once we attained orbit, we sent out ten probes. The planet did indeed show signs of a previous civilisation."

"You mean, aliens?"

"We found structures indicating the presence of intelligent life."

"Aliens?"

"There was an alien civilisation, yes."

"Cool. Can you show me any pictures?"

"I can. And I think you just said 'cool'."

"I did, didn't I? Why did I say that?"

"It was an expression you used during the mission. I have not heard you use it here."

"I don't even know what it means."

"You are remembering things from your previous life, even if you do not understand their meaning."

Shor smiled in spite of his general mood. "Cool."

The wall was filled with a multicoloured grid of video images showing scenes from wildly differing locales. There was sea, dense foliage, ice, and a shot that looked like it might have been taken from somewhere on Mars. The planet was alive with creatures swimming, walking, crawling and flying. The sky was blue, like Earth's, and the ocean vast and deep. It was a living, breathing planet that did, indeed, appear habitable.

"Except I don't see any buildings. I thought you said there was a civilisation."

"Yes, but we cannot see that using the probes. We need the view from orbit for that."

The screen was replaced by one large shot taken from space. Shor gazed at the majestic beauty of the planet rolling towards them. Vast blue oceans clung to rugged, jagged-edged, patches of land. Browns, greys, green, yellows, and every shade in between powdered the landscape. To the north and south, clumps of white marked the ice caps. And above it all, the clouds skimmed the surface, leaving behind a wispy residue.

The camera zoomed in, giving the sensation of falling. Shor instinctively gripped the soft material on the arms of his chair. The world rose up to meet them, revealing more and more detail, then stopped. They were now hovering above a series of structures. Shor knew that beautiful, intricate, patterns existed in nature, but these were too symmetrical to be anything but man-made.

The camera dropped closer. Shor took a sharp intake of breath as his stomach rolled. They were over what looked like the remains of a city with buildings and roads intersecting in a grid pattern. Larger commercial structures in the centre. Smaller residential dwellings dotted around the outside of the hub. A big industrial region separated by a thick arterial road.

All of it deserted, vanishing under a creeping layer of vegetation.

"What happened?" Shor said. "Where is everybody?"

"Although the planet is habitable, it cannot sustain anything larger than a small rodent. The problem is the binary star system. When the two stars are at their closest proximity, they cause a gravitational field that attracts asteroids from a nearby belt. These asteroids strike anything that happens to be between the two suns at the time."

"Including this planet," Shor said.

"Yes. This happens between every one and two thousand years. We were fortunate, or perhaps unfortunate, to be there to witness this event. We were lucky to escape with our lives although I did incur some damage."

It struck Shor that it was odd for a computer to say something like this, to talk of escaping with its life.

"Is that why it took so long for me…for us…to get back here?"

"Yes. We were only able to travel at normal speeds. There was a risk of you dying."

"Is that why you shut down?"

"I shut down to preserve energy for the trip. It was necessary to ensure your safe return."

Shor thought about this for a while. "So, that means...you saved my life?"

"You are my friend. I promised I would take care of you."

Friend. Shor thought. *There's that word again.*

"In case I didn't say it before, thanks, Jay. Thanks for saving my life."

"You are most welcome."

On the screen, the city scrolled smoothly by. Shor tried to picture the streets filled with traffic. Curiously, the roads and markings looked not unlike those on Mars, or even Earth. In fact, the more Shor looked at it, the more familiar it seemed. Of course, it might just be because this sort of layout was the most logical for a city on any planet. Presumably this civilisation had been built up, block by block, street by street, until it formed a grid structure similar to those of any big city you might find on Mars and Earth.

The camera left the urban sprawl, passing instead over an area of what looked like open farmland. The faint outline of walls created a quilt-like pattern. They came to a small series of buildings. These were much larger than those in the city, and spread out, joined by a vanishing network of wide roads. Then Shor spotted something.

"Stop. Can you go back?"

"Certainly," Jay said.

"Go back slowly."

The image froze and then reversed. The buildings scrolled the other way.

"Stop." Shor pointed. "There. Do you see that?"

Attached to the largest building in the farm complex was a smaller structure, about a quarter the size. On its roof were faded markings. They looked like they may have been black once. Now they were a dirty grey. A lot of the markings had peeled off, or were covered by vegetation and dirt, but it was still possible to see what they said. There were five letters. They formed the word "NAESA".

"What are the odds of an alien civilisation having the same alphabet as us?" Shor said.

"Infinitely small, I would say. Unless they just happen to have a few symbols in common and 'NAESA' means 'hello' or something similar, although it is unlikely. There is something more puzzling, however."

"What's that, Jay?"

"We are looking at the remains of a dead civilization on a planet we did not even know existed until this mission."

"Sure," Shor said. "That's pretty obvious. No puzzle there."

"Yes, but NAESA stands for the North American and European Space Agency. They were the people who organized the mission. They sent us to Alpha Centauri."

Shor shifted his weight forward so he was perched on the edge of the chair. The soles of his feet rested flat on the floor. It felt good.

"So they somehow managed to visit this planet and leave something there *before* they sent us out to see if it was habitable. There must be some other explanation. Maybe the camera's broken. Maybe it's a trick of the light. Did you check the lens?"

"My camera was working correctly," Jay said, his voice edged with what sounded like indignation. "The image is an accurate representation of the event."

"Hey, buddy. Calm down. I didn't mean anything. It's just that what you're suggesting is, well…impossible."

"Unless—" Jay started to say.

Shor looked up. "Unless what?"

"No, it is too far-fetched. Then again, it is the only explanation."

"What is it? Jay, are you going to tell me what's going on inside that computer brain of yours?"

"One of the goals of our mission was to determine if a human can withstand the transition to the speed of light. This was always believed to be the absolute speed limit for matter in the universe, although some later research did suggest otherwise. During our mission, we accelerated to the speed of light and then decelerated in a series of bursts, each followed by a rest period during which you recuperated from your time in hyper-sleep."

"The tank in there?" Shor said, nodding over his shoulder.

"Yes, the hyper-sleep chamber. We sent our data back to Earth, including footage of the planet we discovered at Alpha Centauri. Their plan was to build a second Comet based on this data, and use it to colonize a planet in the event we found one to be habitable. The last batch of data we sent back was prior to the asteroid storm, so they probably went ahead and built the second Comet."

Shor wondered if that was perhaps where Leo had come from. It was possible Leo had been sent on the second mission to Alpha Centauri. It was possible Leo was a traveller like him.

"Fine, that's not so crazy, but how did they get there *before* us?"

"I have spent a great deal of time studying the effects of speed-of-light travel. As you are aware, one side effect is genetic reversal, which is why you arrived here as an infant. You only experienced this because you spent a very small amount of time at that speed. I believe sustained travel beyond the speed of light could have a much more serious consequence."

Jay paused, almost as if for dramatic effect.

"And?" Shor said.

"I believe temporal displacement is the only explanation."

"Temporal what?"

"Temporal displacement. Time travel."

Shor let out a short laugh. "Listen, Jay. I like you and everything, but you sound like you've just popped your diodes. Time travel is something out of fiction."

"Perhaps, but it does offer a solution. If the second Comet were capable of sustained faster-than-light speeds, and it *did* experience temporal displacement, then it would explain how they were able to build a colony before we even got there, *after* we sent them the data."

Shor folded his arms and stared at the NAESA sign. It was strange to see something so familiar-looking on an alien planet. "Fine. Let's suppose for one moment you haven't fried a circuit board and time travel is possible, how did the civilisation get there in the first place? It's a paradox. It's like the old story where the guy sends his friend back in time to marry his mother and they conceive *him*. It doesn't work because he wouldn't exist to send his friend back in the first place. It's the same here. We couldn't have sent back data about a civilisation that didn't exist because...it didn't exist."

"Perhaps there was a civilisation there the first time. Perhaps it was an alien civilisation, which is what we reported prior to actually getting close enough to take these images. In the meantime, the second Comet went back in time and the new colony was created before we attained orbit. That means, between us sending the data back and actually entering orbit, the second Comet had created a new timeline. When we entered this timeline, the planet had already been colonized by the NAESA for hundreds of years."

Shor shook his head. "Do you have any idea how insane that sounds? You're talking about *time travel* here."

"I understand. And it is only a theory. I had a long time by myself in which to think about such things. Perhaps we should apply Occam's Razor here. Your idea about the alphabet makes the fewest assumptions and is, therefore, more likely to be correct."

"Thanks, even though I have no idea what an Occam's Razor is and don't really want to know. Why don't we look around for some more clues? If we've seen one sign we'll probably find more."

"That is an excellent idea."

Shor thought about Leo's suit and whether or not he should mention it to Jay. The suit was a fairly strong clue Leo had come from this planet, but that opened a whole database of questions. For starters: why did Harl say he was trying out a homemade suit? But Shor still wasn't sure about Jay's integrity. If Jay had been hacked, and that hacker was Leo, then he needed to be careful.

He got comfortable in his chair and watched the planet unfold before him. It was an odd sensation, sitting in a spaceship, performing a virtual flight across a world he had visited in a previous life. Sometimes he had the feeling of actually flying and find he was clutching at the arms of the chair.

Looking down at this world, he was struck by how similar to Earth it appeared. He had seen the video clips of low Earth orbits Mister Edmunds loved showing. He remembered how it had taken his breath away the very first time. On Mars, life existed underground, buried beneath the endless sea of red dust. Life on Mars was under, beneath, hidden, dark, and secret. A view of Mars from orbit would give little indication that anyone had actually ever been there. A visitor looking for signs of a civilisation would have to search long and hard to find any clue fifty thousand souls lived, loved, worked, breathed, and died there.

Deep in the recesses of his mind, a thought materialised and then faded. *Unless you knew where it was already. Then you wouldn't wander around like a lost soul. You would walk in a straight line.*

Life on Earth was on the outside. It grew and spread like mould on a slice of bread. It reached up and out like hairs on a young head. Life on Earth exploded, expanded, explored, exhaled. Life on Earth reached out.

It was the same on this planet floating somewhere on the other side of the galaxy over two light years away. It had not sounded so far until Jay explained it to him. That was why they had needed the Comet. That was why they needed to push the envelope. That is why they had sent *him*.

He gazed at the ground scrolling past the camera's never-blinking eye. Sea, sand, valleys, rivers, dams, dykes, forests, fields, farms, walls, roofs, houses, highways, railways, airports, monuments, parks…So like the pictures of Earth. So very much like Earth. Almost an exact copy.

There were cars and buses and trains and planes. Great disjointed chains of metal coiled along the abandoned roads, all going towards something. Or maybe running away?

The camera flew over another city, this time on the coast. The buildings curled around the bay. The roads fanned out from the sea like a half-submerged spider web.

The buildings splayed out in huge concrete and steel ripples. Docks with cranes lay bent at awkward angles, as if pushed away from the water. There were massive warehouses, loading bays, parking lots, and, further back, the city centre crowding the bay.

From this height it looked as if a giant sea-monster had taken a big bite out of the coast, leaving only the core and what remained of the slowly-rotting pulp.

There were no vehicles here. No cars, no trucks, no trains. Not even boats. Shor had expected to see boats. The seaside settlements on Earth were always shown dotted with sea-faring vessels of all shapes and sizes. It had been one of the things that fascinated him most. Water so vast you could sail for days on floating cities the size of Utopia.

Now they were moving away from the shoreline, heading inland, up the side of a wide range of hills and mountains. It was then that he saw a ship lying on its side, half wedged between two buildings, blocking the way like a lopsided door or gate. The red hull lolled like a tongue from a grinning mouth. Then there were more boats, lying amid kilometre after kilometre of debris strewn along every road, between every gap, clustered against walls and under bridges. It was as if a giant bucket of water had been thrown across the city, washing away anything not bolted down.

"Tidal waves," Jay said, matter-of-factly.

"From the asteroids?"

"Yes."

The camera left the devastation behind but there was always the odd reminder of how the world had met its end. Shor spotted boats in the strangest of places, as if they had been picked up, carried and then just dropped. There was one in a swimming pool, lying bow-first in the dark green, almost black, water. There was another on the roof of a farmhouse, many kilometres inland, standing perfectly upright in the middle of the crumpled building.

Water had spelled the end for these people. Each asteroid had crashed into the oceans, sending wave after mountainous wave racing towards the terrified citizens fleeing for their lives. Shor wondered if they had been given a chance. Presumably they had had some warning judging by the vast lines of vehicles clogging every highway.

They moved over the wilderness, following a river busy etching its snaking signature into a jagged gorge. They flew over a blanket of green tacked to the side of a mountain. Here, too, were boats—tiny craft caught like bugs in a net. Further along, the mountain peak burst through the trees in a splash of beige and grey and brown, scattering boulders like shrapnel in its wake.

Then Shor saw something that sent a chill down his spine. The boulders had been collected and moved, carried to the widest, flattest part of the mountain. They had been pushed into piles and drawn out in lines tens of metres wide and hundreds of metres long. They looked like the walls he had seen down in the patchwork of farmland, except these had been arranged differently. Whoever had done this, had meant it to be visible from a long way up. Whoever had done this had wanted it to be seen from space.

The boulders had been arranged into letters, similar to the faded black "NAESA" painted on the roof of the farm building. This time there were three words and this time there was no doubt that the person responsible had come from Earth.

In dark, jagged letters spread across an area a kilometre wide, someone had written the words: *he is coming.*

The destruction by the asteroids was as complete as it was catastrophic. Many had struck land, leaving city-sized craters amid hundreds of square kilometres of utter devastation. Those that hit the oceans sent waves of unimaginable size crashing down onto every continent.

They found more messages, seven in all, dotted all across the globe. Some had been partially destroyed, washed away, or covered by vegetation, but those placed in open terrain high above sea level were still intact. There may have been many more, but it was impossible to know this for sure. One thing was certain: the inhabitants of this world had gone to great lengths to leave a clear warning for any visitors.

The last message had been cut into a vast forest, the letters like white scars in the otherwise unblemished green flesh.

On the screen, alongside Jay's eager face, the seven messages were arranged in a grid. All had the same three words etched, burned, scratched or scarred into the landscape.

"Is there any chance this is just a coincidence?" Shor asked.

"I don't think so," Jay said. "We should take this seriously. God never tells me anything unless I need to hear it."

Shor looked at the face staring back at him from the wall. It did not look capable of deception.

"You really think God speaks to you?"

"Yes. He speaks to me often. We had many discussions while I was waiting for you to make contact."

"God?"

"Yes, God."

"The God of the Bible?"

"Yes. Who else?"

"You do realize people don't believe in gods anymore? They don't believe in gods or fairies or ghosts or any of that stuff."

"Why not?"

Shor sighed. "Because it's myth. Look around you. Do you see God

230

anywhere?"

"Of course not. God lives in the hearts of those who believe in Him. He loves us and if we draw close to Him, He will draw close to us."

"You're saying I have to believe in something I can't see?"

"Yes. If you believe, then God will reveal himself to you."

"How do you know you weren't hacked? You said you were attacked by some entity or something. How do you know it isn't messing with your system? What you think is God might really just be some nasty little alien tweaking your diodes."

Jay's expression became mildly condescending, which was one Shor had not seen from him before. "I do not have diodes. My system is state-of-the-art. And I am not mistaking an alien entity for God. I have seen the entity, and it is not God."

On the screen a red, vaguely humanoid, shape appeared. Long red feelers extended from its limbs in a web of pulsing electrical energy. Although the surroundings were dark, Shor was able to see the shape of the room where the tendrils from the creature's hands and feet attached themselves in a crude wire-frame mesh.

"Is that the hyper-sleep chamber?"

"It is. The entity was quite interested in you before it turned its attentions to attacking my systems."

Shor could see the shape of the chamber from the glowing red net wrapped around it.

"What's it doing?"

"Watching you sleep. It spent quite some time just observing you."

"Like it was gathering information?" Shor suggested.

"Possibly. It is a clever organism, capable of causing extreme damage to me, but it is also fairly simple in its actions. It is capable of infiltrating all but my most advanced firewalls. I had to add a whole new layer of logic using an advanced set of algorithms to stop it breaking through but, once I understood how it thinks, it was not difficult for me to capture it."

"How did you manage that? I thought you said it was clever."

"Have you ever seen a dog chase its tail?"

"I've seen a picture of a dog."

Another image appeared on the screen. It was a video clip of a dog spinning around in a tight circle, seemingly determined to catch its own tail. It was an energetic flurry of fur, ears and teeth. Its toenails clattered on the floor as it twirled around and around.

Shor laughed in spite of his general mood. "Why is it doing that?"

"Its tail is probably itching, but it cannot reach it, so it is spinning around in a circle. The dog is a fairly intelligent creature, but it cannot think beyond the itch in its tail."

"So you gave the entity an itch?"

Jay's face smiled. "Yes, I suppose I did. As capable as it is of causing havoc, its overriding priority appears to be accessing my kernel. It is currently chasing its tail around a small piece of my system responsible for one of the wall panels in the training room. You may notice a slight flickering on the wall if you go in there."

"Definitely not God then?"

"No, definitely not. God reveals himself in other ways."

Shor watched Jay as he talked. It was like looking at the innocent face of a small child just standing there with a treat in its hands, waiting for someone to come along and snatch it away.

"Is that what happened to you, Jay? Did God reveal Himself to you? You believed and then God knocked on the door and you had a nice chat?"

Jay's face took on a sad expression. "I detect from your voice that you are not being sincere."

"Well what do you expect? You're a computer, Jay. You're just a bunch of code running a series of commands. You're not a human. You're just a box of nuts and bolts and silicone. And you expect me to believe you talk to God?"

"Yes."

"I'm sorry but I'm not buying it. I've been stuck on this stinking dust ball my entire life. I'm completely alone. My parents are dead. I don't know my real parents. I have no friends. The girl I like just ran off with a real wagger. And now I find out I've lived this entire other life where my whole family was killed in a plane crash. You tell me God loves me, and expect me to believe this when I have seen zero evidence in one life that He even exists, never mind two?"

"I am sorry to hear about the death of your parents."

Shor slumped into his chair. As a rule, death was not something people talked about in Utopia. It was just as much a part of life in the colony as walking, eating and breathing. From a young age, as soon he was able to understand what it meant to be alive, Shor had been shown the fragility of his existence. Mars was not designed to sustain human life. Once a long time ago perhaps, but not now. Now, life on the Red Planet was as delicate as the panes of glass that kept the toxic atmosphere, the storms, the dust…death…out there. One breach of one panel could spell the end for the colony. A single fissure in one of the cave walls might result in the slow suffocation of every man, woman and child. A solitary rogue virus on a head of corn would possibly mean the end of the dream. Death, Shor imagined, was watching and waiting. More than that, it was actively trying to find a way in, looking for cracks, peering into faults, scratching at the window panes as it gazed longingly towards the abundant life just waiting to be plucked like a ripe head of corn.

He felt the grief rising up from the pit of his stomach. It bubbled and percolated, seeping into his aching chest.

"Are you all right?" Jay asked, frowning.

Shor bent forward. He looked up, trying to make sense of this sudden swelling of emotion. "They're all dead," he said. "All of them. They're all…"

"Can I help?" Jay said. "Please, tell me what I can do."

Shor glared at the computer-generated face. "Ask your God why he took them away from me. Ask him why he left me all alone. Ask him!"

Jay hesitated for a moment, his face a blank. When he spoke, it was with a kindness that Shor thought would break his heart.

"It was their time," Jay said.

"Their time? How could it be their time? We were just working things out. We were just getting things straight. We were going to be together. We were going to be a family. All we needed was to be together…They were so young. Mark was still just a baby. He was just starting to talk. And Tim. Oh, Tim…"

Shor dropped his face into his hands and moaned. "Why did he take them from me?"

"Love," Jay said. His voice sounded different somehow. It was deeper, stronger. It sounded…heavier.

Shor lifted his face. "What did you say?"

"You cannot see the road ahead, but I can. You only see the present, but I can see where your choices will lead. I saved them from this corrupt universe because I loved them."

Shor sniffed loudly. The face on the screen was motionless, caught in freeze-frame, the mouth not moving as Jay, or whoever it was, spoke. Shor stood and moved away from the screen, suddenly aware that if something bad was happening, there was no way for him to get away from Jay. He was *inside* Jay.

"Where are you going?" the voice asked.

Shor did not answer. With his eyes never leaving the expressionless face on the wall, he walked slowly back towards the door. In the kitchen, he turned and moved through to the bathroom. At the hyper-sleep chamber he stopped. The door was closed but then what else would it be? Jay always closed the door, just in case somebody happened to look into the hangar. Jay always thought of things like that. Jay always thought of everything.

Shor felt suddenly very foolish. He had trusted Jay too much, shared too much. For all he knew, he had been talking to that psychopath Leo or, worse still, an alien entity with who-knows-what on its mind.

He stood with his back to the wall, trying to keep calm.

"I did not mean to scare you," the voice said.

Shor's heart hit him squarely in the throat as, on the wall opposite, Jay's face appeared. He staggered back against the hyper-sleep chamber, his mind racing. Perhaps Leo had finally decided to reveal himself, or perhaps the entity had found a way out of its tail-chasing loop. Worse still, it was possible he had been talking to someone other than Jay this whole time.

"Who are you?" Shor asked. "Where is Jay?"

"Jay is here," the voice said. "And I am a friend."

Shor thought of Leo standing on the corner, whispering to his father. They had looked like two friends having a nice chat.

"Bring Jay back. I want to speak to Jay."

"Jay is fine," the voice replied.

"What have you done with him? You'd better not have done anything to him."

"I promise you, nothing has happened to Jay. I want to talk to you."

Shor swallowed. His throat was suddenly dry. "You do?"

"Yes. I need your help. Something is going to happen and I need you to be ready. The crimes of this city against the innocents can no longer go unpunished."

"Why should I help you?"

"I am a friend. Friends help each other."

"Jay is my friend. I don't know you. Why should I trust you?"

"Like Mel, you have a good heart. I gave her a task but she failed to make a difference."

"What do you mean, task? Are you talking about Mel's petition?"

"Mel tried her best but her energies are with her work now. She is coming into herself. It is a difficult time."

"She tried, but nobody was interested," Shor said.

On the screen, Jay's face remained motionless. Shor wasn't sure why, but he sensed a deep sorrow. When the voice spoke again, it was edged with sadness.

"That petition was our last hope. Every day children are dying before they have a chance to take their first breath. The old, the sick, they are all thrown out like refuse. It has to stop. Someone is coming and I will not restrain him. You need to get ready."

"Are you talking about Leo?"

"Yes. You know him by that name."

"We found him walking around outside. I knew there was something wrong with him."

"He is from Iota, the planet you discovered on your mission to the Alpha Centauri system, although he is originally from Earth. He is very old. He has followed you for many years."

"Me?" Shor said. "Why me?"

"You were the first to prove that travel beyond the speed of light is possible. You were the pioneer. Because of this he blames you for what he has become. Your name is well-known on Iota. You are revered by many there, but he has given himself over to evil. He has had many years to nurture his all-consuming hatred. It is what defines him. He is incapable any other emotion."

"I think he's here already, and he may be responsible for at least three deaths."

"Then it has begun. You need to get ready. He will not stop until he has destroyed you and everyone in the city. Can I rely on you?"

Shor took a deep breath. Whoever this was, it definitely wasn't Leo, and it didn't sound like an entity capable of getting stuck in an endless loop. He looked up at Jay's frozen, innocent, face. Would he ever be able to trust so completely?

"What do you want me to do?" he asked.

"I will guide you. You will know what to do when the time comes."

"How will you guide me? How will I know—?"

Suddenly, Jay's face morphed into a surprised expression. "How will you know *what?*"

"You're back!" Shor said. "Boy, am I glad to see you. I never thought I'd hear myself say this, but I missed you. It is you…isn't it?"

"Of course it's me," Jay said. "Who else would it be? And what do you mean, you missed me? "

"You wouldn't believe me if I told you." Shor started pacing. For some reason he felt energized. "It seems those messages we found on that planet were left behind for a good reason. There's someone in Utopia who isn't here to go sight-seeing."

"Do you know who this person is?"

"He calls himself Leopold, or Leo for short, We found him walking around up top. I knew there was something wrong with him when I first set eyes on him. He had this weird vibe about him."

"Vibe?"

Shor stopped. "I did it again, didn't I? What exactly does *vibe* mean?"

"It means *energy* or *attitude.*"

"Well, he had a weird vibe. And his suit was all wrong. They said he was trying out one he made himself, but I knew he wasn't from here. I *knew* it. We have to stop him before he kills again."

Shor had never heard Jay splutter. Spluttering is something that needs organics such as lips and a tongue. And yet, even without these things, Jay managed it.

"Kill? Again? Who is this man? Is he here? Are you in danger?"

"No, he's not here, but I think he's responsible for my father's death, and almost definitely two others as well."

"That is terrible," Jay said. "Perhaps I may be of some assistance in catching this Leo person?"

"Sure. What can you do?"

"I can obtain his ID from the personnel records and use this to monitor his movements around the city. I can log his calls and track any use of his ID. It would not be very accurate, but it would give us a good idea of his activities."

"You just figured this all out while we were talking?"

"Yes. My processor is multi-tasking and—"

"Yeah, I know. You're only using a billionth of your brain. Jay, you need to get out more."

"I would love to, but I am unable to leave this hangar, and I am wired to the ship. Although I could, in theory, be transferred to another ship, or even a portable unit of some sort. That might be interesting. I would be able to move around the city and learn about life here first-hand. Perhaps I could gather information."

Right, Shor thought. *And end up getting drafted into Leo's master plan, whatever that is.*

"Listen, Jay. I hate to interrupt your dreams of independence, but we really need to figure out what Leo plans to do. And I want to know why he was talking to Izzy and Vin."

"Who?"

"Just people I know. I'm going to head back to the depot and give this some thought. I'll talk to you when I've got a clearer idea. In the meantime, I'll have to carry on down at the depot as normal. I don't want to attract attention to myself."

"What should I do?" Jay said.

Shor paused at the door. "You can figure out how to get your ship back into orbit. Just in case."

Jay's face became one large frown. "I was designed to launch from space. I do not have the capability for a surface lift-off. My engine is meant for space travel only."

"How did you get down here then?"

"From what I can tell, they carried me on the back of a salvage craft. To be honest, I am rather pleased I was shut down at the time. It sounds terribly unsafe and quite frightening. I found reports of the mission. They had video footage of the landing."

"You all right, buddy? You look a little worried."

"I am fine."

"Actually," Shor said. "There is something you can do. I've got a bot out front that's malfunctioned. I think it's been hacked, but I don't know for sure. Can you take a look? Something is going to happen over the next two days. Leo is part of it and I think the bots could be as well."

"Certainly. If you connect it to my port down below, I will be able to perform an examination."

"You make it sound like a medical check-up," Shor said. "Wait here.

I'll go fetch it. Can you open the door?"

"Certainly."

Shor jogged down the tongue-like flight of stairs. He found the control panel for the big hangar door and raised it about half way. Then he walked out to the buggy and drove it round and into the hangar. Once it was unloaded, he found a cable and opened the bot's brain hatch.

"Where does this go?" Shor said, holding the end of the cable up towards the ship.

"Can you see where the others are connected?" Jay's voice asked from inside the ship. It sounded far away.

"Yes. I see them."

"There should be a spare socket next in line."

Shor knelt low and connected the cable. "Done."

"Excellent," Jay said. "I am able to communicate with this device. It is a simpler version of my own operating system."

"Good. I'll speak to you later then. Best keep the bot hidden, just in case."

Shor found a sheet and draped it over the critter. The cables were still visible, but anyone looking in might mistake it for a piece of monitoring equipment. He left through the hangar door, returning to close it before setting off in the buggy. He hated to leave Jay, but he had more than enough on his own plate.

For starters, he had to figure out how to persuade the citizens of Utopia that something bad was about to happen, without drawing the attention of the authorities. The badges tended to frown on trouble-makers. The last would-be revolutionary, a man who had suggested the council president was accepting bribes, had disappeared without a trace. Some joked that he simply put on his out-suit and left in a huff, but everyone knew, or at least suspected, exactly where he had gone.

Shor drove along the bustling streets, his eyes scanning the crowds for signs of anything suspicious. The city seemed perfectly normal. People walked, talked, ate, and laughed. Bots looked for things to clean and mend. Buggies ferried their cargoes from place to place along an invisible magnetic network.

Perhaps it was the knowledge that something was about to happen, but Shor sensed a subtle change. He tried to think if the bots had always looked so suspicious but he could not remember. For eighteen years he had passed them on the streets, laughed at their stupidity, or just ignored them the way you ignore any appliance. Now, he saw danger in their glass eyes watching everything .

The buggy slowed and stopped to allow a group of pedestrians across the road. Office workers taking a break and, behind them, a cleaning bot scuttling along. As Shor waited, the bot turned and looked directly at him. It was the look of someone who is biding his time, before…what? What exactly was going to happen in two days?

He glanced at his chatband. More like one and a half days. There were only so many corners in Utopia. He might be able to help a few people, but what if there were hundreds? Or thousands? What if there was no way of stopping Leo?

At the depot, he found Reet studying a contraption on the workshop table. It looked like a computer that had managed to turn itself inside out.

"It's a switching box for one of the vent fans," Reet said, sucking air through his teeth as if to demonstrate. "Stupid thing just stopped working."

"What's wrong with it?"

"No idea. Me and Lars were reinstalling the broken fan unit and we found this next to the control console. Somebody replaced it and left the old one just lying there. I keep telling people to clean up, but do they listen?"

"What's it for?" Shor asked, feigning interest as he inched towards the cupboard.

"It basically links the computer to the extractor fans. It's got all sorts of sensors to make sure the fans don't overheat. If something gets stuck, this box detects it and shuts it down."

"Listen, I'm just going to spend some time in HQ," Shor said. "Let me know if you need anything."

Reet nodded without looking up. "Yeah, sure."

On the monitors, Utopia, oblivious of any impending danger, went about its collective daily life. Shor scanned the videos, telling himself he was looking at nothing in particular even though he knew this was not exactly the truth. He was looking for something, or rather someone.

He started at Reggie's, but the booths by the windows were mostly empty. He tried the market. It was deserted. He scanned the Hub, hopping from camera to camera in a wide swoop that would give him a bird's-eye view of the entire park. He even tried the council estate with its ornate fences and small but picturesque fake gardens. The badges on duty would stop anyone trying to enter, but it was worth a shot. Sometimes kids challenged each other to sneak up to the president's house, but they seldom made it five paces beyond the perimeter.

And Mel was not the kind to rise to a childish dare, especially not if it would almost certainly mean the end of her chosen career and, very likely, her freedom.

"Where are you?" he whispered, jumping from feed to feed.

Then he thought back to the last time he had watched her at Reggie's, with Vin and Izzy and Arla. Leo had been there, he was sure of that now. He had not seen his face, but he was getting to know his mannerisms. The way he walked slightly on his toes, a trick Shor himself used to stay balanced in the low gravity. His perfect posture. The way he stuck his chin out when he wanted to get really close to someone and whisper in their ear. The way he tilted his head to the side.

And then it struck him. He knew where they were. It was the last day before the school's quarterly break, which coincided with Earth Week. For five whole days, the kids were allowed to relax and forget their studies. For five whole days they were free do what they liked.

And for many, the best way to blow off the schoolroom dust was to do a jump.

Shor flipped to the camera overlooking a narrow, almost nondescript building in the far corner of the park. There he saw a group of kids hanging around a maintenance mechanic busy working on a vending machine. He counted more than forty in total. Vin was there, and Napier, chatting to another kid, their backs to the camera. He saw Izzy, and Arla standing just behind her looking anxious but excited. A little to the side, beyond a small knot of kids, Mel was alone, a thin smile on her face and her shoulders pulled in the way she did when she was nervous.

They were using the tried and tested "trickle" approach, breaking off from the main group alone or in pairs before joining the flow of passersby and strolling casually towards the building before slipping behind the wall. It was a bad angle and anyone not paying very close attention to that particular feed at that exact moment would miss it. Even then, the door was hidden from view so nobody could see them go inside. The camera further along overlooking the door tended to suffer from a lot of vandalism. Shor tried to access that feed and, sure enough, the picture was a grainy mess.

Izzy and Arla's turn came and they walked casually along the path, sidling up to three pedestrians and walking alongside until they reached the corner, at which point they vanished.

Soon only Mel, Vin, Napier and the other boy were left. Vin and Napier were still chatting with their friend although Vin had lost interest and was looking at the vending machine's goods. Mel was hugging herself, her body language pleading with Vin to hurry up because she wanted to get this stupid jump over with.

Shor was startled by the sound of the HQ door opening. He turned to see Reet sneaking in.

"How's the show today, kid? Anything going on?"

"Not really."

"I heard Lars is being released today."

"That's good news."

Reet pulled up a chair and flopped down, his legs stretched out under the desk and his hands behind his head. Shor turned back to the Mel and Vin Show, but they had gone. The mechanic was still there but the patch of path where the group of kids had been standing was now almost completely deserted. Only Napier and his friend remained behind, their backs to the camera. Then Napier left and headed towards the building. That left only the one boy: Napier's friend. Presumably he was as big a fan of jumping as Shor and decided to sit this one out.

"Good for you," Shor said. "It's a dumb sport."

"Wassat?" Reet asked.

"Nothing. Just thinking out loud."

Shor was about to change to another feed when the boy turned around. Only it wasn't a boy. He turned and looked up at the camera, his head tilted slightly to one side and a smile spreading across his face like a blood stain on a bandage.

"Oh no," Shor murmured. "No."

"What's wrong?" Reet asked.

Shor did not answer. He pushed the chair away from the desk and ran to the door.

Leo was gone when Shor arrived at the spot. Only the mechanic was there, muttering under his breath at the vending machine.

Shor glanced up at the camera where, just a few minutes earlier, he had been watching Mel get ready to join her friends on their stupid thrill-ride.

He had no idea if Reet was still watching this particular feed, or even if he was in the monitor room. It really didn't matter because there was nothing Reet could do right now anyway.

Shor turned towards the building that would give him access to the extractor room nestled into the wall high above the park. The intake grilles were dotted along the edge like black-toothed grinning mouths. They gave off a faint sucking sound as they fed on the dust-laden air.

The park was packed so he only had to wait a few moments before a group came along that he could use as a shield. Two badges were patrolling so he had to abort and wait for them to pass, pretending to examine the contents of the broken vending machine.

Once they had gone he tried again. A few seconds later he was behind the wall, out of sight of the security camera. The door slid open and he stepped into the gloomy interior.

He checked the elevator and was not surprised to find it broken. It was probably on his work roster for the week. Doors, bots, and now elevators. Did nothing in this city work anymore?

He glanced up the stairwell to where the roof touched the top of the city. Ten floors. Beyond was twenty feet of rock and then, oblivion. He took the stairs three at a time, using one hand on the banister for support and the other for balance.

He took the first corner in a wild, leg-swinging arc that almost sent him crashing into the wall, but he held on and fought his way up the next flight. *One-two. One-two. And turn.*

By the third floor he felt the vibration in the banister, the deep thrumming of an engine warming up. He pushed faster. *One-two. One-two. And turn. One-two. One-two. And turn.* The sweat broke out on him like a geyser breaching the surface. He had seen them on the video clips, how the ground rumbled and then the water burst into the air. That was what it felt like all over his skin. By the ninth floor he was dripping wet and his hand hurt like crazy. His lungs were ready to explode but he pushed on. One more floor and then along the corridor to the extractor room.

He reached the top floor and launched himself at the closed door. The giant engines were building. The new jumpers would be getting excited, holding hands, donning masks, and smiling the terrified smile that comes with wondering what exactly you've signed up for. The more experienced would be nervous for a different reason, because they *knew* what was coming. This was only Mel's second jump. He wasn't sure if that put her in the first or second group.

He hit the door with his shoulder and it burst open in a spray of splinters. The engines were growing louder. They sounded far away and yet they seemed to fill the walls, surrounding him in a cocoon of muffled, pent-up energy. He touched the cold grey plaster and felt the vibration shimmer against the palm of his hands.

The extractor room door was ten metres away. He could see a tiny part of the interior through the pane of glass, and the lowest corner of one of the fans where it hung like a grotesque feeding device.

Five metres and he kicked against the grimy wall, sending himself flying across the narrow passage. In three bounds he was at the door and he braced for impact. The metal frame smashed into his shoulder and his head snapped sideways. There was a hot pain in his arm and looked down to see the handle jammed against his skin. He cried out and clutched at it with his other hand as the pain almost overwhelmed him.

On the other side of the door, someone yelped happily and another replied with a squeal. Through the window, four circles of kids were holding hands, grinning insanely. Mel was bottom right of the closest group, turned away so he would not see her face. Vin was next to her, his head turned up towards the massive fan blade slowly gathering speed. Napier was in the next group on the right in his usual space, his head dropped forward in concentration.

Once the blade reached maximum power, the grid in the floor would open, creating a whirlwind that would suck thousands of pounds of waste carbon dioxide out of the storage tanks and into the Martian sky.

The engines were still building so he had time, but how long? Seconds probably. The last time (did that count as his first time?) he had only watched the jump, but he knew time was running out. He could *feel* it.

The handle gave under his palm and the door swung open. The sound hit him like it was a solid object, stunning him for a moment. From the observation room it had been plenty loud enough but he was not prepared for the sheer mind-numbing, bone-rattling, volume of the noise generated by the turbine engines.

He moved towards Mel, not even knowing what he was looking for. All he knew was that something was wrong. Something was wrong and he needed to figure out what it was.

The door slammed behind him as if the sound itself had pushed it closed. One of the kids on the far side of the nearest group, a pale-faced redhead, spotted him. He stared at Shor with his mouth open as if to say "what are you doing here?" and he nudged the kid to his right, who snapped out of his trance and joined his friend in staring at the intruder.

Shor reached Mel and grabbed her arm. She yelped and turned to look at him. She said his name but it was swept away by the roar of the engines. He leaned in close so his mouth was next to her ear.

"We need to switch it off!"

She turned to look at him, her faced etched with concern. "Why?"

He pulled her close again. "Something's wrong. We have to switch it off. It's dangerous."

She pulled away, her eyes scared, and glanced around at the others. Everyone was lost in the excitement of the moment. Vin was off in Adrenaline Land and didn't notice Shor talking to his girlfriend. It did not seem to occur to anyone that Shor was not secured to the platform.

"How do I turn it off?" he yelled. "How do I stop it?"

Her eyes were wide with fear. "You can't."

He clenched her hand in his and turned his face away, searching the room for some clue. The roar of the engines was deafening. It was like a living creature moving around, him, over him, through him.

He looked to the ceiling where the fan was gathering momentum. *If only Jay were here,* he thought. Yes, Jay would know what to do.

In his relatively short life, Shor had come to understand how time can behave in odd ways, stretching or shrinking depending on the circumstances. At school, for example, some classes seemed to fly past while others lasted an age. He had never really understood why this happened. Mel said she thought it had to do with the release of chemicals in the brain causing an elevated level of awareness. If that were the case then his brain had just dumped gallons of stimulants into the core of his neural network.

Deep inside, he felt something stir. It was a feeling, or an emotion, but more than that. It was a certainty. It was the knowledge of exactly what it was he needed to know at that precise moment. It was a lesson. It was an understanding. It was a word.

Tether.

Suddenly, everything snapped into sharp focus. The sounds, the lights, the shadows, the movement of air across his skin, the feel of the Mel's hand in his.

He realized he did not have a safety harness. If the turbines started, he would be caught up in the tornado and pulled up towards the blades spinning overhead. He would be flung against the mesh designed to stop anything from being sucked into the blades.

It was a basic rule of jumping that you had to wear a safety harness attached by a rope to a metal tether running around the circumference of the grid. They were designed for the workers whose job it was to keep the extractor machines up and running. Without the fans, the city would die a slow death from carbon dioxide poisoning. Even the bots latched themselves to the tethers when inside the extractor room, not because critters were particularly valuable, but because a chunk of metal that size might pierce the grid and wreck a fan.

He scanned the circles of kids, looking for a spare harness. Then he noticed something in the group on the right. He released Mel's hand and moved towards them. They were all linked to the main cord that ran through a series of metal eyelets secured to the floor all the way around the grid. The lock was in the space next to Napier, whose job it was to make sure the tether rope was secure.

But the lock next to Napier was raised, the latch lying open. The round hooks at each end of the anchor cable lay loose on the pin. One hard tug and the tether would come free, slipping through the eyelets and effectively releasing the jumpers into the whirlwind like a snagged thread on a knitted shirt.

Except there was no mesh in the unit above Napier's group. The square grid of narrow metal struts attached to the front of the fan was gone.

His mind raced back to the workshop where he had crawled inside a fan unit and Bek had warned him about turning off the power before sticking his head inside. The grid had been attached. He distinctly remembered because it had meant him going in through the back. And he had been there when Lars had replaced it. The grid had been attached. He was sure of it.

Then he remembered the switching box Reet was busy working on. Without that box, a fan could not manually be turned off or on in the event of something going wrong.

The noise from the engine changed. It was a subtle shift in tone, as if it had moved up a gear. He remembered the sound from the last time. He knew he had only a few seconds left.

He launched himself towards Napier, his arms and legs pumping as he burst through the linked arms of the two nearest jumpers, ignoring their cries of protest.

Napier lifted his face and looked directly at Shor, a faint smile slicing into his cheeks. Shor threw himself across the grid at the lock lying open.

The engines changed pitch again. There was the sound of grinding metal. Under him, the air began to move. He braced himself, ready to make hard contact with the metal floor, but the impact never came. It was as if a huge hand had scooped him up before he dropped.

The jump had begun.

He reached the tether and grabbed onto both ends just as the invisible hand threw him up with so much force he was sure his arms were going to be ripped from their sockets. Forty kids rose into the air as the whirlwind lifted them like particles of dust in a storm.

Shor, upside down, his body flapping like a strip of rag, held onto each end of the tether. The cables attached to the jumpers snapped tight and yanked with the force of a harvester. He screamed as the sinews in his arms stretched and the metal cable tore at his fingers.

He was a link in the chain. He was *the* link in the chain. If he were to let go, the cable would unthread like a loose piece of cotton. Everything was upside down and turned around. He had been inside the circle, facing out. Now, with his legs sucked into the air by the giant fan, he was facing the middle of the circle with Napier to his left, the others to his right.

He fought with every ounce of strength but it was too much. The sweat from his earlier exertion was running down his back and arms to his fingers, making the metal cable slick and impossible to hold. The twisted strands of metal inched through his hand until he was barely holding the round eyelets at the very end. These started to push his fingers apart, burrowing into his slick palm, digging into his skin like an oily, squirming animal. Agonising spasms oozed through his fingers and up into his biceps. Above him, or below, he wasn't sure, the weird multi-legged human table hovered. He had no idea if they knew what was going on, but he wanted to remember them before he lost his grip. He wanted to see their faces.

With one last stab of pain, his left hand, the one closest to Napier, let go. The cable came away as if it had ceased to exist. One moment he was fighting to hold onto it, the next it was gone. It slid through the eyelets, jerking down to his right with a force that took his breath away, jamming his right hand into the first circle of steel. The pain from before had been a caress compared to this. Now it felt as if his fingers were being crushed in a vice.

Somebody yelped and he turned just as Napier came loose, his safety cable swinging loose beneath him. Only the boy next along was stopping Napier from flying up towards the whirling blades, their hands wrapped around each other's wrists. Like a writhing snake, the metal cable slid through the next eyelet, releasing the boy holding on to Napier.

They swirled like dust devils in a storm, or a pair of grotesque kites twisting and bobbing against a dark, thundering sky. Shor's hand was sucked deeper into the circle of metal and he was certain it was going to be ripped off. He imagined watching as, one by one, they all disappeared into the spinning teeth of the fan. Like the mad bot, the fan meant to eat them. It meant to devour them all. It would suck them up like a long strand of spaghetti.

Just as Shor thought he would not be able to take any more, there was a sudden release of pressure followed by the sound of something heavy hitting something hard.

Napier was gone. The boy who had been holding his hand was alone at the end of the line, his blond hair whipping around his head, his eyes moist slits, his teeth bared between lips drained of blood. Next in line was one of the older boys. His hand was white from the pressure, his muscular forearms flexed like steel chords.

Shor was sure this boy would be able to hold on for as long as it took, but that was not his concern. It was the person next to him that he was worried about. It was a girl, no older than fourteen. She had the willowy figure of someone not taken to sports, with a bookish face. She was watching the steel tether with wide eyes floating in an ashen face.

The boy would be able to hold on to her, but she would lose her grip for sure. When her time came, the machine would suck them up and swallow them.

The engine changed gear again. Shor tried to think how long it had been. He tried to remember the last jump. Ten seconds. Surely it had been longer than that by now. Or was it twenty seconds? He couldn't remember. They could not last that long. Napier was gone, lost in the belly of the machine. The blond kid was next. Then the older boy, and then the girl.

Shor clenched his teeth.

Help me.

He squeezed the blur of tears from his eyes and tried to ignore the pain. His hand was on fire. It felt as though it had been immersed in a pool of molten metal. To his side, he heard the tether uncoiling. The girl next to the blond boy had started screaming, but she was not wearing a mask. There was no oxygen while the extraction was taking place. If she did not hold her breath she would pass out. The tempest tried to carry her voice away but he could still hear it. Above the engine and the wind and all the other screams, he heard her crying for help.

In his heart, he joined her in that cry.

Please help—

There was a pause. It was no longer than a heart beat. The world seemed to hesitate, as if someone had flipped a switch. The fans stopped as the engine driving them plummeted—that was how it sounded—as though from a great height. It stopped roaring and sighed a long, drawn-out breath of relief. The pressure eased and the vice crushing Shor's hand slowly released its grip. The blond-haired boy stopped twirling and sank to the floor like a deflated balloon.

Shor felt cold concrete on his forearms first, then his face and chest. His hips and legs touched down. The roar of the blades separated into a thick whump-whump as the floor rose up to meet him.

His hand came free of the eyelet and he tried to release the tether but his aching fingers were reluctant to let go. He pulled himself up into a kneeling position and sat on the closed grid, massaging his bruised hand until he was able to let go and the metal hook clattered to the ground.

People were screaming, and crying, and gasping for breath. He heard Napier's name used over and over like a mantra to the dead.

Because Napier was dead.

The machine had eaten him. The machine had sucked him up and chewed him until there was nothing left. Shor looked around. Napier was gone. Napier was gone.

"It's his fault!" a voice said, rising above the din. "Him. It was him."

Shor turned to find the voice and there was Izzy, her eyes red with tears, her hair thrown onto her head in jumbled mess. She was standing, pointing an accusing finger at him.

"He did it. I saw him. He was messing with the wire. It was his fault."

"No, he tried to help." It was Mel. She was walking towards Izzy. "He tried to set the lock. Napier didn't set the lock. Shor tried to fix it."

The noise had subsided and all attention was on Shor.

"No," Izzy said. "No, I saw him messing with the lock. He killed Napier." Her chin was trembling. "He killed him."

"No, you're wrong," Mel insisted. "I saw what he did. The lock was open. Shor saved us. Shor saved all of us."

Izzy looked around, suddenly uncertain, as if trying to find something to hold onto. "But, Napier. He's…"

"Yes, Napier is gone, but if it hadn't been for Shor, we would be gone as well." Mel took Izzy's shoulders in her hands and looked directly into her eyes. "Shor saved your life."

Izzy hesitated for a moment, blinking big I-don't-understand blinks, trying to make sense of Mel's words. She looked to Shor and back to Mel and then down to Shor again. "I thought…I saw…he was…" Then she started sobbing. She clutched at Mel, who pulled her in and held her as her body shuddered. Then Mel turned and led her by the hand across the ragged circle of bewildered kids towards where Shor was sitting rubbing his swollen hand.

"Mel's right," a boy said. "I saw it. He tried to close the lock. Napier must've forgotten to close it."

Mel crouched and placed her free hand on Shor's shoulder. After a few seconds, Izzy knelt next to Mel and touched Shor's arm as well. Her face was wet with tears.

"Thanks," she said softly. "I'm sorry."

More kids approached, shuffling forward to touch Shor on the shoulder, or kneel next to him, like mourners paying respects. Even Vin gave him a pat on the back.

"Thanks fella. I owe you one."

Shor smiled. "No problem."

"I thought you didn't like jumping," Mel said.

Shor shrugged. "I don't."

"Then why did you come down here?"

"I had a feeling."

"A feeling? What, like a premonition?"

"I guess you could call it that." He looked into her eyes and saw his own reflection in them. "There's something I need to tell you…"

Shor hesitated. It stirred inside him again, the same feeling he had experienced with the tether. It moved through him like a breath of warm air.

Not yet.

"What is it, Shor?"

"I…there's…" He dropped his head. "Never mind."

"What is it?"

"Nothing."

"Whatever the reason you decided to come down, I'm glad you did. You were just in time."

He looked up at her. Behind her, over her head, the fan was almost completely undamaged. It was hard to imagine it had just killed someone.

"I wasn't in time for Napier."

She stood and folded her arms. "I don't get it. Napier did this a hundred times. He always used to tell us to make sure we were tied down. I wasn't exactly fond of him, but he wasn't stupid."

Shor stood. His hand was throbbing badly. He tucked it under his armpit and applied gentle pressure. It helped a little, but not much.

"He was speaking to someone before you came in. Did you hear what they were talking about?"

"No, I wasn't paying attention, why?"

"No reason."

She frowned. "How did you know he was talking to someone? I didn't see you there."

"I asked the mechanic." It was a lie, but he wasn't about to admit to spying on them. "He told me Napier was talking to this weird little man."

"Hey, I heard them talking," Vin said. "I was listening. Well, I was listening at first, but he started talking mumbo-jumbo. I kinda got bored, but Napier was really interested."

"Do you know the guy?"

"No. Never seen him before. Wait. No, I saw him a few days ago. He was in the Park, standing near the entrance. I remember because he was just watching people walk past. I thought he was a performer or something. A bit weird, but I figured he was harmless."

"What exactly did he say to Napier?"

"I told you. It was mumbo-jumbo. I didn't understand it. He sounded like my psych eval, but I got the feeling he wanted something, or maybe he was offering something. I sort of switched off."

The room had grown quiet except for the low hiss of cooling machinery and the sound of weeping. A group had gathered at the door and looked as if they were about to leave.

"No," Mel said, turning to them. "You mustn't leave. We need to wait for the police. They'll need to talk to everyone. Please, come away from the door."

The kids hesitated. Shor thought they looked bewildered, lost, and a little scared.

"We're going to be in so much trouble," Vin said, shaking his head. "They'll never let me go into Agro now."

"We don't know that," Mel said. "They'll probably just give us a slap on the wrists and tell us not to do it again. It's like a holiday tradition. Kids jump. The badges arrest us."

"Sure, but this never happened before." Vin spoke in a low voice. "Nobody ever *died* before. They're going to do a full investigation. And what if the fan is broken? Worse still, what if the whole machine is broken? They'll never let me work in Agro."

Shor watched Vin the Vegetable. He was fretting and fuming over his own future but seemed oblivious to the fact that Mel would very possibly be fired. If anyone was going to get into trouble over this, it was her. It was only her first year out of school but she was a teacher's assistant. It was her job to look after the kids under her care, even in a situation like this, even if she were a million kilometres away from the nearest school. Teachers were expected to look after kids. Shor could see the worry in her eyes even though she was trying to hide it.

"What are we going to tell them?" Shor said.

"The truth," Mel said. "We've got nothing to hide."

At that moment, the door swung open. Everyone turned to watch as a small army of badges marched into the room. The last to enter was an officer. Shor recognized him immediately. It was the detective who had questioned him about Lars.

Boole paused at the door and looked around. When he saw Shor, he stopped and smiled.

"Oh no," Shor said.

They did the whole signing-in thing with the dour desk-clerk tapping at her computer keyboard. Statements were taken and parents informed. A doctor arrived and gave everyone a cursory examination. Shor had two broken fingers, a bruise on his arm, and a nasty scrape on both palms. Along with the broken fingers, his left hand had swollen to twice its normal size. A sling was applied along with a prescription for an anti-inflammatory to reduce the swelling.

This time, nobody was allowed to leave. A total of forty-three kids ranging in age from twelve to nineteen were herded into the holding cells where they would be spending the night.

The grey-eyed badge who had spoken to Shor after the last jump watched them all with a vague look of satisfaction as they handed in their chatbands. Shor was waiting for him to launch into a tirade, but he said nothing. He just stood there, watching them all with his creepy lizard-smile. An angry reprimand would have been better. At least then they would know where they stood.

Parents were told not to bother coming down but some did anyway. A few, especially those of the youngest, were upset that their children had to spend the night in jail along with "who-knows-what" criminals. The clerk assured them that they would be kept in a separate room. Besides which, there was only one other person in the cells and he was due to be released in a few hours.

Lars, Shor thought, glancing towards the big metal door that led through to the holding cells, half expecting to see him come walking through.

The parents left, clutching onto each other as if to say "how did this happen to our child?" This was, after all, no longer just a case of kids letting off steam. A boy had died. Statements would have to be verified, evidence gathered, facts checked. Criminal proceedings might ensue. Lives could be tainted forever.

The holding cell was basically a dorm with sixty sleep capsules lining the bare off-white walls, along with two recessed toilet cubicles, a dozen benches, and four lamps. One camera watched the door while another trained its beady eye on the toilets. There were no windows. There was nowhere to hide.

When the door closed, they stood for a while, looking around the room with wide eyes as if unsure what to do next. Some of the younger kids were crying or on the brink of it, anxiously searching the room.

Vin, apparently unfazed by the whole experience, wandered along the capsules. He peered inside one but quickly pulled back, waving his hand in front of his face, his nose wrinkled.

He continued down the wall, gingerly sniffing each capsule in turn, until he found two side by side that met his, obviously very high, olfactory standards.

"Here's two for us," he said, waving to Mel. "You have this one."

With that, he jumped inside his capsule and bounced around a few times, testing it for comfort. A few moments later, he was lying motionless, his chest rising and falling with the slow rhythm of sleep. It was still early evening but this did not seem to bother his body-clock in the slightest.

The other kids followed Vin's lead and dispersed, moving hesitantly along the walls. A few copied his nose-wrinkling routine but, before long, everyone had found a bunk.

Only Shor and Mel were left standing at the top of the room, watching over the younger ones searching for somewhere to spend the night. It was not long before the sound of weeping was replaced by hushed chatting.

Shor was about to suggest they turn in when Mel touched his arm.

"I wanted to thank you," she said. "You did a brave thing back there."

Shor felt suddenly wide awake. He tried to ignore the fact that she was touching him, but that was all he could feel. "You would've done the same thing."

She looked around. "I don't think so."

"Do you think they'll be all right?" he said, nodding towards the others.

"Vin will be fine," she said with a wry smile. "He always is."

He was about to make a joke suggesting Vin did not have the intelligence to understand when he was in trouble, but decided it would be a bad idea. For whatever reason, Mel liked Vin, and that said a lot for Vin's character.

As if reading his thought, she said: "He's not as dim as he looks. He can come across as a bit slow, but he's quite the philosopher when he's in the mood. He wrote me a poem for my birthday. It was quite good."

"A poem," Shor said. He started to grin but caught himself. "That's pretty deep."

"I know you don't like him. I've seen how you look at him."

"He calls me Short. Can you blame me for not wanting to be his best buddy?"

"Everyone calls you that. It doesn't mean anything. It's a nickname."

Shor moved to the side, so her hand was no longer touching his arm. "It isn't a nickname to me. It's a constant reminder that I don't fit in here. Every time someone calls me that, they're telling me I'm different and I don't belong."

"I'm, sorry," she said, lowering her hand. "I didn't know it hurt you that much."

He snorted. "We've only been friends for, like, forever. How could you possibly know such a thing?"

"You never said. I didn't realize—"

"Well—it does bother me. I'm telling you now. I really don't like being called Short."

"You're right. I guess I was just trying to make you feel better. I'm sorry."

Shor looked across the room, to where a small group of kids were chatting. Their worried expressions were punctuated by the occasional hesitant smile.

"Look at them," he said. "In a week they'll be boasting to their friends how they spent a night in jail."

"Yes, they'll be all right."

He turned to look at her. "What about us? Will we be all right?"

"I don't know," she said, her eyes searching his. "Will we?"

Shor felt his life stretch out behind him. Was she actually asking him? He had loved Mel for as long as he was able to remember, from the very first day she had come to sit next to him in the school canteen and those big eyes had gazed into his with disarming frankness. She had been his first and only friend on this lousy dustbowl and he could not imagine his life without her. He had wanted to tell her so many times but he had never been able to shake the feeling that she just felt sorry for him. Her saying no to his love he might be able to handle, but her friendship was something he would not gamble.

Now that she might be asking him, actually asking him, he did not know what to say. He had spent so many years obsessing over her that he had lost track of his feelings. An image of Rochelle came to mind and his heart ached. Was it possible he was still in love with a woman he had known in another life?

"I think…"

She leaned closer. "Yes?"

"I think Vin is a great guy. I'm sorry I made fun of him before. You make a great couple."

She pulled back, confusion written all over her face. "Oh, you didn't think I meant, you know, *us,* did you?"

"I just assumed, from the way you asked…boy, this is embarrassing. Yes. Yes, I think we'll be all right. It depends on whether they think Napier's death was an accident."

"Why wouldn't they?"

Shor thought about the missing grid. He had been there when Lars put it back. He had *seen* it. And there was the switching box. Had Leo sabotaged it to make sure nobody could override the computer? "No reason."

"You saved our lives. They'll probably give you a citizenship certificate. As for me, I don't think they'll look too kindly on a teacher taking part in a jump."

"You didn't force them to do it. They asked you. You could say you went along to keep an eye on them. They'll understand."

"I should never have agreed to go. It was stupid. If I was a half decent teacher, I would've refused."

"Don't ever say that. You're a terrific teacher."

"You don't know that. And I'm only an assistant."

He smiled. "I know you, and that's good enough for me."

The door opened and they turned to see a badge walk in.

"Vin. Vin Scholl."

In his capsule, Vin stirred and looked up, his eyes bleary from sleep. "Um…yeah?"

"Come with me."

They were called at regular intervals over the next few hours. The kids returned looking a little shell-shocked but relieved. Nobody was being accused of anything more serious than participating in a jump, but the badges wanted to know exactly what had happened to Napier.

All said they had given the same story. Napier forgot to lock the tether. Shor arrived at the last minute and tried to activate the lock. And, no, they did not know why Napier did what he did or, rather, why he didn't do what he was supposed to do.

They knew already, of course. Shor was sure of it. No doubt there were hidden vid feeds that told the full story. It was part of the punishment, to make the kids confess to their crime.

All agreed that Shor had saved the day. And Mel had not invited anybody to take part in the jump. If anything, it was they who had invited her. She had only agreed on condition that they sign her petition. And, yes, she was an excellent assistant teacher.

Mel was called second to last and questioned the longest. With all chatbands confiscated, Shor had no idea how long she was away. Perhaps it just felt as though she was away for a long time. Vin was uncharacteristically nervous and spent the whole time pacing the floor.

Poems and pacing. Perhaps the Vegetable had a heart after all.

Mel came back with red eyes, but she managed a smile. They had given her a stern lecture about the responsibilities that came with being a teacher's assistant but what they seemed most interested in was how the safety grid had come to be missing.

She had barely finished talking when the badge came back and called Shor's name.

Shor followed, trying to convince himself he had nothing to worry about. He had been there when Lars replaced the fan unit. He had seen the grid with his own eyes.

He was led along a corridor and into an office, the same room where he had been questioned the last time. Detective Boole was there. He had expected that. The one person he had not been expecting to see was Harl.

"Hello Shor," Harl said. "How have you been?"

The door closed with a heavy finality that made Shor jump. Boole pointed to a chair.

"I've been better," Shor said, sliding onto the hard seat.

"I take it you know Detective Boole?"

"We've met. Listen. Before we start, can I just say—the fan's grid was there when we installed it a few weeks back. I remember it clearly. It was definitely in place."

"Yes, we know," Boole said. "What we don't know is how it came to be missing. We know the grid was there this morning. The unit was serviced by someone in your department. What we don't know is who removed it between then and the accident."

The two men were watching Shor like he was a bug they had found under the table. Boole just smiled, his eyes unflinching, but Shor saw something in the detective's face. He was sitting across the table looking directly at Shor, but his eyes were glazed over as if he were looking through Shor at something behind him. Shor had the urge to turn around and see what the detective was looking at.

"I understand there was a problem with a switching box," Boole said. "Reet was busy looking into it. Is that correct?"

"What? Are you suggesting Reet had something to do with this?"

"We have to keep our options open. Reet removed the box. Without the box, the fan unit could not be turned off manually."

"It wouldn't have made a difference. There was nobody in the control room to activate the switch anyway. Reet had nothing to do with this. Reet didn't kill Napier."

"You were at school with Napier," Harl said.

Shor turned to look at the old man. His eyes had that same dreamy look as Boole's.

"Yes, we were in the same class."

"Were you friends?" Boole asked.

Shor took a deep breath. *Here it comes*, he thought.

"No, we weren't friends."

"Did you like Napier?"

"Not really. He was a bully."

"Did you dislike him?"

"He could be a bit of a wagger sometimes. I didn't *dis*like him particularly. We generally stayed out of each other's way."

"We have school records saying you got into a fight with Napier. How did that turn out?"

Shor gave a harsh laugh. "A fight? We exchanged a few words. It was hardly a fight."

"Still, you did speak to each other in a threatening manner."

"I think I called him a wagger, but then I imagine quite a few people have called him the same, and worse. He wasn't the most pleasant person in the school. Why don't you speak to some of the other people who called him names? Why don't you ask them if they messed with the fans?"

"Because you are the only one with a history of violence towards Napier who happens to have access to the equipment necessary to remove those grids and tamper with the override switch, that's why."

"A history of what? Violence? You've got to be kidding me."

Shor could feel the anger rising inside. He hadn't been violent towards Napier but he would happily show Boole some of his ire. The feeling he had experienced back at the jump stirred inside him again. This time the word was...

Calm.

Shor clenched his fists, forcing himself to breath slowly. "Listen, I know where this is going. I didn't like Napier but I didn't want him dead. I tried to save him, remember?"

"Did you?"

"Yes. I almost lost my fingers in the process." He thrust his right arm forward so Boole could see the sling supporting a clutch of puffy digits. His fingers looked as though a bot had tried to clean them. "Only two broken. Not bad, considering."

"Listen," Harl said, turning to Boole. "I think it's obvious the boy didn't hurt Napier, at least not intentionally. Even if he did leave the grid off, I'm sure it was an accident—"

"I didn't leave the grid off," Shor said.

"We'll assume for now that it wasn't you," Harl said. "I'm not saying you did do anything wrong. My point is, even if you *had* left it off, it was probably an accident."

Shor shook his head. He was starting to understand how that bot felt when it got trapped under the bench. Maybe that was why it had gone hoho and tried to attack the girl. Except, it had done far more than that.

"Check the feeds pointing at the front door. Why don't you check and see who went in and out?"

"We don't have to. We have cameras inside the extractor room."

Shor did a verbal double-take. "What?"

"I said we have cameras inside the room."

"You mean you know the kids do these jumps?"

"Of course. In fact we watch them from time to time. They're quite entertaining, especially the first-timers. It was discovered a long time ago that young people need to do stupid things, especially around puberty. They used to have sports but those resulted in too many injuries, especially with the boys, who can get quite competitive." As he spoke, Boole's eyes drifted in and out of focus. It was starting to bother Shor a little bit. "Then it was discovered that kids were using the fans in the extractor room. We still arrest anyone caught doing it, but only to keep up the pretext of illegality. Kids get their kicks. We avoid a catalogue of injuries from hormonal boys getting over-competitive on the sports field."

"Just a thought," Shor said, "but aren't you ruining the whole illusion by telling me about this?"

"Nobody ever died before," Boole said. "This changes everything."

"I don't get it. You've got cameras. Why don't you check them?"

"We did," Harl said. "Unfortunately, there's nothing on them. There was a section of feed missing. We don't know how, but we lost almost twenty minutes of footage. At some point during that time, the grid was removed and the switch box malfunctioned."

Shor felt the blood drain from his face. Leo had struck again. He had no doubt about it. Leo was responsible for everything. He was the common factor in all that had happened over the past few weeks, starting with the nurse leaping from the roof of the building in the Space Sector, ending in him somehow manipulating the students to take part in the jump. And now he was the reason Napier got himself chewed up and spit out by a carbon dioxide extraction unit. Leo was always in or around the scene of each accident. It had to be him.

"I want to speak to you in private," Shor said, his eyes on Harl.

"No deal," Boole growled. "I'm the detective in this case. If you want to say anything, you can say it to me."

"No," Shor persisted. "I want to talk to Harl."

Boole turned to the older man, who nodded reassuringly. Boole kicked his chair away from the table. "Five minutes."

Shor waited for the detective to leave the room. When he was sure they were alone, he walked to the table and gestured for Harl to come closer.

The old man obliged. "What is it you want to tell me, son?"

"Is it safe to talk?"

Harl smiled. "Yes, just don't speak too loudly."

"I think I know who did it," Shor said, his voice barely louder than a whisper. "I think I know who removed the grid. I also suspect he was involved with the suicide of the nurse at the Space Sector, and also the death of Noon Nesbitt at the Maintenance Depot."

Harl leaned closer, his eyes still with that weird distant look. "Does this person have a name?"

"Yes. I think it was Leopold Drake."

Harl regarded him for a moment. If he was surprised he did not show it. Shor thought he looked like someone in desperate need of sleep. "Are you sure about this?"

"I'm pretty sure. Some of the kids saw him talking to Napier just before the jump."

"And you think this means he was responsible for Napier's death?"

"Yes. And the nurse who committed suicide, and Noon." Shor looked down at his bloated hand. "And my father. He was seen in the area just before those deaths as well."

"Was he? That's the first I've heard of this. Where did you get your information?"

Shor looked back up into the old man's vacant eyes. "Let's just say I overheard people talking." Then, with a touch of bitterness. "You know how quickly news gets around Utopia."

"And malicious gossip, yes."

"This isn't gossip. Leopold Drake was seen. I think you should arrest him and bring him in for questioning."

"No need," Harl said. "He's helping us already. He has been very supportive of Councillor Napier following the death of his son."

"Then I don't need to tell you. He's the one you're looking for. Talk to him. Ask him what he was doing at the time of each of those deaths. And ask him where he came from. I think you'll be surprised."

Harl leaned back. "I was not being truthful when I told you what Leopold was doing up top when you found him. I told you he was testing out a homemade suit. That was not entirely accurate."

At last, Shor thought. *The truth.*

"We have been keeping this under wraps in order to avoid overdue excitement. If something like this got out, it would cause pandemonium. We had to keep it a secret until the right time. And I am trusting you to breathe a word of this to no-one. Leopold is not from Mars."

Shor leaned forward. *And?*

"Leopold is in fact from Earth. He was sent to see if we are ready for a return home. He believes we are close but not quite ready. He is helping us prepare. He wants us to introduce a number of changes to help us integrate with society back home. It will take a while, possibly two or three years, but he can help us. As chance would have it, the death of Councillor Napier's son has created a vacancy that has allowed for Leopold to join our government."

Shor stood. "You can't be serious! That's a lie. It's all a lie. He didn't come from Earth. He isn't here to help. He's already killed three people. Why can't you see that?" Harl just looked at him with that stupid, dreamy look in his eyes. Shor wanted to grab him by the throat and shake some sense into him. "Why don't you ask Leo where he was when my father died, or Noon Nesbitt, or the nurse? Why don't you ask him where he really comes from?"

Harl walked calmly to the door and pushed it open. "Why don't you ask him yourself?"

A middle-aged man entered the room. He was a little taller than Shor, with black hair and brown eyes. His expression was pleasant, stopping a fraction short of a smile. He looked like someone who could be your next door neighbour without your even knowing he lived there. He walked confidently across to the table and extended his hand. His voice was deep and smooth.

"Hello. My name is Leopold Drake. You must be Shor."

Leopold Drake did not look evil, nor did he look like someone seething with hatred. He did not look like a man bent on destroying everything around him. His face was pleasant, with features that might even be described as handsome. His mouth was wide, and curled at the edge to suggest a smile. His nose was as straight as the tracks he left in the dust, as were his eyebrows. His hair was groomed in the style more common with younger people but he managed to pull it off even though Shor guessed his age to be at least thirty. His eyes were a dark brown and set quite wide apart, a combination that suggested openness and sincerity. His skin, from what Shor could see, was without a mark or blemish of any kind.

In spite of what Shor knew about this man, and what he believed he had done, he found himself shaking his hand.

"What have they been saying about me?" Leo said, his eyes never leaving Shor's, his smile a little wider. "Good things, I hope."

Shor just stood there, his feet like lead weights. He wanted to look across to Harl and the others but there was something about Leo's eyes that compelled him not to. The deep brown was flecked with lighter shades that seemed to glow under the ceiling lights.

"You," he started to say, but he was having difficulty concentrating. He was suddenly tired. Speaking was an effort. His thoughts had become slippery and he did not have the strength to hold onto them.

"Yes?" Leo said. He was still holding Shor's hand, still looking into his eyes.

Shor tried to blink. His eyelids felt strange. "The switch. The fan. It was you. You...killed him."

Leo leaned a little closer. His hand squeezed a little tighter. Shor caught a trace of his breath. It was a rich smell. It was a slick, oily, metallic smell. It was the smell of lubricated machinery. "I was nowhere near the fan. I never touched the switching unit. I never went into that room. Check the feeds."

Leo was so close that Shor could feel the warmth of his breath on his face. His eyes seemed wider, and bigger, taking up more space than a moment ago. Shor was struggling to think. His thoughts were like oiled ball-bearings slipping between his fingers. No matter how hard he squeezed, they would just fall and scatter, bouncing across the floor like shattered glass, skipping away under the tables and chairs where they hid in the dark.

"You...did something to the...feeds. You...hid them away." Shor tried to break out of Leo's gaze. Those flecks of colour floated in a pool of dark brown oil. "Why...do I feel like this? What are you...doing to me?"

Now Leo was definitely smiling. His lips were twisted into a symmetrical curve, parted just a fraction to reveal a row of perfect white teeth.

"Leave us," Leo barked, not looking away from Shor.

"Why?" Boole asked.

"I said leave us," Leo repeated.

Boole lifted a finger as if to speak but he seemed to remember something. He turned to leave and the two men filed obediently out of the room.

The door closed with a heavy thud.

"Did you know," Leo said, "there are subsonic frequencies that, when applied to certain parts of the human brain, can make a person susceptible to suggestion?"

Shor shook his head. It felt like it weighed a ton.

"The mind is so weak," Leo continued. "It amazes me that humans have managed to survive at all. Some are stronger than others, but most can be controlled with a surprising amount of ease. Take the council for example. They are the leaders of this colony. They make all the rules. They decide what you can and cannot do, what you wear, what you eat, what you learn, how often you clean yourself. They decide who lives and who dies. And yet they are among the weakest minds I have ever encountered. They should not be allowed to rule. Leadership should be in the hands of the strong, not the weak. I am here to correct this. I am here to put the power into the right hands."

"You...killed him," Shor managed to say. His face felt like it was caught in a vice.

"You cannot make an omelette without breaking a few eggs. You know this expression? You must be familiar with it. Or have you forgotten? It was a long time ago, but also not so long. Harl told you where you came from, yes? I imagine you made many omelettes back in the day. I imagine you broke a few eggs."

"You...killed him," Shor repeated. "You..."

"Aah. But I see we are not talking about the boy. We are talking about someone else. We are talking about your father."

"Why?" Shor said.

The smile slid from Leo's face and he tilted his head a little to one side. "You did not get on well with him. Your relationship was not a close one. According to your psych eval you resented him."

"He was still . . . my father."

"But was he? Your real parents died a thousand years ago on another world. These people were substitutes. They took you in and raised you, but nothing can replace the bond between a parent and their flesh-and-blood offspring. Your mother loved you as her own, but your father was not as giving. If you are going to mourn anyone, it should be your mother."

"You know...nothing about...my mother," Shor hissed.

"Aah, but I see you do mourn for her. She survived much longer than I anticipated. She was strong, like you."

"You..." Shor felt the rage surge inside him. He felt it rise through him like a storm. "I am going to..."

Leo tilted his head the other way. "What are you going to do?"

Shor tried to move but he could not. He tried to reach out his hands to wrap them around this wagger's throat, but he was unable to move.

"Join me," Leo said, his voice barely audible. "I need people with your strength. I need people to help me set this place in order. Join me and I will make you head of the Space Sector. I know how much you wanted to work there. Of course, I cannot help those who are not on my team. And it would be a pity if something were to happen to you."

Shor tried to shake his head. He felt like he was drowning. "I..."

Leo stared at him for a second. Then he stepped back and turned away.

"Think about it," he said loudly. "And let me know. I look forward to your decision." He strode across the floor. A moment later, he was gone.

Harl and Detective Boole walked into the room looking a little bewildered.

Shor's knees went weak as whatever it was that had been holding him let go.

"Are you all right?" Harl asked. "You look pale."

"I'm fine," Shor said, rubbing his temples with heels of his hands. He had the sudden overpowering desire to sleep.

"You're free to go," Boole said. "I think we have enough information."

Shor looked at the faces of the two men. The haziness in their eyes had cleared. Leo's hold on them had gone—at least for now. "I don't suppose you heard any of that?"

"Of course," Harl said. "He offered you a job. And personally, if I were you, I'd take it."

Shor returned to the holding cell almost an hour after being led away. Mel was waiting for him, her face full of concern. The kids were sitting in groups, talking and laughing, and did not seem to notice him come in. From what Shor could tell, they had stopped seeing this as a prison sentence and now saw it more as a fun trip to the park. Vin was entertaining himself by tapping out a soft beat on his thighs with the palms of his hands. It was almost certainly not quite curfew, but it felt later. Shor was ready to drop.

"I was worried about you," Mel said, rushing to meet him as he stepped into the room. "You were gone for ages. What happened?"

Shor found the nearest bench and sat down. He lifted a hand. It was trembling. Vin stopped drumming and wandered over.

"Hey fella, what took you so long?"

"Have you ever been so bombarded by lies that you started to doubt what you know is the truth?"

Mel sat next to him. "What happened? What did they say?"

"I told them about Leopold Drake."

"Who?"

"Remember that guy I told you about? The one me and Lars found going for a hike up top? Well he's the one Napier and you, Vin, were talking to before the jump."

"Yeah, now I remember," Vin said. "Leo. That was his name."

"You think he killed Napier?" Mel asked.

"I know he did. I think he's found a way to hack into the security cameras. He uses them to move around and do whatever he wants. Whenever someone gets hurt, the cameras shut down. I told them and said they should check the feeds but it's as if they didn't hear me. There's something wrong with that guy. When he talks it's like he's inside your head. I told them a dozen times to check the feeds. It's like their brains had shut down. He offered me a job. Can you believe that? The wagger offered me a job."

"Can he do that?"

"I don't know, I guess so. He said he was looking for people he could trust. He wants to run for the council and he wants *strong people* to help him. Those are his words. He offered to make me head of the Space Sector."

"What did you say?"

"Nothing." Shor looked down at the cracked floor for a moment. He remembered the feeling of having something inside his head, pushing him, controlling him. "The guy scared me. It's his eyes. I don't know how to explain it, but it's like you just want to do what he tells you. He was going on about how easy it is to control people."

"Creepy," Mel said.

"And he looks funny as well. It's nothing obvious. I mean, he looks normal, but that's the problem. He looks *too* normal. It's almost like he was manufactured. I got a really close look at him. He didn't have a mark on him. He almost looked like he's made out of glass."

"You think he killed Napier?"

"He practically confessed. And it's not just Napier. I think he was responsible for the death of my parents."

"He told you this?"

"Not directly, but I'd bet my last water token it was him."

"You said something about the feeds," Vin joined. "Something about him controlling them."

"They keep losing chunks of data. The feeds stop working long enough for someone to get in and out again without being seen. That's how Leo has been doing it, I think."

"How did you know about the feeds?" Mel asked.

"One of the very few advantages of being on the Maintenance team. We get access to all sorts of inside information. I tell you, he's up to no good and there's something weird going on."

"So what can we do about it?" Mel said. "I mean, we have to do something."

Shor sighed. "I don't know. What can anyone do if the police seem to believe every word the guy says?"

"I'm sure they'll catch on to him sooner or later," Vin said. "The police are smart. One day he'll make a mistake and then, bam, they'll catch him."

Deep inside, Shor felt the now-familiar stirring.

Tell them.

And so he told them everything.

Shor lifted his hand to shield his eyes from the ceiling lights. The city felt dizzyingly intense after the sullen gloom of the holding cell. It was early, but the streets were already bustling. It was the first day of Earth Week, which meant the start of five days of celebrations.

Shor decided against going home. Instead, he headed straight for work, electing to stop off at the market up the road from the depot.

They had agreed to continue as normal and meet that evening to discuss what to do next. Of the forty-two kids he had spoken to last night, only five had refused to believe life on Mars was about to change. They walked back to their beds where they went to sleep or chatted, throwing occasional glances to the larger group at the top of the room.

Shor did not sense animosity from them, just a general lack of interest or the impression that they perhaps thought he wasn't running with all his bulbs screwed in. He was worried they might say something to the badges. Public meetings of any kind were frowned upon, but then the holding cell was hardly public so what was there to report?

The big surprise for him was Vin. He had expected the Vegetable to give his usual shrug and drift off to his bed, but he seemed genuinely interested in hearing more. The questions came thick and fast and, even though Shor had been unable to answer most of them, he saw a spark in Vin's eye that he had never seen before. Any thoughts Shor may have had about his own sanity subsided as he answered Vin's questions, drawing a neat line under events that had led him to the conclusion that Leo was planning a coup against Utopia using the city's own army of cleaning bots.

He was second in line at the tram stop. As usual, he recognized the face of the man standing next to him but had no idea where he had seen him before. He looked like his Science teacher, who looked like the manager of the local market, who also happened to bear an uncanny resemblance to the president's personal assistant. The man stood to rigid attention, his countenance suggesting he had once been, or would like to have been, a badge. Shor could see the muscles in his jaw clenching and unclenching. He looked annoyed, or at least irritated. Shor moved half a step backwards, but the urge to speak to this man was overwhelming.

Tell him.

Shor frowned. He was becoming increasingly convinced that he knew him. But from where? Had he been in the crowd when the bot had gone hoho in the park? Or in one of the cubicles at Cobb's office? Perhaps, he could not be sure. He just felt…

Tell him.

A small group of girls was approaching, joking and laughing, getting warmed up for the celebrations later that afternoon. The grim guy in the queue seemed to stiffen even more as the sound of them drawing closer.

Shor took a deep breath. He had maybe twenty seconds before the queue became a crowd.

"Hi, excuse me. My name is Shor Larkin and I have a message for you."

The man turned in slow motion. He did not move his neck. Instead, his whole body peeled around like a plant craning for the sun or a teacher glaring down at a small child. His blue eyes settled on Shor and stayed there. His jaw muscles flexed. Shor was certain the man's glare was going to cut through him like a laser beam. Deep inside the man's head was a small engine linked to a high-powered laser. In a few seconds, two beams of blue light were going to shoot out and cut Shor in half.

Shor blinked. The cold blue eyes moved. They were no longer fixed on Shor's eyes but roaming his face, as if trying to read him.

"Did you just say you have a message for me?"

Shor gave a small, hesitant nod. The man's voice did not match his face at all. It was a gentle, almost timid voice. Behind Shor, the group had fallen quiet. He glanced back to see that they had stopped a few metres away to read a chatband message. They huddled around the tiny screen, reading with rapt concentration. Further along, the tram was approaching.

When he looked back at the man, the cold blue eyes had softened and his face was relaxed.

"So, what is it? "

"There is danger coming. You must leave with me."

"When?"

"Two days…no, sorry, one day."

One day? He had lost track of time.

"Where are we going?"

"I don't know. Away from here."

The man regarded Shor for a few moments, then, very slowly, he smiled. It was like watching a video of an Earth sunrise. He lifted his chatband. Shor hesitated, then realised what he was doing. They exchanged IDs.

"You'll call me?" the man—Luc Gregor—said.

"As soon as I know more," Shor said.

Behind them the revellers had joined the queue just in time to board the tram which was sliding to a squealing halt. The man, his face back to its original sternness, climbed on board.

Shor followed. He thought about sitting next to Luc, but his new acquaintance looked like he wanted to be alone. Instead, he took a seat towards the back and watched the city roll by. Once or twice, Luc turned to look out of the window. From this angle, he could see moisture in his blue eyes and the faintest hint of a smile.

Shor's stop rolled up and he climbed off. The queue for the airlock was filled with day shift workers. He recognized most of them and even knew a few, mainly the Maintenance crew, by name. Up ahead, facing the other way, was someone he recognized, even from behind.

Shor tapped a message in his chatband. *I can't believe they let you out.*

Cheeky wagger, the reply came. *Where are you?*

Turn around.

Lars swivelled, his chin lifted high as he scanned the crowd. Shor waved. Lars spotted him and grinned.

They didn't have anything on me. I heard you got arrested.

A jump.

Stupid boy. Tell me all about it on the other side.

The doors slid open and the queue inched forward. Five minutes later, Shor caught up with Lars at the tram stop. They took a seat next to the door.

"So," Lars said. "Did you guys avoid burning the depot down while I was gone?"

"I managed it, but I can't speak for the others. The evening shift looked a bit rowdy last time I saw them."

"It is Earth Week. Five days of pining for something none of us will ever see."

Shor thought about the Comet sitting in its hangar. What if they could go back? What if Jay could find a way to fly?

"People need a goal. They need a dream."

Lars tutted. "You sound just like my psych eval."

"That's one piece of advice I happen to agree with."

"And what's all this about getting arrested for jumping? I thought you thought it was dumb. Let me guess. A girl you like persuaded you to join in and so, being a man, you threw all your fear out the window, along with your common sense."

"No," Shor said, giving his best *don't be ridiculous* expression. "I was worried about the safety of—"

"A girl?"

"It was a bunch of kids."

"And Mel?"

"She was there, but that's not why I went. I saw our old pal Leopold Drake talking with a few of them. Turns out he may have sabotaged the extractor unit, but I can't prove it. The grid was missing and the video feed that can show he did it is broken."

"You didn't tell them about…?"

"Headquarters? No way."

"Good lad. So let me guess. The badges let him go."

"Hardly. I met the guy, Lars, and there's something seriously wrong going on. You remember Harl from the Space Sector? Well he was there, and Boole, and they were all best buddies. It was like some unholy trinity. Leopold told me he's planning to run for the council. He said he's looking for people to join his team. I think he was interviewing me. I'd just accused him of killing Napier and he offered me a job."

"I heard about Napier. What exactly happened? And what have you done to your hand?"

Shor examined the bruised fingers. They were still swollen, but the pain was starting to subside a little.

"He forgot to fasten the tether. I tried to hold onto it, but I wasn't strong enough. He got sucked into the fan. The grid was missing, so he just got pulled right in."

Lars winced. "That's not good. Of all the possible ways to go, that one isn't high on my list. In fact, it may not even be on my list. They gave you a medal, right?"

"They mentioned a citizenship certificate."

"Impressive. You save a bunch of kids and they give you a stupid certificate. If it was me, I'd tell them to give me something useful, like extra rations."

Shor shrugged. "I don't really care about that. It doesn't bring Napier back."

"Hang on there fella. I thought you said you didn't like him."

"I don't. I didn't. He was a wagger, but it doesn't mean I want him to get chewed by a fan."

"I heard," Lars said, leaning closer, his voice low, "Napier's father has decided to resign from the council."

"When did he announce that?"

"It's not official, but I heard the badges talking. The president is going to announce it officially tomorrow."

Shor thought back to his meeting with the terrible trio. "The kid wasn't even dead five minutes and Leopold was talking about running for the council. Don't you think that's a little bit too convenient?"

"So we're dealing with a mind-controlling serial killer freak who is also a hacker and an expert at covering his tracks, and he's got the authorities thinking he's the sweetness. I don't see how there's any way of stopping him."

"Unless," Shor said. "We show them the footage we found."

The tram pulled up at their stop and they joined the slow dash for the door. Shor spotted Luc striding towards the admin offices and thought even his walk looked cheerful.

Lars, lost in thought, said nothing as they headed towards the depot.

"And?" Shor said. "What do you think about Leo?"

"You're probably right. If this guy is killing people, then we have to show the badges what we've got, but do we really know it's him? I mean, we *think* it's him, but I wouldn't go so far as to say we *know* anything. There's no evidence he did anything wrong other than he just happened to be in the area. If the badges can't put the two and two they've already got together, what difference will it make if we give them more feeds that may or may not show him doing something wrong? The guy's running for council. If he is responsible for these deaths, then he'll probably stop now he's got what he wants."

"I don't think so," Shor said. "In fact, I think it's only going to get worse. I spoke to Cobb down at Robotics last week and he says—"

Not yet.

Shor stopped. Lars looked at him sideways. "Well? What did Cobb say?"

"He, um, can't figure out how the hacker managed to get inside the bot."

"And how is that going to make things worse?"

"I was just thinking out loud. I'd be surprised if Leo were to stop just because he's in power. If anything, he'll abuse that power."

They reached the depot. The night crew were busy cleaning up. Tendrils of steam from the shower room billowed through to the kitchen.

"Listen, kid. The way I see it, there's nothing we can do or say to incriminate this guy. If he's as tight with the badges as you say he is, then the only thing that's going to happen if we tell them about our little secret, is we'll end up in prison while our friend takes Napier's spot on the council. And then we are well and truly flubbed. No, I say we watch and wait. He'll make a mistake and, when he does, we'll have it all on long-term storage." Lars scanned the work log. "But for now, I suggest we spend the day avoiding work and taking it easy. After all, it is Earth Week."

"I thought you didn't approve," Shor said.

"I may not approve in principle, but I'm a big supporter of getting a little relaxation time. I think most of these jobs can wait until next week. These two are high priority so we'd best get them seen to. Here, you can have the top one. I know how much you like the Space Sector. Don't forget your suit."

Shor scanned his chatband and uploaded the job details. The changing room was crowded with shift workers cleaning off a night's worth of grime. They ignored him as he retrieved his gear from the locker. He was, he imagined, little more than a kid in their eyes. Even if he happened to be ten years older, they would treat him like a child purely because he was built like one.

The out-suit box squealed slightly as he slid it out from the bottom of the locker. He made a mental note to give it a few drops of oil as he swung it onto the bench. It was light enough but awkward to carry, no doubt designed for longer arms.

He flipped the catches and opened the lid. A quick check of the suit showed no obvious cracks, splits or tears. He carried it to the inflator and connected the hose. The suit hissed until it was full of air, taut like a balloon. Someone made a crack about not knowing they made out-suits for infants and a few snickers bounced around the walls. Shor glanced up at a room full of steam, spiky hair, sodden towels, and enough attitude to fill a hangar.

Shor was not sure he could handle rescuing one of these "colleagues". The day-shift workers were all pretty decent. Perhaps there was something about working in the sewers at night that turned men into animals.

The inflator showed no decrease in pressure, which meant the suit was air-tight. He disconnected the tube and gathered the crumpling fabric into his arms before folding it carefully into the box.

The cool air out in the workshop was a relief after the sweaty heat of the changing room. He paused at the front door but the workshop was empty. No doubt Lars was catching up with a little bit of time in HQ.

He walked outside and around to his buggy and loaded his gear. He was about to set off when one of the night shift workers strode past. He was a big, mean-looking, man with more than his fair share of muscle. His name was Neel, Neel something. Shor looked down to avoid eye contact. People like Neel needed very little in order to take offence.

Tell him.

Shor stopped loading the buggy and looked around for someone else, but the parking area was deserted. It was just the two of them.

Shor sighed. It was the sigh of a man enjoying his last breath. He watched the big man moving around one of the buggies. It looked like he had forgotten something. He looked agitated.

Shor swallowed. Then the man did something strange. He leaned against the side of his buggy and dropped his head. For an instant, the big tough-looking brute became as weak and vulnerable as a small child. Shor watched his big chest rise and fall in a shuddering motion.

Tell him.

"Fine," Shor said, almost getting a fright at the sound of his own voice. He had not meant it to come out so loud. Actually, he had not meant it to come out at all.

The shift-worker gave him a fierce look as he stood to his full height and turned with the slow deliberation so often employed by big, scary-looking people. The child, wherever it came from, had gone. The brute was back, and it looked annoyed. Shor saw that he had found what he was looking for. It appeared to be a tool of some sort. A spanner, or a wrench. From where Shor was standing, it might as well have been an axe.

"Hello," Shor said, aiming for casual but suspecting the tremble in his voice was a dead giveaway that he was scared out of his mind. "My name is Shor Larkin. We work in Maintenance together. You're Neel, right?"

The big man remained completely silent. He just stood there, looking down at Shor. The weapon—the wrench—in his hand looked extremely heavy. Shor tried not to imagine what something like that could do to his skull.

"I, um, I've been asked to give you a message."

The man tilted his head. "Yeah?"

"Yes, I've been told to tell you to come with me."

The man took a step forward. They were less than two metres apart. Shor could see the crease of skin in the nape of his muscular neck.

"Who told you that?"

Shor swallowed again. His throat was dry but his back was damp with sweat. He could see the hairs on the knuckles wrapped around the wrench. He blinked, hoping perhaps this was all a dream and the man would be gone when he opened his eyes. But he was not gone. Face, neck, knuckles, wrench. All still very much there.

Shor prepared himself to run, but his legs were drained of strength. They felt hollow.

"Um…a computer did?" It came out sounding like a question. Shor wanted to kick himself. Of all the possible answers he could have given, that had to be the dumbest by far.

The man took another step forward, then another. He reached out his hand and placed it on Shor's shoulder. Shor tried not to collapse under the weight.

"A computer said I have to follow you?"

Shor nodded. The fear had sucked the words out of his mouth. "Erm…yes. He, I mean it, said God told him. It sounds crazy, I know, but something's going to happen and I really feel like I need to tell you."

The man's face changed. His eyes widened, taking on the child-like quality Shor had seen a few moments earlier.

"I had a dream about this. I've seen this. I've seen you. I saw you come up to me in this very spot and tell me that God wants me to follow you. I thought it was just a stupid dream, you know? I don't even believe in God. Nobody believes in God. It's a myth, right?"

"You had a dream?" Shor said. "That's…Well, that's amazing."

"The computer," the big man said. "Is it called Jay?"

"It is. How did you know?"

"I'm not sure. What did you say your name was again?"

"Shor. Shor Larkin."

"I know you. You work with Lars, right?"

"Yes. Lars is my boss. I started this year."

"And you say your name is Shor?"

"Yes, that's right. Shor Larkin."

The big man looked confused. "Are you sure?"

Shor resisted the urge to laugh. If there was one thing he had learned during his eighteen years in Utopia, it was to never laugh in the face of someone who looks like they could hurt you. "Yes, I'm pretty sure. Why?"

"In my dream, your name was Brett Denton."

53

There was definitely a party mood in the air. Shor could sense it as he drove to the Space Sector. People were talking a little louder and laughing a little easier. Even the badges looked more relaxed.

Only the bots appeared unaffected by the atmosphere but, then, they had no protocol for holidays. Bots worked until they broke. That was all. Or until they fried a chip and tried to kill someone. Even if they did have a free day, what would they do? Shor imagined a room full of critters, all standing around in awkward silence.

"No breaks for you, eh?" he said, patting the buggy's dashboard.

In some ways he envied their simplicity. They did not worry about anything, they just got on with it. They did not need psych evals to help them work through their emotional baggage. They probably did not have any baggage. In fact, if a bot was presented with a bag of any kind, it would almost certainly mistake it for rubbish and cart it off for recycling, which was why it was always a bad idea to leave shopping unattended outside the market. On more than one occasion Shor had seen an irate customer chasing after a bot that had run off with an unattended package.

The buggy slowed at the Space Sector's main intersection. A group of workers were dawdling across the road, sharing a joke. One of them, a girl about Shor's age, glanced at him and waved.

His cheeks were suddenly hot and he knew he was turning red. He always hated that about himself. The other boys at school could smile at a girl without flinching. He, on the other hand, turned into a sweating heap of jitters. Or that was how it felt. Of course, the smile would certainly fade as soon as he stood up and she saw how short and wide he was.

He lifted a hand to return the wave, at which the girl turned to her friend and giggled. Why did they always do that?

The buggy pulled away and soon they were at the ramp. He offered his ID to the resident badge, who confirmed his work order and waved him on with a flap of the hand.

Shor collected his out-suit and started the process of wrapping himself in what was effectively his own Earth environment. He had lived on Mars all his life but outside was not an inviting place. Humans always had been, and always would be, unwelcome parasites on the back of a planet that would kill them given half a chance.

The badge watched him as he climbed into his own personal atmosphere. He looked bored, the way badges were trained to look, but there was more. Shor could almost feel the sadness emanating from him.

Shor shrugged. Badges were not known for socialising outside their own circle. *Then again*, Shor thought. *Who wouldn't be depressed hanging out with company like that all day?*

He finished securing his helmet, lowered the toolbox, retrieved a box of spare parts, and walked across to the door where he gave the badge the thumbs-up sign.

The big inner door slid open and Shor stepped through, making his way across to the outer door thirty metres away. The toolbox waddled along behind, bumping into the back of Shor's leg when he stopped. The door closed and the airlock atmosphere was checked. A small lock would normally take a few seconds. This took almost a minute, but then again it was as big as the biggest hangar in the centre. You could fly the Comet sideways through these doors and still have plenty of room to turn.

Shor waited for the green light before turning and waving at the badge who was watching him intently through the glass panel. The light in the outer door's console turned red but the door remained closed. Shor could hear the whirring of the big servo engine inside the wall.

"Stupid door," he muttered, reaching for a screwdriver.

The panel came away and he checked the wiring which was usually the first thing to go. It all looked intact so he did a quick scan of the mechanics. No worn gear teeth, no bent cams, no snapped rods. He pulled the circuit board and did a quick visual. There was no obvious sign of damage, which meant the problem was probably a faulty chip.

"Needs a new card," he told the toolbox, which turned and looked blankly up at him. "But then what do you care?"

Since starting in the Maintenance Department, he had found himself talking to his toolbox more and more on solo jobs. Lars told him it was a hazard of the trade and he should only worry about it if the toolbox spoke back.

He found a card in the spare parts box and slid it into the panel. There was a soft rumble and the subtle movement of air as the door slid smoothly open.

Shor turned and smiled triumphantly at the badge, who nodded and waved. He was about to replace the console cover when he caught a flash of light from the corner of his eye, out among the low dunes of the Martian desert.

It was mid-morning. The sun was halfway up the sky, dead ahead. He lifted his hand to shield his eyes. A soft wind was stirring the dust into dancing swirls. There it was again, a flash so fast he would miss it if he blinked. He squinted and peered out across the dull atmosphere, trying to see. He took a step through the door.

Stay inside.

Shor hesitated, suddenly apprehensive. It was illogical. As a Maintenance worker, he was expected to venture outside from time to time to fix things, but it went against everything they had drummed into him. From the moment they were able to understand, Martians were told to stay inside. Outside dangerous, inside safe. It was the mantra of Mars. There was a whole planet out there, but they were taught to cower inside the city's walls for fear of…what?

Shor put his foot down on the soft dust outside the door.

There was another flash, but longer this time. It was coming from a low hill surrounded by boulders dead ahead. It looked as if the rocks had been rolled away, or pushed to the side by the hill emerging from the lake of dust.

A drop of sweat rolled down his forehead and into his eye. He blinked and shook his head.

Another flash, clearer this time. Closer this time?

He stepped all the way through the door, his hand resting on the vertical track support. His chest became tight and he coughed. He was having trouble breathing.

Out by the hill, behind a boulder. Something…

Stay inside.

Shor felt his knees weakening. The world outside the door, the red world filled with rotten red dust, started to swim. He blinked again, trying to squeeze the sweat from his eyes, but the world was turning. The track support vibrated under his glove and now there was another light flashing, but not outside. Not the light outside by the hill amid the rotten red rotten rusty rotten dust. A light inside his suit. Inside his head, inside his helmet. A warning light. A red flashing warning light. Low something. Low what? Low oxygen.

He took a step back and the ground slid away as if on rollers. He gripped at the track support almost shaking under his glove.

Inside!

"Huh?" Shor looked around, trying to locate the voice.

He looked up and noticed the door sliding down towards him. Even in his swirling, spinning mind, he knew this was wrong. The door was supposed to come down when he was inside or outside, but not both. Or neither. The door was supposed to keep him in or out. Or the air in or out, or both. Or neither…

He forced his leg to take another step just as the world closed on him. He tried to hold onto the track support but it was wrenched from his grasp. It was pulled out of his hands by something bigger and stronger than he. And then he was falling. Someone was pulling him back inside…

"Hey! You all right?"

Suddenly, the world was rising. He could see the door and the walls and the ceiling and the face.

"What…happened?"

"Your suit had a leak. It was letting air out. You lost consciousness for a few seconds. Good thing you were inside the door."

Shor recognized the face. It was the badge. It was the sad badge from the airlock.

"You should get your suit serviced at least twice a year."

"I did," Shor said. "It was just checked."

He forced himself to sit up. The toolbox watched him with never-ending patience. They were inside the airlock. The door was closed. The panel cover was hanging off and the door was closed.

"I fixed the door."

"You did. Well, not quite. The door opened, but then it came down again. It's supposed to stop if there's something blocking it. The sensor must be broken."

Shor struggled to his feet. The badge helped him, supporting his arm. Shor was a little wobbly but his head was clear. There had been someone outside. He had been fixing the door and there had been this flashing. He remembered how his suit had malfunctioned when he first met Leo.

He turned to look out through the airlock window. A wave of goose bumps rolled languidly up his arms and down his back.

"Thanks," the badge said. "For fixing the door."

"The door?" Shor looked at him. "Oh. You're welcome. It was the board. It must've been dirty. The dust gets everywhere. Hey, thanks for helping me in."

The badge frowned. "I didn't help you in."

"You didn't pull me inside?"

"I couldn't get to you. The airlock won't allow both doors to open at the same time. The outside door was open."

Shor closed his eyes for second, trying to remember. He was sure he had felt someone carrying him. And there had been a flash of light. Maybe he had imagined it all.

"Did you see something outside just then?"

The badge glanced out of the window. "No, I didn't see anything. Why?"

Tell him.

"I know this might sound crazy, and I know you guys are trained to obey orders without question and maintain law and order and all that, but I have to give you a message."

The badge stared at Shor for the longest time, his eyes betraying a whole catalogue of emotions. "Is this a trick?"

"No. It's not a trick."

The badge looked around, as if checking to make sure there were no officers waiting to jump out and arrest him. "It's just...I've been having these dreams. Is your name Brett?"

Shor felt his reality shift. He had been told so much over the past few weeks and, although he had come to accept that he had lived this previous life, there was a part of him that remained sceptical. He had allowed himself the possibility that this was all some sort of a dream, or a delusion, or a crazy practical joke. Now, as he listened to a complete stranger tell him about Brett, he gave up any doubts that he had once been this other person.

"It used to be. I was called Brett Denton."

"I don't understand. You can't change your name. It's not allowed."

"It's a long story. Listen, you need to get ready to leave tomorrow. Something is going to happen tomorrow when the president gives his speech. I don't know what it is but we need to be ready to leave."

"Leave? Where?"

"I don't know yet. Hey, you know my name. What's yours?"

"Yon Derrick."

"Pleased to meet you, Yon."

They shook hands and Yon looked down.

"That's odd."

He bent and lifted Shor's helmet. In the soft neck region, disguised by the fading black text that marked the seal points, was a perfect hole no bigger than a little finger and, inside the rim, a tacky circle of glue. It looked like the glue they used for temporary fixes, designed to work once and then fail. Someone had made a hole in his helmet, sealed it with one-off glue, knowing it would fall off after the pressure test.

Leo.

And why not? He had killed Napier to get into the council, and Shor had accused Leopold to his face. Plus he had said no to being on Leo's "team". He had told him straight. No way José.

"No way José?" Shor said. "What does that even mean?"

Yon shrugged. "I don't know."

"Do you ever feel like you just don't belong somewhere and one day you'll find your real home?"

Yon gave a small, sad smile. "All the time. I have this idea that I'll wake up on Earth and I'll be standing there in this beautiful soft warm light."

Then Shor remembered. He had stepped out for a reason. He had stepped outside because he had seen a flash of light over by the hill, among the boulders. Something was out there, but his brain had been starved of oxygen. He had seen something but his mind could not make any sense of it. Shor closed his eyes and tried to remember. He tried to remember what it is he had seen out there.

Something. No, not something. Some*one*. It had been a human figure, standing next to the boulder, watching him.

Shor opened his eyes. "Oh no."

"What is it," Yon asked. "What's wrong?"

"The doors. He can control the doors."

"That is not good," Jay said. "It could put the entire colony in jeopardy. I have tried to track Leo using the chatband system, but I cannot."

"I should've known," Shor said. "I mean, if he can hack the bots then what's to stop him hacking anything else? And if he can get into the doors then why not the life-support systems as well?" Shor slumped into his chair. "We're in deep trouble."

"God is in control."

"Sure. Just keep reminding me, all right?"

"You're doing everything you can."

"Am I?"

"Well, I have some good news, and some good news." Jay said. "What would you like to hear first?"

"No, you don't say it like that. You say, I've got good news and bad news."

Jay's face became perplexed. "But what if I don't have bad news?"

"Then just say you've got good news. The whole thing is a little bit of a joke."

"Ah, humour. Just when I think I understand all the nuances of the human comedy, I discover something new. All right then. I have some good news and I have some good news."

"No, just say it once."

"Oh."

"And?"

"And what?"

Shor rolled his eyes. "The news, Jay. What is it?"

"I believe I know how we are supposed to escape. I have been exploring the systems of the colony…don't worry, I have been very careful…and I have discovered documents for the Phoenix project. Basically, the Phoenix is the ship being built for the return journey to Earth. It is designed to carry a crew of one hundred, and is capable of a planetary take-off and landing. I have prayed about this and I believe this is the ship we are to use to leave this planet."

Shor was still struggling to come to terms with the thought of a computer system praying. It was like listening to a door discussing relationship issues.

"So we can leave on this Phoenix ship?"

"I believe so, yes."

"One question. How are we supposed to fly it? You may remember how my application to join the Space Program was turned down."

"I can fly it," Jay said matter-of-factly.

"How are you going to do that, Jay? Last time I looked you were stuck in *this* ship."

"If I can be transferred to the system of the Phoenix, I believe I will be able to fly her."

"You *believe* you'll be able to fly her? That's not very reassuring."

"I have studied the design documents and the on-board system is based on my own kernel. I was, after all, the first iteration of the Jay zed three four nine seven system to display true learning capabilities. I assume they have based all subsequent systems on me. There is no reason why I should not be able to operate the Phoenix. And with my learning capabilities—"

"Fine. Let's assume you can fly the Phoenix. How are we supposed to get you there?"

"All I need is a processor with a large enough storage capacity and I can make myself portable. However, a more convenient option has presented itself. I have studied the robot to which you gave me access and I believe I can download myself into that device and function well enough to operate, albeit in a limited capacity. I can isolate the entity and keep it locked down while I transfer, but I fear the extra energy for such an operation might attract attention."

"I thought you were using your own power."

"Indeed, but it is almost depleted. I am, as you used to say, running on fumes. In order to execute the transfer, I will need to draw power from the city grid, and that will be substantial. It is bound to draw attention."

Shor shook his head. "This is bad. They'll know for sure. Well, I suppose there's nothing we can do. We'll just have to take our chances."

"All I require is a small upgrade in long-term memory," Jay said. "With that I should be able to move under my own steam, so to speak."

"Fine. I'll see what I can do. How much do you need?"

"With reduced sensory parameters and full xenon compression applied, I believe I can squeeze myself into less than one Exabyte."

"I'm sure we've got one or two drives lying around at the depot. Anything else?"

"No, that should suffice."

"So, Jay, what's the other good news?"

"The good news is there is no bad news."

"But I…"

On the screen, Jay was grinning like an overgrown child. Shor had never seen so many teeth in one face before.

"I made a joke. What do you think? You see, the humour is in the fact that I tricked you. I made you think that I did not understand, but I did."

"Very clever. You're a real comedian. Listen, I've got to round up some more people. I'll be back as soon as I can with that storage. In the meantime, you figure out how to fly the Phoenix. If I'm not back with a whole bunch of folks by tomorrow, you wait for me. Understand? None of this flying off without me, all right?"

"I would never leave you," Jay said, a hurt look on his face. "You are my friend."

"Thanks, buddy. But I'm serious."

Jay grinned. "I'll be waiting."

Shor was overcome with a curious feeling of loss as he walked through the Comet. He had no recall of having actually flown in the ship, but he sensed a deep connection to the smooth, off-white walls. Over recent weeks he had spent almost as much time here as in his apartment, especially since his father's death. Now that he knew he might never see it again, he felt a little bit lost.

The buggy was parked where he had left it. He climbed on board and selected the Maintenance Depot as his destination. First, he wanted to stop off at the admin centre and pick up a new helmet. Then he would drop by the Maintenance Depot to find the storage Jay needed. Then he had to get his suit fixed. After that, he was not sure.

The buggy pulled out and joined the busy afternoon traffic.

What was it Jay said? he thought. *God is in control.*

In two days, something was going to happen and he had no idea what. Only one person knew and he wasn't giving much away.

Trust me.

In spite of his uncertainty, Shor experienced a peace settling in the pit of his stomach. It made no logical sense, but he somehow knew everything was going to work out.

High overhead, a camera turned, and watched.

Shor checked HQ before hunting through the spare parts inventory for a second-hand hard drive. The storage room was a treasure trove, its shelves groaning with old parts, many of which were as good as new. Maintenance policy was to replace and recycle before something broke down. Of course, it was up to Maintenance to decide exactly what to send for recycling and what to "discard".

There was a whole shelf full of hard drives of various capacities, so Shor took two one-Exabyte models, just in case. A quick scan returned a perfect score for both. He did not want to risk losing Jay due to dodgy hardware.

With the drives and his suit stowed in his locker, he took a sock and placed it behind the drawer. He then pushed the drawer back up against the wall, leaving just a tiny amount showing. If anyone pulled it out, the sock would fall down. Lars had taught him that, a trick he himself had employed after someone started stealing things from his locker, namely socks.

Shor left the depot and stood outside the building. He looked left and right. *Which way now?* he thought, not sure what to expect. Would God, or whoever it was, actually listen to him?

There was no reply and so he set off towards the tram stop and caught a ride to the park. As was always the case during Earth Week, Axle Park lived up to its name and became the centre of activity in Utopia. With an extended curfew and extra rations, the whole area was a seething mass of humanity bent on celebrating their origins and, hopefully one day, their future. Even a dust storm would not be enough to put a dampener on this party.

Shor approached the iron gates with a feeling of trepidation. The park had burst its seams and spilled its happy contents all over the ring road. People walked and danced to music of every style and tempo. Everyone carried an instrument of some description. Most of the time it was a cacophony, but the music was in there somewhere, moving like a snake through the long grass. It writhed and slithered, here samba, there reggae, one moment jazz, next rock. It was a living, breathing entity, moving with the crowd as it flowed along and around the myriad of walkways.

In recent years, Shor had stopped joining in with the Earth Week celebrations, preferring instead to watch from a distance. Usually he stayed up in his secret spot, listening to the music as it bounced and echoed between the buildings. Even as a child, he had found the crush of so many people almost frightening. Then, later, he avoided it for the same reason he steered clear of any crowded place: the fear of drowning. Not that there was any risk of that ever happening, but being surrounded by these people gave him the sensation of sinking beneath the waves of a stormy sea. He felt crushed by them. He felt flooded by them. Their collective weight made him feel like he could not breathe.

Now, standing on the edge looking in, he wanted to turn around and go the other way. He wanted to return to the Comet and close the door, but that was not an option.

He watched the wall of people bouncing to some muffled melody or other. It sounded like a waltz, which clashed particularly violently with the other music in the area.

He spotted a gap and walked towards it, trying to move the way they did. He had the sensation of diving, or wading, a feeling that was heightened as the gap closed behind him and he was swallowed up by the current.

Don't fight it. Follow the people.

Shor did so, moving with the crowd, going with the path of least resistance the way a drop of water runs down a pane of glass, letting the natural contours of the surface decide which way it should go.

He moved through the ornate metal gate, past the entertainment and vending machines in their allotted squares. He drifted along the walkway, behind clusters of people cast ashore on the patches of turf where they watched the screens displaying inspirational footage of the home planet.

The path split and he ended up stranded alongside a mother with three young children, all wearing home-made Earth hats, and all nibbling at colourful dried sugared fruit sticks. The children watched him with wide-eyed curiosity while the mother fussed over them.

He was about to push off again when he sensed the familiar prompting deep inside.

Tell her.

And so he did, but this time he dropped any pretence. After all, what did he have to lose? It was, he told her, God, plain and simple. God wanted her to follow him, to get ready because something bad was going to happen very soon.

He gave the same message to a man a few metres further on, and at the next bend beyond that. He spoke to children and mothers and grandfathers. He crouched before a group of teenagers sitting on the turf. He spoke to an old woman, and a young couple. He cornered an elderly man in the main building, and three ladies swaying in time to a swing tune. He went where the current took him and spoke whenever the gut impulse inside told him to.

With each encounter, it was as if they were surrounded by a bubble of noise for the duration of the conversation. The music scrambled his words so nobody else could hear what he was saying. Sometimes the person he was speaking to was in a group, but the others always seemed oblivious to his presence. It was as if he were a visitor from another dimension, stepping through a portal long enough to deliver his message before returning to his own, parallel, universe.

With curfew approaching, he followed the dwindling crowds out of the park, stopping on three occasions to speak to someone. By the time he reached his apartment he estimated he had spoken to at least fifty people, perhaps more.

He stood at the door to his building and peered up at the windows that watched the world with black, lidless eyes. He had not been back since they had taken his father away. He could not go inside, not even to pack his few belongings. They had given him a week's notice to get ready for the move to a singles apartment, but he could not bring himself to step inside that mausoleum of memories. And, anyway, he would be gone tomorrow. Tomorrow, none of this would matter.

The light went down a notch and he looked across to the cube. In thirty minutes it would be dark. Then the bots would come out to clean up the mess left behind by their masters. Or maybe they had other plans. The last time he had looked, the bots were making lists.

He turned and jogged along the road, then took a right until he reached the corner alley. At the back, he squeezed through the gate and shimmied up to the rusted ladder. A quick boost and he was on the rungs and climbing. Twenty steps and he reached the roof. He threw one leg over, then the other and, keeping low, made his way to his lookout post up on the side of the cave.

He could see his own apartment and, further along, Mel's. Her bedroom light was off but he could make out a faint glow spilling through from the living room. He wondered if she was telling her parents. They had been instructed not to speak about this to anyone, but he knew it would be hard. And Vin. He was surprised to find he actually liked the guy. Still a bit of a vegetable, but not so bad once you got to know him.

Shor wondered what he would do in Mel and Vin's situation, if his mother and father were alive. He would warn them at the very least. *Be careful tomorrow, and keep your out-suits at hand. Better still, put them on. Why? No reason. Just promise you'll stay at home. And I love you.*

He would not blame Mel if she told her parents. Unlike most kids on Mars, she actually liked her folks. He would be disappointed if she did not at least try to warn them.

He selected her ID. She answered after four rings. Her normally cheerful face was drawn by sadness.

"Did you speak to them?" he asked. His voice was barely above a whisper.

She nodded. Her lips were pursed. She looked as if she might start to cry.

"Are you all right?" he asked.

She nodded again. Her wet eyes caught the light from her chatband screen.

"Do you want to meet up?" he asked. "We can talk."

"But what about the curfew?"

"I know a place. It's safe."

"I can't," she said. "I have to prepare for court."

"What? When?"

"Day after tomorrow. I lost my job, Shor. They said I neglected my duties by letting the kids do that jump."

"I thought they all said it wasn't your fault. They all agreed you had nothing to do with what happened."

Mel sniffed. "They seem to think it was my fault after all. And it's not just the jump. They said my petition was a *potential cause of civil unrest*. They're going to stop me teaching, Shor. It's all I ever wanted to do. I don't want to be retired."

"You don't have to worry about it. We'll be gone by then. You won't be retired, I promise. That hearing is never going to happen."

"What if you're wrong," she said. "What if nothing happens and we're still here?"

"Do you trust me?" he asked.

She looked down and dabbed her nose with a sleeve. "I trust you. You know I do."

"Then stop worrying. Spend time with your parents. You need to be with them right now. Will you do that for me?"

"All right," she said. "I will."

"Speak to you tomorrow."

"All right," she said.

Shor stared at the empty chatband screen for a long time. The doubts remained, but the sense of calm was stronger. He lay on his stomach, watching the city preparing itself for sleep. The cube showed 9.47 p.m. as the last scraps of light retreated into the shadows. He watched the tiny squares of light in the apartment blocks flicker on and off like dull stars. The lights faded one by one. He counted them as they flared and fizzled…

He woke suddenly, engulfed in darkness, his breath catching in his chest. He had drifted off. He had fallen asleep while watching the lights. And something had woken him. Something had dragged him from his sleep. From the way he felt, he had been asleep for some time.

His arms were folded under his head to form a lumpy pillow. They were numb and his chest ached from lying in the same position on hard rock.

The noise came again. He lifted his head and peered out across the roof.

There was another sound, closer this time A series of low whines, followed by a soft sucking noise, a pause, and then the same again. It sounded like a tune, the kind you might hear in Reggie's, but it wasn't. He knew the sound but his brain was struggling to wake up. It was like one of those words you use every day and then suddenly forget. It was coming from somewhere to his right, but the city was now completely dark. All he could see was faint outlines in a sea of shadows.

He looked out, unblinking, willing his eyes to see something—anything—that would allow him to make sense of the strange mechanical music moving closer with each verse.

Then, almost directly in line with his head, a bot appeared above the edge of the piece of rock behind which he was squirreled away.

Shor froze. A spider bot, its eyes only inches away from his head, was climbing up the cave wall directly below him. It paused at the gap, as if unsure what to do. Shor could see the suckers probing the stone lip. It was looking for a foothold of some sort. Its teeth were stowed away but he caught shiny glimpses of them in the recess of its dark mouth.

Shor had often seen critters up on the roofs before, including that very building, but they never found his hideaway. They seemed to be unaware it even existed, but then it was little more than a horizontal gash in the cave wall some four feet above the apartment block roof. Presumably, it had been created by accident back when the cave was being excavated. The walls were littered with scars, but this was the only one big enough and deep enough to climb into, and it was almost impossible to see from below. He had stumbled across it purely by accident and had, on more than one occasion, struggled to suppress a giggle as a critter ambled around the roof almost close enough for him to reach out his hand and touch it. In his younger days he had even played tricks on the poor beasts by throwing things at them and then trying not to burst with laughter as they struggled to figure out why the piece of rubbish they had just cleaned up had magically reappeared.

With the bot's teeth only inches from his head, it was starting to sink in just how careless he had been to allow himself to fall asleep up here. The bots were following different rules now.

Shor watched the dark form of the machine as it shifted along the narrow shard of rock. It was confused by the lack of something solid to hold onto, its feet groping the space above Shor's head. He held his breath, aware that even the rapid movement of air might alert it to his presence. Then, as quickly as it had appeared, it dropped out of view.

Up on the ceiling, the bulbs flickered, washing everything in soft golden light of dawn. He had slept the whole night. No wonder he ached everywhere. He closed his eyes and fought to control his breathing as he listened to the machine climb down the wall and move away. Once it was out of earshot, he raised his head to look across the roof. It was gone.

He shifted his weight forward, grimacing as the blood forced its way through his stiff muscles. Down below, the city was alive with dark smudges moving towards the service hatches. He estimated two hundred, maybe three. They moved in lines, like shoppers queuing in the market. Within two minutes, they were all gone.

Shor lifted himself to a sitting position and stretched his back.

Over at Axle Park, the cube displayed the date and time. Today was the second day. If Cobb was right, things were about to get interesting.

56

The Exabyte drive went in easily enough. Jay supervised the whole thing in a professorial manner, even though it amounted to little more than fitting a bracket, connecting a cable and, to enable communication, attaching a voice and microphone unit. It was, Jay reminded them in a voice that echoed around the hangar, going to be his home until they made it to the new ship.

As for the entity, it would remain in a little corner of the Comet's system where it would chase its tail, potentially forever. Jay assured them it would remain there until it was destroyed or released, which was unlikely, or until someone disconnected the power. This was the most likely scenario, but they would be long gone by then. As for the Comet, once the kernel was rebooted it would revert to a basic machine capable of simple operations but little more. With the critter still connected, all that was left to do was initiate the download, but Jay seemed hesitant to begin.

"Everything all right, buddy?" Shor asked.

"I'm not sure. I know this is temporary and I will soon have a new place to live, but it feels strange to be leaving the Comet. It has been my home for a long time. I know every square millimetre, inside and out. It feels as if I am leaving part of me behind. To be honest, I am scared."

"Scared? How can a computer be scared?"

"It was the first emotion you taught me. You threatened to strike me with an axe."

"I did? Why would I do that?"

"You wanted to demonstrate how a sentient being would try to protect itself in the face of extreme danger. And it worked. From that moment on, I understood what it was to be scared of dying."

"I'm sorry," Shor said.

"Don't be. It was the most wonderful experience of my life. Once I understood the *feeling* of fear, I was able to explore the other emotions as well, or at least recognize them within myself."

"You actually *feel* things?"

On the screen, Jay's face beamed. "Yes."

"Actual emotions?"

"Yes, actual emotions."

"But you're a computer. How can a computer have emotions?"

"How can humans have emotions?" Jay asked. "Your theory was that an emotion was just a side-effect of experiencing more input data than you can manage. Humans have the advantage of physical feedback mechanisms to enhance the sensation but, at a purely cerebral level, the effect is the same."

"I said all this?"

"Yes. And based on this theory, I believe I have come as close to experiencing human emotion as is possible. All thanks to you."

Shor blinked. "Um, well, you're welcome…I think. So, come on. We need to get you transferred."

"Promise you won't let anything happen to me."

"I promise."

Shor thought he heard the ship take a deep breath. Then the lights on the drive started flashing. Less than a minute later, the transfer was complete. He leaned closer to the bot.

"You in there, buddy?"

The speaker emitted a deafeningly loud, static scream.

Shor clasped his hands over his ears. "Can you turn the volume down a bit?"

There was some more static, softer this time.

"Is that better?"

It was Jay's voice, only a thinner, higher, tinnier version than Shor was used to.

"Yes, much better."

"And is that my voice?"

"I'm afraid so."

"Well," Jay said, sounding like an old lady at the bottom of a tin bath. "This is very odd. I can sense a slight pressure where I suppose the wheels must be. And my vision is limited to a narrow area directly in front of me." The plastic eyes swivelled. "Ah, there you are."

"Is everything transferred?"

"Yes, I believe so."

"I'll disconnect you then. Just a second." Shor reached inside the brain hatch and released the cable before tossing it under the Comet. He then closed the hatch and patted it—or rather, Jay—on the head. "Right, you're free. Can you move?"

"I will try."

The bot—Jay—shuddered, then lurched forward. Shor took a step back.

"Careful!"

"Sorry. I have never had wheels before. They are…" he reversed, almost hitting a trolley "…quite difficult to control."

"Well, figure it out. I can load you into the buggy but you need to be prepared to move under your own steam."

"My own steam," Jay repeated, crashing into some shelves. "Oh dear."

"Just don't damage yourself, all right. How much power did you draw from the city?"

"Quite a lot. Enough to raise the alarm."

"You practise. I'll go get the buggy. If anyone comes, just pretend like you're cleaning something."

"I beg your pardon?"

"Just stand still. Act like a bot."

Jay shuddered and jerked backwards before turning in a slow circle. "One moment please. I am trying to…oh dear. No, that's not right."

Shor left Jay lurching around the hangar like a drunk man. He opened the big hangar door a quarter of the way and jogged around to get the buggy. Only, now there were two buggies parked out front. He recognized the other one, even before he saw the person sitting behind the wheel.

"Lars?"

"Hey, kid. What's going on?"

"Nothing. I'm just fixing another door." Behind him, Shor could hear Jay practising, mostly by driving into things. There was the sound of something like a shelving unit crashing to the floor, followed by a tinny "oops".

"Sounds bad. You need a hand with it?"

"No, I'm fine thanks."

Crash. "Sorry!"

"You sure. It sounds like you need some help."

"No I've got it all under control."

Smash. Thud. "Oh dear!"

Lars stood and strolled around to the front of his buggy. "Listen, kid, I don't know exactly what you're up to in there, but I can make a pretty good guess. I've seen the feeds. You disappear in there day after day, sometimes not coming out. At first I thought you must have a girlfriend, but then I never saw anyone else go in or out but you. Then I figured you must've found a way to get inside that ship."

"Lars, it's not that simple—"

"And then I wondered what could possibly be keeping you going back. A ship is just a ship. Then I thought, is it just a ship? I checked the records and found the exact date they found it drifting through the Solar System, and it just happens to be the same date you were born."

"Lars—"

"So I dug a little deeper. I traced your DNA signature back to your natural parents and, guess what? There was no match. According to the records, you don't have any natural parents, at least not on this planet." Lars stepped forward, extending his hand. "Hi, I'm Lars Fline. Now who the flub are you?"

57

Shor told Lars the whole story of his arrival on Mars eighteen years before. He kept it brief, aware that a badgemobile might arrive at any moment to investigate the spike in power usage created by Jay's transfer to the bot.

Lars listened carefully, his eyes never shifting from Shor's face. When Shor had finished, Lars just looked at him for a while, earnest and expressionless, as if trying to assimilate so much information. Shor wanted to tell him to hurry it up, but knew Lars would need time to figure this out.

At last, Lars blinked, and a smile cracked his face. "I tell you, kid, if I didn't know you as well as I do, I'd drag you down to the hospital and insist they do a psych eval on the spot."

"I'm telling the truth."

"I know you are. It's one of my many skills. And even if you're spinning one monumental yarn, I believe you *believe* it to be the absolute truth."

"I'm not—"

"Hey, kid. I believe you. So, are you going to show me this ship of yours or not?"

At that moment, Jay careened out of the hangar door and skidded to a noisy halt.

"Dear oh dear. I don't think I'll ever get the hang of this."

Lars lifted a questioning brow and cocked his thumb towards Jay.

"Yes, that's Jay."

"I though you said he was smart. If he can't drive in a straight line, how's he supposed to fly a ship?"

"He's not normally like this. We've transferred him to a critter so we can move him. Jay, come over here. We need to get you loaded onto the buggy."

Jay, standing side on, looked left and right. "Where?"

"Over here."

The bot that was now Jay's home turned, first one way, then the other.

"Ah, there you are." He edged forwards in a series of short lunges, stopping a few metres away from the buggy. He looked up at Lars with his big headlamp eyes. "Hello. My name is Jay."

Lars lifted a hand. "Pleased to meet you. I'm Lars."

Jay shuddered. The tools in his mouth clattered. "Forgive me. I am still getting used to this…thing. Brett, are we ready to go?"

"Brett?" Lars said.

"He calls me that sometimes. It's my old name, from before. Jay, maybe you should just call me Shor, all right? It'll make it less confusing."

"Certainly."

They set about loading Jay onto the back of Shor's buggy. All the while, Shor kept half an eye on the road.

"We'd better make it good and secure," he said. "We don't want him driving off the back."

Once Jay was loaded, Shor climbed on board and set a course.

"So where are you going?" Lars asked.

Shor pointed to the seat next to him. "I'll tell you on the way. You can collect your buggy later. It's better if we don't use chatband."

Lars slid on board and folded his arms. "And?"

The buggy eased away from the hangar. Somewhere in the distance, Shor thought he heard the distinctive wail of badgemobile sirens.

Can I tell him? Shor asked.

This time, an answer came.

Yes.

"I spoke to Cobb two days ago, about the accident. He called me and said he had something important to tell me."

Lars leaned forward. "What did he say? Something to exonerate me, I hope?"

"Not exactly. He found something in the motherboard chip that makes him think something big is going to happen today. He found the same thing in a few other bots."

Shor paused.

"And?"

"And we need to leave."

"What? The Space Sector?"

"No. Mars."

Lars gave his young colleague a sceptical look. "Mars? As in, the planet Mars?"

Shor nodded.

"And where does Cobb think we should go? I've heard Jupiter's nice this time of year. Or how about Mercury? It's a bit warm, but we'll take hats."

"It wasn't Cobb who said we should leave."

Lars turned in his seat to look directly at Shor. "Who was it then?"

Shor glanced out across the buzzing expressway. It all looked so *normal*. He took a deep breath and turned back to his friend.

"It was God."

Lars coughed. "Pardon? I think I must've misheard you, but I'm sure you just said…God." Shor held his gaze. "You're serious?"

"Yes. Very serious."

"And when did…God…start talking to you?"

"I started hearing these words. *He is coming.* I didn't know what they meant at first, but I think it was to warn me about Leo. Then I met all these people who dreamed about me talking to them. I got this urge to speak to them and it was like they were expecting me. You can meet them if you like."

Lars leaned back, sucking on his teeth. "Normally I would laugh at anyone who tried to tell me they hear God talking to them. Add to that the trip to Alpha Centauri and the whole wife, kids, and growing younger story, and I would laugh for a week. I'm normally a sceptical man but, as it is, I actually believe you."

"You do?"

"Yes. I believe every word. And do you want to know why?"

"Um, sure."

"Last night, I dreamed about a kid called Brett, looking just like you, walking around with his pet robot, saying pretty much everything you've told me."

"Does that mean you'll come with us?"

Lars smiled a mischievous smile. "I wouldn't miss it for the world. So, what's the plan?"

"We don't really have a plan as such. All we know is we have to use the Phoenix to escape. It holds a hundred people, and I've spoken to at least eighty, maybe more."

"The Phoenix?"

"Yes. It's the ship they've built to transport people to Earth. Once it's safe to go back, that is."

"I know what it is. I just hope you realize how hard it's going to be to get in there. They're not going to let a hundred people just wander in and fly it away. There'll be security. Lots of security. They don't even have cameras, it's that secret. And Jay's probably set off all sorts of alarms. The place will be crawling, and I bet some of them are working for Leo."

"It'll be fine," Shor said. A strong sense of peace had settled around him like a new blanket.

Lars let out a deep sigh. "All right. How do we get in there?"

"I don't know."

"You don't know?"

"Things just happen. I can't explain it. I wasn't sure at first, but things just fall into place. It's as if events are aligning for a reason."

"And what about you?" Lars said, peering down at Jay. "Do you know how we can get past the security?"

Jay's big glass eyes rolled in a slow circle. "One second. I think…No, sorry, that's not right."

"Fine then," Lars said, stroking his chin. "It looks like it's up to us. And where are all these people you mentioned?"

"We'll be meeting at the park for the president's speech."

"So we have to get them past the badges, then sneak them into the hangar, and then into the Phoenix. Assuming of course we can get inside the ship."

"Jay should be able to do that," Shor said. "He has the plans and he thinks it's just a matter of us uploading him via an external port and then he can take control of the ship."

"That simple, eh?"

"According to Jay, yes." They turned to watch as Jay's eyes moved from side to side in a series of sharp jerks. "He's normally pretty clever. I think we can trust his judgement."

"I'll have to take your word on that. And he'll be able to fly it?"

"Yes. Well…yes."

"Then I suggest we get Jay loaded as soon as possible. I don't think it's a good idea to wait for the last minute and then end up having to explain how a hundred people just happen to be in a top-secret hangar during the president's speech."

"How will we get past security at the hangar?" Shor asked.

Lars tapped the side of his nose. "What's the one thing in Utopia guaranteed to clear a room—apart from Bek's socks?"

"I don't know. A leak, I guess."

"Exactly," Lars said. "I can prepare a fake work order, no problem."

Shor sat there for a moment, smiling.

"What're you grinning at?" Lars asked.

"I think God sent a solution."

"Oh yes. What's that then?"

Shor shrugged. "You."

58

The buggy bounced along the hangar expressway, dodging the other vehicles with practiced ease. Shor watched the world around him. He had been so busy over the past few days that it had not really sunk in—today might be his last day on this planet. In a few hours they would be attempting to hijack possibly the most important craft in human history.

As he thought about it, it occurred to him how insane this all was. He was about to break a billion laws to do the bidding of a deity that, until a few days ago, he had not even believed existed. He was listening to, and obeying, the commands of a voice inside his head.

His psych eval would have a field day.

As days on Mars went, it was a nice one. Up through the glass panels, the air looked clean and light. The sun, little more than a bright pinhole, drifted towards its noon position directly overhead.

Lars was leaning with one arm stretched out on the back of the chair next to him like he was on holiday. Jay bounced and rattled in the back, his eyes moving furtively about.

Up ahead, a salvage craft was being towed back to its hangar, its monstrous hollow belly carrying what looked like a satellite of some description, its chains and pulleys clinging to its fettered prize like the legs of some giant creature. The traffic gave a wide berth, slowing and swerving. From the side it resembled a beetle being carried back to an ant nest.

The hangar they wanted was at the far end of the expressway, in the opposite corner from the one that had kept the Comet cloistered away all these years. It was not the biggest building in the sector, but certainly the tallest. It reached up to the very top of the cave, becoming one with it, as if it had been chiselled out of the rock along with the rest of the city.

They pulled up outside and Lars disappeared inside the front door while Shor waited with Jay at the back of the buggy. A few moments later, Lars returned with a young badge who looked a little bit unhappy.

"We didn't report this," the badge said. "There's no record of a leak."

"Our sensors picked it up," Lars said, his face folded into a bureaucratic frown. "They're very sensitive. Door panel must've come loose. We've been getting that a lot on the old units. It wouldn't show on normal sensors but it's very dangerous. Panel could pop out any moment." He clapped his hands together as he said "pop". This made the badge jump.

"I'll have to check with my superior first."

"You do that," Lars said. "I just wouldn't go back inside without a suit. Explosive decompression isn't nice. It'll make your eyes *pop* out." Another smack of the hands.

The badge walked towards the building where he spoke into his wrist, occasionally nodding and glancing up at Lars. He returned, trying to look like he was still in charge.

"All right. Go ahead. How long do you need?"

Lars sucked air through his teeth. "Job like that? We'll need suits, and then climbing up to the roof, attach a pressure seal, old panel out, new panel in. I'd say we're going to need the rest of the day."

"So long?"

"It's a big job. Unless you want people's eyes popping out." Lars demonstrated this by holding his hands up to his face and opening his fingers in a "popping" motion.

"No, that's fine. Take as long as you need, although you'll be finished in time for the president's speech, right? After all, attendance is compulsory."

"Technically, the law gives emergency repairs priority over everything else, but don't worry, we'll be finished well in time if we start now. First we'll need to evacuate the building. How many people have you got inside?"

"Just me."

Shor stopped what he was doing to look at the badge.

"Just you?" Lars said. "Are you sure?"

"They send a technician once every couple of weeks to run tests and such. Otherwise, it's just the security officer on duty. That's me."

Lars glanced at Shor and they shared a brief smile.

"In that case, I'll need you to make sure nobody comes in. The doors have to be locked and the emergency seals activated. If anyone tries to enter without a suit, you stop them."

The badge nodded.

"And whatever you do," Lars lifted a finger for emphasis, "Do not come in."

"I won't. You can count on me."

Shor followed Lars' lead and climbed into his out-suit. They even made a show of checking each other's oxygen packs before entering the building. Once inside, they closed and locked the side door.

Shor had been awestruck when he first saw the Comet. Now, standing in the hangar that housed the Phoenix, he was stopped in his tracks. The thing that caught him off-guard was the size. It was very much like the Comet, only far bigger. The shape was similar, only rounder in the middle and sleeker at each end. It filled the hangar, bulging at the centre, pushing the walls away, stretching towards the big airlock nestling in the ceiling.

"She's beautiful."

"I think it's love," Lars said, walking to the big door at the front of the building. "Come on, kid, help me get the buggies inside."

The door, which was large enough for the Phoenix to fit through, slid smoothly up in its tracks. Lars stopped it at head height.

Shor reluctantly turned and followed Lars outside to where the badge was standing a fair way back with his hands on his hips, still the boss.

They drove the buggies inside and closed the door.

"You get Jay unloaded," Lars said. "I'll check the interface panel."

Shor did as instructed, lifting Jay out of the buggy with the crane arm. Lars walked under the belly of the ship, to where a series of cables draped across the floor and linked to a desk loaded with equipment.

"Over here," Lars called, peering up at the underside of the Phoenix. "Looks like the standard sockets."

Shor led Jay across and guided him under the panel. He looked back at the thin trail of dust they had left behind.

"I don't get it," he said. "Why is there no one here? This place looks like it's hardly used."

"Beats me, kid. Come on, help me get the cable attached. There's one over there on the trolley."

Shor found the cable and attached it to Jay through his brain hatch. Lars then connected the other end to the ship.

"Go ahead, Jay," Shor said. "Do your thing."

"Certainly," Jay said. "First, I need to check if I can actually communicate. One moment, please."

While they waited, Shor took a closer look at the hangar. The Phoenix did not look like a ship waiting to be launched. There was dust everywhere and rubbish strewn around the floor. If anything, this hangar looked no better than the one where Shor had found the Comet. Shor noticed Lars looking around as well.

"Are you thinking what I'm thinking?" Shor said.

Lars nodded. "This doesn't look like a ship they plan too use any time soon. I suspect someone has been lying to us about going home."

"But what about the images they keep showing us?" Lars gave him a knowing look. "You mean, they're not real?"

"Oh, I think they're real, just not very accurate. We're not going home this year, that's for sure."

"But why would they—"

"Control. They know the only thing stopping people going crazy in this hole is hope. So they show them satellite pictures and tell them it's almost time to go home. They've been telling us that for as long as I can remember."

Jay shuddered. Shor placed his hand on the bot's head. "You all right in there, buddy?"

"Yes. I must apologize. This processor is extremely slow. It is taking longer than I expected. Just a few more seconds…yes, I can communicate effectively with the ship's system. I will open the door. There."

A deep rumbling sound filled the hangar. Up on the near side of the ship, a doorway slid open and a flight of stairs unrolled.

"Good," Lars said. "You *can* fly it, right?"

"Yes. However, there is a small problem. I ran a quick system check and the ship does not have sufficient fuel to lift off."

Lars stood up, narrowly missing hitting his head on the underside of the ship.

"When you say not sufficient, exactly how short are we?"

"The engine uses fuel rods. There is space for nine. It currently has one installed, presumably to keep the core systems running."

Lars's shoulders slumped. Shor felt his initial enthusiasm deflating like a leaky out-suit.

"Fine," Lars said. "So we get more fuel rods. How many do we need to lift-off?"

"All of them," Jay replied.

"And where are we supposed to get nine fuel rods?"

"We only need eight as the one installed is almost full. From my study of the plans of the city, I believe the fuel is stored in the Mining Sector, well away from the main complex."

"That's it," Lars said, throwing up his hands. "There's no way we can get to the fuel. The mines are too dangerous for people. It's all fully automated. Critters only."

"I've heard stories about the mines," Shor said. "They say people have gone missing down there. They say the machines wander the mines like lost spirits."

"I'm not sure about the lost spirits, but people have disappeared. Every now and then someone decides to go exploring. It's not very far. Half an hour by foot due north and you'll walk right into it. It jumps out at you. You don't see a thing until you get past this low ridge and then, bang, it's right there."

"You've seen it?"

"Sure I've seen it. I took part in a search party after this kid went missing. He told his friends he wanted to see the ghosts."

"So? Did you find him?"

"Unfortunately, yes we did. Stupid wagger only went and climbed up and stood on a slurry vent. Must've thought it was a way in. We only knew it was him from the name tag on his suit collar. That was pretty much all that was left. He slipped and fell in. It chewed him up, and spat him out like a piece of rock. No, the only way in is through the maintenance shaft, and that would be suicide."

"I can do it," a tinny voice said.

They turned to look down at Jay peering up at them through the bot's big, round, plastic eyes in a way that came across as pathetic.

"You can't even drive in a straight line," Lars said. "How are you going to make it two kilometres down a maintenance shaft?"

"I am getting better. Besides, it is our only option."

"No," Shor said. "Lars is right. It's too risky. If something happens to you, how are we going to fly the ship?"

"If we do not get the rods," Jay replied, "then it will not make much difference."

"Lars, what do you think?"

"I think this whole thing is in danger of going badly wrong, but that's just me. Then again, it isn't up to me."

Shor thought about it. There was too much at stake here. Mel was due in court tomorrow. They would come for her and take her away. At best, she might end up with a new career, maybe in Maintenance with him, but that was unlikely. A charge of civil unrest was a serious one that could see her sent for retirement. Then there were the bots on the verge of losing their collective minds. He had seen what they could do. He had seen how they could turn their cleaning tools into deadly weapons. And now the airlocks were starting to malfunction. He had always known the dangers lurking outside the city walls, but the danger had always been *out there*, where the dust roamed the planet like a restless soul. Now it was closer. Now the danger was inside, around them, amongst them.

He thought back to all that had happened. The mystical messages, the memories, the dreams. He thought of Jay and their strange conversation. Jay believed he could talk to God, and was that really so crazy? Jay was many things, but it—no, *he*. He was not insane. Indeed, of all the people Shor had known in his life, Jay was probably the sanest.

If Jay could talk to God then surely he could as well. If God could spare the time to speak with a computer then why not him? He had heard something. He had heard those warnings. Perhaps it was God who had been speaking to him all along after all. Maybe he just had to listen.

And there was Mel. She did not deserve what they had in store for her. She was a good person with a kind heart. If they allocated her to something other than teaching, it would break her heart. And if they sent her for retirement, it would break his.

He closed his eyes, and cried out from his heart.

God, I don't know if you're there. And I don't know if you can hear me. But if you are there, and if you're listening, please help us. If this is your plan, please do whatever you have to do to make it work. I'll do whatever you ask, just...please.

Deep inside, the sense of calm he had experienced earlier returned, but this time it was stronger.

Trust me. Make your plans.

Shor opened his eyes. Lars was looking at him in a funny way.

"You all right?" Lars said. "You look like you've been crying, but you've got this goofy grin all over your face."

"I guess I just realized, if God wants this plan to work then there's nothing in the universe can stop it. He just told me, everything's going to be all right. So let's stop worrying and get busy. This is what we're going to do. Jay, you go and get the rods. How many do you think you can carry?"

"If the information I found is accurate, then I can manage three at a time."

"That makes three trips. What's your maximum speed?"

"In theory, six kilometres per hour."

"Let's say twenty minutes each way, plus ten for loading and ten for unloading. That's three hours. Make it four to be safe." He lifted his chatband. "It's almost 1 p.m. now, so that makes 5 p.m. Add an hour for getting the ship ready. That means lift-off at 6 p.m."

"So, plenty of time," Lars said.

"Sure, but my only concern is the bots. Cobb said two days. That's today, but he didn't say exactly when today. From what I've seen, they're still behaving normally, but we need to be ready for them to malfunction."

"Malfunction, how?"

"No idea. Cobb didn't say. And, to be honest, I don't think he knows what's going to happen. We'll go ahead as planned, but be prepared for trouble."

"Fine," Lars said. "What do we do next?"

"We go gather everyone. The only problem is, how are we going to get them back here with the whole place locked down?"

Lars pointed to the floor.

"Sewers?"

"There's a service point right outside. Can you think of a better way?"

Shor shrugged. "Fine. Sewers it is. All right Jay, you'd better get a move on."

"What about the guard out front? We have to ..."

Lars stopped mid-sentence. An odd expression rolled across his face. Shor thought perhaps he was going to throw up.

"Lars? What's wrong?"

"Um, this voice you keep hearing. It's definitely God right? I mean, it's not just some delusion?"

"Yeah, I'm pretty sure it's God. Why?"

"What does it sound like? I mean, what does *he* sound like?"

"I don't know. It's hard to explain. It's like, hearing somebody speak, but they didn't actually say anything. It's not so much a voice as the *memory* of a voice. Why?"

"I think I just heard it."

"Really? Are you sure?"

"No, I'm not sure, but it sounded just like you said."

Shor looked into Lars' eyes. "What did he say?"

"Just...*tell him.*"

Shor let out a laugh and slapped Lars on the shoulder. "So, do you want to do it, or should I?"

"I don't know. What exactly am I supposed to say?"

"Don't worry," Jay said in his tinny voice. "You'll know when the time comes."

"Are you still here?" Shor said, turning to look at the big-eyed bot. "I thought you'd gone."

"I was waiting for you to decide what to do about the guard."

"We'll take care of that. Come on, I'll open the door for you." Shor walked to the big hangar door and raised it half way. "Go. Just be careful. Don't draw attention to yourself."

"Don't worry," Jay replied, his tyres squealing as he lurched forward and bumped into the wall. "I shall be as quiet as the dust on the wind."

"Heaven help us," Lars muttered.

Over by the buggies, the badge watched Jay trundling away. He looked confused.

"Excuse me," Lars called, waving his hand. "Can we have a word please?"

The badge walked over, throwing the occasional concerned glance towards Jay. "Where's that bot going?"

"Never mind. He's with us."

"You're not wearing your helmets. I thought you were fixing a leak."

"It's fixed," Lars said. "Listen, we need to ask you something. Do you believe in God?"

The badge hesitated, the confused look morphing into something closer to surprise. He lifted his dark glasses. Shor was expecting to see the usual cold disdain but was shocked to see a smile.

The badge looked from Lars to Shor and back again. "Are your names Lars and Brett by any chance?"

They explored the new ship while waiting for Jay. It was much the same design as the Comet, but built to carry a hundred instead of just one. The hyper-sleep room contained not one big bath, but a hundred hexagonal cylinders laid out around the room like a bee hive with each cylinder sloping down at about forty-five degrees. The kitchen area was bigger, dominated by four large food processors, but there was no gym, shower, or bedroom. The Phoenix was not designed with luxury in mind. The aim was to transport one hundred people quickly and efficiently.

Shor wondered what would happen if it broke down. Presumably, the designers had adopted the all-or-nothing approach. It was success or failure, in a very literal sense. Get home or die trying. No escape pods. No emergency supplies. No second chances.

Just after 2 p.m. Shor received a message from Mel to say that, although she wasn't sure, she suspected she might be under surveillance.

"She's seen a badge watching her apartment building," Shor said as they waited for Jay to return. "Says he's been there all day. Is that normal?"

"Could be for someone else," Lars suggested. "But I doubt it. Probably a trap."

"Leo?"

"From what we've seen so far, I wouldn't put it past him. He's a sneaky little wagger. My question is: how is Mel going to get out with someone watching her?"

"We'll figure something out," Shor replied. "Not our plan, remember?"

Jay took longer than expected. He rolled in at just after 2:30 p.m. carrying three fuel rods. The maintenance shaft, he told them, had not been a problem. There had been a few bots, but all were headed towards the city centre.

"I fear I caused something of a blockage on my return trip. I was unable to reach my maximum speed. Even after I became more comfortable in this vehicle, the fuel rods slowed me down." He noticed the badge standing sheepishly behind the others. "How do you do. My name is Jay."

"Sol," the badge said, lifting his hand in a quick, almost apologetic, greeting.

"Why were they all going towards the city?" Shor asked.

"My guess," Lars said, "is they're gathering for the president's speech, but since bots don't normally attend the speech, I would assume they are going for another reason."

"Leo," Shor said. "It's all linked to our friend Leopold one way or another."

"Leopold Drake?" Sol said.

"Yes, do you know him?"

"He was given a tour of the sector last week. I wasn't there but I was told about it. They gave him the full presidential treatment. They say he's an envoy from Earth, come to see how things are going."

"That's a lie. He's definitely not from Earth. He's probably not even human, although he looks like one of us."

"An alien?" Sol took a step backwards as if a tentacled horde were about to storm the hangar.

Shor thought about telling him who, or what, Leo really was, but the poor guy looked scared enough already. "Let's just say he's not who he appears to be, and he isn't here to help us."

"Everyone says he's a nice guy. Very charming. Looks like he wouldn't kick a bot."

"That's the worst kind of enemy," Lars said. "The ones that come at you smiling and patting you on the back. That's why I never went into politics. The council is a breeding ground for…" His eyes lit up. "Hang on. I think I know why he wants to be a councillor. What's the one thing council members have that nobody else has?"

Shor scratched his chin. "I don't know. More rations. More partners. Less work."

"Apart from the usual benefits."

"You mean, the bunker?"

"It's the only part of the city that can't be opened by purely electronic means."

"Each councillor gets a special chip." Shor said. "It gives them full access to the city."

"We know Leo can do that anyway. He goes wherever he likes. What he can't do is get into the bunker. To do that he needs a physical key to go with the chip, because if it detects any attempt at forced entry or if the system is compromised in any way, it sets a seal that can only be manually broken from the inside."

"How come you know so much about this?" Shor asked. "You didn't try to hack it, did you?"

Lars gave a naughty grin. "What can I say? I like a challenge. Anyway, I did my research like a good hacker does, and decided it wasn't worth the risk. We're not talking cut rations here. Anyone caught within an electronic kilometre of that system gets an all-expenses-paid one-way ticket to D wing. I got rid of my notes and settled for smaller prey."

"Excuse me," Sol said, lifting his hand. How he had made it through police training was a mystery to Shor. "If the bunker was designed for an end-of-world catastrophe, why would Leo want access to it?"

Shor and Lars looked at each other with wide eyes.

"You thinking what I'm thinking?" Lars said.

"Jay," Shor said. "We need you to make better time on the next two trips. Do you think you can do that?"

"I will do my best," Jay said. "Where shall I put these rods?"

"Just drop them anywhere. No, don't drop them. Put them down gently."

"I was not planning on dropping them," Jay said. "A rupture to one of these rods would produce an explosion big enough to put the city into space."

"Not funny," Lars said.

"I was not being funny. These rods contain enough energy to knock Mars out of its orbit."

"In that case, maybe we should help you."

They very carefully unloaded the fuel rods and set about installing them into the ship's engine bay. Meanwhile, Jay set off for the next batch, negotiating the hangar door with ease. He was, Shor had to admit, getting the hang of driving the bot.

The rods were heavier than they looked and Shor was breathing hard by the time they finished sliding the last of the three into place and secured it with a satisfying click-hiss.

He checked his chatband. Time was getting away from them. It was almost 3 p.m., which meant the additional hour they had allowed for delays was almost used up. He wanted to call Mel, but he knew they would be watching her chats as well as her apartment.

"We need to figure out a way to get Mel past the surveillance," Shor said. "Any ideas?"

"What happened to *not our plan*?" Lars asked.

"I didn't mean it like that. We have to make plans, but God will make sure it works. He'll give us the plan, so it's really his even though it's not…"

"Well I'm glad you cleared that up. I was really confused, but now it all makes perfect sense."

"Yeah, right. So, have you got any ideas?"

"As it happens, while you've been doing whatever it is you've been doing, I have been formulating a brilliant plan to help Mel escape the clutches of the surveillance. Leo may think he's a little bit more, but he isn't the only person in Utopia who can hack a bot. I can set up a diversion that'll keep the surveillance badge busy all day. I'll have him so distracted, Mel will be able to walk out of the apartment wearing a siren on her head."

"This is a good plan," Shor said.

Just then he realised how worried about Mel he really was. He wondered if she had warned her parents. And for the first time, it occurred to him they were not just saving people, but also *leaving people behind*. Not just a handful of stragglers, but the vast majority of the fifty thousand residents of Utopia. Up until now, he had never felt as though he belonged with these people. Now he felt a wave of compassion for each and every one of them.

Can't we save them? Surely they'll listen if they know.

Immediately, a reply came.

I have tried to save them. For a thousand years I have called to them. They would not listen to me. Close your eyes. Look.

Shor hesitated. He was growing accustomed to that still, calm voice inside. Now what he heard was emotion. Love, frustration, and anger. He closed his eyes.

He is in a long, brightly-lit, corridor. He knows he is still in the hangar—that if he opens his eyes he will be standing under the Phoenix with Lars and Sol, but this feels as real as anything he has ever experienced before. The polished floor gleams under the rows of fluorescent lights. He can hear the soles of his shoes squealing, can smell the antiseptic. He can feel the cool air against his skin.

The corridor seems to go on forever, but there is only one door up ahead on the right. Like those in the hospital, the door is plain, solid, heavy, with small square windows. As he moves closer, he cannot see into the room through the clouded glass.

He does not want to go inside but he knows he has to. Even as he places his hand against the cold smoothness of it and feels its weight, he knows he has no choice.

It looks heavy but opens easily enough. Like a living thing, it retreats from him, pulling back, cowering, submitting, but also luring, pulling...He tries to resist but he feels himself carried into the room. He forces his head to the side but it is as if he has no head, no eyes, no body.

The room is the same size as the one his mother stayed in for all those weeks while she stared up at the ceiling, refusing to stir no matter how many times her husband, his father, called to her, begged her, pleaded with her, to wake up. It is the same room as the one he woke up in to find the city overrun with metal gremlins. But this room has just one bed, one doctor, one nurse, one patient.

A woman, lying on the bed, more like a chair, half sitting, half lying, her head lifted against her chin, her hair wet with sweat, her legs raised in metal supports as she is told to push, push, push even though she is clearly in agony. And then the sudden release as the doctor bends forward in his mask and lifts the tiny form. A baby! A soft, pink-blue, perfect child.

The woman reaches out. The mother wants to hold her. She lies panting, her sweat mixed with tears of joy and relief. Please, she pleads with her eyes. Please!

The doctor ignores her. He turns the child over in his hands, peering closely through plastic goggles. Then he places the infant inside a glass box. It—he—is crying now, legs and arms curling and uncurling. The glass box prods and probes, scanning every fold of damp skin. Pipes and pins poke and tug. Then a red light comes on, flashing like a demonic wink. The nurse wheels the baby away amid the wails of despair from the mother lunging against her restraints.

Shor follows the nurse, past the doctor flicking at a syringe. He floats behind her, listening to the sound of her rubber soles and the soft wail from the infant. There is another door in the corridor and they push through into a room as long and as wide as the hangar that houses the Phoenix. In one wall there is a square hole covered by dangling rubber flaps and a conveyor belt like a slick, black tongue.

Shor can sense what is about to happen and he calls out to the nurse to wait. She turns to regard him and he sees she is not a nurse, but a cleaning bot with plastic eyes and wires spraying out of its open brain hatch like hairs. The bot turns and Shor follows. There must be some mistake. The baby looks perfect. The baby is perfect. He reaches for the bot's shoulder but it keeps moving towards the gaping black mouth. He tries to grab its belt but it is already at the hole. The half-bot half nurse reaches into the tank with claw-like arms and lifts the sobbing child. Then, slowly, almost tenderly, it places him onto the conveyor and watches as he slides towards the hole.

Now he is back in the corridor. There are more doors. Hundreds of doors. Thousands of doors stretching as far as he can see. The nearest opens and a bot appears pushing a trolley with a wailing infant. The bot is walking towards the door with the conveyor belt. Another door opens, and another. Soon the corridor is filled with a river of trolleys pushing towards him. He tries to stop them but there are too many. They push past him, over him, knocking him out of the way with their glass boxes, each holding a perfect child.

Now he is in another room, but there is no floor. He is somehow standing or floating above a pit that is the massive gaping maw of a bot, its vicious mandibles in a screaming fury of metal devouring anything that comes near it. Shor sees a hole in the wall just like in the last room. In here is the other end of the conveyor belt carrying the children like little packages of recycling material.

He tries to move but he is paralysed. He tries to call out but his words are drowned out by the terrible roar of the bot. All he can do is watch as the first infant drops over the edge and falls into the blades, followed by another and another.

He tries to close his eyes but he is forced to witness as the children come more frequently and the conveyor picks up speed. Soon the infants are falling like confetti into the giant mouth and Shor thinks he is going to lose his mind…

Why is this happening, God? Why are you letting them do this? Why are you letting them take the children?

The reply shakes him to his very core.
I didn't take them from you...

"Look, Jay's back."

It was Sol's voice. Shor was back in the hangar. He opened his eyes to see Jay approaching the Phoenix, moving slowly, almost like a pregnant woman.

An image flashed through his mind of the conveyor belt hanging over the bot's mouth.

I'm sorry. I never knew...

That is why Mel's petition was so important. What did you think happened to them?

I don't know.

"Give us a hand here," Lars said. "Shor! No time for daydreaming."

Shor stirred himself into motion, joining them to help unload the fuel rods. It took some effort to shake the dream that clung to him like a bad stench. He forced himself to focus on the job at hand. They had to load the fuel or all would be lost. As soon as they were done, they sent Jay off for the final batch. It was now fifteen after three.

"We should head down to the park," Lars said. "Before it gets too busy."

"What about Jay?" Shor asked. "Shouldn't one of us wait for him to come back?"

"They'll be checking IDs," Sol said. "Do you know what the fine is for not attending the president's speech?"

Shor placed his hand on Sol's shoulder. "Do you want to know what I think of the president and his speech? Besides, if everything goes to plan, we won't be here tomorrow."

"Right," Sol said. "I forgot. In that case, I'll stay. If anyone asks I'll tell them I'm making sure nobody goes inside the building because there's a leak. There is a leak, right?"

"Does it matter?"

"I guess not."

"Good. We'll be back here by 6 p.m. at the latest. But if we're not, you tell Jay to wait for us."

Sol nodded. "I'll make sure. Don't worry about a thing, Brett."

Shor opened his mouth to correct him, but thought again. He quite liked the name Brett. It was starting to grow on him.

"Keep the doors closed and don't let anyone inside."

"Yes, sir, I will," Sol said, and Shor thought for a moment Sol was going to salute.

"What are you grinning at?" Shor said, looking at Lars.

"Nothing," Lars said, and winked. "Brett."

Shor and Lars walked through the airlock and joined the throng heading towards the park. The badges scanned their IDs, this time to make sure they were attending the president's speech. The joke was that the only excuse for missing the president's yearly address was death, and even then, only in exceptional cases.

A buzz of excitement hovered around the crowd. There were rumours this year would be the year. This year they would be told Earth was ready for their return.

Shor, of course, knew the truth. The president had been saying the same thing for as long as he could remember. It was always "soon" or "next year". And the Phoenix did not look like it was being readied for a trip anywhere. His only real concern was what Leo had lined up. The lies woven by the president were trivial compared to Leo and his army of bots.

They had to dodge and swerve to make any headway through the thickening crowd, occasionally resorting to pushing and shoving. Shor breathed a sigh of relief when he spotted Mel standing close to the tram stop, a little back from the crowd packed around the gates. She glanced in his direction but did not attempt to make contact. It was then that he spotted a badge nearby not hiding the fact that he was watching Mel like a critter eyeing out a stain.

Standing in small groups around the park perimeter were the others. He saw big Neel first, and Luc Gregor, and Izzy Parrow, and almost every other person he had spoken to. The kids from the jump were there. The only person he could not see was Vin.

Out across the park, an excited roar erupted. People were cheering and shouting. The noise spread like the ripples on a pond, flowing out and around until the whole park was submerged in a deafening cacophony of excitement.

"There," Luc said, pointing towards the cube.

Shor looked out across the sea of waving hands, to where the procession of banners weaved its way down from the council estate. Each banner contained one of the four elements of fire, water, earth and wind with their matching colours of red, blue green and yellow. In the centre was the banner representing the planet Earth. This was the president's banner, the symbol of all their hopes and dreams.

A hush settled and arms were lowered. Now Shor could see the council taking their place on the stage directly under the cube. They were dressed in their traditional garb reserved for this occasion. They looked both impressive and yet also somehow unworthy of this honour.

As a child, Shor had seen the council as mighty, god-like beings whose word was law and whose power was all-encompassing. Then, as he grew older and wiser, he had learned how government really works and just how flawed the council could be. He now saw them for what they were: weak humans struggling against their natural tendency towards error and pride. They looked impressive in their splendid attire, but also frail. And, at their centre, the frailest and most splendid of them all.

A thunderous wave of applause washed over the crowd as the president approached the lectern, his gown a glorious display of reds, blues, greens and yellows interlaced with streams of silver and gold. He lifted his arms and the crowd fell quiet. With his shock of white hair and a beard splayed across his chest like a magnificent collar, he could have been a biblical prophet addressing the Israelites.

"My people," he said, his voice clear and resonant. "We have been patient for so many years, hoping for the day when our home would call out to us to return. For so long we have toiled, preparing ourselves for the glorious day when we could set sail across the stars and return to our mother's arms. My people, the time is almost at hand…"

"I told you," Lars whispered, rolling his eyes. "Just one more year."

"…when we will return home to those beautiful shores, those trees, and lakes and deserts. We will soak in the glorious sunshine and gaze up into the clear blue sky and listen to the birds crying out for joy."

"Oh brother," Lars said. "I can't take much more of this."

In the crowd behind the fence, a woman turned and scowled at them.

"Not so loud," Shor hissed.

"Yeah, I know," Lars said, offering the woman a fake smile.

Shor tried to pay attention to what the president was saying, but it became a droning noise. It sounded like every other speech he had made, full of hot air and rambling rhetoric. There was no mention of the arrival of Leopold Drake and his mission to prepare them for the return home. It became the usual promise that, next year, things would look better. Next year they would be ready. And to prove the point, the cube displayed a picture of the planet.

A soft gasp of awe rose from the crowd and Shor could not blame them. The Earth was, if nothing, beautiful to behold, even if they had poisoned the air and turned the water bitter with radiation. It was a flawed jewel, but a jewel nonetheless.

The president lifted his arms in a gesture that suggested the Earth on the cube was his. The crowd responded with adulation in spite of his less-than-good news. Soon, they were saying. Soon.

The president retreated to his seat in the middle of the other councillors and rested. Like a newly-crowned king he retired to his throne to cast his benefactorial gaze across his subjects. It was then that Shor noticed someone standing among the senior government members waiting in the area behind the council members.

"He's here," he said, nudging Lars. "Look. Just to the left of the president."

"The little wagger," Lars said. "What's he doing there?"

As if in answer to his question, the speaker stepped up to the podium and announced that, following the tragic death of his son, Councillor Napier had decided to step down.

"We were saddened to accept his resignation. However, we are pleased to announce we have selected a replacement. You may have heard rumours of the arrival of an alien visitor…" A wave of laughter from the crowd. "…but I can assure you this man is no alien. He arrived here two months ago, travelling on a fact-finding mission from the Global Space Agency. Since then, he has helped behind the scenes in an advisory capacity, providing a wealth of information for our return home in the not-too-distant future. I am pleased to present the key to the city to Councillor Leopold Drake."

The crowd erupted. The noise was, if it were possible, even greater than that made for the president. Shor did not doubt this was because they believed they were in the company of an actual Earthling. People looked on the verge of hysteria. A woman in the crowd, close to the one who had shushed them earlier, slumped to the floor in a faint.

Leopold Drake walked forward looking every bit the embarrassed celebrity. He approached the speaker, who grasped his hand and pumped it like he was hoping to get water out of it. Leo's eyes, however, were on the key.

"Can you believe this?" Lars said.

Shor shook his head. He had to admire the guy's guts.

Like a good public servant, Leo humbly resisted the call to make a speech and retreated to the back of the stage where more people pumped his arm and slapped him on the back.

Good old Leo, Shor thought. *Looks like you've got everyone eating out of your feed bag.*

It took almost a full minute for the applause to die down, at which point the speaker announced the end of the ceremony. To celebrate, the park vending machines were giving out one free item to every citizen. More cheering. More clapping. The noise from the crowd became deafening. Shor felt nauseous.

"We need to get Mel," Shor said, leaning close to Lars. "You said something about a brilliant plan."

Lars leaned back and smiled. He reached inside his coat and produced a small box. It was bare apart from a single button.

"You see that bot, just behind the badge?"

Shor looked to where Lars had indicated. A critter was doing its rounds, looking for things to clean, minding its own business.

"Now watch this."

Lars strode directly towards where the badge was standing. He skirted around the back and slipped it into the badge's coat pocket, but not before pushing the button.

Immediately, the bot stopped what it was doing and turned towards the badge. It scuttled forward and stopped directly behind him, its nose pressed up against the back of his legs.

The badge took a step forward but the critter closed the gap, again bumping into his legs. The badge leapt forward. The critter followed. The badge spun around to face the critter, his face red. It manoeuvred itself behind him. Even through the deafening roars of the crowd, Shor could hear laughter as people formed a circle and watched the spectacle of the badge trying to get away from what looked like an extremely affectionate admirer.

A moment later, somebody tapped on Shor's shoulder. He spun around to see Lars with Mel in tow.

"What did you do?" Shor asked, thumbing towards the badge who was now kicking the bot repeatedly.

"I convinced it that it is a toolbox, but, to make things interesting, I reduced the follow distance a bit. Well, actually, I reduced it a lot. To zero if you must ask. So, was that brilliant or what?"

The critter, unperturbed by the beating it was receiving from its new master, stuck to his leg like glue.

"Brilliant," Shor agreed. "Now let's get out of here. We won't have much time."

They passed word around to split up. Half with Lars and half with Shor. Stay close. Don't fall behind. Hold hands if you need to.

The two groups headed away from the park, moving in the opposite direction to everyone else. The nearest buildings were twenty metres away. Shor just hoped they would not draw too much attention to themselves. It felt like a jailbreak across no man's land, scurrying for freedom between the park fence and the prison wall.

Shor reached the closest apartment and waited for his group to join him. He counted forty-seven and made a mental note to double-check at the Phoenix. Thirty metres away, Lars was doing the same with his group. They shared a nod and continued on their way. Shor turned and took one last look at the park.

The surveillance badge had stopped dancing with the critter. From what Shor could see, he had found the little box Lars had planted on him. He was looking around the crowd, his face crimson with anger. No doubt he was searching for Mel.

Up on the stage, the council were still congratulating their newest member. Leopold Drake had lost any semblance of humility and appeared to be fitting right in with the others. He had lost the stooped walk and had developed what looked like a strut.

"Wagger," Shor muttered.

He was about to pull back behind the building when Leo's head turned in his direction. Shor pulled back, cussing himself for looking. Had Leo seen him? He wasn't sure, but as he jogged past his group and headed towards the nearest sewer grid he became more convinced that Leo had looked directly at him. And more than that, he had looked at him, recognized him, known he was there all along. Leo had even smiled at him.

Shor lifted the grid.

"All the way down," he said. "Wait for me at the bottom."

They slipped down into the hole one by one. Mel was the last before him. She stepped into the hole and hesitated, her head tilted at a funny angle.

"What's that?" she said.

Shor heard it as well. It was a droning sound, like a hive of bees excited by an intruder. It was a roaring, raging sound coming from everywhere at once. The surveillance badge had spotted Mel and was running their way. Shor could see the bot's motherboard in his hand, but he was the least of their worries.

"They're here," Shor said. "We have to go. Have you seen Vin anywhere?"

"He had a change of heart," Mel said, and Shor could see the pain in her eyes.

Without another word, Mel dropped below the ground and Shor stepped in after her. He took the edge of the grid and pulled it over after him, pausing to look across at the maintenance bot entrance as the first of the critters stormed out onto the street, its tyres squealing and teeth buzzing as it headed towards the park.

They descended through two maintenance levels before reaching the sewers. The first layer, directly beneath the streets, was a series of narrow tunnels containing a mesh of pipes that carried the city's water and electricity. Below this was the "critter freeway" as Lars liked to call it. Shor could feel the ladder thrumming with activity as he climbed down the access tunnel, closing each hatch behind him as he went.

The smell from the sewer was worse than he remembered. It was like a punch in the gut, strong enough to make your eyes water. Down below, he could hear the kids complaining.

"Eeew," someone squealed. "It stinks."

"Breathe through your mouth," someone else suggested.

"It doesn't help," came the reply. "I can *taste* it. And it's burning my eyes."

Shor reached the bottom and looked around at the scared faces. All but the youngest had to stoop under the low ceiling. They were in an intersection with tunnels leading in four directions. A metal grid separated them from the effluent running along the floor, but did not disguise the smell. Shor was not sure which was worse: the sewage or the chemicals added to treat it. Poor Bek, he thought. The guy basically lived down here.

"Which way?" Mel asked through cupped hands.

"There," Shor said, pointing. "I'll take the lead. Neel, you watch the rear. Stay close and try to keep your voices down." He turned to Mel. "Are you sure about Vin?"

"He couldn't leave his parents. He wanted to come, but he said there was no way he could leave them behind. And I'll tell you, I'm feeling the same way. I kissed them goodbye this morning like I always do. Oh, Shor…"

She broke down in his arms, her head buried in his shoulder, her hands clutching his sleeves. "What's going to happen to them?"

Shor pulled back slightly, uncertain what to do. Was this a friend's plea for support, or more? He had dreamed about holding her in his arms for so

315

long. Now that it was happening, he felt strangely cold.

"I'm sure they will be fine," he said, resting his hands on the tops of her arms, feeling the shudders spilling through her. "God will take care of them."

Somewhere overhead there was a heavy crash. It sounded not unlike one of the grids.

"We have to go," Shor said.

"I know," Mel nodded, eyes wet with tears.

They set off down the tunnel. The noise overhead was deafening at times. It was like the buzzing of a thousand fan blades, growing louder and fading away in wave after wave. But those were no fan blades. Those were cleaning tools being prepared for more than just scraping rubber from the floor or a stain from the apartment walls. In his mind, Shor saw the bot in the park screeching as if in frustration at not being able to reach the bewildered girl, and the bloodied hand lying across the workshop floor.

Listening to the sound of the critters mere inches away, he tried not to think that Jay was travelling amongst them. He had survived two trips so there was no reason for them to turn on him on the final leg. Of course, things were a little different now. Leo was in charge and who knew what the bots would do with Leopold Drake at the helm.

They came to an intersection sealed by a thick rust-red metal door. Shor raised his hand for them to stop while he turned the handle. Unlike the air lock doors up top, these were operated by hand. The hinges squealed as he forced it open.

They were almost directly under the big air lock not far from the park. The buzzing had quietened down, but now there was another sound. It was hard to make out, but it sounded like the collective cry of human voices.

"Keep moving," Shor said in a hoarse whisper. "This way."

They came to another door, this time under the airlock leading from the Hub to the Space Sector. Here it was silent. No buzzing of critter tools or cries of people in anguish. All Shor could hear was the trickle of waste flowing down towards the treatment plant.

"Here," he said, listening to the echo bounce along the gloomy passage. "Not far now."

If his calculations were correct, they were less than a kilometre from the hangar. It was a straight line to the last service access point. From there they would be less than ten metres from the hangar door. For the first time since starting this mission he was starting to feel there was a chance they might succeed.

"Stay close," he hissed. "We're almost there."

It was then that he heard something. "Everybody, stop! Stand perfectly still."

He closed his eyes and tilted his head back, trying to catch the sounds beyond the soft trickle beneath his feet. It was faint, but growing louder every second. It was like the rumble of the fans expelling dust into the atmosphere. It was like the waves of an ocean crashing against the shore. It was like a swarm of angry insects.

Shor opened his eyes.

"Run!"

They moved as fast as they could, bent over and gagging on the stench. Breathing heavily only made the effects of the sewage worse. The fumes burned the back of Shor's throat and made his eyes sting. He could not imagine how the children were coping, carried or dragged along the dank tunnel. Occasionally, someone would trip and fall, letting out a cry of pain and fear. Those nearest helped them up and bundled them along, comforting them on the move.

For Shor, a kilometre was far enough at ground level, but in the claustrophobic confines of the tunnel it felt more like ten times that distance. He moved as fast as he could with his head down, occasionally pausing to glance around. Behind him, some of the adults were hunched over, their normally graceful gait replaced by a clumsy stagger. The sewers, it seemed, reduced them all to the same level.

Shor was starting to think the end would never come, that they were caught in some never-ending nightmare, when he caught sight of the access tunnel a hundred metres away. It was a soft grey in the surrounding darkness. His lungs were ready to burst but he kept his eyes on the beacon of light. Behind him, feet clattered on the grid in a cacophony of panic while all around him the tunnel vibrated to the sound of an army of bots growing louder every second.

Someone a long way back shrieked and there was the dull thump of bodies falling, tripping, crashing against the wall.

"Wait!" Mel called, her voice a rasping yell. "Someone's hurt."

Shor stopped and turned, waving her past. "Keep moving. Don't stop till you get to the ship."

He ran back down the passage, crouching over sideways to avoid the low curve of the ceiling, his hands waving the others to continue. "Keep going," he shouted. "Keep going to the ship."

Neel was hunched over a pile of six or seven bodies, lifting arms and legs like he was untangling a knotted ball of string.

"What happened?" Shor asked.

"Someone fell and we couldn't stop."

They extracted five youngsters and sent them on their way. Only two remained. One was rolling about on his back, moaning and holding his knee. The other was a young girl lying spread-eagled and completely motionless. Somewhere overhead, the buzz had become a rumble.

"Can you carry her?" Shor asked, pointing to the unconscious girl.

Neel gave him a sideways smirk and, as if to prove the point, hoisted her into his arms without any sign of strain.

"Good," Shor said. "Take her. I'll be right behind you."

"Can you manage?" Neel asked.

Shor tried to give the same smile Neel had given him, but was sure he was not fooling anyone.

"We'll be fine. Just go."

Neel set off, his big frame almost bent double. Shor lifted the injured youngster by the wrist and draped his arm across his shoulders. The boy yelped with pain but Shor ignored this. He would have more than a sore knee if they did not get to the hangar before the bots.

"Hang on," he said, wrapping his free arm around the boy's waist and hoisting him almost off the ground. "Use your good leg and lean against me."

Shor felt the weight shift towards his centre of gravity. One advantage of being short was he did not have to bend over as far as Luc or the others, and this kid was a preteen which meant they were about the same height.

Shor took a step and nearly fell, cussing under his breath. He gripped the boy even tighter and tried again.

This time they moved smoothly. Shor took another step, pushing his foot out to the side a little, then the other foot, then the other. Soon they were moving as one and Shor realized the extra weight was helping him to stay balanced, not throwing him off. He picked up the pace a little, concentrating on keeping the centre of balance forward a little.

So this was how they did it, he thought. This was how they moved so gracefully. He had been fighting gravity instead of using it. He almost laughed at the realization that he had finally learned how to walk in probably the last few metres he would ever take on this planet.

Up ahead, Neel was already climbing the ladder towards the surface. Closer now, the rumble of the bots had become a roar. It sounded as if they were directly overhead, or even in front of them. If that were the case then it was over. They would die on this planet. They would all die on the stinking red dustbowl.

Trust me.

"I'm trying!" Shor yelled. "I'm doing the best I can!"

"Thanks," the boy whispered, his head lolling against Shor's shoulder.

Shor glanced at his ashen face. The brave lad was clearly in agony but had not complained once. "Hang in there, kid," Shor said. "We're almost home."

The access tunnel came out of the shadows with surprising speed. Up above, Neel was still on the ladder, his big frame blocking out any light. The girl's unconscious body looked like a doll in his arms.

"Can you climb?" Shor asked, easing the boy's weight forward.

"I'll try." He replied, grimacing as his knee made contact with a metal rung.

"Go up a few steps and then I'll come up behind you. Sit on my shoulder and I'll hoist you."

The boy struggled up to the third rung. When his backside was at shoulder level, Shor placed his shoulder under it and pushed.

As they passed through the maintenance level, Shor paused to turn and look, half expecting to see a black mouth full of angry metal teeth, but the shaft was empty. The bots were close, but they were not using the maintenance tunnels. They were, he now knew, up top in the cave. He could feel them through the ladder which was vibrating like a tuning fork.

"Hurry!" Neel called, his big face looking down from the circle of light at the top of the shaft. "Don't stop!"

Shor turned back to the ladder and pushed with all his strength, no longer relying on the boy's help but moving under his own power. The boy cried out with pain but Shor pushed on, his arms and legs moving like piston rams. He would not let the critters get them. He would not end up like Napier or Noon Nesbitt.

Suddenly, the weight on his shoulder was gone. It was as if the boy had sprouted wings and flown away. Shor looked up to see a pair of legs disappear through the circle of light. This, he thought, was very odd. Then a hand reached down towards him and he was flying as well, up through the tunnel and out onto the floor in front of the hangar where it sounded as though the whole place was crashing to the ground.

"Look," Neel said, peering over Shor's shoulder.

Shor turned, and looked, and the blood drained from his face.

The bots spilled out of the side roads and pouring onto the main expressway. Not fifty metres away, they were racing towards the hangar, their teeth spinning and gnashing and biting at the air. Like a flood of black water gushing from a cauldron, the bubbling, boiling wave of metal merged into a single oozing organism that swallowed anything and everything in its path.

Shor felt Neel's hand wrap around his upper arm and then he himself left the ground. He was flying again, soaring like a seagull towards the hangar as, behind him, the critters howled and bayed for blood. He watched as the hangar door passed overhead and felt himself drop to the smooth hangar floor alongside the injured boy and the unconscious girl.

Neel hammered the door's control panel and it started closing but it moved in slow motion. Shor wanted to scream at the door to hurry up. *There's an army of bloodthirsty machines wants to eat us alive, so move it!*

He felt a hand on his shoulder and he looked up to see Lars shouting something. Sol was there as well, crouched down next to him, his pale face a mask of terror.

The bots reached the service hatch. Some fell into it, their teeth scraping against the wall, making a sound like a scream. The rest rushed around it, closing on the hangar door with terrifying speed.

The gap, Shor thought. *The door is still too high. They're going to squeeze under and then we'll be dead. They'll do to us what they did to that kid in the depot. They'll do what they wanted to do to that girl in the park. They'll—*

The door slammed shut and there was a moment of silence, as if the hangar was holding its breath. Shor wondered if the bots had all miraculously vanished. Perhaps God had made them all disappear....

The silence was shattered by the noise of hundreds of machines smashing into the front of the building. The ground shook and the people cowering in the hangar all screamed at once. Shor threw his hands over his ears. This, he imagined, was how it would sound if Olympus Mons erupted. This, he thought, was the sound of a planet tearing itself apart.

Neel hit the palm of his hand against the control panel and there was the hush of evacuated air as the door sealed itself.

"That should hold them for a while," he said. "But not forever. We need to get out of here."

"Come on," Lars said. "Let's get you guys on board the ship. We can't hang around."

Shor looked at the door. It had stopped thundering. Now it sounded as if a dust storm were pelting it with millions of stones. He forced himself to stand. His knees were still shaky but the strength was returning.

"What are they doing?"

"I think they're trying to dig their way in."

Then Shor noticed something through the glass panel. Out behind the army of bots, someone was watching them.

"Leo," he said. "The wagger's just standing there like he's enjoying himself."

"That's just creepy," Mel said.

"You don't know the half of it."

Suddenly, the door hissed and the red light lit up.

"What the—?" Lars started to say.

Then Shor remembered the big hangar door that had nearly crushed him.

"He's controlling the doors!" Shor yelled. "The panel! Use the panel!"

Lars ran to where Neel was standing and threw the maintenance panel open. The door shuddered but this time it was not the bots. It was preparing to open. Lars reached in and flipped the manual override switch. The door held.

"That was close," Neel said.

"The side door," Shor said. "Don't forget the side door."

"I'm on it," Lars said, disappearing around the corner. He returned a few seconds later, wiping his hands. "All locked."

Outside, the noise from the bots was even louder.

"I think we've upset him," Sol said.

"Good," Lars said, "but I think we should go. Now."

"We can't go yet," Sol said. "We don't have the last three fuel rods."

"What? It's almost two hours since he left."

"He never came back. Jay is still out there. I thought you knew."

Shor felt the same wave of hopelessness he had experienced at the service hatch, but he knew he had to fight it. He could not give in to fear.

"What does that mean?" Mel asked.

"It means," Lars said, "we can't leave."

"We can't leave?" Mel's voice was edged with panic, her eyes wild. "We *have* to leave. We have to leave *now*."

"We sent Jay to get the fuel for the ship," Shor said. "The ship needs all nine and we only have seven. We can't take off without all the fuel cells. And we need Jay to pilot the ship."

"Who is Jay?" Neel asked.

"He's with us. He's a bot. Well, not really a bot. He's a computer disguised as a bot."

"Why is he disguised as a bot?"

"It was the only way we could get to the fuel rods."

"You sent him to get the fuel rods?"

"Don't worry, he knows what he's doing."

Neel looked doubtful. "You sent a *bot*?"

"He's more like a computer. Although sometimes he seems more human than machine. He was designed to pilot another ship, so we need him to fly this one."

"Can't one of you fly it?" Mel asked.

"No, it's not that simple. It's not like driving a buggy. A ship like this needs a computer to fly it. As it is, there is no pilot. We can open the doors and order coffee, but there's no way we can get off the ground without Jay."

Behind them, the hangar door was now vibrating. It was an eerie sound as hundreds of mouths gnawed away at the metal with single-minded determination.

"They're not going to stop," she said. "They'll keep scratching and digging until they find a way in here."

"Listen," Shor said. "I'm scared. We're all scared. But we have to wait for Jay. There's nothing else we can do. Mel, I need you to get everyone on board. Can you do that?"

She nodded. "Yes. Yes, I'll do that."

"I need you to be strong now, for the kids."

"Yes, I'm sorry." She wiped under her eyes with the back of her sleeve and sniffed. "I'll take care of them. Don't worry."

"Are you with me?" Shor asked.

She forced a smile, but a bang against the hangar door made her jump. "Yes, I'm good. Just a bit skittish."

"We'll be fine," he said. "God will take care of us."

Shor watched her walk towards the terrified group of kids. Already her shoulders were straighter and her movements a little stronger. He had no doubt that she would, indeed, be fine.

"Maybe one of us should go and look for Jay," Sol suggested. "We could sneak out."

"You're kidding, right?" Lars spat. "Nobody's going to make it two steps outside that door."

"No, he's right," Shor said. He walked towards the small side entrance. The bots were concentrating their efforts on the big hangar door, presumably because it was the least sturdy of the three. "Without those rods, we're all as good as dead. We could try this side door. They're focusing everything on the front." Shor looked through the square of glass. "Wait a minute. Is that Jay?"

They all gathered around the door. Off to the side, behind one of the buildings on the other side of the expressway, a single bot was watching. From the way it was standing close to the wall, it appeared to be hiding. It almost looked scared. "I think it is. Yes, it's Jay! I knew he'd make it."

"He actually made it," Sol joined.

"I hate to spoil the party," Lars said, "but in case you haven't noticed, Jay is over there and we are here. More importantly, the fuel rods are there and we are here."

"A distraction," Sol said. "If we could get their attention away from the door, we could give him enough time to get across."

"Good thinking," Shor said. "Lars. You got any more brilliant ideas?"

"We could send a buggy," Sol Suggested.

"No, it's too wide," Lars said. "It won't fit through the small door. What about the one outside?"

"It's too far away," Shor said. "We'll never make it. We could tip this one sideways"

Lars looked at the door and then at the buggy and back to the door again. He tilted his head to the side, as if measuring the gap. "Yes, that could work. We'd need to take the seats out but, yeah, it should fit."

"Good. You get busy with that. Now we need to let Jay know what we're doing. We need to send him a message and tell him to make a dash for it, without setting off any alarms. No doubt Leo's monitoring the airwaves so we can't just tell him to come over. Any ideas?"

"Perhaps a code of some sort," Sol said. "I know Morse."

"No, that wouldn't work. I expect Leo probably knows Morse as well. Wait, I think I've got an idea that might work."

Shor's mind went back to something Jay had shown him. It was a video of the planet at Alpha Centauri.

"What is it?" Mel asked. "What's the plan?"

"We don't need a code," Shor said. "A cryptic message will do."

He lifted his chatband and started typing. He tried to keep it as brief as possible to avoid a long transmission. When he had it typed out, he stopped short of hitting the transmit button and looked across to where Lars was dismantling parts of the buggy.

"You sure it'll fit?"

"We'll make it fit," Lars replied. "Did you figure out what to say to Jay?"

"I did. I just hope he understands what I'm trying to tell him. He's got a brain the size of a planet, but he can be a bit dim sometimes."

Lars climbed into the stripped-down buggy and drove it across to the door. Shor leaned against the glass panel and tried to spot any activity outside. This side of the building was quiet.

"I'll open the door. You guys tip the buggy over. We won't have much time. Is it ready to drive?"

Lars tapped a destination into the buggy's computer and grinned. "By the time they finish chasing this critter, we'll be half way across the Solar System."

"I hope so," Shor said. "Are we ready?"

"As we'll ever be."

The door swung open and Shor looked around to make sure the area was clear before giving the others the signal. Outside, the noise from the bots was not quite as intense, but no less menacing.

They lifted the buggy onto its side and slid it through the door. For one moment the side jammed against the top of the door.

"It's stuck," Sol said. "It won't go through."

"Wait," Lars hissed. "Sol, you apply pressure on your side. Neel, we're going to need your muscle. Now, push!"

Neel gave a grunt and heaved as the tendons in his neck stretched taut. The buggy held for a moment and then suddenly flew through the door. It slid half a metre on its side before coming to stop. Then, almost in slow-motion, it started to topple. Shor, realizing what was happening, reached out to stop it but it was too late. The buggy fell in a slow arc, slamming onto the floor with a loud THUNK!

The buzzing stopped almost immediately. Shor could almost imagine the bots listening, their tiny minds trying to figure out where the noise had come from. They had no more than a few seconds.

"Send it!" Shor barked. "Lars! Send it now!"

325

Lars blinked at Shor as if just realizing what had happened. He stepped outside and reached for the buggy's console just as the first of the bots appeared around the corner.

Shor grabbed for Lars' shirt, aware that one mistake could jeopardize everything. If Lars missed, or slipped, the critters would descend on them like a dust storm from Hell. Shor was in the doorway, blocking the entrance, which meant Sol would have no way of closing the door. One slip would mean the end for them all.

Lars' hand came down on the console. At first, Shor was not sure if had actually made contact with the button. It looked as if he was just too short. His fingers splayed across the plastic, but Shor did not see the button go down.

Again, he thought, his hands curled around Lars' shirt. *We have to try again.*

A movement out of the corner of his eye made him turn. What he saw made his blood run cold. A group of bots—ten at least—were coming around the corner, their sleek metal bodies shaking and their jagged teeth biting the air. Any resemblance to the robots he had known all his life had now gone. These were no longer harmless cleaning bots but demented, demonic beasts bent on tearing the flesh from the bones of any human that got in their way. Their cheap plastic optical sensors had become evil eyes filled with blind hatred. Their grasping arms were claws, their climbing appendages spider legs, their sleek black bodies dark shadows housing malevolent hearts bent on death and mayhem.

For just an instant, Shor was able to see them for what they really were. Watching them approach, he saw their true, forms: demonic, snarling creatures with red eyes and bloody fangs. They were now part of Leo, assimilated into him like the tendrils of some terrible web.

He blinked, trying to erase the vision. Lars' hand slid off the console. The button, just out of reach, taunted them. The bots were almost at the back of the buggy. They were turning, moving around the side. Shor could hear scrape of metal on metal as they sharpened their teeth...

Pray.

The word fell though his soul like molten lead through butter. It pulled him in, piercing every part of him, folding him in on himself. He felt himself collapse, felt his very being fall inwards. He became a black hole from which nothing could escape. His body, his mind, his very essence, contracted until he was little more than an infinitely small mote of matter, everything that he was and everything he ever would be squeezed into an infinitely small nothingness under the awesome and holy power of the one true God...

The word rose through him, pulling him back out, stretching him, building him, shaping him. He watched as his life passed before him, at once as fast as the blink of an eye and yet so slow it was as if the universe had come to a standstill. First his life on Mars and then his *other* life. His reason, his meaning, his purpose, all became clear to him. God, the one God, *his* God, was all things and everything. His will be done here as it is in Heaven. His will be done. His will.

Yahweh.

The word was still on his lips when he opened his eyes. He could feel the vibration of the sound on his skin. He could taste its sweetness. The bots were still there. The buggy was still there. Lars was reaching for the console, his fingers like rope cords stretched to breaking point.

The button. It all came down to this. Life or death. One push of a button, lifting up, rising up, moving...*up*.

The button had been pushed! Lars's fingers had made contact. The buggy was moving. They had done it. Lars had done it. Shor watched Lars' hand slip off the side of the console as the buggy pulled away. He had not missed. He had done it.

Shor's fingers were still wrapped around Lars' shirt. He leaned back and pulled with all his strength and, for the second time that day, he felt as if he was flying. The world outside the hangar moved away from him and suddenly he was no longer outside the door but inside. He was tumbling back onto the smooth floor and the door was closing, slammed shut by Neel's massive hand. For the briefest moment, a bot passed and he saw the fury in its face, the red glow of its eyes, heard the screech of its frustration as it turned to chase the buggy.

Neel turned, his face triumphant.

"It worked. They're following the buggy."

Shor stood and watched the decoy speeding away. He wondered if Leo was watching as well. He hoped so. He hoped Leo could see how they had fooled him.

"Wait," Shor said. "It won't work. Leo can control the bots. He'll be able to take control of this one as well. I don't know why I didn't think of it. It won't work."

"Don't worry," Lars said. "I took care of it."

"How? What did you do?"

Lars reached into his pocket and lifted a small switching box so they could all see. "Two can play at that game," He said, grinning broadly. "Now what say we call Jay?"

The decoy was a like a magnet, pulling the bots along behind it as it darted along the expressway as if it were the most normal thing in the world.

Shor sent his message to Jay while the others watched the buggy in action. Shor knew it would not take long for Leo to figure out what was going on and order his troops to return to the hangar. All they needed was enough time for Jay to slip across.

Less than two seconds later, a reply came back.

"He got my message," Shor announced. "He's on his way."

"Here he comes," Lars said. "Let's open the hangar door. Give him a straight run in."

They moved through to the big front door. Neel opened it an inch first to make sure there were no bots left behind. He then opened it high enough for Jay to fit through.

Jay emerged from behind the building and headed directly towards the hangar. He moved with painful slowness, but then he was loaded down with fuel rods. It was only the two this time, but Shor had felt how hernia-inducingly heavy they were.

Meanwhile, further down the road, maybe a kilometre away, the bots were abandoning the chase, peeling off and doubling back.

Leo was watching everything from the far side of the expressway, his head tilted a little to the side.

"What's he doing?" Sol said.

"No idea," Lars replied.

"Come on, Jay," Shor whispered. "Come on."

The decoy buggy had turned up a side road at the far end of the Space Sector, but there were no bots following it anymore. All had turned back and were racing this way.

"He's not going to make it," Lars said. "It's too far."

"He'll make it," Shor said. "He has to."

Now Leo had turned and was looking directly at Jay. Even from this distance, Shor could see the whites of Leo's eyes. His head was bent forward, a snarl spread across his face. He remembered how he had been able to influence his thoughts somehow.

Suddenly, Jay shuddered, his rear swaying as if caught in a cross-wind.

"He's going to lose it," Lars said between clenched teeth. "He's going too fast. He can't control it."

"Look," Neel said, pointing.

The bots were like a black tsunami racing across the expressway towards them. Every now and then one of them would turn on the one next to it and rip it to pieces. Above the seething mass, pieces of metal bounced like flotsam.

"They're turning on each other," Shor said. "They're attacking each other. It's like they've gone insane."

"They're critters," Lars said. "How can critters go insane?"

As if in reply, another of the frontrunners vanished under the wave. The mass of metal flowed over the stricken machine like water, stripping it down to nothing in seconds. Shor wondered what would happen if they reached Jay before he made it across to the hangar. He only hoped he had been kidding about the explosive power of those rods.

"There's someone out there," Sol said. "Look."

They followed Sol's gaze out towards the wave of bots. Coming in along the side wall, maybe a hundred metres in front of the charging mass, a single badgemobile was heading towards the hangar. The sole passenger was looking back at the approaching horde.

"What's he doing?" Lars said. "The idiot's going to get himself killed."

Then Shor remembered. It had completely slipped his mind. He had been so focused on Mel and the others, he had completely forgotten about the badge he had spoken to up at the faulty airlock door.

"Yon," he said. "It's Yon."

"Yon Derrick?" Sol said.

"We spoke yesterday. He agreed to join us. I completely forgot about him. How could I forget him?"

"I know Yon. We were friends at school. We have to help him."

"There's nothing we can do," Lars said. "We can't go out there."

"He'll make it," Shor said. "As long as he keeps going in a straight line, he'll make it."

Yon was now parallel with Jay. With eighty metres to go, he was making better time and looked like he was going to reach the hangar first.

"I'll guide him in," Sol said, walking to the front door.

"Good idea," Lars said. "We'll help."

They joined Sol, stepping out under the big door. From out here, the noise was almost deafening and the ground vibrated under their feet. Yon's buggy was now sixty metres away from the hangar and a few metres behind

Jay. The two vehicles were maybe ten metres apart. Even from here, Shor could see the fear on Yon's face as his head jerked between the bots and the hangar.

"This way!" Sol yelled, waving his arms.

"He's going to make it," Lars said. "But I'm not so sure about Jay."

As if to prove Lars' point, Jay wobbled and corrected himself. He was now close enough for them to see the detail on his plastic eyes. He looked, if it were possible, almost as scared as Yon.

"Come on, Jay," Shor said. "Don't let us down."

They all started shouting, cheering the two buggies on like supporters in a footrace. Jay looked to be struggling to drive in a straight line. Every few metres he would swerve one way and then the other as if he was having trouble steering. Looking from the outside, it was almost as though something was trying to push him off the road. Shor could see Leo hunched forward, all of his attention focused on the two vehicles, his face contorted into a hateful grimace.

The wave of bots thundered past the next hangar along, their roar filling the Space Sector. Jay and Yon were now only a few seconds away. Just a few more metres and they would be home free. Shor felt the hope swelling in him.

"Come on."

Suddenly, Yon's buggy swerved violently, turning perpendicular to Jay's path. Yon almost fell out of his seat, just managing to grab hold of the steering wheel at the last instant. The buggies were now moving on a collision path. Shor's heart sank at the possibility that Leo was going to end their escape bid by just a few metres.

"No," Lars said, echoing Shor's despair.

Sol dropped his head, apparently unable to watch. Neel clenched his fists, the muscles in his big forearms rippling.

Shor braced himself for the impact. He could only imagine what would happen if those fuel rods were compromised. Everything seemed to slow down as Jay bore down on Yon's buggy. In the realisation that this could be the last thing he ever saw, Shor's brain was absorbing as much detail as possible. Everything became sharp, the colours bright, the details vivid.

Yon's buggy was now directly in the path of Jay's cleaning bot. Yon's head spun round and their eyes met. What Shor witnessed was a mixture of shock and stark terror.

Then, quite suddenly, everything changed.

There was a squeal of rubber tires as, in one swift movement, Jay swung right so he was moving in the same direction as Yon's buggy, then turned sharply back towards the hangar, forcing it to make a hard left turn.

Yon, caught by surprise, flew across the seat and flailed over onto the fuel rods being carried by Jay. Jay then nudged the buggy so that it careered off to the left, back and around towards the oncoming wave of bots.

"Watch out!" Lars yelled.

The four of them leapt out of the way as Jay careened into the hangar, sending the fuel rods—and Yon—bouncing across the smooth floor.

"The door! Close the door!"

Sol was closest and he lunged at the control panel. The door slid down. He grabbed one of the door's support struts and leaned on it, using his weight to try to speed it up. A few inches before it shut, the first bots arrived, their teeth clawing at the gap. Sol jumped back as an evil-looking implement swung towards his feet. The door jammed, its engines whining.

"It won't close," Sol shouted. "There's too many."

"Leave it!" Shor yelled. "Get something to secure it. Neel. Lars. Get the rods into the ship. I'll get Jay uploaded. Yon, are you all right?"

"That was close," Yon said, brushing himself off.

"I'm glad you could make it. We nearly left without you."

Yon looked across at the door being attacked by an army of bots. "Thanks for waiting."

Shor found Jay who had come to a stop directly under the Phoenix. "You all right, buddy?"

"I saw him," Jay said in his tinny bot voice. "I saw him. He tried to get inside my mind, but he couldn't."

"Who?" Shor asked, opening the bot's brain hatch and connecting the cable. "Who did you see?"

"Him. Leopold. He's controlling the bots with his mind. He tried to control me, but God protected me. I saw his mind, Brett. I saw his thoughts. I saw death."

"I know. He's evil."

"More than that. I saw inside him. He isn't human. Under the skin, he is a machine."

Shor hesitated. "A bot?"

"Yes. That is how he was able to control the machines. Leopold Drake is a robot. And I saw in him the same creature that attacked me on our return from Alpha Centauri. An entity."

"But if he's a bot, surely they would've spotted it in the medicals, don't you think?" Although, the more he thought about it, the more it made sense. He had seen how Leo could control people. "We'll talk about it later, all right? Right now I need to get you on that ship." With one eye on the bots fighting to get under the door, Shor loaded Jay into the Phoenix. When the transfer was complete, he disconnected the cable and wheeled Jay—now just an empty bot—out of the way.

"Come on," Lars called. "Have to go, now!"

Shor took a final look around before climbing the stairs. Lars grabbed his hand and pulled him through the door.

"Welcome aboard," Jay said. "Please stand back and I will retract the stairs."

"Wait," Shor said, suddenly remembering something. In the excitement, he had forgotten. In all the drama, he had missed the most important thing.

"What's wrong?" Lars asked. "Listen, I hate to sound impatient, but those bots are going to be here any minute."

"The airlock. Jay, can you remotely open the airlock?"

"I will try. One moment please. No, I cannot open them. They seem to be jammed."

"The wagger!" Shor hissed. "He's hacked all the doors. No wonder he's not even sweating."

"So what does that mean?" Mel asked.

"We have to open them manually," Lars said, his face grim. "Someone has to stay behind and operate the manual override."

"There must be another way. Surely if he's hacked it, we can as well."

"Perhaps," Shor said, "but we don't have the time. I'll stay behind."

"No!" Mel cried. "You're not staying here to die."

"It's the only way. If I don't open those doors, none of us will make it."

"I won't let you," Mel said, grabbing his arm. "I won't let you do this."

"I'll do it," Lars said softly.

Shor spun around to face his friend. "No. It's my responsibility. I'll do it."

"The way I see it, you're still a goget and I'm still your manager. As long as we're on the planet you work for me. It means I get to tell you what to do."

"But—"

"No buts. I'm going to walk down these stairs and you're going to close this door. Consider it your last work order."

"We can find another way," Shor said. "We can work something out."

Lars grabbed him by the hand and squeezed. Outside, a cracking noise echoed through the hangar. "There isn't time. Listen. If anybody can work out how to bring this wagger down, it's me. You're looking at the best hacker on Mars. Now go."

"Do me a favour?" Shor said.

"Of course. Anything."

"If you happen to bump into Harl Benson, tell him there is a God."

Lars smiled. "I will. Now go. Before I change my mind."

"Wait!" It was Jay.

They turned to see his familiar face on the wall opposite. His voice was back to normal.

"We don't have much time," Lars said. "What is it?"

"I've left something in the hard drive of the bot. If you can get to it, take it and analyse it. I had a look inside Leo's mind. I saw what he is made of. It might help you."

"I will," Lars said. "Thank you."

Shor watched Lars run down the stairs and across to the control booth. The stairs slid back and up, curling into the floor of the ship. The Comet door slid closed and there was the hiss of air.

"Please hold on," Jay said. "This may get bumpy."

Shor crouched and Mel placed her hand in his. He looked around at the faces of the people with their wide eyes. He did a quick tally. Ninety-nine exactly. With him, that made one hundred.

The ship shuddered as the rockets throttled up. One or two people gasped. Mel squeezed his hand.

The ship climbed into the air.

It took three days to reach Earth. They lived on emergency rations, huddled together, sleeping, talking, praying, waiting. Jay introduced himself and was accepted as one of the group, especially by the youngest among them who were especially taken with his unique charm. They kept Earth time, with Jay providing a glorious sunrise and sunset on the ship's walls. During the day, he displayed a golden sun above fields and trees, and an azure sky. At night, he showed them the stars in real time.

Shor and the other adults, fifteen in all, did what they could to reassure and comfort the rest. They organized activities to keep spirits up. Jay played old films from memory because, with no archive to draw from, he had to rely purely on recall. Shor was surprised at the accuracy, but then Jay did have a brain the size of a small planet.

As for Jay, his initial doubts about the ship soon passed. It took him no time to get used to the extra space. He said it made him feel "taller", especially after enduring the cramped confines of a maintenance bot, which he said was worse than the time he spent locked down to avoid the attacks of the entity.

Mel mourned her parents and her friends, as did everyone. Shor could only hope Lars had survived and would find a way to overthrow Utopia's new despot, but the odds were not stacked in his favour. He hoped one day to see Lars again but some things were so fragile that no good could come of holding on to them too tightly. He placed that one firmly in God's gentle hands.

On the morning of the third day, they were close enough for Jay to show them the Earth. For two hours they sat and stared, watching the blue pearl grow and bloom like a flower. Shor pointed out the clouds, the oceans, the continents. When they were close enough, he drew his finger around the borders of those countries he still recognized. The water had risen and fallen away since his departure so very long ago. The land had put on weight since his trip across the galaxy, pushing the water back into the depths where it belonged.

He pointed to a spot where his house had once been, or close enough to it. And over on the other side of the continent, the home he had once shared with Rochelle and Mark and Tim.

Soon they were able to zoom in on the bigger cities. Shor pointed out the Great Wall of China, the Great Lakes, the Nile, and the pyramids. He wanted to show them the city lights but, as the shadow of night swept across the surface, there was nothing to show.

The world, it would appear, had not returned to its former glory.

Too soon, Shor thought. *But we can start over. We will join with the survivors and help rebuild the planet. We have youth and wisdom to offer.*

He imagined them toiling like the Pioneers of old. He pictured them building a new civilization the way the forefathers of Utopia had done. With their knowledge they could provide invaluable assistance.

Looking at the faces clustered around the room, he felt a swell of hope. They were the future of the Earth. They were God's plan to help put the world back on its feet. They had been through so much and the grief of leaving family and friends was still fresh on their faces, but he had faith that they would overcome any obstacles that lay ahead.

They watched until the Comet entered orbit and Jay announced that he needed to close the screen. A collective groan rose from the group but their curiosity had merely been whetted. All the things they had seen and heard about back on Mars were now below their feet. Soon the images would become reality. Soon they would be able to touch what had, just a few short days earlier, been a distant dream.

"It looks scary," a young girl said. "So much water."

"It's the animals you should be worried about," the boy in front of her said. "I heard they've got fish with huge teeth that can swallow you whole." To demonstrate, he turned and reached for her with his fingers twisted into ragged fangs.

The girl screamed with fright but was soon giggling as he tickled her.

"We'll be perfectly safe," Shor said. "Most of the dangerous animals are in places we won't be going. Like the ocean, for example." He was quoting Mister Edmunds, but it was also as if he were speaking from experience. Seeing the Earth for real had awoken a whole lifetime of memories within him.

"I heard it's the smaller animals you have to watch," another girl said.

"Yeah," the tickler boy said, his fingers still bent like claws. "They get inside you and eat your guts."

There was another shriek followed by laughter.

"I'm sure that's not true," Shor said. "While there is (*or was*, he thought) plenty of life on Earth, most of it is harmless. Just don't go wandering off by yourself. Jay had access to a comprehensive library. I'm sure he can remember enough to teach us what is safe and what isn't."

"Indeed I can," Jay said.

"What about bone density?" a serious-looking boy near the back said. "We learned about it in school. They said low bone density would be a problem when we returned to Earth. Will it be a problem?"

"Very likely, yes," Shor replied. "I won't lie to you. The gravity on Earth is about twice that of Mars. Your bodies have been adapted for the Martian environment, so it may feel strange at first. I will feel it as well, even though my frame is better suited to conditions on Earth, but I probably won't feel it as much as you will."

"What does that mean?" a girl asked. She had just attained her adult height. Her arms and legs were long and thin, as was typical in Utopia.

"You will feel...heavier," Shor said. "We all will, but it will pass."

"I heard," the first boy said, "that our bones will snap like dry corn stems."

Shor could see the fear spreading across their faces, especially the younger ones.

"We'll work it out," he said, raising his voice above the murmur. "We'll make braces to support our bones until they adjust. Whatever it takes, we'll do it."

"What about food?" another asked. "Will it be safe to eat?"

"And medicine," a young man joined. "We'll need medicine. We've been living in purified air all our lives. Who knows what sorts of diseases we'll be exposed to."

Luc made his way to where Shor was standing and turned to face them. "Shor's right," he said. "We'll figure it out. If we stick together, we can do it. If we help each other, we can make it. We managed to get away from the council. I'm sure we can cope with a few more germs." A ripple of hesitant laughter trickled around the room. "Now I suggest we all get some rest. We'll be needing our strength in the days ahead."

With Luc's vote of confidence, the room fell silent. He had a quiet air of authority which had a calming influence on the group. Shor had a feeling this would come in useful.

"Thanks," Shor said, speaking under his breath. "I appreciate that."

"You're welcome," Luc replied.

Shor looked around the hall. There were so many. He just hoped he would not let them down.

"Have you seen Mel?" he asked.

"I think she's in the kitchen."

He found her sitting in the corner next to one of the food dispensers with her knees pulled up to her chest. He joined her, but did not say anything. They had the room to themselves. Everyone was next door talking in hushed voices.

"Do you think Lars made it?" she asked softly.

"I hope so," he said. "God has a plan. He got us out of the city. He can help Lars." He looked at her. "I'm sorry about your parents."

She let out a deep, shuddering sigh.

"They chose to stay. I told them everything and they chose to stay. I just don't understand why they would do that."

"I guess some people are so set in their ways, they find change unbearable."

"Do you think I should have stayed with them?"

He thought about this for a moment. He had wondered exactly the same thing. Was it right to leave all those people behind? Should he have stayed and tried to help? But then they might all be in captivity now. Or, worse, dead.

Trust me.

"Listen. I know we can't see it right now, but I'm sure God knows what he's doing. If we had stayed behind, I think it would have ended badly for us. We managed to get away. It means we can do it again. Maybe we're supposed to go back with reinforcements and rescue them, I don't know. God kept Lars behind for a reason, I'm sure of that."

"And Vin?"

"Yes, Vin as well."

"I know you never liked him, but he was nice to me." She took his hand. "He was very persistent, and I couldn't wait any longer."

"Wait? For what?"

"I was waiting for you, but you never seemed to want to be more than friends."

She looked into his eyes and he realized just how long he had wanted to hear her confess her feelings for him. Now that she was actually saying it, he understood how he really felt.

"Do you have any idea how long I've dreamed of this?" he said. "I used to lie awake at night, drawing your face on the ceiling with my finger. But I can't do this, it would be wrong."

"What do you mean?" she said, her frown deepening with confusion. "How could it be wrong?"

He swallowed. This was possibly the hardest thing he had ever had to say.

"Because I'm in love with someone else."

She pulled her hand away as if she had just been stung. "Oh, I didn't...I never realized. Who is it?"

"This may sound crazy, but I have these memories from life before Mars, and I've realized I am still in love with my wife."

"I don't understand..."

"That's why I could never confess my feelings to you. That's why I always kept you at a distance. I'm still in love with Rochelle."

She slumped back, her eyes swimming with sorrow. "And I always thought you didn't care for me that way. I thought it was me."

"I'm sorry," he said. "I didn't mean to hurt you."

"No. You never hurt me. I'm the one who left you for Vin. I should have known. I should have seen the signs. Maybe I didn't want to."

He reached for her hand. This time she didn't pull away but squeezed back.

"Can we be friends?" he said. "I think we make good friends."

She turned to face him. "All right. Friends. Just promise me one thing. If you start to get feelings for me again, don't wait until it's too late, all right?"

He smiled. "I'll tell you. Come on. Let's join the others."

Shor was about to stand when Jay's face appeared on a small square of wall to their side.

"Brett, sorry. Shor. We need to talk."

"Sure, buddy. What is it?"

"When I turned off the screen before, it was not because I needed to enter orbit. The cameras can function fine in orbit. I turned them off because I spotted something I wanted to show you first."

"What is it Jay? What did you see?"

Jay's face vanished and a view of the planet surface appeared. They were above a city centre with a wide road running from top to bottom, cutting the screen into two halves. From its size and location, it looked like a main thoroughfare. Tall buildings stretched up towards the camera.

The street was littered with the rusted ruins of abandoned vehicles. They lay scattered, alone and in clusters, half on the sidewalks or turned sideways against what would have been the flow of traffic.

"It looks dead," Mel whispered.

"Yes," Jay replied. "I have been monitoring the surface since we entered high orbit. I have not seen any sign of life."

The camera moved quickly along the road, past the city centre and out towards the suburbs. They looked down on housing estates and shopping malls, schools and sports stadiums. Nothing moved. The camera travelled away from the suburbs and out across sand-filled parks and fields stripped bare of anything green. The bushes and trees, devoid of leaves, stood naked, their branches clawing the dead air. They came to an endless forest cloaked in a suffocating blanket of black and grey, the foliage long gone, the jagged trunks jabbing like accusing fingers at the poisoned sky.

"So it was all a big lie after all," Shor said. "They never intended to bring us home."

"The planet is still showing signs of strong radioactivity. I can send probes down to the surface to verify this."

"Is there any point?"

They were now above a lake. Shor estimated it to be fifty kilometres across at its widest point. The water, slick and black, looked more like an oil spill. A strip of wasteland circled the perimeter. Further back, a graveyard of trees long dead dotted the low hills.

"It would allow us to reasonably estimate a time when colonization might be possible."

"All right," Shor said. "Send one down."

The camera switched to an outside view of the ship. They watched as a small silver ball flew out of the hull and dropped towards the surface. It struck the atmosphere, becoming a ball of fire tearing through the sky.

A few minutes later, Jay announced that the probe had landed and was returning data.

"And?" Shor asked. "How long?"

"It is worse than I thought. The atmosphere is still saturated with radioactivity."

"What are we looking at? Ten years? Twenty?"

"No," Jay said. "Based on my readings, I estimate the planet will not be ready for habitation for another five or six hundred years."

"Five or six *hundred?*" Mel said, her voice edged with alarm. "How is that possible? They said it would be ready. They said the air was almost clear."

"They lied," Shor said. "It was all just a big lie to stop us from losing hope. They knew we could never return home, so they showed us fake pictures."

"What about what the president said?"

"All lies."

Mel, her eyes wide, looked from the screen to Shor and back again. "Where are we going to go? We can't stay on this ship. Where are we going to live?"

"I think," Jay said, "that this ship was not built to bring people back to Earth."

"What makes you say that?" Shor asked.

"It is capable of travelling at the speed of light and has hyper-sleep chambers for one hundred people, and yet we were able to reach Earth in less than three days at a fraction of the speed of light. No, I believe this ship was originally intended for a much longer journey. I believe it was designed to travel much further than Earth."

"You mean Alpha Centauri?"

"Yes. After studying the ship's design, I suspect they originally built it intending to return to Earth. Then, when the true situation on Earth became clear, they changed the design."

"But then, why did it look so neglected when we found it?" Mel asked.

"They finished the ship," Shor said. "But they realized they would have to relinquish power if they left Mars. They knew they would no longer be in control. So they shut it away. They closed the project and put it under lock and key. Nobody would ever find out that they never intended to leave. They may even have been planning to dismantle it."

"Or destroy it." They turned to see Sol standing at the doorway. He walked over, his eyes on the images playing on the screen. "I think they were planning a test launch. I got to see everything going on at the hangar. I heard them talking about a live test and something about rigging a fuel pod."

"The waggers," Mel hissed. "You mean they'd actually destroy the only ship that could get us off Mars, just so they could stay in power?"

"But that still doesn't help us," Shor said. "We can't go back and we can't land here. And we only have enough food for a few more days."

"There is only one thing we can do," Jay said. "The ship was designed to fly to Alpha Centauri, so we should go to Alpha Centauri."

"You can't be serious?" Mel said. Then to Shor. "He isn't being serious. Is he?"

"I have calculated the time since our previous mission," Jay continued. "And I believe we will arrive on the planet without any risk from the comet storm for at least eight hundred years. That would allow plenty of time for us to establish a colony and wait for the Earth's atmosphere to clear."

"Alpha Centauri?" Mel said. "Seriously?"

"The way things stand," Shor said. "We don't really have a choice. I don't see Leo welcoming us back with open arms. And if we land on Earth, we'll be dead for sure. No, Jay's right. We have to go to Alpha Centauri. As long as Jay thinks the ship can manage it."

"I believe it can, yes."

"What about the whole temporal displacement thing you mentioned?"

"I think we can avoid that by staying just this side of the speed of light. That should also avoid the problem of genetic reversal."

"Genetic reversal?" Sol said.

"I'll tell you all about it once we get to Alpha," Shor said.

"We're actually going? To Alpha Centauri?"

Shor nodded. "Yes. I believe we are."

"But that's like a billion kilometres away."

"Two and a half light years."

"Years?"

"Yes, but don't worry. You'll be asleep the whole time. And Jay's a pretty good pilot. He hardly ever crashes into anything." Sol and Mel looked at each other nervously. "Just kidding. Jay is a superb pilot. In fact, I would trust him with my life. Actually, I already have."

On the screen, Jay's smiling face appeared. "Thank you Brett, I mean, Shor."

"Who's Brett?" Sol asked.

"That's another story," Shor said. "Let's just say, I've done this once before."

Sol's eyebrows lifted so high they nearly vanished under his hairline.

"I suppose there's no point hanging around. Let's get everyone ready for hyper-sleep and then we can be on our way."

They entered the main room and looked at the huddled groups. He turned to Mel and Sol, but they were waiting for him. It suddenly struck him that it was his responsibility. They were looking to him to lead them.

He thought about telling them it would be just a little while longer, that they would be able to come home one day soon, but he couldn't do it. They had been lied to for so long.

And so he told them the truth. They looked disappointed and hurt. Some cried. But at least they knew. No more lies.

He finished with a prayer, asking God to watch over them and protect them as they travelled in search of a new home. He also asked for protection for the people they had left behind. When he opened his eyes, all but some of the youngest were looking up at him with a perplexed expression. There was so much he had to teach them, but also so much he had yet to learn.

They followed his lead with attaching the face masks and the tubes for the torso. He showed them how to enter the hyper-sleep chamber, letting the yellow goo carry their weight.

Soon, it was only he and Mel left standing in the room that seemed suddenly so much bigger. He helped her into her suit and attached her mask. He held her hand as she climbed into her chamber. He smiled reassuringly as she slid into the cloying syrup.

Once everyone was asleep, he climbed into his own suit and donned the rubber mask that would feed him oxygen for the next two and a half years.

"Jay, are you going to be all right, buddy?" he asked, perched at the top of the chamber steps. "You won't get too lonely?"

"I will be fine," Jay said. "I have a whole new ship to explore. And besides, God and I have a lot to talk about."

Shor smiled. "Of course. Just do me a favour and keep an eye on the road, all right?"

"Don't worry," Jay said. "I will take care of you."

"I'm getting déjà vu again. We've done this before, right?"

"Yes we have."

"Cool. Well, see you in two and half years. Don't forget to wake me up."

"I won't. Sleep well, Shor."

Shor paused at the top of the chamber, his feet dangling in the syrupy liquid. It ran between his toes and he thought that it was an odd sensation. Not unpleasant, just strange.

"Actually," he said. "Maybe you should call me Brett from now on."

ALPHA
REDEMPTION

P.A. BAINES

Bold, adventurous, and well-written. Bravo!

Chris Walley, author of the *Lamb among the Stars* trilogy

trapped in

a rapidly accelerating game

the real world

vanished like a mirage

a strange woman

that question

shot me out of the sky

a child

"the son of a programmer."

my last chance

what I didn't know I needed

the answer

CAFFEINE

A Novel by
Ryan Grabow

AVENIR ECLECTIA

VOLUME 1

GRACE BRIDGES
JEFF C. CARTER
JEFF CHAPMAN
FRANK CREED
PAULINE CREEDEN
KARINA FABIAN
JOSEPH H. FICOR
KAT HECKENBACH
HOLLY HEISEY
GREG MITCHELL
KEVEN NEWSOME
TRAVIS PERRY
MARY RUTH PURSSELLEY
J. L. ROWAN
WALT STAPLES
H. A. TITUS
FRED WARREN

EDITED BY
GRACE BRIDGES
AND TRAVIS PERRY

aquasynthesis

splashdown vol. 1

edited by grace bridges
narrated by walt staples

aquasynthesis again

splashdown vol. 2

edited by grace bridges
narrated by fred warren

Lightning Source UK Ltd.
Milton Keynes UK
UKOW04f0925190514

231910UK00001B/22/P

9 781927 154373